WESTERN

Rugged men looking for love...

Fortune's Secret Marriage
Jo McNally

Home To Her Cowboy
Sasha Summers

MILLS & BOON

Jo McNally is acknowledged as the author of this work
FORTUNE'S SECRET MARRIAGE
© 2024 by Harlequin Enterprises ULC   First Published 2024
Philippine Copyright 2024   First Australian Paperback Edition 2024
Australian Copyright 2024   ISBN 978 1 038 91752 2
New Zealand Copyright 2024

HOME TO HER COWBOY
© 2024 by Sasha Best   First Published 2024
Philippine Copyright 2024   First Australian Paperback Edition 2024
Australian Copyright 2024   ISBN 978 1 038 91752 2
New Zealand Copyright 2024

® and ™ (apart from those relating to FSC®) are trademarks of Harlequin Enterprises
(Australia) Pty Limited or its corporate affiliates. Trademarks indicated with ® are
registered in Australia, New Zealand and in other countries.
Contact admin_legal@Harlequin.ca for details.

This is a work of fiction. Names, characters, places, and incidents are either the
product of the author's imagination or are used fictitiously, and any resemblance to
actual persons, living or dead, business establishments, events, or locales is entirely
coincidental.

MIX
Paper | Supporting
responsible forestry
FSC® C001695

Published by
Harlequin Mills & Boon
An imprint of Harlequin Enterprises (Australia) Pty Limited
(ABN 47 001 180 918), a subsidiary of HarperCollins
Publishers Australia Pty Limited
(ABN 36 009 913 517)
Level 19, 201 Elizabeth Street
SYDNEY NSW 2000 AUSTRALIA

Cover art used by arrangement with Harlequin Books S.A.. All rights reserved.

Printed and bound in Australia by McPherson's Printing Group

Fortune's Secret Marriage

Jo McNally

MILLS & BOON

Award-winning romance author **Jo McNally** lives in her beloved upstate New York with her very own romance hero husband. When she's not writing or reading romance novels, she loves to travel and explore new places and experiences. She's a big fan of leisurely lunches with her besties. Her favourite room at home is the sunroom, where she enjoys both morning coffee and evening cocktails with her husband while listening to an eclectic (and often Irish) playlist.

Visit the Author Profile page
at millsandboon.com.au for more titles.

Dear Reader,

I finally got to write a cowgirl heroine! This is my first honest-to-goodness Western rancher romance. And they're *both* ranchers! And yes—I am excited. I grew up dreaming of horses and cowboys. In my teens, I got my first horse, and spent years riding, showing, training and raising them.

So when Harlequin asked me to write another *Fortunes of Texas* book, I was thrilled when I discovered the heroine, Dahlia, is a horse lover, lives on the family ranch and raises sheep. And the guy she wakes up married to in Las Vegas? Well, Rawlston Ames is the cattle rancher next door. They share a fence line *and* the huge secret of their impulsive Vegas wedding (spiked punch may have been involved). Dahlia's in a hurry to end the sham wedding, but Rawlston keeps coming up with excuses not to sign those annulment papers she keeps waving in his face.

I want to thank my El Paso in-laws for hosting us and helping me understand Texas, and my brother and sister-in-law for joining me on a giant Texas adventure last fall—from Houston to Dallas. I'd like to thank editor Susan Litman and my agent, Jill Marsal. And I'd like to thank my very own cowboy, Himself. He never lets me forget that he won a blue ribbon at his first horse show, while I came in second! I was, and am, so proud of him. He's my biggest cheerleader, and my very own Happily Ever After.

Jo McNally

DEDICATION

This book is dedicated to my lovely Texas cousin-in-law (and avid reader!), Judy.

CHAPTER ONE

DAHLIA FORTUNE'S WESTERN boots clicked on the marble floor like stilettos as she strode across the lobby of the Indigo Blaze Casino and Convention Center. Heads began to turn, and she slowed her pace. She didn't usually move quite so…aggressively…but her dislike of Las Vegas was showing.

She was a Texas cowgirl through and through. She liked open vistas and the smell of saddle leather and horses. And just because she was staying in a luxurious suite at the hotel this week, she really wasn't one for the trappings of the rich and famous. She supposed she *was* wealthy, but thankfully *not* famous. Crowds weren't her thing, and she definitely didn't want to be the center of attention.

She could handle it when needed, of course. After all, she was the daughter of a ruthless businessman—who was *not* a Fortune—and he'd raised her and her five siblings to be ready to take on the world without showing any sign of weakness. That didn't mean she *liked* it. Dahlia would rather be riding a horse or sitting alone working on her needle felt art. But the national sheep farmers convention was winding to a close, and she didn't want to miss the Best in Show competition coming up.

Her pace slowed again as she found herself stuck behind yet *another* wedding party. She'd been bumping into brides and grooms all week—yet another reason to dislike Vegas. There were weddings happening *everywhere*.

Elvis weddings, superhero weddings, grunge weddings, champagne weddings... The only thing they *usually* had in common was one or both wearing some sort of wedding veil. The gift shops were full of the things, in every color, length and price point.

The couple in front of her now had brought friends, and the whole crowd had clearly been partying for a while. They were carrying champagne bottles, waving them in the air as the hotel staff watched warily to make sure the bottles weren't open. The two grooms each wore white tuxedo jackets over... Speedos. Their veils matched the swim trunks—one orange and one green. She guessed they were Irish, and it was confirmed when one of their pals started step-dancing.

Vegas weddings were ridiculous. But she'd yet to see a newly hitched duo who didn't look ecstatically happy and in love. Well...a few of them were too drunk to be sure about the *in love* part. Those couples got sloppier as the nights grew later, sometimes barely holding each other up. But they seemed happy. And they were, well...married. Something *she* hadn't managed to accomplish in her thirty-two years on this planet.

Dahlia managed to work her way past the Irish wedding and turned down the hallway leading to the exhibition arena. She was hoping that whole *unmarried* issue would be resolved as soon as her boyfriend, Carter Powers, returned from his business trip to Europe. It seemed like she was always waiting on Carter to show up lately, with all his business travel and now, talk of running for office. He'd been a little distant emotionally, too, after her move from Cactus Grove to Chatelaine and changing her last name from Windham to Fortune.

Carter wasn't big on being *impulsive*, and she'd been nothing *but* that over the past few months—ever since her father's death and Mom's stunning discovery about her past. Turns out Wendy Fortune was a long-lost member of the well-known Fortune family, meaning her children were Fortunes, too. Dahlia and her siblings had all been dealing with so many changes in their lives at the time, so why not honor Mom's request that they take the Fortune name and move to Chatelaine to be closer to other members of the Fortune family? Although, admittedly, some did so with more enthusiasm than others.

Dad had been...difficult. Hard. Cold. Demanding. Still, a name change was a big step. But he was gone and their mother was here. And when sweet Wendy Wind—er, make that Wendy *Fortune*—wanted something, she had a way of making it happen. In this case, she'd done so by buying a massive working ranch on Lake Chatelaine with six luxury lakefront log homes on it. One for each of her children.

Dahlia couldn't blame Carter for being overwhelmed with her life choices in the six months since they'd met. But she still had a hunch he was coming back from Europe with an engagement ring. He was always talking of what a great match they made. In fact, he said that more than he mentioned how much he loved her. He tended to talk about loving *them* together more than loving *her*. But despite her father's personal faults, she respected Carter for being a hard-driving businessman like her dad had been. If he was approaching marriage from a practical point of view, she had no problem with that. It *was* a merger of sorts. It wasn't like *she* was all emotional about things, either. She cared for Carter. And as far as she was concerned, that was a solid foundation for marriage.

Some people got too caught up in the mushy romance stuff instead of focusing on compatibility. Her parents had lived largely separate lives, but they'd made their partnership work...for the most part. Dahlia entered the exhibition center, smiling at her naked left hand as she pushed the door open. Soon she'd be sporting a diamond—she was sure of it.

The Best in Show competition was just starting, and she hurried to the main arena. The Dorper sheep were so cute, with their black faces and floppy ears. They looked like the *Shaun the Sheep* character in the popular animated TV show. But *cute* wasn't a factor in her decision-making this week. Instead, she searched for Sally Mathison and her award-winning Texas Merino sheep. It was no surprise to find the older woman in the arena with a beautiful, fluffy ram with short, curly horns. The ram had already won Best of Breed and, just as Dahlia walked up to the fence, Yellow Ross of Texas won Best in Show.

Dahlia applauded with the other sheep farmers watching, satisfied that she'd made the right decision. Ross would be moving to the Fortune Family Ranch next week, along with thirty ewes. Another fifty sheep would arrive from two other farms farther north, in Texas Hill Country. They would be the beginning of Dahlia's dream coming true—raising her own sheep and selling their highly prized merino wool. And, of course, she'd use the wool for her own crafts, too. She caught Sally's eye and gave her a thumbs-up across the ring. Tomorrow, she'd head home to Texas and inform her family that she'd be adding sheep to the ranch livestock.

Across the sheep pens, she saw a tall man with a vaguely familiar stride moving through the crowd. He wore a well-worn cowboy hat and a dark blue Western shirt. She froze.

No. It couldn't be…

At that moment, he looked up as if she'd called out to him. His gray-eyed gaze slammed into hers from forty feet away. It was him. Rawlston Ames. *Damn it*. The guy had been her nemesis since grade school, floating through life with his *aw-shucks* charm and deep Texas drawl. Always outdoing her in school and in most of the livestock shows. She'd work herself to exhaustion and he'd stroll into the ring and flash that killer smile at the judges, then waltz out with the blue ribbon.

To be fair, the guy was legitimately smart and his family had a successful ranch in Cactus Grove. He'd been an only child with adoring parents. So yes, she might have been just a bit jealous. Rawlston had such a knack for showing up at the most annoying times, though. It wasn't until after she'd agreed to move to Chatelaine with her family that she discovered Rawlston owned a large ranch there. One that bordered the Fortune Family Ranch. Just her luck.

And now, here he was in Vegas. At a *sheep* show. She turned on her heel. Maybe he hadn't recognized her.

"Dahlia! Wait up!"

She kept walking, hoping she was just imagining that was Rawlston's voice. She was having a good day, and if that guy had suddenly decided to be a sheep farmer, too, she'd absolutely lose it.

"Dahlia! Wait!"

He was closer now, and she stopped. Running from him would be undignified. He was almost at her side by the time she turned. She couldn't help noticing the random women watching him with interest. Yeah, he was that kind of guy. Tall and lanky, with a stride as smooth as his voice. A man's man who made the ladies swoon. So *irritating*. She put her hands on her hips.

"What the hell are you doing here?"

RAWLSTON CHUCKLED IN surprise. Leave it to Dahlia Windham Fortune to waste no time in setting him back on his heels. She'd been doing it since high school.

"I think what you *meant* to say is 'Hi, Rawlston, how nice to see you again.'"

Color rose on her porcelain cheeks. "That's the thing, though," she answered. "I keep seeing you everywhere lately. Even after I moved to Chatelaine—surprise—*you* now live in Chatelaine. I decide to raise sheep, and suddenly you're here at the sheepherding convention in Las Vegas. I thought you raised cattle?"

"I do, and I'm not planning on changing livestock anytime soon." Rawlston nodded off to his right. "I was in town for a farm equipment convention and stopped by to say hi to a navy pal who's a vendor here for animal husbandry supplies." He reached out and touched her shoulder, moving the two of them out of the way of a teen boy pulling a cart loaded with hay bales and bags of feed. Exhibitors were packing up now that the show was over. "Are you really looking to raise sheep?"

Some of her brittleness eased, and her chin rose in pride. "The Best in Show ram will be moving to Chatelaine next week."

"Congratulations. I didn't know the Fortune Family Ranch was branching into the sheep biz."

She gave a flippant one-shoulder shrug. "They don't all know about it yet. But it's a big ranch. I'm sure they can handle me raising a few sheep on my portion."

Rawlston wasn't so sure about that. The Windhams… he caught himself. He knew they were Fortunes now, but he'd known them as Windhams his entire life. Whatever their names were now, they could be a prickly bunch. Their dad, Casper Windham, had been a real SOB. Arrogant, greedy, detached. His one love was Windham Plastics, a mega producer of plastic products that had been the target of environmentalists for years. Casper had seemed to regard his six children as assets more than family.

That kind of upbringing affected a kid. Rawlston had gone to school with Dahlia and her siblings, and each of them seemed to absorb the stress of their cold, demanding father differently. But they'd all come through it intact, as far as he could see. They'd each developed their own defense mechanisms, from being driven and competitive to overpleasing. Dahlia fell closer to the driven end of the spectrum. She'd always been fiercely independent.

An older woman walked up to them, giving Dahlia a quick hug. The woman was obviously a rancher, with her trim jeans and well-worn boots and hat.

"How about that Ross, huh?" the woman said, beaming. "You bought yourself a champion!" She turned to Rawlston. "Sorry to interrupt you two. I'm Sally Mathison, owner of the Mathison Ranch outside of Dallas. And you must be the boyfriend—"

"No!" Dahlia almost shouted the denial, making Rawlston smile. He'd rarely seen her get flustered. "This is *not* Carter. This is…" She glanced at him, then away again. "This is just someone I used to know in high school." *Ouch.* "He has a ranch near mine in Chatelaine. We're neighbors, I think…"

She was starting to babble, so he held out his hand to Sally. "Rawlston Ames. My ranch borders the Fortune ranch. I stopped to say hi to a friend and ran into Dahlia."

"Well, if you're a neighbor you're still invited."

"Invited to what?"

"There's an exhibitor's reception near the pool to celebrate the end of the show. Dahlia is officially a sheep rancher now, and her ram just won Best in Show, so the two of you should join us."

"Oh…" Dahlia stammered. "I… I appreciate it, but—"

"We'll be there," Rawlston said.

"Great! See you both there!"

Sally hurried off, and Dahlia was staring at him in fury.

"What?" He splayed his hands wide in innocence. "If you're gonna raise sheep, you need to build relationships with people in the business. A casual reception like this is a great opportunity for you."

"If there's one thing I don't need, it's some man making decisions for me. And what do *you* get out of it? I have a boyfriend, you know. A *serious* one. Carter Powers."

Rawlston did his best not to let his disgust show. Carter was a world-class jackass. The dude thought he was some brilliant businessman, but most of his success had come from riding other people's coattails, stealing other people's ideas and bamboozling his clients. One of those former clients was Rawlston's dad. He had no idea why Dahlia was with the guy, but her taste in dating had always baffled him.

Truth be told, Rawlston had had a mad crush on her in high school, but she'd always gone for the nerds or the superrich boys. The kind of boys her father would approve of. She'd never given a jock like him a second glance. Stung at her rejection, he'd dated casually, earning a reputation as a ladies' man. It was what was expected from the high school quarterback, but he'd never been serious about anyone. However, he'd always known when tall, elegant Dahlia entered a room. She'd walked down the halls like she owned the place, and students would make way for her as if she was royalty.

"Free food and drink?" He finally answered her question, pushing aside thoughts of his childhood crush on her. No good could come from those memories. Besides, if she was the type of woman who dated a guy like Carter, she wasn't the woman for him. "Look, I was already going. My pal Mike invited me. So we can walk there together or separately. Your choice. And for the record…yes, I know you have a boyfriend."

Dahlia studied him for a moment, then relaxed. Had she really thought he'd been hitting on her? "Fine," she relented. "There's nothing wrong with two neighbors walking to a reception together."

Two neighbors. Not even *two friends*. He watched her walk away, her blond hair swinging in time with her hips. Still tall and slender, wearing simple chinos and a denim jacket, Dahlia had somehow picked up even *more* elegance through the years. But old, unrequited feelings aside, there was no escaping the fact that the two of them had always been lifelong competitors, in everything from grades— she was valedictorian, he was salutatorian—to livestock competitions.

She could outride him in the horse ring, but he had the prize cattle every year. He smiled to himself. One year she'd decided to raise piglets, so he'd convinced his parents to let him do the same. His litter won at the county fair.

Rawlston stopped. No wonder she hadn't been thrilled to see him. He'd been kind of a jerk to her back then. It was high school stuff, but still. Maybe he'd deserved her anger. Dahlia glanced over her shoulder, and he hustled to catch up with her.

They were neighbors, after all. Tonight he'd show her he knew how to be a *good* neighbor. Maybe even a friend. Nothing more than that…no matter how tempting.

CHAPTER TWO

WHEN DID RAWLSTON AMES become so fascinating?

Dahlia took another sip of her fruit punch and stared into his mesmerizing gray-blue eyes, trying to pay attention to the story he was telling about buying his prize bull. Those eyes were really something. And his deep voice and slow drawl…

She sat up straight and gave herself a mental scolding. Rawlston had *never* been her type, and he wasn't going to start now. She was just tired. It had been a while since she'd relaxed and just let herself have a good time. For whatever reason, that was what had happened tonight.

She and Rawlston were in a booth near the appetizer table at the poolside exhibitor's reception, although the actual reception had wound down an hour ago. Most of the food had been cleared, other than a cheese and cracker tray and the bowl of virgin fruit punch sitting at the end of the table.

They'd headed in separate directions when they'd first arrived. Rawlston went to chat with his navy buddy near the bar, and Dahlia had followed his advice and networked her way around the room. She'd talked with sheep ranchers from all over the West, and some who had traveled from as far as Canada. She might be new at this business, but she wanted to show she was serious and that she'd done her homework.

As the evening wore on, she'd found herself with a

group of women who'd glommed onto a group of guys, which included Rawlston and his buddy Mike. Dahlia wasn't there to hook up with anyone, so when Rawlston gave her a tip of his head as if to say *let's leave these young'uns* she'd followed him to the far side of the pool. The table near the food was her choice—she needed something to absorb the chardonnay she'd been drinking all evening, and the fruit punch was mighty refreshing.

They'd talked about relocating to Chatelaine, and Rawlston told her where the farm supply and feedstore was and which businesses to check out, like the upscale LC Club. Apparently the town was often a comparison of opposites—dusty ranches amid the mansions of the wealthy. He told her about his herd of prize beef cattle at his Chatelaine ranch. Of course, he just had to mention the *prize* part—competitive as ever. Then he shared how he and his dad had come to Chatelaine for a fresh start after Rawlston's mother had died of cancer back in Cactus Grove.

Rawlston refilled their punch glasses whenever they were empty, and the conversation rolled along so easily that she began wondering if she'd misjudged the man. He was witty and charming, with an easy smile and such great stories. *So many* stories, and they were great. All of them. Really great.

Dahlia had shared some stories, too. She was actually surprised how talkative she'd become. She wasn't usually this chatty unless she'd been drinking. She told him about the discovery of her mother's past—that Wendy was a secret baby from long ago, and the woman who'd raised her wasn't her mother at all. The woman was a babysitter who'd raised Wendy as her own after her parents died in the tragic mine collapse that was such a big part of Chatelaine's history.

The mine collapse had killed fifty men. There were

signs all around Chatelaine saying *Remember the 50.* There was even a small museum dedicated to the incident. History-loving tourists came to Chatelaine to learn more about the mining disaster. But it turned out there were actually fifty-*one* people who had perished. The fifty-first was a woman—Wendy's young mother, Ariella, who'd rushed to the mine to tell the father of her child something urgent. Their relationship, and the baby, had been a secret, because Ariella's father, Wendell Fortune, had forbidden them from seeing each other. The baby—Dahlia's mother—became an orphan that day.

Wendy had never known, until this year, that she'd been the secret illegitimate granddaughter and heir of the recently deceased Wendell Fortune. That discovery came on the heels of the death of Casper Windham, and everyone's tangled feelings about Casper made them more receptive to move as a family to Chatelaine for a fresh start, just like Rawlston and his father had done.

So…they had *that* in common. Which was funny, right? It must have been funny, because they were both laughing so hard about it right now. Or…laughing about something. Who cared what? It felt good to laugh again, and Dahlia put her hand on Rawlston's arm and leaned closer. Which wasn't hard to do because they were now sitting side by side in the booth. He'd joined her on her side of the table after refilling their punch glasses again. Such a clever guy. Why had she ever disliked this man? She couldn't remember. *Damn, this punch is delicious.*

Rawlston took her hand and wound his fingers into hers. That was nice. Wait…she wasn't supposed to be feeling nice with another man. She was engaged, well, almost. She snort-laughed at herself. Almost didn't count, right?

"This isn't horseshoes." She hadn't intended to say that out loud, and the sound of the words in her oddly elevated voice made her giggle. Rawlston grinned. He had a fantastic grin, especially when he let it show in his eyes, which were twinkling right now.

"Uh, no," he said. "This is definitely not horseshoes. Would you like it to be?" He scooted closer to her, putting her back to the wall. "Do you want to get points for being close?"

There was a dim voice in the back of her mind warning that this was a really bad, possibly disastrous, idea. Rawlston leaned in, his shirt brushing her chest. His hand touched the corner of her mouth lightly. Was the room spinning, or was that just her?

He held up his thumb, where he'd wiped a drop of punch from her chin.

"You're wasting perfectly good punch, Dahlia."

She licked it from his thumb and felt a shocking jolt of white-hot desire sweep through her. Rawlston felt it, too—his eyes went from gray to cobalt in an instant.

Bad idea! Horrible idea! Abort! Abort!

She straightened, breaking the moment. He sat back enough to give her some space and a chance to shake off whatever had just happened between them.

"Whew, is it getting hotter tonight or what?" She fanned herself with her hand, then reached for her glass and drained it. "If it wasn't for this punch I'd be melted into a puddle. Speaking of which…?" She held up her empty glass. Rawlston took it with a smile.

"I don't think it's the heat that's melting you, Dolly. But it's probably time to call it a night." Ever the practical cowboy, doing the right thing, even when neither of them wanted tonight to end. He took their glasses. "But this *is* damn good punch. One more to clear our heads, okay?" He slid out of the booth to get refills. He was just sitting back down when there was a commotion behind him.

"Spencer!" A woman's voice was nearly shrieking. "What in the blue blazes are you *doing*? Oh my gawd…"

The woman, with a teased bubble of white-blond hair and a sparkly gold jacket over a white leather miniskirt, was confronting a young teen boy. They were having a heated discussion while Rawlston and Dahlia toasted each other with their punch glasses.

"Here's to a new friendship between former rivals." Dahlia wondered why her voice was all soft and sultry. Sure, they'd had lots of sparks in this booth tonight, but it didn't mean anything. It wasn't real. Just two acquaintances innocently finding a friendly connection. Even if she *did* want to see how that firm mouth felt on her skin. She flushed and downed her punch in one gulp. *This isn't real.*

Rawlston chuckled. "Here's to hot nights, cool punch and beautiful women." His eyes never left hers as he drained his glass. Why was she thinking she wanted him to swallow *her* like that—like a man starved for a woman?

Another mental reprimand—*Stop it.* Rawlston Ames was gorgeous and rich. He could have any woman he wanted, and he'd never once wanted her. Not in high school. Not in college. Not now. A sudden wave of melancholy washed over her. For some reason her emotions were all ramped up tonight.

"Hey…" His voice, smooth as butter and warm as whiskey, broke through her thoughts. "Why the frown?" His fingers touched her chin and lifted it. "I like happy Dolly better."

She'd never liked that nickname, and he kept using it. She should be mad, but instead, it felt intimate and nostalgic. She blinked back the moisture in her eyes. Was she *crying*? Something was definitely off with her. Rawlston was right, it was time to get back to her room and get some sleep.

They left the booth and made one last stop at the punch bowl, both giggling as they grabbed nearby water glasses and filled them to the top "to go." As they were leaving the table, the bubble-haired lady in gold sequins stopped them. She was weaving, and her eyes seemed a bit unfocused. Or was that Dahlia who was weaving?

"Is that the punch from the poolside table?" The woman was almost whispering, which did nothing to dim her thick Southern accent. "I'm pretty sure my knucklehead nephew poured vodka into that bowl. Like…a *lot* of vodka. He took a full bottle from our room. Actually, it might be more than one." She closed her eyes with a dramatic sigh. "I was just headed to tell the hotel staff that I saw a mouse in the punch or something so they'll throw it out. I mean, Spencer's an idiot, but he's only fourteen, and I don't want him in trouble. Besides, we were supposed to be watching him while my sister and her husband go to her husband's brother's wedding, which is one of those Elvis circus weddings that will never last."

Dahlia and Rawlston looked at each other and each raised a brow. This woman's story was endless.

"My point is, I can't in good conscience let you drink too much of that punch without knowing the truth. Consider yourselves warned."

She dashed away, leaving the two of them staring from each other to their glasses. They'd already been drinking that punch for two hours. *Weird.*

Rawlston spoke first. "That lady's crazy. If this punch was spiked with that much vodka, you and I would be on the floor by now." As if to prove his point, he gulped down the punch in his glass, then gave her an exaggerated, lip-smacking sigh of satisfaction.

Dahlia nodded in agreement. "I was thinking the same thing. That kid sure has her fooled." She took another healthy sip from her glass. "He probably drank the booze himself." Then she drained the rest of it. *See?* She felt totally fine.

Rawlston took her arm and leaned in. *Damn this man smells good.* "Probably. But just to be safe, let's see if I can walk you to your room without us accidentally falling into some Vegas wedding chapel."

Dahlia clutched his arm—his thick, hard, warm bicep— and laughed. Was her laughter suddenly extra loud?

Must be the empty hallway.

"As tempting as being married by Elvis would be, I think I'll be able to avoid buying a hot pink wedding veil and saying *I do* to you, Rawlston Ames."

RAWLSTON WOKE UP with a pounding headache. Even worse, there was a blazing bright light shining on his face. He raised his arm to shield his eyes. *What the hell is that?* He winced and blinked a few times before he realized it was the sun. Looking around his suite at the Indigo Blaze Casino, he saw it was daytime, and well into it judging from the height of the sun in the sky. He'd clearly forgotten to close the drapes before going to bed last night. Oddly enough, he didn't remember getting back to his suite or getting undressed. But he definitely felt naked under the sheets right now.

He glanced down to confirm and his whole world came skidding to a halt. Including his heart.

It wasn't a blanket keeping him warm.

It was a *woman*, sprawled across him like a starfish. She was lying face down, her head turned away from him.

Rawlston touched her arm and she made a soft sound and shifted slightly. Okay, she was breathing, so this wasn't an episode of *Law & Order: SVU*. But who the hell *was* she? He scrubbed his hand down his face and tried to remember what happened after he walked Dahlia to her room last night.

He must have gone back down to the bar, because he and Dahlia had been drinking punch while they'd talked for hours. Furrowing his brow, he winced as his head pain increased right between his eyes. Sure, that weird lady had told them the punch was spiked, but they'd both dismissed it. They hadn't been drunk. Another throb of pain. Or *had* they?

Nah. He must have gone drinking after and picked up some woman at a club. Not his finest moment, but not the end of the world, either.

He shifted gently to sit up, eliciting another groan from his bedmate. To his relief, there was a used condom on the floor. Even in a drunken romp, he'd used protection. The woman's left hand moved to the top of the sheet. She was wearing a wedding band.

He muttered a curse. It was one thing to have a random one-night stand in Las Vegas. But he wasn't the kind of guy to bring a *married* woman to his room, no matter how drunk he'd been. Maybe his drink had been drugged? He looked around the room. No, he hadn't been robbed. He could see his wallet, phone and laptop. Besides, she wouldn't spike her own drink, and she was still passed out. He reached out to touch her hand, and had another shock.

He was wearing a wedding band. And it matched the one on *her* hand. They were both platinum, with a center stripe of textured gold. He yanked his off like it was burning him. It was inscribed inside—*RA and DF Forever.*

He glanced at the long blond hair sweeping across the sheets. *No. It couldn't be.* He touched the woman's hair and she made an annoyed sound and turned her face toward him, eyes still closed in slumber.

Dahlia Fortune.

He blinked a few times, as if that was going to change what he was seeing. *Dahlia* was naked in his bed. They were wearing matching wedding bands, and she was wearing a sparkling diamond engagement ring. There was a long bridal veil draped over the desk chair in his room. Some fake pink roses, edges gilded with gold glitter, were scattered on the floor. They were in Las Vegas. It didn't take much of a leap to realize what had happened. But *why*? And...*how*?

For some reason, he slid the ring back onto his finger. In between head throbs, he was starting to piece together snippets of memory from last night. Laughing at all the bridal couples. Seeing the gift shop... No, they went *into* the gift shop. Dahlia was trying on veils and chortling something about wanting his opinion on what color she could get. Then she'd found one that not only sparkled, but *lit up* with tiny LED lights. They'd been acting silly—uncharacteristic for either of them.

He remembered being surprised that the shop actually had a small selection of high-end rings, including diamonds. Another couple rushed in, breathlessly grabbing a hot pink veil and a matching bow tie the groom put on above his grunge rock T-shirt. When they'd left, Rawlston couldn't remember if it was Dahlia or him who had said something like, *If you can't beat them, join them.* The words were a dare neither would back down from. He did now recall a pink chapel. A female officiate wearing pink tulle. An elevator ride that was a blur of kisses. And judging from the rumpled look of the bed, they'd had one hell of a night.

As a *married* couple.

He closed his eyes tightly, shaking his head. What had they been thinking? How many bottles of vodka had that kid poured into the fruit punch? This was going to be a mess of epic proportions. But Rawlston was a problem solver at heart, and there had to be a solution to this one. Surely these things happened a lot in Vegas, and could be quietly annulled. First, he needed to wake Dahlia and see how much she remembered about their very busy night. His hand hesitated above her shoulder.

He had a hunch she was *not* going to be thrilled to wake up as Mrs. Rawlston Ames.

CHAPTER THREE

DAHLIA HEARD HER name being spoken, but she did *not* want to wake up. She was warm and comfortable and her body felt heavy from physical exertion. She muttered, "Go away," and turned her head. A hand touched her shoulder.

A *hand* touched her shoulder. There shouldn't be any damn hands in her hotel suite.

She jolted awake, shocked to find she was sharing a bed with someone. Not just someone...a *male* someone. And he was touching her. And she was *naked*. She catapulted out of bed with a scream, twisting the sheet around herself like a toga.

"Where am I? Why am I naked? Did you *drug* me? Oh my God. Where's my phone? Where's my stuff?" Panic choked her words, and all she could think was that the worst had happened.

The man moved and Dahlia shouted at him. "Don't you move! I don't know what happened last night, but I'm calling the..."

"Dahlia." The voice was firm and steady. And familiar. For the first time, she dared to look at his face.

"Rawlston?"

Confusion replaced her panic. She couldn't imagine him doing anything to purposefully harm her. And yet... they'd been naked in bed together. And she had no memory of coming to his suite. She sat on the far corner of the large bed, her legs no longer willing to support her. She clutched the sheet around her body.

"I don't understand..." She felt foolish for admitting that, but she needed answers. His response was to hold up his left hand and waggle his fingers. He had a wedding band on. She rolled her eyes. "Yes, I know you were married. But isn't it time to take that thing off?" She'd heard he and Lana divorced a few years ago.

He seemed shockingly unperturbed by this...this *situation*. In fact, he looked downright amused. What was she missing? He nodded toward her hand. She looked down and inhaled sharply.

She was also wearing a wedding band. And it matched the one on Rawlston's hand. Above it was a diamond solitaire.

"No-o-o-o-o..." The protest came out as a moan of disbelief. This wasn't possible.

"I hate to argue on our honeymoon, but...apparently yes." A corner of the comforter was covering his private parts, but there was a whole lot of Rawlston Ames on display. Some remote corner of her mind noted, even in crisis, that he was a fine specimen of a man. Lean and hard and tanned. *Wait.* Did he just say *honeymoon*?

"We cannot be married. It makes no sense. I don't even remember." She narrowed her eyes at him. Maybe he wasn't as trustworthy as she'd thought. "Why can't I remember?"

Rawlston gave her an understanding smile. "It took a bit for it to come back to me, too. Do you remember that lady who claimed her nephew spiked the punch we'd been drinking for hours?"

Dahlia's head was throbbing and fuzzy, but she did recall the woman in leather and sequins. She nodded and Rawlston continued.

"We were so sure she was wrong, but now I can see that was the vodka talking. Think about it—we were talking nonstop for hours, and laughing up a storm. You and me. We're far from friends." He glanced at the bed. "Well, we're *more* than friends now, I guess, but you know what I mean. It was out of character—booze-fueled—and it didn't end when we left the reception."

She closed her eyes tightly, willing this to all go away. But as bits and pieces of the evening came into focus, she realized he was right. They'd been laughing and giggling like little kids. She'd been fingering his biceps and getting lost in his eyes. Then more things came to mind. The gift shop. The jewelry counter. A laughing dare…

"Does pink tulle spark any memories?" he asked softly.

Her eyes snapped open.

"The chapel," she breathed. "Everything was covered in pink tulle. I had a veil…"

He pointed to the chair, where a long white veil was draped. "It lights up."

A horrified laugh bubbled up. Was it possible that she'd gotten drunk and had a Barbie wedding in a battery-operated veil? That Rawlston Ames was actually her *husband*? She put her hand down on the bed to support herself, suddenly dizzy. She was *married* to one of the most annoying men she'd ever met. Her fingers tightened on the sheet. And they'd clearly had quite a night together in this bed. Her body was aching, but in the nicest way. She straightened at one more horrifying thought.

Carter. She tried not to question why it took this much time for her boyfriend's existence to enter her mind. But they *were* dating, and he'd been hinting at a future together. How the hell was she going to tell him she was *married*? And why had she and Carter never left a bed looking this disheveled or her body feeling this sated in their six months together? *No, that isn't important right now.*

"I can't be married to you. I have a boyfriend, Rawlston."

"Cheating on your husband already, eh?" His smug grin infuriated her.

"This is *Not. Funny.* This is my *life* we're talking about, and none of my life plans included marrying *you.*"

"And yet, here we are." He raised his hand when she started to argue. "I get it—it wasn't on my bingo card, either. But the fact is, you and I did get married last night, and we can't turn back the clock to change our lousy decision-making, so getting hysterical won't help."

Dahlia went still. "Did you just tell a woman not to get hysterical?" Uncertainty clouded his eyes as she continued. "It is *not* hysterical to be concerned about telling the man I'm dating that *oops*, I accidentally married someone else. That is a genuine and legitimate problem for me, Rawlston. And my family…"

As if her mother and siblings hadn't dealt with enough this year, now she was going to add a scandalous Vegas wedding to the mix. Instead of wooing the future governor of Texas, she'd be letting them down by marrying some rancher. Of course, *they* were technically all ranchers, now, but still. She'd been a constant disappointment to them over the years. Or at least, to her father. He'd never missed a chance to tell her she was "wasting herself" by being a lowly horse groomer or worse, wanting to raise sheep. She'd started dating Carter just before her father's death, and Casper Windham had been thrilled that she was linking two prominent Dallas-area families together.

For the first time, Rawlston lost his aura of calm acceptance. He was scowling now, his jaw working back and forth.

"Okay. Yeah, you're right. I didn't mean to diminish the seriousness of what we've done. But every problem has a solution, and we'll figure this out." His gaze slid down her body and she felt an odd tingle on her skin. He looked away with a sigh, staring out the window. "I think we'll tackle it more maturely with clothes on, don't you? Why don't you use the shower first, and I'll order us some breakfast. Brains work better on a full stomach."

Every problem has a solution.

Brains work better on a full stomach.

He was always so full of practical platitudes. His calmness could be grating, but he was right. Breakfast, a shower, and clothing sounded like a good idea. But there was one thing she didn't need to wait to make a decision on. She stood, holding the sheet in front of her with one hand and pointing at him with the other.

"We can't tell *anyone* about this, Rawlston. Not a soul. I will *not* go back to Chatelaine as Mrs. Rawlston Ames." The thought gave her a chill. "These things must happen all the time in this town, so there has to be a way to annul it quickly and easily. No one else needs to know."

He stared at her for a moment, studying her face intently. "I'm not sure how quick and easy it will be, and it sure won't happen before we go home tonight. So technically, you *will* go back to Texas as Mrs. Rawlston Ames." He cut her off before she could object. "But I promise not to call you that there. It'll be our little secret."

There was nothing *little* about this mess, but she was satisfied with his answer. She turned toward the bathroom and stopped by the dresser. Their marriage certificate was sitting on top. She groaned and slid the rings off her finger, leaving them on the pink piece of paper and giving him a pointed look.

"One thing you can do before we leave is return these rings."

There was a pause, then he called out as she walked into the bathroom. "Does that mean no conjugal visits once we're in Chatelaine, Mrs. Ames? It looks like we had fun… *Ow!*"

He ducked from the box of tissues she'd thrown at his head, and it bounced off his shoulder.

"That is your one and only time to call me that. Whatever happened last night will *never* happen again. Return those rings."

"Yes, ma'am!" He was cackling when she slammed the bathroom door closed. *Jackass.*

She was trying to suppress any bits of memory from their night in his bed, but she knew her body was going to be remembering his touch long after they were no longer married.

RAWLSTON STEPPED OUT onto his back porch with a mug of coffee in one hand and a rawhide bone in the other. Tripp, his Australian cattle dog, was right at his heel, watching him intently. Correction—watching the *bone* intently. After a few feints, Rawlston tossed the bone far into the yard and the black and white dog tore after it. That would give him a few minutes to himself before Tripp demanded more attention. Tripp had spent four days with Rawlston's dad while Rawlston was in Vegas. He'd no doubt been sleeping on the furniture and being fed hand-cooked slices of chicken and beef. That fool dog had had more of a vacation than Rawlston, but Tripp was still playing the victim now that they were home.

Smiling despite himself, Rawlston walked across the

patio and stared out over the range behind the low-slung barns. The sun was just peeking over the horizon. The main cattle herd was nowhere in sight, but that wasn't unusual on a fifteen-hundred-acre ranch. They were probably out by the creek that ran near the border of his ranch and the Fortune ranch. In a smaller pasture near the barns, a few cows and calves were grazing.

Instead of the more common Herefords, he raised Brahmans. Originally from Africa, Brahman cattle had distinctive humps above their shoulders, and the males were often used in rodeos for bull riding. But they were good beef producers, and tolerated the Texas heat well.

Rawlston's red brick house was long and low like the barns, but at least twice as old. He'd bought this place for the land, not the amenities. It was just a house—nothing fancy. It kept him cool and dry and held the comfortable, overstuffed furniture that he liked. He'd furnished all three bedrooms but two of them had rarely been slept in. A few high school or navy pals and his dad were the only people who occasionally stayed over if the talking or drinking ran late. When he bought the ranch a few years ago, the real estate agent had assumed he'd use this house for staff housing and would build something more impressive for himself. But he wasn't into impressing people. The dog let out a bark, standing on alert as he watched a jackrabbit tear across the back of the yard.

"Stand down, dog." Three-year-old Tripp was a well-trained herding and hunting machine, and he knew when he had permission to run and when he didn't. He quivered until the rabbit was out of sight, then heaved a sigh and came back up into the shade. It was going to be yet another hundred-degree early August day.

Tripp might have been spoiled staying with Rawlston's dad, but he still hadn't had as exciting a weekend as Rawlston had. He'd come home from Vegas a married man. Albeit temporarily. He'd agreed with Dahlia's demand that he remove the wedding band, but he hadn't returned the rings. They were all together in a small box tucked into his sock drawer.

He sat on the bench and watched the sun rising higher in a clear sky. Hoping it would give him clarity. Because in all honesty, he wasn't sure why he'd kept the rings. Dahlia was right—they needed to end this sham marriage right away. He had zero interest in ever being married again to anyone, and she'd made it clear that she felt the same about *him*. Rawlston scowled into his coffee mug. She wanted that sleazeball Carter Powers. Carter was another reminder that Dahlia wasn't the kind of woman he'd ever be compatible with. Sure, he'd always admired her cool confidence back in school, and basked in her beauty as she grew into her willowy body and developed curves in all the right places. He'd also admired her competitiveness with him—they sharpened each other as they tried to outdo one another.

That said, her total lack of interest in his charms had cooled that crush pretty quickly. He didn't need a prickly girlfriend he had to work to get. Not when the other girls were more than happy to be one of his many dates. He wasn't into relationships back then, just good times. Rawlston finished his coffee and sighed. But when he'd finally committed to a real relationship as an adult, it had ended in betrayal and divorce, ending the naval career he might have pursued and sending him back to ranching. Which wasn't a bad thing—a man could be alone out here day after day. He was okay with that.

His phone pinged with an incoming text, and he knew without a doubt it had to be Dahlia. She'd been blowing up his phone since they got back to Chatelaine, swearing him to secrecy repeatedly and updating him on her progress in divorcing him. He pulled out his phone and saw his guess was right.

Talked to an attorney yesterday afternoon, and he filled me in on what we need to do. Got time to meet today?

Sure. Why not? He'd planned on heading to the farm supply store anyway. He tapped his response.

Going to Longhorn Feed this morning. Coffee at the Daily Grind in two hours?

Her answer was immediate.

The sooner the better. See you there.

She was not only awake, but ready to roll this morning. Probably because she was so determined to end things with him.

THE COFFEE SHOP was just across the two-lane highway from the feedstore. This was the "townie" side of Chatelaine— no mansions or resorts out here like there were in the ritzy Chatelaine Hills neighborhood on the other side of town. Just ranchers and the folks who worked at the mansions for the millionaires on the other end of Lake Chatelaine. This was blue-collar Chatelaine. *Dusty* blue collar. Rawlston slapped at his jeans to shake the dust off from loading bags of feed into the back of his dual-rear-wheel pickup truck.

This was his favorite side of town. He was successful enough that he could afford to hang out at the fancy LC Club on the water with all its tourists. But dressing up and listening to everyone brag about what they owned wasn't his idea of fun. He'd rather have coffee with the folks at the Daily Grind and talk ranching.

Once a modest home, the square, one-story building with a wide front porch had been converted to a restaurant back in the 1930s. The interior hadn't changed much since then, even as the place changed hands and formats a few times. Thirty years ago, it was reborn as a coffee shop that catered to ranchers, opening at six in the morning and closing in the early afternoon. Being right across the road from the feedstore made it the ideal spot for ranchers to stop by for a cup of strong coffee, something sweet and all of the best local gossip.

The shop was busy when he stepped inside, and he immediately spotted why. Beau Weatherly was at his corner table by the window, with a handful of people waiting for him. A small folding sign on the table read Free Life Advice. Rawlston checked his watch—the man's free advice time was running long today. He usually started at seven and answered people's questions until eight thirty or so. On the mornings when Beau was there, the Daily Grind would attract those who wanted advice and those who wanted to see who was asking for advice.

Beau was an interesting guy. The tall, gray-haired, stately gentleman was a salt-of-the-earth rancher with an unassuming demeanor who also happened to be a genius-level investor who'd made millions. His generosity had helped Chatelaine in many ways. He'd donated to numerous local charities, and had also quietly helped individual ranchers and local businesses when they needed it. That last part was just rumor, but Rawlston had heard it often enough to figure it was true. Not that Beau would ever admit it.

Beau's wife had died shortly after Rawlston arrived in Chatelaine, and Beau had been lost without her. He'd let his ranch slide, and word around town was that he'd stopped doing much with his investments. He just sat in his massive house and stared at the walls, ignoring friends as well as business.

After a year or so of sitting in limbo like that, he'd suddenly decided to give life advice to people for free at the coffee shop. He said that helping people was what his wife would have wanted him to do, so he answered people's questions on whatever topic they wanted to know about. Would it rain next week? Should they buy XYZ stock? Would they ever reconcile with their grown child? What should they cook for a family barbecue that weekend? Beau had earned a reputation for wisdom on all subjects.

Rawlston removed his hat and gave Beau a nod from the doorway. The whole thing was a little too woo-woo for him, but it didn't seem that Beau was hurting anyone, and if he made people feel better, what was the harm?

The coffee shop was small, with a few square tables and a counter along the back with wooden stools. There were more tables on the front porch. It was simple but cheery, with its whitewashed shiplap walls and red gingham curtains. They not only served the best coffee in the county, but also had a selection of bagels and pastries that went perfectly with that oversize mug of coffee. A glass case displayed desserts—it looked like today was cream pie day.

Dahlia was already here, at a table on the far side of the room with one of Daily Grind's giant red coffee mugs in front of her. Her long, blond hair was pulled into some sort of knot on the back of her neck. She was in a pair of stonewashed jeans and a flattering dark green top, with Western boots. She had her share of the Windham wealth, in addition to probably inheriting a good sum from her grandfather, Wendell Fortune.

Dahlia could not only afford the LC Club action, but

she'd fit in there like a natural with her supermodel good looks and the aura of growing up rich wrapped around her. Her clothes said working rancher. But her ramrod straight posture, carefully manicured nails and that porcelain complexion screamed *I should be on a yacht somewhere*. She'd always been out of his league. And yet—he bit back a smile—she was his wife.

"I highly recommend the banana cream pie," he said as he slid into the chair across from her.

"For breakfast?" Dahlia made a face.

"Trust me." A wiry older woman hustled over to take his order. "Hey, Sylvie. I'll take a big coffee, black, and a slice of that banana cream pie with two forks."

"Sure thing, Rawlston honey. You sure you want to share?" Sylvie eyed Dahlia through narrowed eyes. Sylvie was a mother hen to regulars like him, and she'd probably never seen the Fortune heiress before. "You usually have no problem eating our pie all on your own."

Dahlia was staring daggers at him as Sylvie headed back to the counter.

"Why do I get the feeling she doesn't like me?"

He huffed out a laugh. "Sylvie? She just doesn't know you. And to be honest, you're not the first woman I've been here with. She has no problem expressing her distaste for most of them." Lifting a shoulder, he muttered, "Sylvie thinks I need to find a nice rancher woman for my bride."

Dahlia smiled. "Don't tell Sylvie, but…you kinda did."

"That's true. But you don't look like a rancher. You look like a movie star."

Her eyebrows arched high. "I'm in jeans and boots, and I started the day in my brother's horse barn, checking on his favorite mare. I also have thirty sheep arriving later today, with more on the way. That's not exactly an A-lister lifestyle."

"I'm not saying you're not the real deal. I'm just saying you don't *look* like the real deal. You look like…" *A vision*. He blinked. High school had been a long time ago, but she still didn't want him. Time to focus. Sylvie saved the day by bringing a towering slice of banana cream pie to the table, along with his coffee.

"Extra strong, just the way you like it." That meant she'd added a shot of espresso.

"Thanks, Sylvie. Oh, we need another fork." She'd only brought one. She grumbled something and pulled the other out of her apron pocket and put it in front of Dahlia. Sylvie had seen him here with other women, but she'd never once seen him share his pie. "Sylvie, this is Dahlia Fortune. She's part of the Fortune Family Ranch, and she's starting a sheepherding operation there. She's great with horses, too. Won the junior state barrel racing championship back in high school."

Sylvie put her hand on her hip and reassessed Dahlia. For some reason Rawlston needed the waitress to know the woman sitting across from him wasn't a one-night stand of his. She was a rancher. And, secret or not, she was his *wife*. He wouldn't have her dismissed. Dahlia stared right back at the older woman, not defiant but not intimidated, either. Finally, Sylvie smiled, looking between the two of them at the table.

"Okay, then. Welcome to Chatelaine, Miss Fortune. Your momma has been in here a couple of times. She seems like good people."

"She's the best." As soon as Sylvie moved on to a different table, Dahlia slid a large manila envelope across the table toward him. "Annulment papers. Sign them."

CHAPTER FOUR

"Way to change the subject, Dolly." Rawlston's voice was light, but there was tension around his eyes. He couldn't possibly be surprised, Dahlia thought. They both wanted this, and it was the reason they were sitting in this coffee shop so early in the morning.

"Stop calling me that. Someone's going to hear you and then it will stick and I am *not* anyone's Dolly." Her fingers were still resting on the envelope for some reason, and she slid them off. "The annulment or divorce or whatever will take a month or so to finalize, but if we start the process now, no one needs to know. It'll just…go away."

He was still staring at the envelope, as if it held something terrible.

"Rawlston?" She leaned forward, lowering her voice even further. "We can't dillydally here. That whole night was one big, drunken, foolish mistake, and we have to fix it. I have a *boyfriend*. This could ruin everything that Carter and I have together."

It wasn't until she said Carter's name out loud that Rawlston looked up. He took another bite of the pie, then gestured for her to do the same. She rolled her eyes and did it, just to humor him.

Holy banana tree. This was the best pie of *any* kind that Dahlia could remember eating. Rich but not too rich, sweet but not sickeningly so, creamy without being heavy, with just the right amount of banana flavor. She blinked, then noticed Rawlston's quick, slanted grin as he watched her. Was he trying to sidetrack her from the annulment papers with *pie*?

"Yes, fine, it's very good pie. Are you happy? Now please look at the paperwork. The firm I hired sent a list of all the reasons people can legally choose to annul a Vegas wedding, and broke down the whole process. The only thing we're signing today is the agreement to retain their services for the annulment, and—"

"What *do* you and Carter have?"

"What?" The question came from left field.

"You said this could ruin everything you and Carter have together. Are you two that serious?"

"I…" She realized her mouth was hanging open and snapped it shut. "I don't see where that's any of your business."

"Well, you *are* my wife, so—"

"Shh! I swear you're trying to let every gossip in here know what we did!" She was hissing the words at him. "Carter and I have been dating for six months."

Rawlston sat back in his seat. "Congratulations. But I asked what you *have*. Are you in business together?" He frowned. "You haven't invested any money with him, have you?"

"I don't know why you care, but no. I haven't invested with Carter."

It wasn't for the lack of opportunity. Carter had asked her for money more than once, either as a straightforward investment in his company or to help fund his political action committee for the campaign that hadn't been announced yet. But Dahlia had always declined. Money complicated things, and she didn't want things to become muddled between her and Carter. It was one of the few relationships in her life that was *un*complicated. Two grown-ups who were compatible. No drama. No fuss.

Rawlston nodded thoughtfully. "So you two *are* serious?"

"We're getting there, yes." Carter had hinted pretty heavily that he was going diamond shopping. Which meant there'd be a wedding proposal shortly after he got home. The idea didn't make her heart go pitter-patter or anything, but Carter was a good guy. He'd had a hard time adjusting to her move from Cactus Grove to Chatelaine, but he would come to see that it made her happy. That said, it *had* rubbed her the wrong way when he'd laughed at her announcement that she was going to raise sheep here. He'd called her Bo Peep. She knew he would come around on that, too, in due time. She'd jokingly told him it would be good for his campaign if he had a rancher girlfriend, and he'd responded by saying he'd have the campaign run a focus group on it. Romantic? No. But he was just trying to be practical. She understood that.

"So you're going to tell him about us, then?" Rawlston took another bite of pie, chewing it while waiting for her response.

"There is no *us*," she snapped.

"The marriage certificate on my desk at home says otherwise."

Her teeth clenched. "What I tell him or not is none of your business. God, Rawlston, you and I haven't spoken in years and now you think you can tell me what to do just because..." She looked around the quiet coffee shop and lowered her voice. "Because we got drunk in Vegas and made a mistake. Mistakes can be erased, and that's exactly what will happen once you sign the paperwork and we get the annulment."

She tapped her fingers on the manila envelope, but his

gaze remained on her face, his expression impossible to read. Finally he shook his head and picked up the envelope.

"You're right—it was a pretty big mistake. But if you're in that serious of a relationship, it seems like you'd want to tell him. I thought good relationships were based on honesty. But hey, maybe I'm wrong."

Her conscience twitched just a little. She had to tread carefully with Carter. She needed to pick the right time, and frame it in a way that wouldn't upset him. Did that bode well for a long-term relationship? Maybe not, but then again, being thoughtful about if and when to share information made sense. And, in truth, she had no idea how she was going to explain her Vegas wedding in a way that would make it seem like good news for either one of them.

"I'm not saying I won't ever tell him. It's probably something we'll laugh about years from now. I'm just saying I'm not going to spring it on him as soon as he gets off the plane in a few weeks—*Guess what, honey? I accidentally got married while you were gone!*"

A slow grin curved one corner of Rawlston's mouth, and his gray-blue eyes darkened. "Don't forget the accidentally-slept-with-the-guy part."

An odd tingle danced across her skin. She only remembered snippets of that night, but the snippets were hot. Wild. Funny. Tender. The sex couldn't possibly have been that good. It must have been her imagination filling in memory gaps. But there was something about his heated gaze right now that felt very familiar. She needed to deflect this conversation.

"No good can possibly come from talking about that night. With Carter *or* with you. Let's just…forget it."

"Forget it?" His voice was level, but she heard a mix of humor and disbelief behind it.

"Look, it happened. We can't deny it. Thank God we

were aware enough to use protection." She swallowed hard. "We have to deal with the marriage part, but we do not need to relive the rest of that night. It's…it's humiliating for me."

The heat and humor vanished from his eyes in an instant. He sat forward and put his hand over hers, then glanced around and slid his fingers back so that just their fingertips were touching.

"We had no idea we were getting blackout drunk from that damn fruit punch, so our judgment was obviously impaired. But *what* we did…at least what I remember…" he almost smiled but seemed to catch himself "…we were two adults having safe and rather spectacular sex."

Dahlia's face heated. In fact, her whole body did—a flush that rose from her belly to her cheeks. He thought she was spectacular? She gave herself a mental shake. It didn't matter what Rawlston thought. That night was *never* going to happen again.

"Hey…" His gruff voice made her meet his gaze. "I was out of line, telling you how to handle things with Carter. I'll support whatever you want to do, including never telling a soul for the rest of our lives. But just so you know… I'll *never* forget it."

If she thought she was warm before, her skin was on fire now. From his words. His steady gaze. The touch of his fingers against hers. Which was ridiculous. She snatched her hand away, then picked up her fork and stabbed the pie slice so hard that some of the whipped cream topping sprayed on the table. She took the bite in her mouth and sat back, trying to regain a semblance of balance.

"I can't help what goes on inside your brain, Rawlston, but no one can know about this. Just…sign those papers and get them back to me so we can get the annulment started, okay?" She glanced at her watch and pushed away from the table. "I've got to get back to the ranch. My sheep arrive in a few hours."

"How'd the family take that news?" he asked.

"Some didn't care. Some did. But I didn't get any push-back."

As long as she didn't count her brother Nash's loud insistence that sheep were not moneymakers and that she'd made an "impulsive" decision. She'd dealt with her father's skepticism about her dreams her entire life, so she hadn't let Nash's opinion bother her. If anything, it was extra motivation to bring her plan to fruition. She'd learned to use men's opinions of her as fuel. Dad didn't think she should barrel race? She became state champion barrel racer. Dad and her brothers called her "contrary," but she didn't see it that way. She simply didn't like anyone telling her what to do.

She turned to leave, but Rawlston stopped her. "My father's having a big cookout this weekend. You should come."

"As what, your *wife*?" She shook her head, but he answered before she could continue.

"As my *neighbor*. You could meet some of the locals. If you really want to get this wool business going, you'll need to have customers." He tapped the envelope. "Maybe I'll have this signed by then."

She wasn't sure what to think about the invite, but she knew what she thought about that paperwork. "You could sign that right now. It's just to get things rolling."

"My daddy taught me not to sign anything I haven't read carefully. Dad's barbecue is at three o'clock on Sunday. I'm sure he'd like to see you there."

"I'll think about it." She left Rawlston to finish the pie and drove back to the Fortune Family Ranch.

Home, even if it didn't feel that way yet.

DAHLIA SAT BACK in the brightly patterned chaise lounge with a heavy sigh.

Her twin, Sabrina, started to laugh. "Life as a rancher getting to you already?"

They were sitting on Dahlia's spacious back deck, overlooking a long, narrow lap pool and beyond that, Lake Chatelaine. A timber-framed roof extended out from the log house to shield most of the deck from the sun, and a large fan hung down from the peak to keep the hot air moving. With the temperature over a hundred degrees for the third day in a row, the fan wasn't helping much. She took a sip of her sangria, looking over the rim at Sabrina.

They weren't identical twins, but their looks were very similar. Both were tall, slim, blond and blue-eyed. They had what their father had once described as "Betty Boop" faces—heart-shaped with large eyes and pouty lips. He'd assured them from childhood that the world would fall at their feet at just one look from them, as if their appearance was their best feature. Casper envisioned them successfully married—as in married to a rich man—not as successful individuals with plans of their own.

Sabrina was more of a numbers girl. She'd been an accountant at a children's charity in Dallas, and was now managing the finances for the Fortune Family Ranch. Dahlia, on the other hand, understood numbers just fine, but didn't want to spend her life looking at them.

"What?" Sabrina asked. "Why are you staring at me?"

Dahlia set her glass down on the teak side table. "I don't know. I guess I'm wondering how we got here, living in neighboring log houses on a lake and running a ranch."

Sabrina nodded. "It's been a wild year, hasn't it?" She paused. "Any regrets yet?"

Other than marrying Rawlston Ames?

"Uh…no." She shifted in her seat, adjusting her sunglasses. "I still stumble over my new last name since we changed them. But the houses on the ranch are very nice, and I'm beginning to be able to find my way around the ranch and around town. The sheep are settling in their pastures. And most importantly, Mom seems *really* happy here in Chatelaine."

"I am glad for Mom, but you know how I felt about the name thing. Nothing against the other Fortunes, but a name change was a big deal for me." Sabrina had always been closer to their father than Dahlia had. "But I have to agree that these houses are pretty sweet."

When Wendy Fortune bought the ranch for her children, there were already six luxurious log homes along the lakeshore, in addition to the large main house where she lived. These weren't cabins—they were basically waterfront mansions with log exteriors. Most had a contemporary feel, with cathedral ceilings, open floor plans and walls of windows facing the lake. Like Dahlia's, the others had big, multilevel decks in back, with pools and/or docks on the water so they could have boats if they wanted.

"This house is a major upgrade from my old condo in Cactus Springs, but let's face it—Chatelaine is not Dallas by a long shot. It's growing on me, though." Even though she'd moved here with five siblings, Dahlia felt the place offered new opportunities for her individually. People didn't know her here, so she wasn't saddled with their expectations.

Back in Cactus Grove, everyone had assumed she'd want to do something with horses—raise them, train them, race them. No one took the time to learn that she loved creating things with wool, or that she'd started dreaming of raising her own sheep.

But here, no one blinked an eye at the news. She was a Fortune, but there were Fortunes everywhere in Texas. It honestly didn't carry the pressure of being Casper Windham's daughter in Cactus Grove, where he'd been more infamous than adored.

Dahlia sat up. "Want me to heat some carnitas? I picked them up from that little Mexican place on the far side of town, along with some chicken taquitos."

Sabrina nodded then followed her into the kitchen, with its hickory cupboards and swirling brown quartz countertops. The four-bedroom house was a little masculine for Dahlia's taste. There was a lot of brown, but she hoped to change that when she had a chance to do some redecorating. Which wouldn't be anytime soon, since she had another truckload of sheep arriving the following week. Her dream was becoming a reality, and so was the workload. She warmed the food and set out a basket of chips with salsa and guacamole.

They ate inside to enjoy the air-conditioning, talking about the sheep and their latest wool projects. Sabrina loved to knit and crochet, and she often tackled some of the toughest patterns. Dahlia's preferred woolcraft was needle felting, where she basically painted scenes with wool across a wool background or on an embroidery hoop. Her rebellious streak carried over to her art, so working with patterns left her feeling constrained. With needle felting, she created her own vision and could alter it as needed.

"So how soon until I can get my wool directly from you?" Sabrina asked, pouring more sangria into their glasses from the pitcher on the counter. Dahlia couldn't help thinking of the night she and Rawlston kept refilling their glasses with spiked punch, and how it ended with them married. And in bed. She straightened abruptly.

"What?" She tried to remember what her twin had asked. "Oh, I might do some shearing this fall, but most of it will be done next spring. Bender gave me contact information for some good shearers up near Waco, and they have me on their spring schedule."

Bender—his real name was Bobby—Grant was one of the ranch hands for the main barns. He worked the cattle now, but also had a lot of experience as a younger man raising and caring for sheep. Her brother, Nash, acting as foreman of the ranch, was in charge of the workers, and he'd agreed Bender could work for Dahlia on a part-time basis to help with her sheep. Bender had been on the Fortune ranch property far longer than any of the Fortunes had, and longer than the previous owners, too. He'd spent most of his life here, living alone in one of the trailers clustered together near the main barns and office. He was a quiet guy, but he seemed genuinely happy to be in charge of the sheep herd.

"Don't worry about wool, though," Dahlia continued. "I'm buying it in bulk from Sally Mathison, the woman I bought some of the herd from, so I'll have wool for you. But it will be raw, not spun yet. And not dyed, although I may start playing with dyeing over the winter." Her dream was to sell not only her art and Sabrina's clothing items, but also to sell spun wool to other crafters.

Dahlia was clearing the dishes when Sabrina took her by the wrist. "Okay, sis. What's going on?"

"W-what do you mean?"

"My twin-sense is going off like crazy. Something is different with you, and it's not just the changes we've all been through lately." Sabrina pursed her lips. "You're acting funny, like you're not telling me something. What gives?"

Dahlia pulled away. "I don't know what you're talking about. Everything's fine. *I'm* fine." She glanced at her bare left hand, where a wedding band had been not that long ago.

"Does it have anything to do with Rawlston Ames?"

"I…no… I…*what*?" The mention of his name short-circuited her brain.

Sabrina stared hard for a moment, her eyes narrowed. "So it *is* him. Someone said they saw you two at the Daily Grind the other morning, and that you left in a hurry. The last I knew, you two were arch rivals, but high school was a long time ago. So I'll ask again. What's going on?"

Dahlia was still frozen. Her mind was spinning, but it wasn't conjuring any words to say. Just images of Rawlston—striding across the exhibition hall in his Stetson, laughing with her at the secluded booth near the punch bowl, swooping in for a kiss in the hot pink chapel, slowly sliding her top from her shoulders in his suite—

"Holy… Are you *blushing*?" Sabrina stood and came around the kitchen island. "I didn't even know you two were in contact with each other. What did he do? What did *you* do?"

"Nothing!" she insisted, trying to turn away, but Sabrina stopped her. Dahlia couldn't look her twin in the eye and lie. So she tried to tell some *little* truths in order to avoid the big truth. "We bumped into each other in Las Vegas, and spent a little time catching up, that's all. Did you know he owns the neighboring ranch to ours? Anyway, we talked about my plans for the sheep, and he…" She was losing track of her own story. "And he…wanted information. When we saw each other at the Daily Grind, I gave him that…information. And then I left, because that was the day the first load of sheep arrived, remember?" She chewed her lip, knowing she hadn't sounded very convincing.

"So you spent time catching up. In Vegas." Sabrina paused, then brightened. "Oh my God, did you and Carter break up? Do you *like* Rawlston now?"

"No, and definitely no. Carter and I are still together."
Even if she was technically married to someone else.
Minor detail. Totally fixable. "And I do *not* like Raw-
lston. I mean, I don't hate him, but he's….inconsequential."

Her twin smiled smugly. "You only use big, fancy words
like *inconsequential* when you're nervous. What really
happened when you guys met up in Vegas?"

Dahlia stared straight up at the ceiling, trying and fail-
ing to find a way out of this. But she couldn't hide the
truth from Sabrina.

"We accidentally got married."

Sabrina's mouth fell open. "I'm sorry, did you just say
you *married* Rawlston Ames in Las Vegas?"

"What in the hell did I just miss?"

Sabrina and Dahlia turned to see their younger sister,
Jade, standing near the front door. Her eyes were round
with shock. *Perfect.* Dahlia muttered a curse. Why hadn't
she at least *tried* to lie? Jade rushed to join them in the
kitchen.

"Tell me everything! Right now. Does this mean Carter's out of the picture?"

Her sisters had never hidden their disdain for Carter.
Jade once said he was a miniature version of their father,
and that Dahlia had some sort of reverse Oedipus complex
that drew her to him. Total nonsense, of course.

"Carter is *not* out of the picture. In fact, I'm pretty sure
he's going to propose when he gets back from Europe."

Sabrina snorted. "Won't that be a little crowded if you're
already married to Rawlston? And what do you mean, you
accidentally married him?"

After a heavy sigh, she gestured toward the island. Her
sisters sat in rapt attention as she gave them the highlights
of her so-called wedding night. The spiked punch, the

hours of conversation, the barely remembered trip to the chapel, waking up in his bed—

"Wait," Jade interrupted. "Are you saying you two actually consummated this accidental wedding? Like you just took a wrong turn into the chapel and then *oops*, your clothes fell off?"

"How was it?" Sabrina took Dahlia's hands in hers. "He's matured into one hot man. Was the sex good?"

"I don't know! We were basically blackout drunk by then." The truth was, she was remembering more and more pieces of that night and they were all very, very good. But there were some things even her twin didn't need to know.

"So *now* what?" Jade asked.

"Now we get an annulment, just as quickly as possible." Hopefully Rawlston had signed the attorney paperwork so they could get started. Tomorrow was that cookout he'd mentioned was happening at his father's place. Maybe she should go after all, just to get the promised signatures from him. She straightened, giving her sisters her most threatening look. "No one else can know about this. I'm serious. Do not tell a soul. Got it?"

"So…" Sabrina started "…you're just going to quietly end the marriage and not tell anyone? Not even Carter?"

"That's the plan. There's apparently a whole branch of Nevada law built around ending Vegas weddings, and the process is pretty straightforward. That's why we met at the Daily Grind—so I could give him some preliminary documents to sign."

Jade squinted, looking thoughtful. "You sure you want to do that? Rawlston's a catch. He's a huge improvement on *Carter*." Her mouth twisted when she said Carter's name, making her feelings very clear.

"Yes, I'm sure." Dahlia rolled her eyes. "I barely *know* Rawlston, other than how annoying he was in high school.

Carter and I have been dating for six months now, and we're really good together, so give it a rest, Jade."

"*Really good together?* What does that even mean?" Jade waved her hand in dismissal. "It's hardly a declaration of undying love."

Dahlia frowned into her glass. Jade had a point. It didn't sound quite right, considering she was hoping to marry Carter.

But…if she truly *loved* Carter, she had a feeling all the alcohol in the world wouldn't have been enough to get her to marry another man in Las Vegas. And that man, Rawlston Ames, wouldn't be haunting her dreams the way he had been all week.

CHAPTER FIVE

"DAD, I'M NOT trying to tell you how to grill, but—"

Rawlston's father shook a pair of metal tongs in his direction. "Don't ever approach another man's grill with unsolicited advice, son. I taught you better than that."

Keith Ames was a big man, and people tended to listen to him. But Rawlston wasn't "people" and he nudged his father to the side. "I know a thing or two about steak, and I'm telling you the flame's too high. You're going to end up serving shoe leather."

His dad nudged him right back, rocking him back on his heels. "Boy, I was grillin' steak before you were a glimmer in my eye. I'm putting a sear on, then I'll lower the heat and close the lid. It'll be fine. Go bother someone else."

Rawlston shook his head with a low chuckle. He hadn't seen his dad this animated in a while. They were just playing with each other, of course. They'd been razzing each other about grilling for years. But since Rawlston's mother died five years ago, Dad hadn't been as jovial as he seemed to be today. There was a brightness to his smile and a twinkle in his eyes that hadn't been there in a long time.

The veranda surrounding the pool behind Dad's home was filling with people. This cookout was looking like an event, and Rawlston wondered what the occasion was. Dad had been very mysterious about the whole thing, just saying he had something to announce to his friends and family. Rawlston figured his father was going to take a trip somewhere and just wanted to let people know. He'd been talking about a fishing trip to Alaska. But this was a bigger and more well-heeled crowd than Dad usually hosted.

"What is this big announcement about, again?" he asked. Dad just laughed, never looking up from the thick slabs of steak on the grill.

"Nice try, kid. I told you—it's a surprise. I don't want to tell the story over and over, so everyone who might care was invited. And even a few I didn't invite." He gave Rawlston a sideways glance. "That pretty Fortune lady said *you* invited her."

Dahlia? His eyes immediately scanned the people milling around with cocktails and hors d'oeuvres, provided by servers. Other than his precious steaks, Dad had left the rest of it to the caterers.

Dad snorted. "So it's true. I remember her from when you were in high school. Are you and her an item now?"

Well, they would be if anyone found out about their marriage. "No, Dad. She has the ranch next to mine and I told her this would be a good place to meet more Chatelaine residents." He gave his father a pointed look. "And that's all there is."

"You're slipping, son. She's a looker, and I heard she's smart as a whip, too. The two of you would be—"

"Don't even think about playing matchmaker, old man. Dahlia and I are friends." And barely that.

"That's too bad. It's about time you found a good woman and settled down."

His jaw went tight. "I tried that, remember?"

Dad basted the steaks with melted butter and herbs. Aromatic smoke rose up from the grill. "I said find a *good* woman. They're out there, you know. Everyone has a someone, even if they haven't met them yet."

"What is it with you and all the touchy-feely talk

lately?" His father had started acting differently in the past month or so—smiling, whistling, and waxing poetic about life and romance.

"Maybe I'm gettin' wiser in my old age, son. Maybe I have a newfound appreciation for the mysteries of life and the rhythms of love." Dad was waving the basting brush in the air. "And maybe you could learn a thing or two from listening to my *touchy-feely* talk. Oh, there she is."

Rawlston followed Dad's gaze to the veranda above them and saw Dahlia staring back. She wore a gauzy skirt and top in shades of beige and soft blue. Her hair was long and straight, looking almost white in the Texas sun. She gave a quick wave with her fingers. He excused himself from his father, ignoring Dad's smug laughter. No matter what his old man might think, there were no cupid's arrows between Dahlia and him. But he had to admit there *was* a pull there, drawing him to her.

"Rawlston." Her voice was low and thick.

"Dahlia." He couldn't help smiling at her. "I'm glad you could make it."

She glanced around. "You and your dad are the only people I know here."

"Your brother Ridge is supposed to stop by, and Arlo might, too. I saw them the other day and invited them."

She arched a brow. "You seem very invested in helping us Fortunes get to meet people in Chatelaine."

"Well, you're all trying to get settled, and they *are* my brothers-in-law now." He couldn't resist teasing her.

Her eyes narrowed dangerously. "Stop it!" she hissed. "We are *not* family. In fact, the only reason I came today was to pick up the attorney papers I gave you. You've signed them, right?"

He hadn't, actually. He'd read them, then slid them right back into the envelope. As she'd assured him the other day, the papers weren't a big deal. It was just an agreement to be clients of the law firm for the purpose of annulling their marriage. Signing them would allow the attorneys to start the legal process. But still…he hadn't signed.

"They're out in my truck," he finally said, not exactly answering her question.

"Good. The sooner we get things moving, the better. Carter's back from Europe in a few weeks, and I want this as close to finished as possible." She looked around the spacious yard and pool area. "Your father's place is nice."

He followed her gaze. "Dad and Mom planned to move to Chatelaine Hills together. This little hobby ranch was supposed to be their retirement home. Then she got sick and they stayed near Dallas for her treatments. She designed this place, but never had the chance to enjoy it. Dad moved here shortly after we lost her, and I followed a year later." After his divorce. His voice dropped. "Mom would have loved seeing all these people here."

"I was really sorry to hear about her passing. She was always so sweet."

"She was, thanks." He met her gaze. "I remember seeing you at the memorial. Thanks for that, too."

He'd been wrapped up taking care of his father and handling his own grief back then. He didn't remember if he spoke to Dahlia at all after the service.

"Your dad looks like he's doing well."

He glanced down to where Dad was grilling what looked like the last batch of Angus steaks. Leave it to him to make it clear he preferred his own Black Angus beef over Rawlston's Brahman cattle. But his father *did* look good. He had a beer in his hand, and he was laughing at something Beau Weatherly was saying. He and Beau had both lost their wives, and the experience had created a bond between the men that had deepened into friendship.

At that moment, Rufus Wilkins walked up to Rawlston and Dahlia. The older man owned a ranch a little farther out from Chatelaine, where he raised some of the best quarter horses in Texas, which was saying something. Rawlston started to introduce him to Dahlia, but of course, they already knew each other. She'd worked for Rufus as a groom and trainer on the racetrack, and the mare she'd won so many barrel racing awards with had come from his ranch. As the two began talking horses, Rawlston excused himself and went to catch up with another rancher. He mingled and socialized through dinner, and so did Dahlia.

She was never completely out of his line of sight as she made the rounds, introducing herself and chatting with her new neighbors. She didn't need his help with networking—she was a natural. Dahlia put her hand on some woman's shoulder and laughed, her hair tossed back and her eyes bright with humor. He caught her eye and, instead of the coolness she generally aimed his way, her gaze was warm and relaxed. Moments later, she made her way through the crowd toward him.

Everyone was nibbling on desserts now, and cocktails had been replaced with coffee and brandy. His father was up on the edge of the veranda, and he clinked his spoon against his glass for attention. Rawlston had almost forgotten there was an announcement coming. He gave a quick nod to Dahlia as his father began to speak to the hushed group.

"Ladies and gentlemen, thank you for coming to my little picnic today."

Someone shouted out from near the pool. "Picnic? More like a feast!"

Keith Ames grinned and held his glass up in a mock toast. "I'm glad you enjoyed it, Tommy. I'll confess I threw this party for purely selfish reasons. I have news to share, and I only want to share it once."

Rawlston frowned. That made it sound like bad news. Was his father ill? A ripple of unease went through the partiers, as if some of them felt the same way.

"No, no," Dad said, "it's nothing like that. This is good news, but it's also news that's going to get tongues wagging, so I want to get ahead of the grapevine and give you the facts straight up." He paused, a smile slowly spreading on his face. "I've met someone."

This time, the ripple going through the audience was one of excitement. But Rawlston went very still. He'd had no idea Dad had started dating. In all honesty, he didn't *hate* the idea. He didn't want his father to be alone the rest of his life. But if he was making an announcement this grand...

"And I'm getting married." There was a collective gasp. Dad's smile deepened. "And no, none of you have met her. Because *I* haven't met her yet...at least not face-to-face."

"He's kidding, right?" Dahlia asked softly. "Is this his way of saying he's going to start dating or that he *has* been dating?"

"I haven't a freakin' clue," Rawlston growled. He was on edge, but also concerned. Dad's health might be okay, but was his mind starting to go? He and Dahlia weren't the only ones asking questions, and his father raised a hand to silence everyone.

"Here's the deal. I stumbled across a dating app that's just for farmers and ranchers. I wasn't looking to date as much as just...find someone to talk to. The evenings get long and quiet around here, and I missed discussing the news of the day, or the workings of the ranch, with a woman. Ever since Kathy died, I've been mighty lonely." He looked at Rawlston. "My son and my friends have done their best, but they can't be here all the time, and I don't want them to be. They have their own lives."

Dad cleared his throat with a cough. "Anyway, I had correspondence with a few different women, and it was nice, but it wasn't until I met JoAnn that everything just shifted for me. She and I have been texting and talking for five months now, and she has made my life so much brighter and lighter. JoAnn's a widow from Vermont. She and her late husband had a dairy farm for forty years, so she knows all about livestock and the farming life."

He paused, then rushed ahead again. "I proposed and she said yes. She's moving to Chatelaine next week, and I expect every single person here to welcome her with open arms." He stared right at Rawlston on that final sentence and remained fixed on him. "JoAnn and I hope to be married by the end of August. She's kind and funny and adventurous, and… I like her very much. I want her in my life, which means she'll be in your lives, too."

"Oh, wow," Dahlia breathed. She rested her hand on his arm. "Did you know anything about—"

"Not even a hint." Rawlston had very rarely in his life ever been angry with his father, but right now all he could see was red. Why hadn't Dad said anything? What if this lady was a con artist? What if she was just after Dad's money? How *dare* he just move some random stranger into what was supposed to have been Rawlston's *mother's* home.

"Rawlston…" There was warning in Dahlia's voice now, as if she felt his rising rage. "Look at him. Your dad seems happy. Don't spoil his moment by—"

He pulled away, looking at her in shock. "You, of all people, shouldn't be talking about stopping someone from rushing into a disastrous wedding." She glanced around to see if anyone heard him, her face paling. He dropped his voice, but it was still vibrating with anger. "This sham of a marriage isn't going to happen. If it *does*, I'll end it just as fast as you're ending ours."

Rawlston stormed away, doing his best to keep his expression neutral as everyone began applauding his father's ridiculous news. He drew Dad away from the crowd of well-wishers as quickly and quietly as possible, finally wrangling him into the study and closing the door with more force than he'd intended.

"Easy, son."

Rawlston stood for a moment, head down, hand on the doorknob, trying to compose himself. When he thought he was ready, he slowly turned to face his father.

"Are you okay, Dad? Do you need to talk to your doctor? Have some blood work done? Maybe get some pills for depression or an altered mental state? Because there's clearly something wrong if you think you're marrying some random woman you've never even met face-to-face."

Dad smiled. "I had a full physical last month, and the doctor said I'm in prime condition for my age. There's nothing wrong with my brain, either, but thanks for your concern." His expression sobered. "And JoAnn isn't just 'some woman.' She and I have been corresponding for months. We've been video-chatting before bed almost every night for weeks. We know things about each other that no one else in our lives knows. Including you." His father leaned back against his oak desk. "I know every book and movie she loves. She knows I'm obsessed with all those *Law and Order* shows, and she's wild about *Yellowstone*. I had to make it very clear to her that I am not Kevin Costner."

Dad winked, but Rawlston didn't return the smile. "She writes poetry and she likes to grow flowers. And she loves history. She wants to take me to *Greece*, of all places, just so she can visit some old temples or something. Son, she's made my life… Well, she's made it a life worth living again. I actually look *forward* to getting up every morning now, and I haven't felt that way since we lost your mother."

"And what *about* my mother?" Rawlston demanded, his voice rising. "What about your wife?"

"Watch your tone, son." Dad's eyes went flint hard. "Your mother isn't here anymore. I mean, she'll *always* be here—I loved her more than the air I breathed. But I can't be alone anymore, Rawlston. I can't do it. I'm asking you to understand that."

"And you couldn't tell me this was all happening?"

"I *could* have, but I chose not to. Look at how you're reacting right now. I didn't want your disapproval coloring how I saw JoAnn. I wanted it to just be me and her for as long as possible, without the outside world pushing us one direction or another."

Rawlston paced the room, rubbing the back of his neck in agitation. "Okay, fine. You want companionship. That's fair. First, there are plenty of women in Chatelaine—hell, in all of *Texas*—that would be willing to be your companion. Be on your arm at parties. Go to dinner with you. You didn't need to reach all the way to New England for that. Secondly, it's okay to like a woman. It's okay to like *this* woman. That doesn't mean you have to rush into *marriage*. Why can't you just take things slow?"

Keith Ames nodded, then straightened, making sure he was looking Rawlston right in the eye. "Man to man? I'm not getting any younger, son. And I miss having a woman in my life…for more than just friendship."

"I get it." Rawlston held up his hand. "But why do you need to *marry* her? Marriage is painful and complicated to get out of. Trust me, I know." He was referring to Dahlia, but Dad thought he meant Lana.

"I know your one experience with marriage wasn't great," Dad started. "But I believe in marriage. You think I'm dishonoring your mother by marrying JoAnn, but I'm actually honoring the things Kathy and I valued in life—fidelity, commitment, partnership."

"You can have those things without getting *married*. Bring this woman to Texas…call her your girlfriend if you want. Have a good time. And when it's over, send her back to Vermont with only what she came here with, and not a penny more."

"Worried about your inheritance, Rawlston?" There was a warning edge to his tone.

"Dad, I don't need your inheritance. But *you* do. And for all you know, this stranger is thinking a lonely old man is an easy mark."

He knew the words were a mistake the minute they crossed his lips. His father was only sixty-five, and he'd earned an MBA from the University of Texas, as well as a degree in finance. He'd never been a stupid man, but he *was* a proud one. "Dad, I didn't mean—"

"Oh, yes, you did. Don't BS me now that you've spoken the words out loud. Own them." Keith Ames didn't often intimidate his son, but right now he was so angry and tense that it took all Rawlston had in him not to step back. His father poked him hard in the chest. "You think I'm some doddering old fool who's been hoodwinked by a dame. Nice to know my own son thinks so little of me."

"Dad—"

"Be quiet. Just—" he sighed heavily, then patted his hand on the spot he'd just poked "—be quiet. I know you're trying to look out for me, son." His voice softened. "And I blindsided you with this, mainly because I was afraid of having this exact conversation. But that time gave me a chance to be sure without any pressure. I'm *sure*, Rawlston.

JoAnn is a good woman, and I want her to be my wife. Not my gal pal. Not my partner in the sheets. My *wife*."

Rawlston blinked and glanced away, taking a step back. While he couldn't wrap his head around his father's decision, he couldn't fight him anymore, either. He started muttering to himself, eyes tightly closed as he tried to come to terms with it all. "It's been quite a month, with the two of us getting married and probably the two of us racing toward divorce, too." Divorce. Annulment. What was the difference?

"What did you say?"

Uh-oh. Had he just said that out loud? He cleared his throat loudly. "What? Nothing. I just hope your marriage lasts longer than…" He coughed. "Than the summer."

His father's eyes narrowed on Rawlston. "You said the 'two of *us* getting married.' What the heck did you mean by that?"

There was a long beat of silence in the room, although the party seemed to be going strong outside. Music was playing and there was a steady hum of laughter and conversation. He did his best to look his dad in the eye and act as if nothing was awkward at all. He failed.

"Remember when I was in Las Vegas a week ago?"

"Yeah." Realization began to dawn on Dad's face. "Aw, hell. You didn't marry some showgirl or something, did you?"

"Worse. I married Dahlia Fortune."

It was hard to track all the emotions that crossed his father's face. Shock. Disbelief. Concern. And then…absolute, unadulterated delight. Dad let out a laugh that morphed into a whoop of celebration as he clapped his hands together and started laughing for real.

"Son, I swear to God if you're pulling my leg, I'll take you out behind the barn like I did when you were ten. But if you're *not*, then *praise Jesus*, because that's the best news I've heard since JoAnn accepted my proposal!"

Rawlston gestured for Dad to be quiet. "Keep it down! No one knows, and no one *can* know. It was a mistake, and we're fixing it."

"Why? Dahlia's a great gal."

"Dahlia's dating Carter Powers, and she intends to *keep* dating him." Maybe even marry the jerk.

His father's face fell. "Really? Well, that's disappointing. She's clearly never done business with the guy."

Keith Ames had been pulled into one of Carter's so-called investments, which had basically been a well-disguised Ponzi scheme. By the time his father realized it was all smoke and mirrors, he'd lost over two hundred thousand dollars. It would have been a lot more, but Dad had pulled his money out when he saw the red flags. Carter had mocked him for not having *the guts to invest with the big dogs*.

His father sat on the corner of his desk again while Rawlston filled him in on the Las Vegas story—the spiked punch, the wedding veil that lit up, the bright pink chapel and the legally binding marriage certificate sitting on his dresser when they woke up the next morning.

Dad thought for a moment, then his smile returned. "She can't get serious with Carter as long as she's married to you, right?" The same thought had crossed Rawlston's mind. "So why not *stay* married a while longer? You'd be doing her a favor in the long run, and hell, you might just find the two of you are a good match. Who knows, you might fall in love and stay married for *real*." He gave an exaggerated shrug. "After all, love and matrimony are in the air for the Ames men this month."

Rawlston felt his anger flaring again. He was mad at himself for even being tempted to consider the crazy idea.

He was mad at his father for marrying a total stranger. He was mad at a world that seemed determined to convince him there was anything *good* about marriage. Because there *wasn't*. He'd given up his navy career for Lana and she'd left him anyway. And even if he *did* believe in marriage at all—which he did not—he was currently married to someone who didn't even want him. He'd already had *one* marriage like that. He'd be damned if he'd consider a *second*. He turned his back on his father and jerked open the door.

"Rawl—"

He slammed the door shut behind him, refusing to listen to any more of his father's nonsense. Marriage was for suckers. It was a long con that ended in broken dreams.

CHAPTER SIX

DAHLIA HAD BEEN hanging around the living room, worried about Rawlston's confrontation with his father. He'd obviously been stunned by Keith's news, but she wasn't sure where exactly his anger came from. Was it because he hadn't known, because he didn't want his mom replaced or because he was so anti-marriage in general? It was probably a combination of the three, but she didn't want him blowing up at his father.

Keith Ames had always been a bit of a revelation to Dahlia. He was so incredibly different from her own father. Where Casper Windham had been cold and demanding, pushing his children to win at all costs, Mr. Ames had been quietly supportive of Rawlston, encouraging him to find his passion and supporting whatever his son chose to do. Not in a screaming-from-the-sideline way, but in a gently encouraging, do-your-best way.

As a teen, she'd been envious of Rawlston because of his father, and because he was an only child. Her dad not only wanted his children to win, he wanted them to compete with each *other*. No wonder Rawlston seemed to do so well all the time—he was the solo, golden child in his home, and both parents adored him unconditionally.

Dahlia could hear angry, raised voices coming from down the hall. She wasn't close enough to overhear words and, frankly, she didn't want to be. This was a family matter between the two men. Things got quiet. Then she heard

Keith laughing loudly, and then raised voices again before Rawlston stormed out. Dahlia barely had time to duck into the kitchen with the caterers so that he wouldn't see her lurking. She worked her way outside, hoping to bump into him casually, but Rawlston was nowhere to be seen.

She jumped when she felt an abrupt tap on her shoulder ten minutes later. She'd barely turned when a folded piece of paper was slapped into her hand.

"Here," Rawlston growled. "I can't wait to be done with this marriage."

"Wait…" But he was gone as fast as he'd appeared. She opened the paper to see his signature, agreeing to allow the law firm to begin the process of dissolving their marriage. It was what she wanted. So why did she feel like chasing after him?

She didn't, of course. She reminded herself that whatever was going on between Rawlston and Keith Ames was none of her business. And there was Keith now, mingling with his guests with a big smile on his face. So the two hadn't killed each other, and Rawlston's bad behavior hadn't dimmed his father's joy. She wouldn't let it dim hers, either.

WHEN DAHLIA OPENED the gate to the new pasture, a hundred sheep galloped through the opening, looking like bouncy cotton balls against the green grass. With a nudge of her heel, the buckskin mare she was riding stepped forward so Dahlia could reach over to close the gate. The well-trained old mare sidestepped obediently until the gate was closed and latched.

"Good girl, Bunny." Dahlia patted the horse's neck. "Chasing after sheep is a lot easier than chasing racehorses, isn't it?"

Bunny—officially King's Sweet Bun—had been Dahlia's mount when she'd worked at the racetrack near Dallas. The mare had been a calming influence on the young colts and fillies Dahlia worked with as a groom. Of course, they didn't all want to *be* calmed. She and the mare had been bitten and kicked at numerous times in the eight years they'd worked there. But sturdy Bunny had always been unflappable around the high-strung youngsters.

Dahlia figured the move to the Fortune ranch was the equivalent of retirement for the thirteen-year-old mare. She'd use her for the occasional check on the herd, just to keep her in shape, but most of Bunny's time would be spent in the partially covered paddock near the stable. Dahlia's daily mount would be her paint stallion. Unlike Bunny, Rebel wasn't a calming influence on *anyone*, especially sheep, which he seemed to have a particular dislike for.

Maybe the stud thought herding sheep was beneath his dignity as a champion cutting horse—a competition that involved herding and outwitting grown cattle. Then again, Rebel hadn't liked the cows much, either. He was a grumpy soul trapped in a gorgeous black-and-white paint body. That was how Dahlia had come to own him. His last owner had given up on him and labeled him *dangerous* after he'd charged at the man's wife, mouth wide-open, with clear intent to do serious harm.

Dahlia had realized a long time ago that stallions are all about ego. And misbehaving ones were more egocentric than most. She'd learned to honor that ego rather than try to break it. Tough horses wanted respect, but they also *gave* respect to humans who didn't respond to them with fear or anger. Rebel was only five, and he had a lot to learn, but he'd come to trust Dahlia.

She saw the top of a tall cottonwood tree just visible

beyond a rolling hill and trotted Bunny in that direction. The sheep seemed content where they were, barely lifting their heads from the grass as she rode past them. As the tree came fully into sight, she was surprised to see a man and horse near it. The horse was in the shade, but the man was working on a nearby fence line. She thought it might be one of the ranch hands, but when he took his hat off, wiped his brow and turned to face her, she was surprised to see it was Rawlston.

"Good morning, neighbor!" She called out to him. He didn't answer, but he gave a slight nod. Was he still in a mood from his father's party? She looked over at his dark chestnut gelding, standing by the tree. "Will he be okay with company?"

"Malloy? Yeah, he's fine with sharing the shade."

She dismounted and tied the reins loosely to the saddle so Bunny could graze by Malloy. She was glad she hadn't ridden Rebel out here today, as that would never have happened. A mottled black-and-white dog came running over to her.

"Who's this?" She knelt to pet the dog, whose stub of a tail was wagging wildly, making his whole butt wiggle.

"That's Tripp. He's an Australian cattle dog. Fearless little guy." Rawlston smiled down at Dahlia and Tripp. "You're gonna need a herding dog of your own, aren't you?"

"I've been thinking about it, yes." She loved dogs, but she knew nothing about using a herding dog. "I need to learn what to do with one first. I've heard it's a science." She stood.

"I know a border collie breeder outside Houston. Bonnie has raised some champions, and she'll teach you how to use them with the sheep. I'll get you her number. It's just a matter of learning their commands." He made the slightest of hand signals, and Tripp promptly moved to sit at his side. "Herding dogs are hyperintelligent and energetic. They make good companions."

As he leaned over to pet his dog's head, Dahlia couldn't help wondering if that companionship was more important to Rawlston than the work. He had no siblings, and he'd told her in Vegas that he only had a few hired hands on the ranch. He had to be lonely. She checked herself. That wasn't her problem.

She walked to the fence line. "I believe you're on the wrong side of this fence, mister."

He shook his head with a slow smile. "I won't swear to it, but I'm pretty sure that old tree is on the property line, so technically if you're on this side of the tree, *you're* the one trespassing. But you're welcome to do so." He looked past her, his smile fading. "You're bringing your sheep up into this range?"

"Well, it's my range, so…yes, of course I am. Why?"

He gave a slight shrug of one shoulder. "Sheep and cattle don't mix. They had whole range wars about it in the old days."

"Well, then, I guess it's a good thing you're keeping this fence repaired. My sheep will stay over here, and your cows can—" She looked toward his side of the fence. "Oh, are those Brahmans? I didn't know you raised rodeo bulls!" The big, grayish-blond bovines, with long ears and humped backs, were well-known on the rodeo circuit as some of the toughest bulls to ride.

"I don't raise anything for the rodeo, and I only have two bulls at the moment." He followed her gaze to the distant cattle on his side of the fence. "Those are what we call 'gentle Brahmans.' They've been crossbred with Angus and Herefords to take the attitude out of them. I wouldn't recommend trying to *ride* one, but they're actually as gentle as kittens, despite their size."

"What made you go with Brahmans? My brothers said Black Angus was the way to go for our ranch."

"Angus is a good cow, and the meat is in demand. But I like the Brahmans because they can handle the heat of southern Texas so well. The breed originated in Africa." His smile returned. "And I think they look cool."

"They *are* cool. That's one of the reasons I went with the Texas Merino sheep—they can handle the summer heat." She turned to face him. "Oh, and just FYI... I got an email from the law firm, and they'll be sending us the papers to sign within a couple of days. After that, the annulment only takes a few weeks to process."

She expected him to be thrilled, but his face went blank. "That's what you want?"

Did he really just ask that?

"You're the one who barked at me that you couldn't wait for the marriage to be over. Now it will be, and we can both go back to living our lives."

He slid his hat back on with a sigh. "I'm sorry about my attitude on Sunday. Dad just...stunned me. It was a reminder of all the reasons marriage makes no sense as a concept. People aren't meant to pair up forever. It's not sustainable."

She stared for a moment before responding. "Wow. I thought *I* was the cynical one. Clearly *our* marriage makes no sense, but marriage in general is... Well, it's about making a commitment to a person you love. And long marriages do happen, so it's not impossible."

"It's impossible for me."

She'd heard some vague gossip about his marriage to Lana, but couldn't remember the details—only that the divorce had been ugly.

"It's impossible for *us*, I agree. But this will be just a blip on the screen of our lives, Rawlston. You'll find your someone someday."

CHAPTER SEVEN

HER WORDS WERE meant to be comforting and encouraging. They only left Rawlston feeling numb.

"You sound like my dad," he muttered. "I tried those rose-colored glasses once, and got trampled on, so forgive me if I have no interest in trying again."

"What happened with you and Lana, anyway?" Dahlia's voice was soft. Gentle. But her question cut like a dull knife on a salted wound. He braced against the sting, reminding himself it wasn't her fault for being curious. She wasn't being intentionally hurtful...unlike his first wife.

"I'd already enlisted in the navy when Lana and I got serious." He gestured for Dahlia to follow him into the shade near where their horses grazed. Tripp was already napping there, curled into a ball. "But I guess she hadn't thought through what that meant. She loved me wearing my dress white uniform at the wedding, but she had a fit the first time I deployed. She acted as if I had a choice in where I went or for how long."

Dahlia took a bottle of water from her saddlebag. She offered it to him, but he'd brought his own and dug that out.

"Why *did* you choose the navy? You were always the cowboy-est of cowboys when we were teens."

"That was why. I wanted something totally different. My dad thought it was defiance, but it was more...curiosity. I wanted to visit some of the places we'd learned about in school, and I wanted to see the ocean, so it seemed a

great way to do both. And I loved it. I worked in naviga-
tion and it was different from anything I'd ever done."

"But Lana wasn't impressed?"

He huffed. "To say the least. Lana wanted to be the center of everything. At the time, I saw her ego as strength,
but it was really a weakness of hers. She was only happy
when everyone's world revolved around her. And I couldn't
do that from the Atlantic Ocean. She told me I 'wasn't
present' for her."

"Did she send you a Dear John letter?"

"I wish she had." He saw the surprise on Dahlia's face.
"If she'd just ended things, I'd probably be on a ship somewhere today. Instead she begged me to come home, making me think we had a chance to make it work. That was
back when I thought marriage vows meant something."

Lana had acted like being in the military was a job he
could just quit whenever he'd wanted, but it didn't work
that way. "When my time was up, I left the navy and came
home to save our marriage. Two months later, she left me
for the guy who lived next door to us. His wife was a navy
pilot, and apparently Lana and Ted had been keeping each
other company whenever we were deployed." He took a
long drink of water, hoping to wash the bitterness from his
throat. "I lost a friend, my wife *and* a career I'd enjoyed."

"You don't enjoy ranching?"

The question surprised him. "That's what you got from
that whole story? I love ranching now. But for a while, I'd
had a different dream, and Lana stole that from me."

"I'm sorry about your marriage, of course. It just surprises
me to hear you mourning a navy career while we're standing
here." She gestured around. The cottonwood tree sat atop a
small hill, so they had quite a view of ranges sprawling out
around them in greens and browns. He nodded.

"I've gotten over that part of the loss. Ranching's hard

work, but rewarding. I have no regrets about the life I have. But marriage? No thanks. Four years later, that wound is still raw."

Which made it even more bizarre that he'd stumbled— no matter *how* drunk—into another marriage in Las Vegas.

Dahlia glanced at her watch. "I should head back before the temperature gets higher. I don't want to stress Bunny too much in the heat." She flashed a quick smile. "I should have those papers soon, and we'll make ending *this* marriage less stressful than your last one."

He stepped up to help her mount the buckskin mare, then remembered who she was. Dahlia was a champion, and didn't need his help with horses.

"I heard you bought that ornery paint stud from Hal Templeton. How's he working out for you?"

"Rebel is slightly less ornery these days, at least with me. But he's still not very social. And oddly enough, he doesn't like sheep."

He laughed at that. "He was bred to be a cattle horse, not to chase around a bunch of stuffed squeak toys." She started to object, but he raised his hand to stop her. "I'm not making fun of your livestock. I'm just saying what that paint horse probably thinks of them." He patted her mare's shoulder, right next to Dahlia's leg. "I'd like to take a look at him sometime. I've got a bay mare I think would be a good cross with his bloodline." He stepped back with a grin. "Maybe we can make his breeding fee part of the divorce settlement."

"It's an annulment, not a divorce." She corrected him like a schoolmarm. "And I take breeding fees seriously in my stable, so if you're really interested, stop by and we can talk. I might even give you a neighborly discount."

She turned her horse and trotted off down the hill away from him. He caught at the reins of his own trusted horse,

Malloy, just in case he got any ideas about following. Dahlia's blond hair was free under her Western hat, fluttering lightly as she neared the bottom of the hill. She sat straight in the saddle, like she was born to be there. She'd been riding and showing horses since she was a kid.

Dahlia was a good person. She deserved a better husband than him, for sure. He frowned. She *definitely* deserved a better husband than Carter Powers. Dahlia was smart, but she didn't seem to see how sleazy the guy was—he'd do just about anything for more money and power. The fact that she was now going by the name *Fortune* probably made her all the more enticing to Carter as a spouse. Would she really say yes if he asked?

He mounted Malloy and headed down the fence line in the opposite direction, to a gate at the base of the long slope. Tripp was trotting along behind him. Dahlia couldn't say yes to Carter if she was still married to Rawlston. As much as he disdained the institution, his dad was right. He could use it in order to protect her. Carter would move on in a hurry once Dahlia rejected him—the guy didn't know how to handle losing.

And as soon as that happened, Rawlston could sign those papers and set them both free. It was an absurd idea, but it might just work.

DAHLIA WAS DREAMING about Rawlston when her phone began to ring. She blinked, looking around in consternation until she remembered she lived in a log mansion these days. She'd fallen asleep in the overstuffed easy chair near the fireplace, thinking about her conversation with Rawlston under the cottonwood that morning. That was probably why he'd sauntered into her dreams, holding her close and kissing...

The phone rang again, forcing her to wake up for real

and find the damn thing. It had fallen into the cushions. She dug it out and frowned at the screen. What was her brother Ridge calling her about at midnight?

"What's wrong?"

Her brother chuckled softly. "Nice greeting, sis. Sorry to do this, but...can you come over to my horse barn? Livvie's not acting right. I'm worried it could be colic..."

She sat up and reached for her boots. "Have you called the vet?"

Just because she'd worked as an aid for the track veterinarian for a few years didn't mean she was qualified to diagnose anything officially.

"I did, but both vets are all the way out in Billington. There was a barn fire and a bunch of horses were injured in the evacuation. They won't make it to Chatelaine for a couple hours yet, and I know how fast a minor case of colic can go bad." Ridge had lost a prize broodmare to the intestinal condition last year. "I'd really appreciate the help, sis."

She tried to push the horror of a stable fire out of her head. It was every horse owner's worst nightmare. "I'm on my way."

They'd begun using golf carts to get around the ranch. It was their mother's idea—something she'd seen on another ranch in the area. Wendy had bought all six of them new golf carts with headlights, comfortable seating and a small cargo basket in back, where golf clubs would normally go. At first they'd all rolled their eyes behind Mom's back. It was a sweet gesture, but it felt silly.

Until they'd started trying to walk the long roadway to each other's homes, or worse, to the main barns over a mile away. Not an impossible distance to walk, unless you were carrying something or were trying to avoid a hike on a hundred-degree August day. But too short to make driving their cars worth it. Within a few days, they'd embraced the golf carts, and started tricking them out for fun.

Dahlia had found dahlia stickers online in a variety of colors and sizes, and had covered her cart in the flowers. Her name was considered unusual by some, but it was a Windham family name from generations back. While there was no proof, everyone had assumed it had originally been inspired by the large, colorful flowers.

The lights were on in the low stable across from Ridge's home, and she found him inside, walking a dapple gray mare up and down the main aisle. Lonestar Livvie was a three-year-old thoroughbred, and she'd won quite a few races. Ridge had high hopes for her, both on the track and as a future broodmare. He looked up in relief when Dahlia walked in.

"Thanks for coming so fast. I heard something on the intercom, so I walked over to the barn to check it out. That's when I saw Livvie biting at her side and I got nervous." All the barns had cameras or intercoms installed. The ranch staff monitored the main barn cameras, but Dahlia and some of her siblings kept monitors in their homes for their own smaller stables, just so they'd hear if something unusual happened during the night.

Dahlia ran her hand down the mare's neck and stepped close. A horse with stomach colic often had pale gums and lips, and an inward look to their gaze. Dahlia checked her mouth, and Livvie's gums were pink and healthy looking. Her eyes didn't look distressed as much as just nervous, and her pulse was close to normal. Dahlia was relieved to discover that the mare's stomach wasn't bloated, and she didn't react when Dahlia pressed against it in a few spots.

"I don't think this is colic, Ridge." Livvie whipped her head around to bite at her side. "But something's definitely bothering her." Dahlia examined the area Livvie had tried to bite. There was a small, hard lump there. When she tried to look more closely, Livvie's ears went flat back. "It looks like a bug bite or maybe even a—" she pressed against it and the horse tried to bite *her* "—yep, it's a bee sting. Probably burns and itches like crazy, doesn't it, girl?" Livvie wasn't ready to forgive her quite yet, shaking her head and stomping a front hoof in anger. "She doesn't seem allergic, but I need to get the stinger out and see if we can make her feel better. Do you have tweezers and ice packs?"

"In the first aid kit on the wall. How would we know if she's allergic?"

Dahlia went to the first aid kit. "Just like humans, really—swelling, increased pulse, lips and gums turning blue. She doesn't have any of that. She seems more ticked off than sick, but the vet may want her to have a steroid to be safe." She returned to Livvie. "In the meantime, let's hold cold compresses on it to get the swelling and pain down." She held up the tweezers. "Hold her head so I don't get bit while I try to find the stinger and get it out."

She was able to do that fairly quickly, and only had to dodge one sideways kick from Livvie in the process. They were taking turns holding compresses on the bump when they both heard something near the open back door of the barn. It was a soft, mewing sound.

"Did you hear that?" Dahlia asked. "Was that the yearling squealing or…?"

Ridge frowned. "The colt's right here across from Livvie. There aren't any horses in those back stalls. Might be a cat or something. There are a few around."

They dismissed it and returned their attention to the mare, whose mood had definitely improved. She was snatching hay from Ridge's hand and chewing it contentedly.

"I think you can save the veterinarian a midnight drive," Dahlia said. "She looks fine now."

Ridge agreed and put her back into her stall. He was finishing a voicemail to the vet when they heard another sound from the back of the barn. This time the sound was more clear, but it made no sense, because it was definitely the sound of an infant crying. They hurried toward the sound, which was coming from an empty stall Ridge used to store bales of hay. They both came to an abrupt halt at the open door.

There was a woman lying on the floor, her back against the stack of hay bales. On her chest was an infant carrier, and inside that carrier was an unhappy baby crying loudly. The petite brunette wasn't responding to the child's cries. Dahlia rushed forward. The woman was unconscious, with a nasty bump on her forehead.

"She's hurt. Call 9-1-1!" Instead, Ridge knelt at her side, staring at the woman. Dahlia looked over at him. "Ridge, do you know her? You need to call someone."

"Just…wait." Her brother reached out to remove the baby from the carrier, cradling the infant in his arms. "Let's figure out what's going on first. The baby looks healthy. Looks like a girl, with hair just like her mom."

They did both have the same auburn hair, but Dahlia was more of a skeptic than Ridge. "We don't know if this is the baby's mother. Maybe she's a kidnapper or…"

"She's not a kidnapper. Look at her neck, at that birthmark. And look at the baby."

He was right—the woman and child had matching birthmarks, shaped almost like a star, on their necks.

"Okay, maybe she's the mom. But look at her! She needs medical attention, and why is she hiding in your barn? Who's she running from? It could be a custodial battle or—"

"Or maybe she's protecting the baby from someone, Dahlia. You don't know."

"Neither do you!" The baby's cries got louder, and Dahlia lowered her voice. "This is for the authorities to figure out. This woman needs help. If you're not going to call, then I will." She pulled her phone from her back pocket, but Ridge put his hand on hers, stopping her.

"She has a bump on the head, but the bleeding has already stopped. I've got a friend I can call." He looked straight into Dahlia's eyes to make his case. "A *doctor* friend who lives in Chatelaine Hills. I know Mitch will come over. If he thinks she needs a hospital, then we'll take her. She ended up in my barn for a reason, and I'm not going to put her at risk of being found until I know for sure who's after her."

Ridge was the baby of the family, and tended to be pretty lighthearted in his approach to life. He also had a reputation as a bit of a playboy. But she'd never known him to be this impractical or impulsive. Not that he wasn't a loving brother and a good man, but watching him bouncing an infant in his arms and arguing for *not* calling the police to handle this situation was a bit of an out-of-body experience for Dahlia. Against every instinct she had, she felt compelled to support him. At least for the moment.

"Maybe there's something in the baby bag." It was a small bag, but she was relieved to find a baby bottle in there with milk in it, a small container of formula, diapers, and a few items of clothing. But nothing that would identify the mother.

"Look!" Ridge said. "On the flap of the bag." He tugged at the flap of the pink-and-white-gingham bag. There was a name embroidered there in minty green thread. *Evie*.

"Well, I think it's safe to say that's the baby's name. I'm guessing little Evie is around three months old." Dahlia held the mother's wrist, checking her pulse. It was strong and steady. Her breathing was steady, too. She lifted her eyelids and checked her eyes—they also seemed fine. "The woman doesn't seem to have any other injuries than the bump on her head. But, Ridge—"

"I'll call Mitch right now to come check her out. And I promise I'll follow whatever medical advice he gives me." The baby was quiet, content in the warmth of his arms. He was staring down at the little girl. His expression was soft...sweetly intimate in a way that made Dahlia smile. He looked up. "I just can't shake the idea that they might be in more danger if we report this to the police. Not *from* the police, but from whomever she's running from. If they know where she is, they might try to take this baby from her, or...worse." He looked up at Dahlia. "I can't take that chance. Not until I know."

"It's a huge risk, Ridge. You're taking responsibility for them both."

"Trust me, sis. Please."

She'd never known her brother to beg. She let out a long sigh. "Okay. But I'm not leaving until I see you call this doctor friend of yours."

DAHLIA CALLED RIDGE first thing in the morning. He assured her that not only were his surprise houseguests still there, but they were both awake and doing fine. In fact, the mother had woken while his doctor pal was there last night. Her head wound only required a couple of stitches, but there was one big problem. She claimed not to know her own name or who she was. Ridge tried to explain it away as something his doctor friend said was probably temporary amnesia, but Dahlia had her doubts.

"Don't you think it's a little convenient that she can't give you her name?"

"Look, even if she *does* know her name, I can't blame her for being cautious about sharing it." He huffed out a breath. "Like I said last night, I'm convinced she's hiding from someone or something."

"Does she remember Evie?"

"Yes. As soon as she saw her, she knew the baby's name and knew she was her child. She's very protective of her. She told me this morning that she knows they're in danger, but she doesn't know why or who the threat is."

"So, where is she going to go?" Dahlia asked.

"They'll stay with me for now. They'll be safe here while she works on getting her memory back."

"Ridge, you can't just take them in like that."

"Well, I just did. I named her Hope."

"*Excuse* me?"

"The woman. I have to call her something, so I've named her Hope." He paused. "I'll protect her, Dahlia."

"Yes, I'm sure you will. But who will protect *you*? Be careful, Ridge."

He promised he would be, but she couldn't help thinking it was too late for that. She'd promised to trust his decision, so she hoped for the best. But she also promised herself she'd keep an eye on all of them.

She'd been scrolling through her emails on her laptop as they talked, and she opened one from the Nevada law firm as soon as they hung up. Attached to the email were annulment papers. She sat back and smiled. All she had to do was sign them, get Rawlston's signature, and their so-called marriage would be over.

Ridge's problems might just be beginning, but hers were about to be over.

CHAPTER EIGHT

RAWLSTON READ DAHLIA'S text again, after finishing his first morning coffee and starting on his second.

Papers attached. Sign and return them and we'll be single again. Yay!

There was an attachment to the text. All he had to do was send it to his printer, sign it and get it to Dahlia for her signature. He'd be free of marriage. She'd be free *to* marry. To marry Carter Powers. He scowled at the phone. Carter would only use Dahlia—her beauty, her name, her money—to advance his own agenda. Rawlston had heard rumblings that the guy was looking at a run for political office.

She couldn't say yes to Carter as long as she was wed to Rawlston. The thought kept rolling over and over in his head. It would mean telling lies. Little ones, perhaps, but a lot of them. To Dahlia. And it would mean staying legally married, at least for a while. That would be wrong.

But if he was doing it to *protect* Dahlia…wouldn't that be a noble cause? Would it be worth a few little white lies to keep her from walking into a disaster with Carter? It wasn't like he'd be trapping her—or himself—in marriage forever. Carter had a short attention span, and he'd need a partner before his campaign started. As soon as Dahlia said no, the jerk would be on the hunt for someone else. And *then* Rawlston would sign those damn papers and set them both free. He was only talking about another month or two.

Rawlston took a sip of his coffee, surprised that he was seriously thinking about this.

He couldn't tell Dahlia he *wanted* to stay married. She'd get the wrong idea and it would backfire. After all, she didn't want to have a relationship with him now, any more than she had back in school. He wasn't looking to court the woman anyway. So he'd have to just…stall her for a while. Similar to riding a good cutting horse in competition, whenever she tried to break past him, he'd have to move fast to hold her in place. Metaphorically, of course. He was *helping* her, not keeping her as a hostage.

Oh, damn. This was actually becoming a plan. One he couldn't tell anyone about. He set his coffee mug down and picked up the phone, tapping a response.

Printer's on the blink. I'll have to go to town but can't til tomorrow earliest.

He winced as he hit Send. It was a tiny fib, but still. There was a pause before he saw she was typing.

My printer works. You wanted to see Rebel up close, so come to the ranch later and I'll have the papers ready.

Rawlston scrubbed a hand down his face, mulling it over. He really was interested in seeing that stallion. And also had been wanting to see the Fortune Family Ranch. He sighed. This plan was going to be more challenging than he'd thought. But he had to find a way to hold her off a little bit longer.

Can't today. Tomorrow afternoon?

That would give him time to decide if any of this was a good idea. Her response was quick.

Fine. Anytime after 3 works.

RAWLSTON WAS IMPRESSED with the Fortunes' ranch. It was hard *not* to be, with thirty-five hundred acres of prime range land, multiple barns and *six* big log homes on the north shore of Lake Chatelaine. That was in addition to the large main house, where Wendy Fortune lived. She'd also inherited an actual castle from her grandfather, Wendell Fortune. Rawlston had heard Wendy was busy converting the castle into a boutique hotel and event venue.

Each of the housing lots on the ranch was spacious, with a long driveway leading off from the main road. The log houses were similar, but still unique. They didn't look like cookie-cutter homes—each had some feature or roof angle that the others didn't. Dahlia told him her home was the last one at the end of the road.

As he continued driving, he realized that, just like her rangeland, the lot where her contemporary log home stood bordered his land. They were technically next-door neighbors, even if his house was another mile or so over the gently rolling hills, and away from the lakeshore.

Dahlia's home wasn't massive, but it was a lot of house for one person. The center looked like an A-frame, with single-story wings extending out to the sides. Large windows went up to the peak, giving the impression you could look right through the house to the lake. He didn't turn into her driveway, though. Instead, he went to the barns across from her house. There was a golf cart parked there covered with dahlia stickers, so he assumed it was hers.

The stable had a narrow loft above the main level, and the sheep barn behind it was one-story. Both had horizontal panels under the roofline that were raised up and fastened to allow air to move through. The stable had doors that opened from each stall into small, individual paddocks which were partially shaded. It was a nice setup for the horses, allowing them more space to move while sheltering them from the blistering mid-August sun.

The sheep barn looked like it was mostly open—more of a shelter than a barn, since sheep were generally out to graze, unless they were ill or the weather turned nasty. Dahlia walked out of that sheep barn and seemed surprised to see him getting out of his truck. She took off her leather work gloves and gave him a smile that made his heart skip a beat.

"Oh, hi. I was just tossing some feed to a couple of moms and their lambs. I'll be weaning them soon. Give me a minute to switch gears to horses, okay?" She gestured to the stable. "Rebel's in the back corner stall. Be careful—he's not crazy about men, for good reason. He was abused as a colt. He still likes to bite once in a while, but most of the time he's bluffing."

Rawlston understood what she meant when he got to the stall. The big paint horse was built like a Mack truck, with a long mane that whipped when he shook his head menacingly. He blew out a sharp snort and stomped a front hoof, then made a short charge at the opened top of the stall door. Rawlston stepped back, for his own protection and to appear less threatening to the stallion.

"Easy, big guy." He kept his voice low and steady. "I'm thinking of bringing you a girlfriend, so play nice."

"He *is* nice." Dahlia walked to Rawlston's side. "He just likes to test people he doesn't know."

"Looks like you have your hands full with him, but someone told me you were a 'stallion whisperer.'"

She chuckled. "That all started at the racetrack. There

was a three-year-old colt who was an absolute menace to the trainers, grooms and jockeys. Everyone tried to subdue him, but he wasn't the rogue they labeled him as. He was just smart and bored, which made him mischievous. I started giving him different stall toys to play with and we upped his exercise time to burn off some of that excess energy. I showed him he wasn't scaring me. He eventually settled down, and people started calling me to help with *their* rambunctious colts." She shrugged. "And a reputation was born."

"And what about Rebel here? Is he just being playful?" Rawlson asked.

"No, Rebel's being defensive. That makes him a little more dangerous. He was abused—not by Hal, but on the ranch where he was born. Then Hal and his stable hands treated him like a killer stallion, so Rebel's never learned how to relax and behave properly. He's great in competition, but in the barn, he thinks everyone's out to get him. Isn't that right, pretty boy?"

Dahlia walked confidently to the stall door. Rebel shook his head and snorted, then showed his teeth in a mock bite attempt. But she calmly talked to him and ran her fingers down his face. He lowered his head, still tense, but giving her access to the top of his head. She started scratching behind his ear and the horse began to settle. He brought his head over the half door and bumped Dahlia affectionately. His mouth began moving in a chewing motion, which signaled he was relaxed and trusting. She slid a halter over his head, snapped on a lead and brought him out of the stall. "Do you want me to saddle him up, or do you want to see him move free in the round paddock?"

"Moving free is fine—no need to go through a lot of fuss. I can already see how impressive he is," he replied.

It was no exaggeration. The horse was drop-dead gorgeous. Close to sixteen hands tall, broad chested and muscular, with a striking black-and-white coat. His conformation was near perfect, and his head was refined—not too long, broad between the eyes and sculptured. Rawlston knew without seeing the horse move that he'd be a great cross with his mare in the spring.

Dahlia led Rebel out the barn door and to the sturdy round pen. The posts were like telephone poles, and the wooden rails were tall enough to contain a stallion who might have a wandering eye. It was larger than most training pens, probably seventy feet across. Rebel started prancing as they neared the gate, but he never pulled on the lead in Dahlia's hand. The stallion was high-spirited, but well-mannered. It was an attractive combination.

The dynamic between horse and woman was pretty damn attractive, too. Dahlia might *look* Hollywood, but she was a genuine horsewoman through and through. Rawlston had a hard time taking his eyes off of her.

When Dahlia latched the gate and unfastened the lead, Rebel let out a loud snort and charged away from her, head and tail high. Dahlia joined Rawlston, sitting on the top rail to watch. He had to remind himself that he was there to see the *horse*.

"I can see why they named him Rebel," he remarked. One of the horse's black patches covered both eyes, like a mask.

"Yes," she nodded. "I imagine it was really cute when he was a foal. His full name is Mendelsohn's Rebellious Heart. He came from the Mendelsohn ranch up in Oklahoma. That's where he was handled so badly." She turned to face him. "Oh, hey—don't let me forget that I have those annulment papers in the barn."

He kept his face carefully neutral. He'd been hoping

she *would* forget, and he had no intention of reminding her. He asked about Rebel's pedigree, hoping horse talk would distract her.

DAHLIA SLAPPED HER computer shut with a muttered curse.

"Whoa," Sabrina laughed from the kitchen. "What did that laptop ever do to you?"

"It's not the laptop, it's the email I just read from Rawlston Ames." The man was beginning to get on her very last nerve. "He has more excuses than the Gulf of Mexico has water!"

"Excuses about what?" Her twin came into the great room and handed her a glass of wine. "Arlo said he heard Rawlston might be breeding one of his mares to your Rebel. Is he trying not to pay for it or something?" Sabrina sat. "Oh, is this about the annulment?"

"Yes! He's making me crazy! I texted him the papers and he said his printer was broken. He came to the stables to see Rebel at the beginning of the week, and I had the physical papers ready to sign, and get this—" she stared up at the ceiling "—he told me he'd forgotten his *special pen*. Can you believe it?" She stared at Sabrina. "Apparently, he uses a special lucky pen his grandfather gave him to sign important documents, and he didn't have it with him. He refused to sign them without it!"

"Well, people can be superstitious about things like that," Sabrina said with a slight shrug.

"But I *told* him I'd have the paperwork, so he knew I wanted him to sign them. Why wouldn't he bring his damn lucky pen? And now he just emailed me saying he can't find the papers. He *lost* them."

"Sis, I know you're in a hurry to put this marriage in your rearview mirror, but it's clearly not a priority for Rawlston." She added gently, "That doesn't mean he's plotting against you. It just means he's not feeling as urgent about it as you are. You're living your own lives as if nothing happened, so the marriage isn't affecting him one way or the other."

"That's nice for *him*, but I need to get this done before Carter gets back."

"Ah, yes. Good old Carter. Are you missing him yet?"

"What kind of question is that?" Dahlia huffed. "Of course I miss him…"

When she thought of him. Which admittedly wasn't as much as she probably should. But she blamed that on the stress of this damn Vegas wedding. She took a sip of wine, then told Sabrina that Carter texted her nearly every day, which was a slight exaggeration. Carter seemed so absorbed in this business trip—the exact nature of that business wasn't clear to her—that he'd only reached out once or twice a week.

"Oh, wow." Sabrina rolled her eyes. "How romantic."

"It's *attentive.* And he called just last night."

She didn't elaborate on how well, or *not* well, that conversation had gone. She knew her twin's dislike for Carter, and directed the conversation back to knitting patterns and preferred types of wool.

After Sabrina headed back to her own house, Dahlia refilled her coffee mug and went outside to the deck. Sabrina had insisted from the start that Carter was "just like Dad." Craving power and success at any cost. Dahlia had seen some of those things, of course, but that was just part of being a businessman.

Yes, Carter was a little secretive about the details of his work in finance. And he'd done it in a way that made her feel patronized, as if she wouldn't understand his big, complicated world. But he'd insisted that she was his shelter from talking about all of that. Busy with her move to Chatelaine, she'd let it slide.

She'd heard rumors about his integrity, but trash talking was just part of being in business. Her father had dealt with all of that, too. Her coffee mug stopped halfway to her lips. Which meant Carter really *was* like Dad. And most of the rumors about Dad's ruthlessness in business had been true. What if the rumors about Carter were, too?

She shook off her doubts and headed to the barns to check on a few ewes and lambs she'd brought indoors because they'd seemed stressed. Between the stifling heat last week and being moved from their original home in the Texas panhandle to the Chatelaine ranch, some of the ewes with the youngest lambs had lost some weight, so she wanted to give them good alfalfa hay to build them back up again before rejoining the herd. The heat wave had eased now, and they all seemed rested and content this morning. She figured they could go back out to the range by tomorrow.

And speaking of the herd and the range—she hadn't seen the herd since yesterday morning, and even then, they were nearly out of sight on one of the farthest little hills. They had thirty-five hundred acres to roam, but she figured she'd better go check on them, just to be sure all was well. It would be a good excuse to give Rebel a ride and burn off some of his perpetual energy.

The Fortune ranch was feeling more like home every day. The main barns and office were up and running, keeping her siblings busy. Nash was the ranch foreman, Arlo was the overall planner and manager, Sabrina was keeping the books, and Jade wanted to open a petting zoo of some kind. Ridge was working his way through all the jobs on the ranch, learning the ropes. Dahlia was making plans to sell wool and woolen arts and crafts by the holidays. Next spring she'd be bringing in shearers to harvest the wool from her very own sheep, and then her business plans would really be rolling. Which brought her thoughts back to Carter as she saddled Rebel.

Last night's call had been unsettling. Carter was in Italy this week, and sounded like he'd had too much espresso—he was talking a mile a minute, without giving her much opportunity to respond. His trip was going well, he was setting up business connections, but more importantly, *political* connections. Apparently he was getting support from "very important people," whatever that meant. He was excited, so she was happy for him.

At least, she *had* been until he made an offhand comment that they could be living in Austin soon. That was hours away. She reminded him that she was just getting settled in Chatelaine, and Carter had laughed. He'd *laughed*.

"Don't get me wrong, Bo Peep—the ranch, the sheep and all of that is cute, but come on, you don't really expect us to *live* on your family's ranch, do you?"

He had a point—Carter was no rancher. It was odd… she hadn't once pictured Carter in her home. Or on the ranch at all. Rawlston had walked into her stables to see Rebel with an ease that Carter would never have. Carter didn't even like to ride.

It seemed she and Carter had a lot to work out before she thought about accepting a ring from him. But she had to deal with this pesky marriage to Rawlston first.

She led the stallion out of the barn and mounted, spending a moment settling his prancing down to a more sedate walk before she tried to tackle opening a gate from the saddle. It took a few tries, but she finally got Rebel through it, then managed to latch it. Afterward, he was as ready for a good run as she was, but she kept him working between a walk and trot for the first part of the ride.

He didn't like it, but Dahlia gave him just enough leeway to get out his friskiness without disobeying her commands. The big horse started to settle after a few minutes. He was paying attention to her leg cues now, and his head dropped as he relaxed. Eventually he stopped tugging on the reins. The sun was hidden behind clouds at the moment, making it more comfortable for riding.

She located the sheep herd near the tall cottonwood tree by the fence line. And just like the last time she'd been there, Rawlston was working on the fence line. She let Rebel have a gallop up the hill, scattering the sheep along the way. By the time she reined him in as they reached the tree, the horse was snorting and prancing, ears back at the sight of Rawlston's horse grazing. The chestnut was unconcerned and unimpressed.

Rawlston stood, his hands on his hips. He looked…annoyed. That was an emotion she didn't often see on his face. Not only did he *look* something like Matthew McConaughey with his light brown hair and lanky appearance, but his *attitude* was a lot like McConaughey's, too. Laid-back and always seeming vaguely amused, as if he might break out with an "alright, alright, alright" of his own. But right now he did not look chill at all. She wondered if he was angry about her riding Rebel up here, but his horse didn't seem to care.

"You looking for your sheep?" he asked sharply.

"Well, yeah. But I found them back there. What's—"

"You didn't find all of 'em."

"What are you talking about?" She didn't like his accusing tone, especially when she had no idea what she was being accused of.

"Take a look. Tripp's rounding up the last of 'em now."

He gestured across the fence line toward his property. She could see a dozen or more cream-colored Brahmans grazing. And… *Oh, no.* There were at least six of her sheep with the cattle. The small dog was skulking around behind the sheep, moving them away from the cattle, who were ignoring the drama.

"How on earth did they get over there? Was the fence down?"

Rawlston grabbed the lower line of barbed wire and pulled it up, pointing to the tufts of white wool attached to it. "The fence is just fine. For *cattle*. But your sheep have discovered they can get *under* it, and onto my range."

She dismounted, tucking Rebel's reins through her belt loop. One tug and he'd pull free, but she'd been training him to stay close. She didn't dare let him graze freely— he wasn't *that* well trained. She inspected the fence, her heart dropping.

"Damn, that's a lot of wool. Your fence is shearing my sheep!"

"My fence is…" Rawlston stared at her. "Your sheep are grazing on *my* land!"

"Oh, calm down. They're sheep, not vacuum cleaners. I don't think your precious cows will starve because a few sheep spent a little time over there."

"Dahlia, Tripp's already brought a dozen or more of your little darlings back where they belong. These are the last of them." The dog expertly nipped at the heels of the protesting sheep, who hurried under the wire Rawlston was holding up for them. "This is a serious problem. Sheep don't eat the same way cows do. Sheep yank grass up by the roots, and they can ruin grazing for cattle."

She tugged at the large clumps of wool hanging from the fence, ignoring Rawlston's glare. She tucked the wool into her pocket. "Nonsense. If sheep pulled grass up by the roots, I wouldn't have any pasture left."

He followed her gesture to the range behind her, which still had plenty of green grass. Then he shook his head sharply. "Maybe you still have pasture because they're over here eating *my* grass."

"You're being ridiculous." She folded her arms on her chest. Lord save her from impossible men this week!

"Really? I told you before that entire range wars were fought over sheep and cattle competing for the same grazing land." He took a beat, and his shoulders eased. "Look, I'm not saying they've destroyed my pastures today. I was up here two days ago and the fence was wool-free. But we do have to solve this." He seemed to notice Rebel for the first time. "You brought the stallion. I thought he hated sheep?"

She looked over her shoulder at her horse. "Did you see how flat his ears were when the sheep trotted by? He's not a fan, but he knows he'd better behave when I have the reins."

"And you think your belt loop will stop him if he doesn't?"

"I told you he's not the killer horse everyone made him out to be." She reached out and scratched Rebel's neck. He nudged his head against her.

Rawlston's eyes softened. "Because of you."

She hesitated, then nodded. She'd never been a fan of false modesty. "I suppose so, yes. So what do you think we should do about my wandering sheep?" She smiled at his dog, now sitting attentively at his side. "Other than employ Tripp on a daily basis."

"Tripp and I can't be running this fence line every day—I have a thousand other acres to tend. Besides, he's a cattle dog, not a sheep dog."

Rawlston seemed especially testy this morning.

"Is there something else bothering you?"

He rubbed the back of his neck and sighed, staring at the ground.

"It's my father."

Alarmed, Dahlia reached out to hold his arm. "Keith? Is he okay?"

"Physically? Fine." He scowled. "Mentally? I'm honestly not sure. I met his so-called fiancée, JoAnn, last night. They're getting married next week, and the whole thing is just absurd!"

CHAPTER NINE

RAWLSTON TRIED TO hang on to his rising temper. He'd been agitated—no, more like *furious*—all morning. He'd woken up this way, after a fitful night of dreams that bounced between his mother and Dahlia and stupid weddings. His mother, being replaced by JoAnn marrying his father. Dahlia, being kept from marriage because she'd married *him*.

"Rawlston?" Dahlia's voice was low and soft, snapping him back to the present. They were standing on the hill between their properties. His gelding was nearby, grazing quietly. Rebel was on alert behind Dahlia, nostrils flared and ears up, but standing still.

And Dahlia was staring up at him, concern clear in her blue eyes. The sun was coming out from behind the clouds, so he nodded toward the cottonwood tree. "Let's go in the shade. Will your horse be okay with Malloy nearby?"

She began walking toward the tree. "He'll be fine. Rebel likes the ladies, hates other studs, but pretty much ignores geldings." Sure enough, the stallion followed her quietly. His reins were just pulled through a belt loop on her jeans, but he acted as if he was tied to her. Enthralled with her. Enchanted by her.

Or maybe that was just Rawlston.

"Don't get me wrong—I want Dad to be happy. But this marriage is a mistake on so many levels." He just couldn't figure out how to stop it.

"What's she like?" Dahlia asked.

"She's…different. She's nice enough, but—"

Dahlia pursed her lips in thought, tipping her head to the side. "But she's not your mom?"

He got Dahlia's point, but he disagreed. "I don't expect her to *be* my mom. I'm not clinging to Mom's memory and thinking no one can live up to her or anything like that." That might not be true deep down but he was certainly not gonna admit it. "I'm all for Dad finding someone. But JoAnn is this sturdy New England farm woman."

"I don't know what that means." Dahlia pulled up a handful of grass and fed it to Rebel.

"She's…" He couldn't figure out how to describe his father's wife-to-be. "If you remember my mom, she was quiet and…dignified. She did charity work and served on the library board. She was afraid of horses, so she took care of the house while Dad handled the ranch work."

Dahlia nodded. "Your mom always looked so classy and put-together, even at horse shows. Dressed to the nines and never a hair out of place. She wasn't a snob, though," she rushed to say. "She was sweet. I never realized she was afraid of horses, but now that you've mentioned it, she *did* stay up in the stands when we were in the ring. But…you keep describing your mom when I'm asking about JoAnn."

"Take everything I just said about Mom and flip to its opposite, and that's JoAnn. She's loud and outgoing. She's already been out in the barn cleaning stalls and she and Dad went riding yesterday. She's also making plans to double the size of the vegetable garden, and said she'll build the raised beds herself." His mouth turned downward. "JoAnn's got a very…casual…style. She was wearing this long denim skirt and her hair was in braids." He stopped, hearing his words and cringing a bit. "And all of that sounds superficial, doesn't it?"

Dahlia raised one shoulder. "Pretty much, yeah. You can't hold it against her that she's not your mom—that's not her fault."

"It's not about what that means to me as much as what it means for my dad. Why would he fall for someone so completely different? It's like he intentionally sought out Mom's opposite, and now he wants to *marry* her. They have nothing in common!"

"Actually, it sounds like they have a *lot* in common. She rides, she works outside, she's outgoing like he is…" Her words slowed to silence. "And you don't want me debating this, do you?"

He didn't. But damn if she wasn't right on all counts. "I want you to agree with everything I'm saying. But I think I *need* to hear your viewpoint." He sighed heavily. "Does it mean he and my mom *weren't* suited for each other? He always said she made him complete, like a piece he didn't know was missing until he met her."

Dahlia leaned her back against the tree and removed her Western hat to wipe her brow. The sun's reappearance after last night's rain had caused the temperature and humidity to start climbing again. Rawlston went to his saddlebag and pulled out a couple bottles of water, handing her one.

"Your mom and dad were terrific together," she assured him after she took a sip. "They looked at each other with a love I never saw between my own parents. They really were a perfect fit. But…" She looked up at him with a soft smile. "Puzzle pieces have more than one side. They can fit perfectly together with more than one piece. JoAnn fits differently with your dad, but that doesn't mean they're not right for each other. My advice is to trust your father's judgment on this."

That was going to be easier said than done, even if he suspected Dahlia was right.

"I'll try." He opened his water and took a swig. "Marriage just seems like a drastic step."

After a pause, Dahlia gave him a pointed look. "Speaking of marriage, we really do need to get those papers signed. I texted you a pdf file yesterday for you to print and sign. I texted the same file two days ago. And I emailed it to you two days before that." She sighed, and he braced himself to hear all about Carter again. She watched Malloy snatch at some tall grass at the base of the tree. "I don't like lying to everyone."

No mention of Carter? *Interesting.*

"My internet's been screwy lately, but I'll check when I get home."

They both knew he was lying. Usually, this was where Dahlia got mad. Instead, she rolled her eyes and opened her water bottle.

"Yeah, I bet you will. God, it's getting hot again." She took a gulp of water and stared at the bottle for a moment. Then she dumped all the water over her head, letting it run down her face and neck, soaking the pale yellow knit top she wore. "That's better."

The water made her top transparent, along with the lacy bra beneath it. Rawlston knew he should probably look away, but he was a hot-blooded man. And he was her husband. She caught his expression, then glanced down at her chest.

"Dude, you saw me naked in Vegas. This shouldn't shock you all that much."

"Trust me," he said, doing his best to keep his gaze on her eyes. "That is a sight I'll never forget. When I woke up to you wrapped around me, nothing but bare skin… You were—you *are*—beautiful."

Her lips parted in surprise at the compliment. Something shifted in her posture. She seemed to let her guard down a bit, and her voice softened.

"Is that why you won't sign the annulment papers? You want another night together?"

"Why? Are you offering?" His body responded immediately to the thought of making love to Dahlia again.

"Of course not." A pause. "Unless it will help me get your signature. I'd have to at least think about it if that were the case, but I'd lose all respect for you in the process."

That night with Dahlia had been all he'd thought about since leaving Las Vegas. But bartering for sex was wrong on every level. He stepped closer to her. She pressed back against the tree, but her eyes never left his. It was almost as if she was daring him to do this. To kiss her. Was she *hoping* he would?

"I'd never use sex like that, Dolly." Rawlston pushed a strand of her hair behind her ear, then left his fingertips brushing against her neck. He could see her pulse beneath the thin skin there. "But I may just kiss you. Just enough to remind myself how sweet you taste." His head dropped close to hers, and their noses brushed against each other. "Would that be okay? If I kissed you?"

She placed one hand over his heart, and he figured she was holding him off. Pushing him away. Instead, she twisted her fingers into his shirt and tugged him closer. Bringing him near enough for her to stand on her tiptoes and touch her mouth to his.

Yes, please.

His arms slid around her waist, his hands gliding up her spine. Was this really happening? Her lips pressed on his and his mind stopped analyzing. He only cared about sensation now, not thoughts. Not doubts. He returned the kiss, his tongue pushing past her willing lips to taste her. It was as if he'd been struck by lightning. Every moment of their wedding night came back to him—every kiss, every touch, every orgasm. They'd been amazing together, and it felt amazing now as her arms wrapped around his neck. Their heads turned, seeking better access to each other. She lifted her chin, exposing her long neck, and he traced kisses and nibbles all the way to her shoulder.

He didn't want to stop, but they were outdoors, with two horses, a few dozen cattle and a hundred sheep watching them. Rawlston pulled back, but her fingers tangled in his hair, preventing him from getting away. With a muttered curse, his mouth covered hers again. Let all those watching eyes be damned. He wasn't going to stop until she did.

His beautiful wife.

DAHLIA HAD NO idea what she was doing, or why. And *she* was the one who'd started this. Sure, it was Rawlston's idea, but he wouldn't have pressed it if she hadn't kissed him. Once their lips connected, it was all over for both of them.

He kissed a trail down her neck, interspersed with nips of his teeth on her skin. Her body was on fire, raging with desire. She was surprised the tall grass around them hadn't burst into flames by now. Rawlston hesitated, but she held him close, gripping his hair. She needed this. She wasn't sure why, but she needed his embrace. Needed his kiss. Needed *him*.

He drew back again, staring down into her eyes, looking as dazed as she felt. With the slight bit of space between them, the heat cooled enough for her to think more clearly. And she definitely should *not* be jumping Rawlston's bones like this. Bad idea. Big mistake. Not the way to end their marriage. She straightened, and he stepped away, respecting her space. Of course. Always the gentleman.

He cleared his throat sharply. "We probably shouldn't—"

She huffed out a laugh. "We *definitely* shouldn't. I'm not sure what just happened, but let's…forget it, okay?"

One corner of his mouth lifted in amusement. "You think I'm going to forget that? I'm betting you won't, either. But we can agree not to do it again. I was agitated about my dad and—"

"Please tell me you didn't kiss me because of your father."

"I'm pretty sure *you* kissed *me*, madam."

"That's true. Sorry." She turned away, pretending to check the horses, who were both just fine.

"Don't be sorry," he said thickly. "It was exactly what I needed, along with your commonsense advice, of course."

"Advice and a kiss. More than you'd get from Beau Weatherly at the coffee shop. Think I should set up my own table there?" She was feeling almost giddy, as if that kiss gave her a shot of adrenaline.

Rawlston took her arm, turning her to face him. "Don't go giving those kisses away, Dahlia Fortune."

Still feeling playful, she patted his hand. "Why? Do you want them all?"

He started to answer. She could swear he started to say *yes*. But he caught himself, clamping his lips together and moving away from her. There was a sudden thread of seriousness to the conversation. *Did* he want all her kisses? Did he want all of *her*? She couldn't decide how that made her feel. Why was her heart racing?

And just like that, things turned awkward. Her amusement flipped to irritation, probably because she had no idea what was happening between them. She gathered Rebel's reins and put her foot in the stirrup, swinging up into the saddle.

"I should get back before it gets any hotter."

A spark of humor shone in Rawlston's eyes, picking up

on the unintended double meaning. "Wise decision. But we haven't decided who's going to pay for fixing the sheep problem. I'm going to have to add a lower strand of wire to keep them off my land."

"You made a point of telling me the fence is on your land, so my guess is you'll pay for it."

"But they're *your* sheep."

She looked down the hill to the herd of fluffy sheep grazing her land. "Maybe it was a one-time trespass." She met his gaze. Darn...she'd done it again. Her cheeks heated.

"Maybe." Rawlston nodded, pretending to be considering the idea. "But maybe it'll happen more than once."

"It won't." She slapped the reins on Rebel's neck, turning him for home. "I'll make sure of it."

DAHLIA STABBED AT the muslin stretched on a large embroidery frame. Sometimes she thought the main reason she enjoyed wool art was that it involved stabbing. Lots and lots of stabbing. She reminded herself to pay attention. The special felting needles were not only incredibly sharp, but they were also barbed. When stabbed into a ball of loose, raw wool, each motion in and out created knots in the wool fibers. Eventually the loose wool would be tightened into a firm shape, guided with her hands. In this case, she was creating the trunk of a tree. She'd already formed dozens of tiny leaves in fall colors that would become part of the three-dimensional scene she was creating on the muslin.

Her siblings were talking about opening a small shop near the office, featuring ranch products, and she and Sabrina had offered to showcase their art there. Dahlia's needle felting had started with her creating cute little animals and ornaments ten years ago. Then she went to a wool show and discovered people were creating beautiful scenes on stretched muslin, with swirls of colored wool and the occasional three-dimensional accent. It felt freeing to start something without a specific pattern to follow. She couldn't do it "wrong" if it was freeform.

Dahlia knew that was a holdover from growing up with Casper Windham as a father. Everything had to be the best, the winningest, the most perfect. It was a pressure that she'd never handled well. She'd honed her competitiveness while showing horses and doing rodeos, and her father had always been happy when she came home with blue ribbons. Anything *less* than a blue ribbon would earn her a lecture on trying harder. Coming in second out of fifty competitors was *losing* in Dad's eyes.

Creating art, where there was no *right* or *wrong* was something that just didn't compute in her father's mind. What was the point of sculpting a dog out of wool if it wasn't a photo-quality likeness of the actual dog? Or if it couldn't be sold for lots of money? Making the effort for the "fun of it" was pointless to him, which made her more determined to do things like be a groom at the track rather than own the horses and make the money. Or why she'd rather raise her own sheep in order to create her own wool for her personal artwork.

And yet… She'd never quite succeeded in quieting her father's voice in her head, whispering that whatever she was doing wasn't good enough.

Her mobile phone rang at her side, snapping her out of her own head and making her jump just enough that she managed to stab her finger. She was still cursing as she swiped the phone, not bothering to look at the screen.

"Is this a bad time?" Rawlston was laughing on the other end of the call.

"No, I just stabbed myself."

His laughter was gone in an instant. "Are you okay?"

"It's just a needle poke. I'll live." She checked the time—it was almost 9 p.m. "Why are you calling?"

"I just… I wanted to apologize for this morning."

"Which part? Having a hissy fit about my sheep or kissing me?"

"I was thinking more of the part where I dumped all my feelings about my dad and JoAnn on you." He paused. "Do I need to apologize for the kiss?"

"No. I kissed you, remember? And you don't need to apologize for talking about your dad, either." She glanced at the kitchen island and saw a folder sitting there. "But if you feel like making amends, you could stop by and sign the annulment papers."

There was a *long* pause this time. Finally, he just said "Tomorrow night?"

She felt an odd little thrill at the idea of Rawlston coming to her house. At night. To talk over dinner and wine. She gave herself a mental shake. There was a purpose to this meeting.

"Six o'clock. I'll have dinner ready. Don't forget the lucky pen."

"The what?"

"Your grandfather's pen? The only one you use for important contracts?"

"Oh…that. Yeah, of course. I won't forget."

CHAPTER TEN

RAWLSTON DROVE UP to the front of Dahlia's house the next night, not sure if this was a good idea or not. But he *did* feel like he needed to make amends for his behavior by the cottonwood tree. He'd been petulant about the sheep getting under the fence, and then he'd blathered on about Dad and JoAnn. And moments later...they'd kissed. A kiss that rattled him right down to his core. Which suggested that it wasn't just the spiked punch that made his memories of their wedding night so steamy. They had some *wild* chemistry.

She called out when he rang the doorbell that the door was unlocked. Her house had a wide-open floor plan, with soaring cathedral ceilings. The great room included the large kitchen, a giant fieldstone fireplace, and a seating area divided into both dining and relaxing. There was also what seemed to be a reading nook, with a large, overstuffed chair and low bookcases below the windows. The deck and lakeshore were visible through the tall windows.

Dahlia was in the kitchen, her hair twisted into a messy knot on top of her head. She looked frazzled as she bent over in front of the open oven door, waving absently at an open bottle of wine and two glasses on the island.

"Help yourself. Sorry, I ended up running late and then I forgot about the roast while I was upstairs getting dressed." She straightened, wrinkling her nose. "I'm afraid it may be a little on the well done side by the time the veggies are cooked through."

He poured wine into the glasses, sliding one in her direction. "I'm sure it will be fine. What had you running late?"

"Peter Knight stopped by to look at Rebel. He said he was thinking of sending a few mares over for breeding in the spring."

Knight was another one of the top horse breeders in Texas. "Impressive."

She gave him a look, one eyebrow raised sharply. "Not terribly impressive, no."

"Why?"

She checked a pot on top of the stove. "He was a bit of an ass."

Rawlston suddenly saw red. "What the hell does that mean?"

She glanced back at him. "Relax, big guy. I just meant he was a misogynist. Very condescending about 'a pretty thing like me' handling a big, mean horse like Rebel, blah blah blah. He even tried to step up and take the lead from me when Rebel had one of his little tantrums, as if the guy had to save me. Which, of course, just fired Rebel up more." She huffed out a breath. "Knight was just generally annoying. Ah, I think the carrots and potatoes are done. Let's eat, and then you can sign those papers."

Despite his resolve to do the right thing, he did *not* want to sign off on the annulment yet. He told himself it was only because of Carter Powers, but he was beginning to think there might be another reason he wanted to stay married to Dahlia a while longer. He didn't want to examine that reasoning too deeply. Instead, he worked on keeping the conversation as far away from Vegas, annulment and signatures as possible. Surprisingly, it wasn't difficult. Just like that night at the reception, conversation flowed easily between them as they sat at the table to eat.

They talked about horses, sheep, cattle and what the plans were for the Fortunes' ranch. She asked about *his* ranch, and he told her what it was like to raise Brahman cattle and the fact that the house was nowhere near as grand as hers, but it was comfortable. He didn't mention how lonely it sometimes felt, especially since their return from Las Vegas.

Dahlia grew more animated as she spoke about her mother remodeling the Fortune castle into a boutique hotel and spa. Her siblings were all sliding into their roles on the ranch.

By the time she brought her homemade blueberry cobbler to the table for dessert, they'd moved on to more general topics—favorite books, movies, TV shows. It turned out that they were both slightly geeky. They ended up debating which space dramas were better, with him defending Star Wars as Dahlia argued for Star Trek.

He sat back in his chair and patted his stomach. "Woman, that was some damn fine cooking. That roast beef could be sold at the LC Club for top dollar."

She smiled, looking away as if to dismiss the compliment, but her cheeks went a pretty shade of pink. "Thanks. I loved spending time in the kitchen with Mom as a kid, and I picked up a few tricks. That was Angus beef, like what we'll be raising here on the ranch."

"Along with your sheep," he pointed out.

"Yes, along with them. Some people don't take the sheep very seriously, though."

"Your brothers?" That didn't sound like the Fortune guys. They were fiercely protective and supportive of each other and their sisters.

Dahlia started to answer, stopped, then finally spoke.

"The boys have been good about it, and so have my sisters. Sabrina can't wait until we shear in the spring and she can get her hands on the wool for her knitting. It will be fun to create from product grown right here on the ranch."

He wondered who it was that wasn't taking her choice in livestock seriously. Which prompted him to ask if she was a knitter, too, but she shook her head. She pointed to a framed piece of art on the wall—a landscape with swirling shades of blue, green and brown, with mountains in the distance and a river flowing in the foreground.

"That's what I create with wool. And little things like those sleeping mice in the bowl on the buffet."

Rawlston was stunned. The mice were cute, and so realistic that, if he'd noticed them sooner, he might have thought they were real. But the landscape was incredible. He walked over for a closer look. Sure enough, it was wool, not paint, that created the scene on tightly stretched fabric.

"This is beautiful, Dahlia. Forget being a restaurant cook, you've found your calling as an artist. This should be in a museum somewhere." There was a smaller work in progress near the chair in the corner of the great room, and he went to check it out. It was a fall scene, more three-dimensional than the other work. A tall, dark tree was on one edge, with textured leaves on the branches and on the ground beneath it. He looked up to find her next to him. "Seriously—this stuff is good. No wonder you want to raise sheep. For you, they're raw material."

It was like looking at a whole new person. He'd had no idea she was an artist. He'd always thought of her as uptight, controlled, sharp. But no one like that could do anything like this—the sweeping, swirling colors, the texture, the *vision* to create something out of nothing. She was holding papers in her hand. *Oh, damn.* But she didn't hand them over. She was looking at him as if he'd just said something amazing. Surely she knew how good she was?

"Dahlia? I'm not exaggerating. This stuff is awesome."

"Not that many people have seen my pictures. I'm..." She blinked a few times. "I'm glad you like it."

She set the papers on the table and showed him how she worked the wool by stabbing at it with a long, barbed needle with a wooden handle. He'd never seen anything like it. He'd never seen anyone like *her*.

He helped her clean up the kitchen while she told him of picking up the hobby a few years ago when she was feeling stressed. Her dad was giving her a hard time about not coming to work for Windham Plastics and being a lowly groom instead, which he'd said was basically a "horse servant."

Rawlston had only met Casper Windham a handful of times, and on one of the occasions, the man had been scolding Dahlia for only placing third in a competition of thirty barrel racers. He was a hard man, and seemed especially so with his children. The polar opposite of Rawlston's own father. If anything, Keith Ames was *too* kindhearted. That was probably why he'd become so enamored with JoAnn—he believed the best of everyone.

Rawlston took Dahlia's soapy hands in his and looked her straight in the eyes. "You are no one's servant. I'm sorry he said that to you."

Her lips parted slightly, and it took all of his strength not to kiss her. But this wasn't the time for that. He needed his words to sink in, without distraction. She needed to know he thought her father was wrong about her. About a lot of things, but all Rawlston cared about was Dahlia.

It wasn't until he was driving home shortly after that he realized she'd never once asked him to sign those annulment papers.

"HOW COULD YOU *FORGET?*" Jade asked, accepting the coffee mug Sabrina handed her. The three sisters were in Sabrina's kitchen. It was two days since Rawlston had been to her house for dinner.

Dahlia waved her hand in a half-hearted shrug. "I don't know. We just got talking about stuff and I forgot to ask him to sign. And Lord knows, he isn't going to volunteer. I don't know why he's stalling, but he clearly is."

Sabrina sat down with Jade and Dahlia. "Has it ever occurred to you that he doesn't *want* to end the marriage? That maybe he likes being married to you?"

"He's *not* married to me!" Dahlia set her mug down with a thump. "I mean, yes, we're legally married, but we're not living as husband and wife. No one knows about it besides you two."

Jade snickered. "You mean you haven't snuck off for one single kiss since spending your wedding night together in Vegas?"

Dahlia kept a straight face. At least she tried. She might have fooled Jade, but her twin could read her like a book. Sabrina leaned forward, staring straight at Dahlia.

"Oh my God, you *have* been sneaking kisses! What else have you two been doing?"

"Nothing!" Dahlia protested. "I swear, we haven't done anything. Other than argue."

Sabrina cleared her throat dramatically, and Dahlia conceded. "Okay, there was *one* kiss. Out on the range, by the big tree near the property line. It just…happened. We were talking and it was hot and—"

Jade snorted. "Oh, it was hot alright!" Sabrina joined in the laughter.

"We're not thirteen, ladies," Dahlia said. "You're over-reacting to one simple kiss. He and I agreed it was a mistake that wouldn't happen again."

"And what about Carter?" Sabrina asked.

"What about him?"

Dahlia knew the reply was a mistake as soon as she said it. Her sisters' eyes went wide as they looked at each other and then to her, waiting for her to elaborate. She didn't want to tell them that she had been rethinking her relationship with Carter. Not because of Rawlston, or at least, not because she was falling for him or anything like that. But she couldn't get over the way he'd looked at her the other night when he saw her artwork, and how he'd been so horrified at one of her father's many criticisms of her.

Carter had never done either of those things. Not once. He'd dismissed her plans for raising sheep, mocked her artwork as a *cute little hobby*, and now he was rejecting the idea of even *living* in Chatelaine. She deserved a man who respected her choices the way Rawlston did, and she was beginning to realize Carter would never be that man.

"Dahlia?" Sabrina took her hand. "Are you and Carter over?"

"No!" She said it more forcefully than intended. "Nothing has changed."

"So you're still expecting a ring when he gets back from Europe?"

"Probably…"

She just wasn't sure she'd accept it. And not because of this wedding mess with Rawlston. She was having serious doubts about a future with Carter. But she couldn't discuss it with her sisters, because they were *not* impartial on the subject. They'd be thrilled if she admitted they'd been right about him all along. She needed to be sure before she dealt with their reactions.

"And… Rawlston?" Jade asked quietly.

"Rawlston is going to sign those papers. We got distracted and I forgot the other night, but that won't happen again. I'm going to his ranch this afternoon and I'll make sure I get his signature, with his *special lucky pen*, on the papers I've printed out for him. No more excuses."

SHE WAS SURPRISED when she drove up to Rawlston's house. It was more humble than she'd expected—a smallish one-level stucco home in front of large cattle barns and a stable. He'd never been one to go for a flashy house or car. But she'd heard from her brothers that Rawlston had been successful when he took over his dad's ranch in Cactus Grove, and even more so with his Chatelaine ranch. She'd envisioned a different type of home—larger, newer, more upscale. Then again, Rawlston had been surprising her ever since he'd walked up to her in Las Vegas.

His dog came bounding off the front veranda as she got out of her car, barking loudly before rolling over on his back for a belly rub.

"Hi, Tripp!" She obliged with a scratch of his belly. "No sheep for you to chase today, huh?"

"I keep telling you that he's not a sheep dog, he's a cattle dog." Rawlston came around the corner of the house. "Come on inside, out of this heat."

It was another scorcher, with the temperature forecast to hit triple digits again. She grabbed her folder with the annulment documents from the car and followed him. From behind, she took in his broad shoulders. His long, confident stride. His light brown hair, curling from sweat and the heat. He was one of a kind. And she was married to him.

The house was at least fifty years old, but it was clean and neat inside. The large terracotta floor tiles and arched doorways gave it a Southwestern feel.

"This was built as the ranch foreman's house," Rawlston explained, giving her a quick tour. "This was all originally part of an even larger ranch, and their main house was on the lake. That burned down years ago and they never rebuilt. They sold the ranch instead."

She looked around and smiled. "This suits you."

His eyebrows rose. "Small and simple? Old and tired?"

"No. It's... practical. It has what you need, and nothing you don't."

"Fair enough. I figured I could always build a new house on the ranch someday, but so far I haven't seen the need."

"Where does your foreman live?" Most ranches of this size had working cowboys on it.

"I'm pretty much the foreman," he answered with a shrug. "But I have a few local ranch hands who keep their horses here or trailer their own in."

"Again—practical," she pointed out. They were in the kitchen area, and there were plates set out with shredded lettuce, cooked ground beef, tomatoes, chilies, cheese and salsa.

"I put together a little taco bar for us for lunch. You want iced tea or beer?"

"Iced tea would be great, as long as it's not sweet tea."

"Something we have in common. I don't do sweet tea, either." He opened the refrigerator. "Grab a plate and help yourself."

They sat at the nearby table and laughed as they tackled their messy tacos. He'd added a shot of hot sauce to his, but she declined, letting him know she didn't think food should hurt you.

Just like the other night, they settled into easy conversation about the weather, his house, ranching and some casual Chatelaine gossip. She'd been getting to know some of her newfound Fortune cousins, and Rawlston knew most of them, too. He was actually good friends with West Fortune and his wife, Tabitha. They were raising one-year-old twins, which was apparently a Fortune family trait. Dahlia wondered aloud if it was her mother's Fortune genes that led to her giving birth to Sabrina and her.

"What's it like being a twin?" Rawlston asked. She'd been asked the question so many times.

"I don't know what it's like *not* to be a twin, so I never know how to answer that." She sipped her iced tea. "Sabrina and I definitely have a strong connection. I guess it's what they call *twin-sense*. But it's not magical—we're very in tune to each other's moods and stuff, but we don't read each other's minds. I got tossed and broke my arm when I was working at the race track, and she didn't suddenly feel the same pain or anything like that."

She looked up, surprised to see how intently he was listening. She always felt like she babbled uncontrollably around him, but he seemed genuinely interested. It was nice to not have to censor or edit herself around him. "Being a twin is complicated. On one hand, it's great to have someone who knows you so well and reads you like a book. But on the other hand, it can be stifling to have someone who's that close and who knows that much. It's hard to keep secrets."

He stared for a moment. "Does she know *our* secret?"

She felt a stab of guilt. "Um…yes. Sorry."

"Don't be." He lifted a shoulder and murmured matter-of-factly, "I figured you might have told her, being twins and all. I think it must be nice, having someone like that to share everything with."

"What's it like being an only child?"

"Just like being a twin, it's both a blessing and a curse." He refilled her tea, then set out a plate of warm sopaipillas for dessert. "You get lots of attention as a kid, and you hang out with adults a lot, so you grow up fast. But it can be lonely. And there's a level of pressure there. When you're the only child, you know you're all your parents have. You don't want to disappoint them, and when you *do* disappoint them, you can't point to a brother or sister and blame them. It's all you, all the time." He gave her a rueful grin. "I was jealous of all of you Windhams, with your big, noisy family full of kids."

It never occurred to her that anyone looked at her family as something to covet. She adored her siblings, but as a teen, it often felt that she had to compete for attention. It was easy to feel lost.

"And I was jealous of *you*, having a nice, quiet home with such calm, loving parents."

"I guess we always want what we don't have, right?"

Like the way she wanted *him* right now. Which was silly.

"Maybe so." She bit into a sopaipilla and moaned. "These are delicious!"

There was a heat simmering in his eyes as he watched her bite into the fried pastry that suggested he was thinking silly thoughts, too.

"Thanks." He cleared his throat sharply. "I picked them up this morning from a little Mexican cantina in town."

"Carlitas? Oh, I love that place. Their carnitas are next level." How interesting that they liked so many of the same things and places. "Another thing we have in common is that we both grew up with interesting names. Where did *Rawlston* come from?"

"It's my mother's maiden name. She was the last of her father's line of Rawlstons, and she wanted to carry the name on for at least one more generation. I don't mind it now, but it was a mouthful as a kid. It sounds so formal, and there isn't a good way to shorten it."

"Rolly?"

His eyes narrowed. "The kids who tried that one usually ended up with black eyes."

She laughed. "Message received. You know I feel the same about being called Dolly." Although it didn't sound so bad when Rawlston said it.

"Rolly and Dolly," he snorted. "We should put that on our wedding announcement."

"Oh, thanks for reminding me!" She turned to grab the folder from the countertop. "Get your lucky pen, mister. We're ending this marriage."

CHAPTER ELEVEN

Rawlston did his best not to make a sour face at his own stupid mistake in mentioning the marriage. He got up to search for a pen nice enough to be his "lucky" pen, and took his time doing it. The more time they spent together, the less he wanted to sign those papers, and he hadn't wanted to sign them in the first place.

The only thing that had changed was his reason for delaying. He still didn't want to think about Dahlia with Carter. But he was starting to *like* the idea of Dahlia with *him*. Despite his feelings about marriage, he was in no hurry to end this one.

While he "searched," she asked how he got Tripp, who was sprawled on the tile floor in the kitchen. The dog was usually there when the weather was this hot. The house had air-conditioning, but Rawlston didn't want to spend half his income keeping the temperature as low as his dog wanted. So Tripp took advantage of the cool tiles.

He told Dahlia how he'd gone to a friend's ranch outside San Antonio and had stumbled across a stall filled with a wiggling litter of puppies. Tripp had trotted over to Rawlston and sat down, looking up as if to say, *Here I am, Dad*. His friend Dan had tried to direct him to puppies with more energy, but Tripp just had a look that told Rawlston that he was the one. He'd been a great herding dog, and good companion, for three years now.

"Have you found that magic pen yet?" Dahlia asked

sharply. He'd stopped pretending to look while talking about Tripp.

"It's not magic. It's just lucky." It also didn't exist. He fumbled around and finally pulled an old ballpoint pen from the junk drawer. "Here it is!"

He was running out of distractions to offer to keep her from getting his signature. She was standing now, her hand on the documents, staring at the pen in his hand.

"It's not exactly the fanciest lucky pen, is it?"

"Luck comes in all shapes and sizes."

The jig was finally up. He was going to have to sign the papers and annul their marriage. It was the right thing to do. He had no use for the institution, so delaying this any longer would be pointless anyway. He felt a small sense of relief at the idea that this performance would finally be over. The dishonesty was getting to him. He reached for the papers, and his pen clicked against the rim of his iced tea glass.

The glass flipped over in less than a heartbeat, sending iced tea all over the annulment papers. And he hadn't even been trying. Dahlia let out a cry, then tried to save the papers, but it happened too quickly. They were saturated with tea.

She glared at him as he tried to sop up the mess with a kitchen towel. "I swear you're doing this on purpose!"

He held his hand up to pledge his innocence. At least he wasn't going to have to lie about it. "Hand to God, that was an accident."

She stared hard, testing his sincerity and finally finding it acceptable.

"Fine. I can send a fresh copy to your printer. You got that fixed, right?"

"Uh…no." Technically, that wasn't a lie, either. He hadn't fixed it because it was never broken in the first place.

"Rawlston."

"Yes, Dahlia?"

"Every day makes me regret marrying you even more."

DAHLIA WAS SADDLING Bunny to ride out to check the sheep when Bender shuffled into her stables. It was impossible to define the man's age. It could be anywhere between fifty and eighty, with his leathery skin and deep wrinkles that spoke of a lifetime on the range. He was short and stocky, and had an ambling walk, as if he'd spent so much time on horseback that his legs stayed in that position.

She and Bender were becoming pals. At first, it was because Bender was one of the few ranch hands who had experience with sheep. But she and he were developing a friendship built of mutual respect. He liked Rebel and the way Dahlia handled the stallion. In turn, she liked the way he could wade into a sea of sheep without spooking them. And could spot a potential problem in an instant.

Last week that problem had been parasites. Bender saw the telltale weight loss in a few ewes and lambs, and had singled them out of the herd for treatment. He'd held the sheep while instructing Dahlia how to administer the oral paste dewormer. That was one of the other things she liked about Bender—he treated her like an intelligent rancher, not a "pretty girl" who shouldn't be messing with livestock.

That was the phrase Carter had used in his email to Dahlia two days ago, after their tense exchange about living in Chatelaine. He clearly thought he was helping his cause by explaining that doing the gritty work of ranching wasn't going to be helpful to his campaign. It was fine if she wanted to be the "pretty girl on horseback, or in front of a herd of cute sheep," but he didn't want her getting dirty, or ruining her "porcelain complexion" doing actual ranch work. The *last* thing Dahlia needed in her life was another opinionated man telling her what to want or how to behave.

Bender patted Bunny on the rump. "If yer ridin' the old mare for pleasure, go ahead. But don't worry about those sheep. I rode out and checked the herd this morning, and they're all good. The medicine did the trick with the sick ones, and it doesn't seem to have spread."

"Oh…thanks, Bender," she replied. "You didn't have to do that, but I'm glad you did. And it's awful hot for a pleasure ride, so I'll let Bunny hang out here in the shade instead." She tugged the saddle off and put it on a nearby rack.

He shrugged. "I'm a ranch hand, and those sheep are on the ranch, so I reckon it's part of my job to check on 'em." He spit some chewing tobacco into the dirt. "I've been ridin' out there to count heads and see how they're doin' every morning since they got here. Mr. Arlo and Mr. Nash know and are okay with it. They told me that when it comes to the sheep, I report to you, not them."

Usually Dahlia was not keen on people taking care of her business without her approval. But this didn't feel like that. This felt like her brothers knew she'd taken on a lot with basically an overnight herd of over a hundred sheep, and good old Bender had been keeping an eye on things. They were just looking out for her. Something she wasn't really used to.

Her brothers and sisters, of course, cared about her and would defend her against trouble in a heartbeat. But, sometimes, even siblings could be overbearing in their "caring." She thought of the time Jade had signed her up for theater class without telling her, because she thought Dahlia would be good at it. And of course there had been dear old Dad, who'd constantly pulled strings to get her better jobs with more prestige. He couldn't understand why she didn't want those *better* jobs with *better* people.

Maybe some of them would have been good opportunities for her, but she wanted to find those opportunities for *herself*. She didn't want them handed to her, or worse, her being bulldozed into them.

"Thanks so much, Bender. It's a relief to know I've got someone who knows what they're doing with sheep. It was ambitious of me to jump in with so many right off the bat."

Bender spit again. "The number don't make no difference really. Just more to count, but sheep are pretty independent. You're hiring shearers in the spring?"

"Yes, I'm already on their schedule. I wouldn't tackle that job myself."

"Smart. That's where people get themselves in trouble with sheep. They take too long, they stress the sheep, they get themselves hurt. The pros spend a couple minutes on a sheep, while amateurs waste half an hour or more. Multiply that by a hundred, and you're talking a week versus a day. Big difference."

Bender walked over to look at Rebel, who laid his ears back and made a false charge at the doorway. The ranch hand didn't flinch, so Rebel went back to eating his hay.

"Yeah, it's no fun to play those games with someone who's not afraid of you, is it?" Bender laughed at the stallion. "You're all bark, you big dummy."

"You've got his number. He's not exactly a marshmallow inside, but he's not the killer everyone tries to make him out to be."

"The best studs got some spirit in 'em. Don't need to be mean spirit, though. Just that big old ego that makes them act like cock of the walk." To her surprise, Rebel allowed Bender to scratch his neck, and then his head, although his eyes were still wide and cautious. "Oh, relax, big guy," Bender muttered. "You ain't impressin' me."

She put the mare back in her stall, then opened the gate to the covered outside run. The runs gave them more space to move around safely. She looked at the older man as she came back into the barn, latching the stall door behind her.

"Do you mind if I ask where you got the name Bender?"

He didn't look away from Rebel and the spot behind the horse's ear where he was lightly scratching with his fingertips in a rhythmic, circular motion. The stallion looked like he was in heaven.

"Cowboys love nicknames, Miss Dahlia. But you can't pick your own—it gets picked for ya'. I was a wild one in my younger days, and I liked my booze. Some mornings I came straight from the bar to the barn and saddled up without a wink of sleep." His voice was low and melodic, and she realized he was doing that for Rebel's sake, keeping the horse mesmerized. "One of the guys back then would say, *Bobby's been out on another bender*, and after he said it a few times, a nickname was born." He stepped back from Rebel's stall door and gave a shrug as he walked away. "Stuck on me for forty years now."

She did a quick calculation after he left. If he was old enough to drink, and had that nickname for forty years, Bender had to be around sixty, if not older.

Dahlia brushed dust off of her jeans and decided to visit her mother now that she had unexpected free time. Mom wasn't at the main house, so she drove to her mother's pet project—Fortune's Castle.

She pulled up in front of the place and stared at the unusual stone structure rising from the Texas dirt. It was an honest-to-God castle. Wendell Fortune had left it to his long-lost grandchild, Wendy Fortune. It had been a year of inheritances for Dahlia's mother. First, Casper Windham had died, and left most of his estate to Wendy. He'd sold Windham Plastics in the months before his death, so the amount was substantial for Mom and for all six of her children.

Then the Fortune castle and money had fallen into Mom's lap, along with a new name and new family. It had been…a lot. But Mom had handled all of the changes and surprises with her usual grace. That's who Wendy Windham Fortune was. She was always tasteful, kind, soft-spoken and almost ethereal in her mannerisms. But that gentle exterior hid a spine of titanium. She was strong-willed and smart. And knew what each person needed to hear in order to be persuaded to do her bidding, especially with her children.

"Hi, sweetheart!" Mom rushed out to give Dahlia a warm embrace. "I thought maybe you'd forgotten how to get here. I haven't seen you in a week." She held Dahlia at arm's length. "You look fabulous—the ranch life agrees with you. Do you have time for an early lunch? I can have the kitchen make up some sandwiches for us."

Dahlia was doing quick calculations in her head, cringing as she realized her mother was right—it had been over a week since she'd been here. The castle was only a short drive from the ranch—she drove past it every time she went into town. She'd been so distracted with the annulment and Rawlston's efforts to avoid moving forward with it that she'd lost track of the days.

"I'm sorry. It's been hectic. How are the renovations coming?"

"The renovations are making me pull my hair out," Mom answered. "But it's taking shape very nicely. You should stay for the afternoon. The Perry triplets were just here for a tour this morning—Haley's doing a story for the newspaper about our soft opening coming up. You know the three ladies, right?"

Dahlia had become friends with Haley, and had briefly met her sisters, Tabitha and Lily. She'd connected with Haley at a luncheon for new members of the Lake Chatelaine Business Owners Association, and they'd hit it off right away. The newspaper editor, Devin Street, had introduced them, and Haley had quietly filled her in on everyone's backstory-slash-gossip. She'd liked Haley's straightforward approach and dry humor. She was a very good observer of people. It was over a wine lunch last week that Haley had told her about a possible missing brother. The triplets didn't learn until recently about a rumor that claimed a *fourth* sibling might still be alive somewhere. According to an older woman who worked part-time at GreatStore, there'd been a baby Perry *boy* adopted out at birth. Were they quadruplets? Was he older? Younger? Did he exist at all?

The ladies were on the hunt for him, even though the old woman struggled with bouts of dementia. It could all be an elaborate fairy tale in her mind. Just in case, they'd done DNA testing to see if they could locate him through one of the popular genealogy companies.

"I can't stay long, Mom," Dahlia said, "but a quick lunch sounds nice."

They ate at a small table on a private stone veranda. The elaborate castle had hidden rooms and staircases, and was filled with quirky little clues built into the stones. The number fifty was a recurrent one—the number of men killed in a mining disaster back in the 1960s. It turned out that a woman had also died in the mine that day—Wendy's mother—leaving infant Wendy with a babysitter who'd raised her as her own. The true number of dead was fifty-one. Wendy had had the new number engraved into a stone on the veranda. They were sitting in the shade of a grape arbor, with a soft breeze to cool them. Dahlia sipped her tea, smiling to herself about her and Rawlston both being fans of the beverage in its pure form, without sugar.

"That's a secretive little smile you're wearing, Dahlia. Do you have a forbidden lover stashed away somewhere?"

She choked on her tea, laughing to hide her shock. "*Mom!* What on earth made you suggest that? I've been here for all of three weeks—hardly enough time to find a forbidden lover. Or a lover of *any* kind. I'm busy on the ranch, not running around dating a cowboy somewhere."

Unless she'd met him in Las Vegas and married him there, of course. But they weren't lovers. Not past that first night, except for one scorching kiss under a cotton-wood tree.

Her mother was studying her now. "That was a long, detailed denial for a casual joke. What's going on with you?"

"Nothing." Dahlia did her best to look calm and composed. "There's nothing going on for me except lots of wooly sheep bouncing all over my range."

There was a long pause, Mom's examination unwavering.

"I don't believe you, Dahlia," she finally said, sitting up straight. "Spill it. Now."

If twin-sense was bad, mom-sense was even worse. She couldn't hide anything from her mother, and she no longer wanted to. She needed her mom's wisdom, and the only way she'd get it was to tell the truth.

"I sort of ran into Rawlston Ames in Las Vegas. We kind of got drunk and we…well—"

"Oh my God, you slept with him!" Mom exclaimed, looking surprisingly happy at the thought.

"Well…" Dahlia let out a long sigh, then told the story as quickly as possible. "Only *after* we got married. In a hot pink chapel in a midnight ceremony neither of us remembers very well."

Wendy Fortune froze, her tea glass just an inch from her mouth, which was now wide-open in shock. She slowly set down her glass, and all the while her forehead was wrinkled in deep thought as she stared at Dahlia.

"You…and Rawlston…*married*?"

Dahlia nodded. "Believe me, no one was as surprised as him and me the next morning. And no one knows about this, except Sabrina and Jade. We're getting it annulled, of course."

"Why?"

Now it was Dahlia's turn to look shocked. "*Why?* Well, for one thing, I barely know the man. I've hardly seen him since high school. For another, we were drunk out of our minds on spiked punch. And most importantly, I'm dating *Carter*, Mom!"

A brief flash of some emotion crossed her mother's face. There'd been the tiniest wrinkle of her nose in distaste, and the lines around her mouth had deepened as if she was struggling to maintain her composure. Did *everyone* dislike Carter? Was it possible that Dahlia had been so wrong about him? Or had been in such denial, which seemed more feasible? Her mother reached out to take her hands.

"Tell me how this all happened."

She did, skipping over the hot wedding night of lovemaking, and the kiss out on the range. She told how fate seemed to be conspiring against Rawlston signing the papers, with one thing after another going wrong.

"Are you sure it's fate interfering, and not Rawlston?"

She'd wondered the same thing, but it made no sense. "Rawlston despises the institution of marriage, Mom. His first marriage was a hot mess, and there's no way he wants to stay hitched to me. I think we've just had bad luck."

"And what about you and Carter?"

"Well…" It was a very good question. "He's been dropping a lot of hints lately, and I'm expecting him to propose when he gets home."

"That's a very factual description of your status together. Do you love him?"

"I…uh…" Dahlia's shoulders slumped. "I'm honestly not sure, but I think we make a good couple—on paper, at least." They were both wealthy, successful, mature adults who had ambitions for their lives. Those ambitions were completely different, though. That was becoming more and more apparent every time they communicated.

Her mother patted her hands before releasing them and sitting back. "The problem is, people don't *live* on paper, dear. And your voice has no excitement at all when you speak about Carter. But when you talk about Rawlston, you sound—"

"Irritated? Frustrated?"

"Maybe." Mom paused. "But at least those are *real* emotions. The kind of emotions that keep you awake at night, thinking about the man. Does Carter make you feel that way?"

She didn't hesitate.

"No, he doesn't."

"But the man you're married to does?"

"Mom, we can't build a relationship on irritating each other!"

Her mother smiled that all-knowing mom-smile of hers. "You'd be surprised what you can build a relationship on, Dahlia."

CHAPTER TWELVE

Rawlston gave two short whistles, sending Tripp scurrying around the left flank of the cattle. The dog nipped at a few heels, deftly dodging some corresponding kicks, and started the herd moving away from the fence line.

It had become an almost daily routine with this subset of his overall herd. They loved coming to the top of the hill between the Fortune and Ames ranches and grazing with however many of Dahlia's sheep managed to scurry under the barbed wire and onto his property. It was as if the cows and sheep had become friends somehow, and he couldn't afford to let that happen. Every rancher knew that cattle and sheep didn't mix.

He nudged Malloy forward, and between the horse and Tripp, the cattle moved into a jog away from the hilltop and back down to the level ground, where there was also plenty of grazing. Rawlston's fear was that the sheep would eventually wander this far, and end up ruining some of the best grazing ground he had. He turned to ride back to the house.

It had been three days since he'd innocently spilled iced tea on the annulment papers. He was surprised Dahlia hadn't been back the next morning with a fresh set, but so far she'd stayed away. Salty old Bender Grant had been checking the sheep for her. Rawlston had seen him yesterday and this morning, riding through the herd, counting heads. He was glad to see she was getting some help. Dahlia had always been so fiercely independent, scorning other people's help and advice. Not that that had ever stopped her brothers and sisters from offering it.

Just yesterday, he'd run into her sister, Jade, at Great-Store. He'd nodded when they'd made eye contact, figuring she'd go on her way without stopping. They barely knew each other. But she'd rushed over to him, wide-eyed and animated.

"Rawlston! Oh, it's so good to see you! How's everything on your ranch these days?"

"Uh...fine. And how are you doing, Jade? Settling in okay in Chatelaine?"

"Yes. It's been a big change, but I like it here." She'd looked around the giant box store and wrinkled her nose the same way her sister liked to do. "I wish the shopping was better, but other than that, it's all good."

He'd nodded. "We have everything we need, but not much more than that."

She'd given him a funny look, which made him uneasy, then put her hand on his arm. Another trait like Dahlia's.

"Okay, I won't beat around the bush here." She'd glanced around to make sure no one else was in the canned food aisle. "I know what happened in Vegas."

He wasn't thrilled that Dahlia had told another of her siblings about the wedding she wanted kept secret. He rushed to reassure Jade.

"We're getting it annulled."

"Don't."

"What?"

Jade had given him a conspiratorial wink. "You seem to be dragging your feet on the annulment, and I think you should keep stalling for, say..." she'd looked up in thought "...maybe another month?"

"Until after Carter gets home." Her eyes had brightened when he hit on the truth.

"Something like that, yes." She'd looked around again. "Is that why you've been avoiding signing anything?"

"It was, originally, yes. But it doesn't feel right. She and I screwed up, and I can't use that mistake to interfere with what she wants."

"Sure you can." Jade's laughter had brightened. "Her and Carter are all wrong for each other, and you know it. He's another Casper Windham, and that's the last thing Dahlia needs in her life. Her relationship with our father was messy, and she let him get into her head. If you don't sign the papers, she can't say yes to Carter when he gets back."

He'd told Jade the delay felt like a wasted effort, since Dahlia would just run to Carter as soon as the annulment went through. The thought ate at him like acid, but she had the right to make her own choices, and his tactics had been making him squeamish lately.

"Carter's not the waiting around kind," Jade had pointed out. "He has a very short attention span. He'll move on before she can finish asking him to wait."

She'd probably been right about Carter, but Rawlston hadn't made her any promises about the annulment. The more he got to know Dahlia, the more he liked and respected her. Then again, if she was the type to prefer Powers, then maybe he didn't know her all that well after all.

HIS FATHER'S TRUCK was at the ranch when he got back. Dad got out of the driver's side, and someone opened the passenger door. Dad had brought JoAnn here, to Rawlston's home. He remembered what Dahlia had said to him—he couldn't hold it against JoAnn that she wasn't like his mother. He'd done some digging, and she seemed to be exactly who she'd said she was. JoAnn Henderson from Rockslide, Vermont. A widow who'd been running a farm stand for years—first with her husband, then alone after he'd died.

Tall and buxom, she looked up at Rawlston with a hesitant smile as he rode Malloy over to the car. Dad walked to her side, giving him a warning look as if to say, *Be careful, son.* Rawlston dismounted and greeted them.

"Dad, JoAnn. Did we have something planned today?"

"Nah," Dad said. "I was telling JoAnn about the ranch and decided I should show it to her—" he gave a pointed look "—rather than wait for an invitation."

"Oh, yeah. Sorry. It's been busy and..." He floundered for an excuse and finally gave up. "Come on in. I'll throw some burgers on the grill for us." He turned to JoAnn, who was carefully keeping her distance. She was giving him his space, respecting his doubts about her. Which made him feel like a jerk. His dad was determined to marry this woman, and Rawlston needed to at least *try* to honor that. He smiled at her. "Come on in, JoAnn. Just uh…forgive the mess, okay? The house is nothing fancy."

She seemed to relax a bit. "Rawlston, I lived in a hundred-and-eighty-year-old Vermont farmhouse most of my adult life. I don't give a hoot about fancy *anything*."

They ended up having a nice afternoon. His dad told stories about raising Rawlston in Cactus Grove, and JoAnn talked about her two children. Her son was in Maine, and her daughter lived in a Boston suburb. She had three grandchildren, and Rawlston didn't miss the look his father gave him. He wouldn't mind giving his dad a grandchild or two, but it wouldn't be happening anytime soon. JoAnn insisted on clearing the table after they ate, and while she was out of earshot he got another one of those looks from Dad.

"What?" he asked. "You're obviously dying to say something, so just…say it."

"I'm wondering how your, uh, marriage is going."

"It'll be going away pretty soon. We have the annulment papers, and just have to get them signed and sent
back to the lawyers."

"You sure you want to do that?"

He wasn't, but he didn't want to admit that to his father. Or to himself. "It needs to be done, Dad. She wants
someone else. Story of my life."

"Quit feeling sorry for yourself, son. Not every woman
is Lana."

"What's the point of marriage, anyway?" Rawlston
complained. "Mom was your one and only, and now that
she's gone, along comes JoAnn, who's the complete opposite of everything you loved in Mom, and you're going
to marry *her*. It makes no sense to me."

His father's face was stony and silent for a long moment.
Then he slowly shook his head. "Boy, you really don't get
it, do you? JoAnn has the same exact quality I loved in
your mother—she's genuine. She is who she is, through
and through. Her version of being genuine is admittedly
different from Kathy's, but their honesty and openness are
identical. There weren't any games with your mother, and
there aren't any with JoAnn, either." He leaned forward to
make his point, staring straight at Rawlston. "I initially
thought I wanted to be with JoAnn because we were compatible and I was lonely. But now that she's here, in person... Well, I didn't think it could happen again, but... I'm
falling in love with her."

Rawlston was surprised, but his dad had always been
a romantic. "Aren't you afraid you might be setting yourself up for heartbreak? I mean... Mom was sick. You told
me JoAnn's a breast cancer survivor, and..." He felt like
a jerk for even bringing it up.

"And she could get sick again?" Dad nodded slowly.

"She could. Or I could. Or *you* could. None of us knows what the future holds. There's no guarantee of happily-ever-afters for any of us. Falling in love is probably the biggest gamble a person can take. But the rewards are so great that it's worth it."

"It wasn't for me."

"The problem with you and Lana was that you were in love with different things. You were in love with *her* and she was in love with *marriage*. She was a borderline bridezilla about your wedding, spending a fortune so she could be a fairy-tale princess. She envisioned the fairy tale *after* the wedding, too—picket fence, two kids and a dog, hubby coming home every night. And as it turned out, she wasn't built for sitting around alone while you went off and had your adventures at sea."

He wasn't wrong. Lana had thrown huge red flags during the wedding planning. She'd told him more than once that it was *her* day, and refused to listen to his opinion that it should be *their* day. But his friends had assured him all women wanted to be the star of their wedding.

He thought of Dahlia in that ridiculous electronic veil in a bright pink chapel in Las Vegas. Completely at ease and in the moment. Yes, they'd been drunk, but he had a feeling that was who Dahlia was. What was the word Dad used? *Genuine.*

"Son," his father started, "you need to find someone to love who loves you back. *Then* you'll understand why people want to be married."

"Yeah, well…that's not Dahlia." If he thought there was a chance with her, what would he do?

"Maybe not. But don't close the door on her until you know that for sure."

He was going to argue that *she* was the one closing the door, but JoAnn rejoined them and he let the subject drop. After they'd left, he sat on the patio and sipped a good Southern whiskey, wondering what a *real* marriage to Dahlia would be like.

DAHLIA HADN'T BEEN to the Daily Grind since that first meeting with Rawlston. Going out for breakfast wasn't her thing. But Haley had invited her to breakfast, and she'd decided forging a new friendship was worth a change in her routine. Haley said Dahlia needed to be seen in the Daily Grind if she wanted to be considered a local.

"The LC Club is great for networking with the upper crust, but the heart of the real Chatelaine beats inside places like the Longhorn Feedstore and the Daily Grind," Haley said. "Sit with Beau Weatherly and ask him a question or two. Make friends with Sylvie. You're a rodeo gal, so they'll accept you in no time at all. And once you're accepted, *all* the doors will open for you."

Dahlia had loving brothers and sisters, but she'd left her few close friends behind in Cactus Grove, and she was missing them. A woman needed a friend who wasn't family. Otherwise, who on earth would she talk to *about* her family? And sometimes, a person needed to do that, no matter how much she loved her siblings.

So here she was, walking into the Daily Grind at 7 a.m., ready for coffee. She'd opted for ranch wear—jeans, her everyday boots and a blue gingham Western shirt. This was who she was, and she didn't want to network as anyone other than herself. Beau Weatherly was seated in the corner, with his Free Life Advice sign on the table. A woman was sitting with him and they were laughing over something. A man waited patiently for his turn with Beau.

Rawlston had told her Beau's unusual story. He'd been a successful rancher and an even more successful investor. He had a sixth sense about which businesses were going to take off and which ones had run their course. He and his wife had built themselves a wonderful life on a spacious ranch in Chatelaine. Then Susan Weatherly had died unexpectedly, leaving Beau wallowing in grief. His wife had been a big believer in giving back to the community. It was her way of paying it forward and sharing their bounty with others.

Beau started coming to the Daily Grind to be around other people, and customers would ask him for his advice on things. He enjoyed sharing his wisdom, and pretty soon people were coming to the coffee shop just to see Beau. With the shop's permission, he made his appearances official, coming in most mornings to answer whatever questions people had. Rawlston had explained that sometimes his advice was tongue-in-cheek, like when people asked if it was going to rain that day, and he'd answer, *It's gonna rain somewhere, for sure.*

It was a sweet gesture that had become a beloved tradition. And it had apparently helped Beau as much as it had helped the town. It gave him a reason to get up in the mornings, and Rawlston said Beau had seemed more like his former happy self in recent months.

Dahlia had just taken a seat when her phone pinged with a text. It was Haley, telling her she couldn't make it because the paper was covering a story about an overnight house fire somewhere. She told Dahlia to "mingle," but that felt too much like political schmoozing. She wasn't running for office—she just wanted to get to know people here. She ordered a large cappuccino and a raspberry scone, which arrived drenched in butter and smelling heavenly. She'd just taken her first bite when she made eye contact with Beau, two tables away.

He gave her a smile and a nod before turning back to the young man at his table. There was no one left in line.

She thought about getting up to wait, but that felt silly. Dahlia didn't need anyone's advice, and she didn't want anyone thinking she did.

Taking another bite of the delicious scone, she looked over toward Beau's table and found him watching her again. The young man was gone. No one was waiting. Beau smiled and nodded at the empty chair, inviting her to join him. Knowing it would be rude to refuse, she gathered her plate and mug and moved to his table.

He jumped to his feet to hold the chair. "Good morning, Dahlia. I know who you are, but it's nice to meet you in person. I'm—"

"Beau Weatherly," she finished for him. "Everyone knows who you are, Mr. Weatherly."

"Everyone also knows to call me Beau. What brings you to the coffee shop at this early hour?"

"I was supposed to meet Haley Perry, but she had to cancel."

He shook his head. "That gal is always on the run. She's a good'n, though. How are those sheep of yours doing?"

"They're doing well, thanks." She wasn't sure how much to share with him.

"And the ranch is doing well for your family?"

"Oh, yes. We're still settling in, but it's good."

He stared at her for a long moment.

"Then what's troubling you?"

She straightened. "Nothing! Everything's fine." Then she realized why he was asking. "Oh, I didn't come over for advice, Beau. No offense—I'm sure you're great at it, but I'm okay."

He stared again, then smiled as he set his coffee mug down. "If you say so, Dahlia. But let me give you some free advice anyway." He waved Sylvie over for a refill, then waited for her to leave, which the older woman did reluctantly.

Dahlia had no idea what kind of advice a total stranger thought she needed. But his eyes were warm and kind. Almost…fatherly. The idea shocked her. She didn't even realize she'd been *looking* for a father figure. But here she was, staring at Beau Weatherly, wishing she'd had a dad like him. And feeling guilty about it.

"Thanks, but I… I should go." Emotions welled up in her, and she needed time to sort through them.

"I understand." Beau's smile deepened. "Let me just say this—it's good to keep an open mind when life puts a chance at happiness in front of you. It might not be the future you imagined or even one you think you want, but life is funny that way." He winked. "Have a good day, Dahlia, and remember—love shows up in the strangest places."

CHAPTER THIRTEEN

RAWLSTON WAS GOING to sign those papers. He drove onto the Fortune ranch and headed for Dahlia's house at the end of the road. She wasn't expecting him, but he couldn't keep dragging this out, despite what his father had said about fate and all that nonsense. If anything, it was because of those comments. If Dad wanted to marry JoAnn, fine. Fine for *Dad*. But the conversation had reminded Rawlston that marriage wasn't for him, and he couldn't keep up this charade any longer.

Dahlia had stopped pressuring him about the annulment lately, but he had a feeling that was just reverse psychology. Pestering him constantly hadn't worked, so now she was backing off, making him come to her. And it was working, because here he was, driving to her house unannounced. He imagined the surprise on her face when she opened the door at this late hour to find him standing there, pen in hand. Tonight she was going to get exactly what she wanted.

He saw lights on in the stable, and slowed. Her golf cart was outside the barn door. It was after nine o'clock, and he grew concerned. Was something wrong with one of the horses? Or was it the sheep? He parked his truck by the barn and walked to the open door. Dahlia was there, with the paint stallion standing on the crossties. She was brushing Rebel slowly down his neck and shoulders, almost like a massage, and she was speaking low and soft.

The stallion, normally fidgety and raring to go, looked surprisingly mellow, with one hind leg relaxed and his head down, eyes half-closed.

Rawlston took another step forward, then heard Dahlia say his name. To the horse. He paused to listen.

"I just don't get it, Rebel. What is it about Rawlston that makes my pulse jump like a jackrabbit every time we touch? I know we were drunk in Vegas, but if it had been anyone else in the world, I can't imagine going so far as to *marry* them. Rawlston just felt…*safe*, you know what I mean?" The brush moved rhythmically over the big horse's coat. "And I don't mean safe in a boring way. He's got this laid-back-dude thing going, but at the same time, he pushes me. Or pushes my buttons, at least. None of it makes any sense, but I just can't help wanting to be with him. Wanting to be in his arms. It's stupid, right?"

Rawlston stepped into the light from the doorway. "I don't think it's stupid."

She spun, and the quick movement had Rebel laying his ears back in agitation. Rawlston had interrupted a perfectly good massage, and the horse was clearly not happy about it. But Rawlston's eyes were on Dahlia, and only her. There was a blush of pink on her cheeks, and her perfect lips were parted just enough for him to know she was feeling the same aching desire that he was. Then her eyes narrowed.

"You scared ten years off my life! What are you doing here?"

He closed the distance between them. "I couldn't stay away."

"Are you *drunk*?"

"Not this time, Dahlia…" He slid one hand behind her head and the other behind her back. He waited, needing to be sure before he made another move. She stared up at him, then moved closer, stepping into his embrace. "You wanted to be in my arms, and now you are. What's next?"

Her eyes deepened to blue velvet, and her arms slid around his neck.

"Now we kiss," she whispered.

And they did. Gently at first, with their lips caressing and their tongues tangling in a slow, sultry dance. Neither one of them was in a hurry, and it made the kiss all the more satisfying. She let out a soft moan as she turned her head to give him easier access. He took advantage of it, taking her mouth and tasting the heat of her desire. She wanted this. She wanted *him*. And he was very much okay with that.

His arms tightened around her, lifting her from the floor as the kiss turned more frantic. She hooked one long leg around his hips and he tugged her higher until both of her legs were wrapped around him. He gripped her tightly and she moaned again, grinding against his hardness.

Spots of bright colors burst behind his tightly closed eyes. For the first time since he was a teen, he worried about losing control before he ever got his clothes off. She was setting him off like a firecracker.

"The house," he muttered, nibbling on her neck as he gasped for air.

"The horse," she answered breathlessly. "Let me put Rebel away. Put me down. And then—" she clasped his face between her hands "—*then* we go to the house."

She ushered the stallion back into his stall, and Rebel rolled an annoyed look at Rawlston as he passed him. Rawlston accepted responsibility for the horse's interrupted grooming session, and had no remorse. Zero. None. Dahlia had barely latched the stall door when Rawlston turned her and pressed her back against it, kissing her hard. She returned the kiss just as eagerly, then whispered against his ear.

"Too many clothes…"

When the lady was right, she was right. They *did* have too many clothes on. He tossed off his T-shirt and helped her tug her blue knit top over her head, revealing a lacy pink bra that matched the soft blush high on her cheeks. They both froze, staring at each other hungrily. She was the first to reach out, tracing her fingers in a zigzag pattern down his chest, flicking at his nipples with her fingernails, sending a jolt of electricity down his spine. His shorts were suddenly uncomfortably tight, and he growled a curse as he grabbed her wrist and pulled her close.

It was his turn to tease *her* breasts now, and she let out a cry as her head fell back. She bit her lower lip as he ran his tongue around and around before settling his lips on the peak and drawing her into his mouth, right through the lace. She hooked her leg around his thigh again, getting herself closer to where he was pulsing inside his shorts, desperate to be inside of her.

But not here. Barns were only good for sex in the movies. The reality? Hay was scratchy, not soft. And full of bugs and spiders. Besides, it was hot out here, and not the sexy kind of hot. The sun may have gone down, but the air was thick and still with humidity. There was a tropical storm spinning somewhere out in the Gulf of Mexico, and it was pushing hot, charged air into Texas. He'd heard thunder rumbling in the distance when he'd walked to the barn. Besides, making love while her horses looked on was a bit of a buzzkill.

"House!" He gasped the word against her skin before taking one more lap around her right breast.

"Yes!" she cried. He wasn't sure if it was agreement or ecstasy. She pushed on his shoulders. "Let's *go*."

It was a wild dash to the house. But unlike Las Vegas, he remembered every single detail. Their lips were locked together most of the trip, as clothes went flying. Their shirts were in the barn. Her bra landed somewhere outside. They jumped on the golf cart, where she straddled his lap as he tried to drive. She tugged his belt off and tossed it somewhere in the dark, then buried her fingers in his hair and kissed him so hard he almost drove into a pomegranate tree in her yard.

He wasn't exactly sure when her boots came off, but when they stopped in front of the lakeside house, she'd stepped out of her jeans easily, kicking them into the shrubbery in her bare feet. *His* boots came off in her doorway, with one landing outside on the porch and the other inside the door. Her panties and his boxer briefs left a trail down the hallway to her bedroom.

He barely registered the room she led him into. It was big. There were windows. The only thing he cared about was the king-size bed. He tossed her onto it and climbed on, kneeling over her like a starving man staring at a feast. Before he could get any closer, she held her hand up, her fingers against his mouth. He went still. *Oh, damn.* Too much? Too fast?

"Condoms." She tipped her head in the direction of an arched doorway. "Bathroom. Bottom drawer."

He closed his eyes in relief. She wasn't stopping what was happening. She was just being smart about it. He could live with that. Because he really, truly, absolutely did not want to stop.

DAHLIA WATCHED RAWLSTON'S very fine ass vanish into the bathroom, then heard him opening and closing doors and drawers frantically.

"Bottom drawer!" she called out, but before she finished, he was hurrying back to the bed, a length of condom packets hanging from his hand. She couldn't help chuckling. "Feeling optimistic, are we?"

He tore one off and tossed the rest onto the nightstand. "I've always been a positive thinker, babe."

He rolled the condom on, then settled his weight over her. She'd pushed back against the pillows, and he held himself up on extended arms, his hips against hers, his erection twitching between her legs. She closed her eyes in anticipation, but then…nothing happened. She opened them to find him staring at her.

"What's wrong?" she asked.

"Nothing at all is wrong. This is…" He looked down at her naked beneath him. "This is everything I've dreamt about for weeks now. It's perfect. But…what are we doing? Are you sure we're okay here…"

There was a flash of light, and thunder boomed outside the windows. Even the weather was turned on.

She reached up to cup his cheek with her hand. "I know consent may have been a little sketchy on our wedding night, for both of us. But I'm stone-cold sober tonight, and I think you are, too." He nodded as she continued. "I'm fully capable of making decisions for myself. I want this, Rawlston. I want *you*."

"Thank Christ." He entered her as his mouth covered hers, capturing her cry.

All those fragmented memories of that night in the Las Vegas suite came together in her mind like a Rubik's Cube snapping together in perfect symmetry. He moved inside of her, nipping the skin at the base of her neck as they rocked together, building a fire that became the center of her universe. She reveled in the realness of this moment with him. Vegas had seemed like a dream—something that couldn't possibly have been that good. But here she was, with Rawlston, feeling that fire building and feeling a scream rising up inside of her. Like she was trying to contain an explosion that wouldn't be stopped. This couldn't be happening. It couldn't be *Rawlston* who made her feel this way.

She clung to him as they both fell off a cliff of urgent, magnificent passion that consumed them both. Why weren't the sheets on fire? Why weren't the smoke alarms going off? Why wasn't there a choir of angels singing in her bedroom?

Dahlia was barely coherent when a flash of lightning lit up the room again, followed quickly by a crackle of thunder that seemed to rumble on indefinitely. Was it real, or had their lovemaking made her dream up the sudden storm? Rawlston shuddered in her arms, then collapsed against her with a loud groan.

"Damn, woman. I guess it wasn't just the spiked punch that made us so good together. We're the real deal."

She wanted to argue, but couldn't. She'd never had a man's touch light her up the way Rawlston's did. There was something deep between them. Something unlike anything she'd ever felt before. It was thrilling. And terrifying. She shivered, and he reacted immediately.

"You okay?" He slid off her and pulled her into his arms, his warmth chasing away any doubts for now.

"I think so. It's just…that was…a lot."

"Too much a lot, or the kind of a lot that makes you want more?"

"The second. But I'm not sure if I *should* want more. Rawlston…"

He snuggled her in close, resting his head on hers. "It's okay, babe. We'll figure this out together." She closed her eyes and absorbed his warmth. He was her safe place. He was…home.

CHAPTER FOURTEEN

RAWLSTON WOKE UP ALONE, in a strange room. He blinked a few times in the darkness before he realized he was in Dahlia's bed. Just like in Vegas, their lovemaking had scrambled his brain. And something else that was just like Vegas—they'd been *incredible* together.

He lay back against the pillow, remembering every detail this time around. Every touch. Every look. Every whisper and every cry. They knew what to do to please each other without saying a word, and they both focused on that—pleasing the other person. Was he physically satiated and happy? Of course. But he felt far more satisfaction knowing that he'd absolutely rocked her world tonight.

At least…that's what he'd thought. But she wasn't in the bed. And the bathroom was dark. He got up and looked for his shorts, then remembered they'd shed their clothes last night like Hansel and Gretel had left a trail of crumbs. He snagged a towel and wrapped it around his waist, following the soft light out on the deck, which he could see through the bedroom's open French doors.

Dahlia was curled up on one of the upholstered lounge chairs near the gas-fueled firepit, where low blue flames rose up through clear glass pebbles. Wearing a very short pink robe, she was sitting in the covered section of the deck, away from the rain that was falling now. Thunder rumbled in the distance—another round of storms were rolling in.

"Hey," he said, not wanting to startle her.

She lifted her head and stared at him for a moment before nodding back. "Hey."

He thought she might be looking for alone time, but she slid over in the lounge, making room for him to join her. He did, wrapping his arms around her and pulling her close, her back to his chest. "You okay?"

"I'm not sure." She'd almost whispered the words. "I mean, yes—there's nothing wrong with me. Like I said before, it's—"

"A lot?" He finished the sentence for her. "Yeah, I know. We're pretty amazing together, Dahlia."

She snorted. "Yes, we are." She pulled away so she could look him in the eye. "But what does that mean?"

He shrugged. "Does it have to mean anything other than that? Just because we can't define it, that doesn't mean it's a bad thing."

She relaxed back against him again, staring at the flames. "No, but it's not necessarily *good*, either. It's… unexpected. I'm not big on surprises, and what we have going on is a huge surprise to me."

He kissed the top of her head. "Me, too."

It was one thing to nurse a crush from high school. But he'd never in his horniest dreams thought they'd be *this* good together. That she'd be the one woman to shatter him in bed and put all the pieces back together so he was better than before. What she'd done to him was magic, pure and simple. And he wanted it to happen again. Right now. And again after that, because he had a feeling he'd never, ever have enough of her.

"So what happens now?" she murmured.

"If you're asking what I *want* to have happen now, then my answer is we go back to bed and do that all over again. More than once. Slower. Faster. Harder. Softer. I don't care—I just know I need more of whatever that was." She didn't answer right away, and he started to worry. "Only if you're interested, of course."

She turned onto her back, sliding her arms up around his neck as he leaned over her. "I'm interested. I'm *terrified*, but I'm interested. My only question is—" Her back arched up toward him. "Why do we need the bed?" Lightning flickered across the sky, and Rawlston groaned, suddenly hard and aching for her. *Yes, please. Right here!*

He kissed her, softly at first, then growing in intensity. She pressed her body against his, and he wasn't sure if it was thunder he heard or if it was his pulse pounding in his ears. He worked her robe open and she shrugged out of it as he tossed his towel aside. They fit together so perfectly. The new storm grew closer, and he couldn't imagine anything better than this—making love to Dahlia outdoors with a Texas storm brewing. Except for one thing...

"Damn it," he moaned through gritted teeth. "Condom."

There was a beat of silence before she answered. "I'm on the pill, Rawlston."

He lifted his head. "Are you saying what I think you're saying? You want to...?"

"I'm healthy and I assume you are, too. I have birth control taken care of. Technically, we are husband and wife, so..."

"Oh, hell yes."

He was on top of her, and then inside of her, in seconds. His eyes closed at the feeling of skin against skin, warm and wet. It was all enough to make him lightheaded for a second, but a mist of rain brushed across his back and snapped him back to reality. The wind was gusting, sending soft sheets of warm rain under the roof of the deck and onto the lounge. There was another flash of lightning, much closer and brighter.

Dahlia looked up at him, her eyes wide and dark, shining with intensity. She might be as turned on by the storm as she was by him. He began to move in her, and she raised her legs and wrapped them around his waist. The position made it even easier to thrust inside her, and he did. She called out his name as she met him move for move. Soon he wasn't sure what was real and what wasn't. Was it raining? Was that thunder? Was the wind moving things on the deck, or was that all part of the vortex that was him and Dahlia?

He held back as long as he could, waiting for the storm to be right over them. Waiting for her to beg him for release. Both things happened at once, and not a moment too soon. With a garbled yell, he came in her, quivering and thrusting again and again, until there was nothing left to him. Nothing but Dahlia, still wrapped around him, making soft purring sounds of joy.

"Christ, woman." He tried to gather his wits, but they were scattered in the wind.

"I know," she answered, gently patting his back, now damp from the rain and wind. "That was even better than earlier. Better than Vegas. The hands-down best."

"Best between us or your best ever?" He couldn't help asking. She gave him a throaty laugh, then kissed his neck.

"Both."

Rawlston smiled in quiet pride. "Best sex ever, eh?"

"Yes, you egomaniac," she laughed. "A new benchmark has been achieved. Wanna see if we can break it before the sun rises?"

"I've heard trying is where the fun is, so why not?"

They made love again on the lounge chair, then went back to her bedroom for more fun before collapsing in each other's arms in complete exhaustion. She was sprawled across him in a position nearly identical to that morning in

Las Vegas. He ran his fingers through her hair and down her back, and her skin twitched like a cat. She moaned something that ended with his name, but he didn't pick up on the first few words. He only knew she sounded happy.

Rawlston shifted so that he could hold her in an embrace, and she reciprocated without waking, sliding her arms around his body as she snuggled close. This was a brand-new sensation for him—a mix of physical pleasure and emotional contentment so intense that it scared him. Partly because he was afraid it wouldn't last. And partly because he was afraid it would, which would mean changing all of his most firmly held beliefs on women, relationships and marriage.

He'd been convinced he didn't need or believe in any of it. Until tonight, when Dahlia showed him what a future with her might look like. And he, like an addict, was ready to fight to keep it.

To keep *her*.

DAHLIA WOKE TO the sun streaming through her bedroom windows. She blinked a few times, wondering why the sun was so bright. Then she checked the time and sat up abruptly. Eight o'clock? That wasn't possible. She *never* slept this late. She scrambled out of bed and into the bathroom to splash water on her face and untangle her hair, which looked like she'd been making crazy love all night long. She paused, staring at her reflection, expecting to see more of a change than messy hair. Nope. Same Dahlia looking back at her. But on the inside, she was a different woman.

All because of Rawlston Ames.

Her bed was empty, but she knew he was still here. She could hear him whistling in the kitchen, and heard pans and dishes being moved around out there. Smiling to herself, she pulled a cotton sundress over her head then went looking for him. His back was to her as he worked at the stove. He wasn't wearing a shirt, and his shorts were unbuttoned and hanging low on his hips.

"I could get used to this." In more ways than one—the breakfast *and* the view.

He glanced over his shoulder, taking in her ponytail and yellow sundress. "Me, too. Western eggs okay for breakfast? Your fridge was nicely stocked with everything I needed."

She saw a stack of carefully folded clothing on one counter stool, including her bra, and sagged in relief. She'd forgotten about their wild, stripping dash from the barn to the house. What would Bender have thought if he'd walked into the barn and found her *underwear*?

"You're welcome." Rawlston had seen her eyeing the clothes. "I did a quick search when I got up. I think I found everything. Coffee's ready."

"Sounds divine." She slid onto a counter stool as he pushed a coffee mug across the island to her. "Wait, are we both morning people?"

"Looks that way. I think it comes with the territory when you're a rancher."

"Not necessarily," she said. "My sister Jade is nonfunctioning in the mornings."

He scooped the eggs onto two plates and joined her at the island. "But Jade's an accountant, right?"

She took a bite of her breakfast and moaned. "Oh, this is delicious. No, it's Sabrina who's an accountant. Jade's an animal-lover who wants to open a petting zoo on the ranch."

He chuckled. "Still, not the same as you and me. We have livestock to care for and a full day's hard labor waiting for us every morning."

She nodded, too busy enjoying breakfast to say anything. But she was thinking how nice it was to be with someone who understood. Not only understood, but *embraced* the same life that she did. Being outdoors all day. Worrying about the weather and the livestock. Spending hours on horseback. Backbreaking work that left a body aching and tired. She wouldn't trade it for anything, and she had a feeling Rawlston wouldn't, either.

They finished eating in an easy silence, then cleaned the kitchen together. She noticed he'd tossed a kitchen towel over the folder holding their annulment documents, and she decided to leave it there. She hadn't planned on springing those on him after last night, anyway. She was putting the clean dishes up in the cupboard when she felt his hands on her waist, gently pulling her back against his chest.

"What are we doing here, Dolly?"

"Oh my God, stop calling me that." It was automatic, but to be honest, she liked the sound of her hated nickname coming from him.

"You're avoiding the question, *Dahlia*." He brushed a light kiss against her neck. "What are we doing? Because I've gotta say, I'd like to keep doing it."

A warm glow washed over her. He wanted her—not just now, but ongoing. It was one more thing they had in common, because she wanted that, too. Even if she had no idea what that meant. For once, she didn't want to put her plans in a spreadsheet to be managed.

"Do we need to define it?" she asked quietly. "Can we just be two adults enjoying each other's company for now?"

He went still. "And how long is *for now* going to last?"

It was interesting that Mr. Laid-back was suddenly so concerned about getting all the details right, and she wasn't.

"Can we just take it day by day for now?"

"Again…what does *for now* mean?"

She turned in his embrace, sliding her arms around his waist. "Until one of us decides it's time to stop?"

He studied her face for a long beat, then nodded. He didn't look enthused, but she could tell he wasn't going to fight her on it. "I guess that works. I just… I don't want to share you. If we're together, we're together, period. I can handle temporary, but—"

"We're committed to each other while in our noncommittal relationship? That works for me." She reached up to cup his cheek. "I know we have a lot of stuff to figure out, but I want to enjoy this, *whatever* it is, for now."

"There are my favorite two words again." He grimaced. "But yes, I want us to be able to enjoy being together, too."

"And one more thing…" she started.

"Let me guess—we can't tell anyone."

She smiled. "Doesn't that make it more of an adventure?"

"Or a dirty little secret you're ashamed of."

"I'm not ashamed," she assured him. "Not of us. Not after last night. But…"

"But you don't want anyone to know…*for now*."

CHAPTER FIFTEEN

RAWLSTON STRODE INTO the LC Club Saturday night, feeling an uncharacteristic pulse of anticipation. Not just because of the annual summer reception for area ranchers tonight. It was an event he'd come to enjoy, mainly because it was more casual than the ritzy cattlemen's Christmas ball in December. The summer reception was more for mingling and laughter…and he didn't have to wear a tuxedo. Sport coats were acceptable, and, while the women certainly liked to dress up, it was more cocktail or tea dresses than formal gowns.

He was happy to be there, but the anticipation he felt was because of one person. Dahlia was going to be here, along with the Fortune family. They'd made their plan that morning—they'd arrive separately, mingle for half an hour or so, and then bump into each other. Dahlia reasoned that if they pretended to be surprised to see each other, no one would suspect they'd been spending their nights making love on pretty much every surface in her house. And his.

Rawlston was doing his best to live in the moment, rather than worrying about the time when *for now* would come to an end. It wasn't hard to do when they were naked together, focused only on pleasure. But during the day, when he was working his ranch and she was working hers, the worry crept in. She hadn't mentioned the annulment once since before their first night together, but that didn't mean she didn't still want one eventually. Meanwhile, he didn't want their marriage to end. Not yet…maybe not ever.

He entered the reception area, which took up the ballroom and a veranda overlooking Lake Chatelaine. He was scanning the crowd for a tall blonde when his father walked up to him, with JoAnn on his arm. This was her first time meeting all of the ranchers, and he thought she might be intimidated. After all, she'd come from a small Vermont dairy farm. At least, he'd assumed it was small, but he'd never asked. JoAnn looked totally at ease as she was introduced to people, though. She was wearing a softly shimmering purple pantsuit, with a long, loose jacket over a simple white top. Her pewter hair was pulled back into a twist.

It was a good reminder that he really needed to check his less-than-generous assumptions about the sturdily built farm woman. He was coming to like her, but he'd still assumed she'd look or feel out of place with the well-heeled LC Club crowd. Instead, she looked like she'd been here for years, cool and confident.

"Hey, son!" Keith Ames pulled Rawlston into an enthusiastic hug. "I was afraid you might have blown this off like you did last year."

"I was at my friend's wedding in Norfolk, Dad. I don't consider that *blowing off* the reception. I just had somewhere else to be that weekend. Hi, JoAnn. You look lovely."

"Thanks, Rawlston," she replied warmly. "You clean up pretty well yourself."

"You might want to keep that outfit handy for Thursday," his dad said, giving JoAnn a conspiratorial wink.

Rawlston couldn't think of anything going on that week. "What's happening on Thursday?"

"JoAnn and I are tying the knot down at the courthouse, and I'd like you to be our witness."

"Already?" He knew the word was a mistake as soon as he said it. His father glowered at him, and JoAnn looked anywhere but at Rawlston. "Look, I'm sorry for the way that came out. It's just happening…fast. But you two are very much adults, and it's your decision to make, not mine. I'm happy for you."

Was he also still a bit *concerned*? Heck yeah. But he tried to set that aside. JoAnn had given him absolutely no reason to doubt her sincerity. "I'd be honored to stand up for you, Dad."

His father beamed. "I was hoping you'd say that, son, because you were my only choice. Be there at two o'clock. We'll schedule a small reception at the house when her kids can get away to join us. Jo and I just wanted to make everything official. It's important to us."

Dad's look was a warning to Rawlston, and he rushed to assure them. "Of course. I understand." They were from a different generation, and they didn't want to *live in sin*.

Another group of cattle ranchers joined them, but the whole time he was chatting, he was searching the room for Dahlia. He spotted some of her siblings in the crowd, but not his wife. It wasn't a formal sit-down meal. Instead, it was what they called hot *hors d'oeuvres*, with food stations and bars scattered around the ballroom. There were numerous tables, including taller café tables to stand at, and round dining tables with seating. A band was setting up on the far end of the room, near a small dance floor. But Dahlia was still nowhere to be found. He excused himself from the group gathered around his father. He had a feeling both the women and the men were curious to meet Keith Ames's new bride-to-be.

The Perry triplets were at one dining table, laughing with their spouses. He wondered if they'd learned any more about the mystery of possibly having a brother somewhere they'd never met. He caught a glimpse of long, blond hair across the room, and headed that way eagerly. It wasn't Dahlia, though. It was her mother, Wendy Fortune, who appeared to be deep in conversation with Beau Weatherly.

Looking at Wendy, it was easy to see where Dahlia and her sisters had gotten their tall, willowy good looks from. He'd only met their mom a few times before their move to Chatelaine. She had an aura about her that was intriguing. She was soft-spoken and kind, but he'd sensed there was an underlying strength to her as well. Maybe it was because she'd uprooted her life and her adult children to start fresh in Chatelaine. She'd embraced her newfound Fortune relatives, and the feeling was mutual. West Fortune had told Rawlston they all adored her.

Beau Weatherly saw Rawlston approaching, and stepped away from Wendy, apologizing to her for monopolizing her time with his stories. She laughed brightly, sounding just like Dahlia. Then she turned to Rawlston, and there was something in her gaze that said, *I know all about Vegas.* He held in a sigh. For someone who'd insisted on keeping the marriage and relationship top secret, Dahlia seemed to have spilled the truth to her whole family.

"Hi, Rawlston," Wendy said, extending her hand to him. "How lovely to see you, although I almost didn't recognize you out of your jeans and boots. You cut a fine figure, young man."

"And you look stunning, Wendy." He took her hand and gave a slight bow. She was in a flowing chiffon dress in a deep orange color with tiny yellow polka dots. It reminded him of something royalty might wear to a garden party. All she was missing was a wide-brimmed summer hat. "How are you liking your first rancher's reception?"

She glanced around the room before answering. "It's

wonderful, but then I've thought that about everything I've experienced so far in Chatelaine."

"And how are the renovations coming at Fortune's Castle?" Dahlia had told him all about her mother's plans to convert the place into a venue.

She rolled her eyes and laughed again. "Right now, it's a dusty mess, but I can tell it's going to be beautiful when it's done. I've hired a marketing firm to start attracting customers." She glanced at Beau, who was standing nearby. "If you two gentlemen will excuse me, I'm going to go say hi to a friend I just spotted. Enjoy your evening!"

After she left, Beau gave Rawlston a searching look. The guy was sometimes downright spooky in the way he could read people. His expression went from one of curiosity to a knowing grin. *Damn.* Did he know, too? He couldn't imagine Dahlia telling him, though. He wasn't family.

"How're things going, Rawlston?" Beau took a glass of bourbon from a server and drank from it. "Those Brahman cows doing okay for you? I've always favored the Herefords myself, but I heard the Brahmans handle our Texas summers well."

"Yes, sir, they're working out fine for me, and all is well in my world."

"I'll just bet it is," Beau answered.

Rawlston frowned. Maybe the guy *did* know something. Nevertheless, he was determined not to feed the gossip machine. "And how are things with you, Beau? I heard you're cutting back your herd a bit."

They talked for a few minutes about the challenges of raising beef cattle. Beau had sold off a portion of his herd, but he assured Rawlston he wasn't leaving ranching.

"It all still fascinates me," Beau confided. "Balancing the weather, the price of beef, the cost of raising cattle, getting good working horses to use on the range. I love ranching, but I'm reaching a stage of my life where I want to make time for other things."

Rawlston wondered what new endeavors the older man had in mind.

"You know," Beau continued, "I was just reading an interesting article on cattle ranching last week. All those wars that were fought over range space back in the eighteen and nineteen hundreds between cattlemen and sheep ranchers."

Rawlston worked to keep his face neutral as he nodded. What *did* the guy know? "Yes, I know about it. The sheep farmers came west, and the cattlemen didn't want the sheep ruining the range for their cattle."

He hadn't said much to Dahlia, but her sheep were regular trespassers onto his range. He'd started riding the fence line every day, looking for telltale tufts of wool, and then he'd send Tripp out to herd them back to her property. He was going to have to add a lower strand of wire to keep them on their side.

"That's just the thing," Beau said. "All that fighting was for nothing. Turns out sheep and cattle *can* graze the same range without a problem, as long as the population of each is properly balanced."

He had Rawlston's attention now. "That doesn't sound right. Sheep rip grass up by the roots and kill it."

Beau tipped his head to the side with a smile. "Now think about that, son. How could golf courses and parks use sheep to mow the lawns if they killed the grass they ate?"

Dahlia had said something similar that day when he'd been so cranky about finding her sheep with his cattle. If sheep killed grass, her range would be destroyed, and it wasn't. Beau was still talking.

"...turns out sheep have pretty sharp teeth, and they'll bite the grass off close to the ground, whereas cattle eat from the middle up. So it looks different, but they're not killing anything. Of course, if you have too many sheep mixed with cattle, the cattle will have less tall grass to eat. But with the right combination, the cattle chew the tops and make it easier for the sheep to graze, and the sheep eat it down to the ground, prompting new, healthy growth to start the cycle all over again. I can email you the article if you'd like."

"Yeah, sure," he answered, then caught himself. "Not that I'm planning on adding any sheep to my cattle herd, but it sounds interesting, if only for the sake of...science."

It wasn't the smoothest recovery, and Beau chuckled. "For science. *Right.* Because you've always been such a science guy." He leaned in close. "By the way, she's out on the veranda, wearing a pink dress that'll make your eyes pop."

Rawlston's pulse jumped. He didn't need to ask who Beau was talking about, and the older gentleman didn't need to explain. Giving up on pretending, he quickly excused himself and headed outside.

DAHLIA WAS TALKING to her brother Ridge in a quiet corner of the veranda. *Lecturing* was more like it. She was concerned for her little brother and his big heart. The mysterious woman and her infant daughter were *still* living at his place, and he was still fiercely protective of them.

"Ridge, tell me the truth—is Evie actually your daughter or something? Did you have a relationship with that woman? Is this all some ruse to ease her into the family?"

He rolled his eyes dramatically. "As if I wouldn't be crowing from the rooftops if that beautiful baby girl was mine? Come on, Dahlia. Get real."

She pointed to herself. "Me? You want *me* to get real?

You're the one possibly harboring a fugitive and her child at your *home*."

Ridge pulled her closer to the corner, with its spectacular views of the lake. He looked around, as if he thought the trees might be hiding spies. "Keep your voice down," he urged. "There are only a few people who know about Hope and Evie, and I want to keep it that way until she remembers more."

Dahlia tried to wrap her head around what her brother was doing. "But Hope isn't even her name!"

Ridge was annoyed. "What was I supposed to do—call her *Hey You*?"

She put her hand on his arm. "Honey, naming her is the least problematic thing you've done. I'm worried for you getting emotionally involved with this woman."

"*This woman* is intelligent, caring and frightened for her child's safety. What kind of man would I be if I didn't help her?" He stepped away from her touch, staring out at the water. "And it's not like I'm hiding her in a cave somewhere. The family knows she's there. My doctor friend knows she's there. I just don't want to go to the police yet, until we know more about what happened."

He turned to her. "What if Hope has some wacko husband who's trying to harm her, or kidnap Evie, or both? Have some faith in me, Dahlia." His expression brightened. "Why don't you stop over for lunch this week and meet her? It will make you feel better, and I think you'd like her. Oh, hi, Rawlston."

Her heart thumped in her chest, and it was all she could do not to spin with a bright smile to greet the man she'd been sleeping with for days now. Instead, she composed herself and turned slowly.

"Hi," she said, her voice deliberately cool. "It's good to see you." She stuck her hand out to Rawlston, and immediately regretted it. Her thought was that it would make them look like a pair of ranchers who barely knew each other. What she hadn't anticipated was that he would take her hand in his and hold it, with a wicked gleam in his eyes. His forefinger traced over the pulse point on her wrist, and her knees trembled under her long skirt. Rawlston's touch did that to her now. One fingertip on her skin could light her whole body up with red-hot desire. After holding her hand for what seemed like forever, he shook it formally.

"Why, Dahlia, what a pleasure. How are you and your family settling into Chatelaine?" The corner of his mouth twitched. She pulled her shoulders back and mirrored his movement, sliding her finger across the thin skin of his wrist. Two could play that game. The humor in his eyes turned to heat. *Touché.*

Ridge was babbling something about the ranch and the town and whatever, but she and Rawlston were locked in a moment meant only for them. There was no LC Club filled with ranchers. It was just him and her. He was taking in her dress, which she'd worn on purpose. They'd agreed to pretend to be acquaintances, but she hadn't been able to resist the body-skimming candy pink dress—the same color as the chapel in Las Vegas. The draped neckline was just low enough to be interesting, with tiny sleeves that draped off her shoulders. The hemline flared a bit, brushing her calves above white stilettos. She blinked, realizing they'd been silent too long. Ridge was staring at the two of them.

"Is everything okay between you guys? You *are* neighbors, you know." Oh, she knew. She knew that Rawlston rode Malloy to her ranch every evening, stabled him in the barn, and spent the nights with her with no one else being the wiser, then he'd ride his horse back to his place in the mornings. No telltale truck driving on or off the ranch to raise questions from Ridge or anyone else. She pulled her hand away and looked at her brother.

"We're having a bit of a range dispute, Ridge. My sheep are going through Rawlston's fence and he seems to think that's *my* problem. He's afraid my—what did you call them?—*fluffy squeak toys* will ruin the grazing for his precious cattle."

Ridge frowned. "Well, sheep can be a problem, sis. If they're trespassing on his land, technically he could shoot them."

She took a sharp breath. "He wouldn't dare!"

Rawlston gave her a lazy grin. "No, *he* wouldn't. And actually, I'm hearing it may not be as big a problem as I thought. I have more research to do on that. You look lovely tonight, Dahlia."

"Thank you." She did a mock curtsey, knowing she was giving him an extra special view of the dress's neckline. She wondered about his comment about the sheep, and made a mental note to ask him about it later. But tonight wasn't the right time. Haley Perry walked up to them, and Dahlia turned to greet her friend while Ridge and Rawlston talked cattle.

"That dress is stunning." Haley took Dahlia's hands and held her at arm's length, examining the dress. "That color suits you."

Dahlia caught Rawlston's eye. He was suppressing a grin at the comment. They both knew exactly why she'd worn that shade of pink—a color that hadn't been a big part of her wardrobe before.

"Thanks," she answered. "It was an impulse buy—I saw it and just had to have it, you know?"

Rawlston coughed, and she turned her back on him to avoid laughing. "How are things going with your search for your possibly-maybe brother?"

Haley shook her head sadly. "Nothing yet. We've sub-mitted our DNA to two different companies, so if he does the same, we hope he'll reach out or that we'll find him." She shrugged. "*If* he exists, and *if* he wants to be found. The thing is, I have this really strong feeling that he's out there, and my sisters feel the same way. But I've checked every source I can think of, and there's no record of quads being born around our birth date. That doesn't make it im-possible, though. As you've learned, the Fortunes are full of secrets, surprises and mysteries, and I guess that goes for anyone who marries into the family."

The two women chatted a bit longer, then Haley went off to greet someone else and Ridge left, probably rush-ing home to Hope and Evie. Rawlston was gone, too, but she quickly spotted him heading back her way, two drinks in hand. He gave her one, and they walked back into the ballroom, where the band had begun to play. She told him what Haley had said about "secrets, surprises and myster-ies" and he'd agreed.

"From what I've discovered, she's spot-on. The Fortune name seems to attract drama." He smirked at her. "That explains a lot, actually."

She gave him a light smack on the arm, making him laugh. This was uncharted territory for her—a relationship filled with laughter, fun and complete acceptance of one another. It was new yet, but still, he supported her choices, even when he didn't understand them. He said they were her decisions to make. She couldn't remember *any* man in her life ever saying that to her. They'd either blatantly told her she was making bad choices—like her father—or had quietly manipulated and gaslighted her toward doing what *they* wanted her to do. Rawlston made her feel secure in being herself. It was a very nice feeling to have.

They stood together quietly and watched as couples

danced to a hip-hop tune. There was another fast song, and then the band slowed with a cover of Ed Sheeran's "Perfect." Rawlston took the glass from her hand and set it next to his on a nearby table, then led her to the dance floor. She started to resist. This was very public, and people might get the wrong idea about them. Or…the *right* idea, but one they'd agreed to keep secret for now.

Fortunes and their secrets.

Rawlston raised one eyebrow, waiting for her to decide what to do. The fact that he left it up to her, without pressure, was what propelled her into his arms. And just like that, they were dancing for the very first time together. Like everything else they did, it felt as if they'd done it all their lives. Easy. Comfortable. Requiring no effort as they glided across the dance floor. Her hand on his shoulder, his hand on her hip. Their eyes locked on each other and nowhere else. They started at a respectable distance apart, but by the time the chorus began, they were pressed against each other, drawn like magnets to be touching in every possible way. He twirled her gently, then dipped her deep at the end of the song.

Was anyone else dancing? She couldn't say. Was anyone else even in the ballroom? She didn't care. He straightened and she stayed in the hold of his arms, so strong and sure. And in that moment, brief as a heartbeat, she fell in love with Rawlston Ames.

The band started a line dance and the floor soon crowded with people. She and Rawlston went back to their drinks, as if nothing had changed. As if she hadn't been shaken to the core by doing the last thing she'd expected or even imagined possible.

Dahlia had fallen for her husband.

CHAPTER SIXTEEN

Rawlston stood outside the Chatelaine courthouse and watched as his wife strolled toward him on the sidewalk from where she'd parked, a block away. She was in one of her flowy skirts and ruffled blouses, with flat sandals. Dressy, but not overly so. Her hair was straight and free, the way she knew he liked it. She looked perfect. As usual.

He'd been surprised how easy it was to convince Dahlia to join him at his father's courthouse wedding. After they'd danced at the reception, close and intimate, she'd seemed preoccupied and quiet. Not upset, just a little withdrawn. She'd told him nothing was wrong when he asked, but something was going on with her. He hoped it wasn't regret, because he'd hate to see their relationship end.

It was pretty funny, actually. He was the one determined to avoid relationships, and now he was fretting that *she* might choose to walk away. They'd agreed not to define what they had. Not to make it permanent. Just keep it day-to-day. *For now*, as she'd said over and over. Until one of them decided to end it. He'd been okay with that then. Not thrilled, but okay. Every night they spent together made it much less okay.

His horse knew the ride to Dahlia's place by heart now. Every evening, he'd saddle up and head her way. Every morning, he'd saddle up and ride home. And every day, it got harder and harder to leave her. To play their little game of not telling anyone. She'd told him what Haley said about Fortunes having secrets, surprises and mysteries.

He and Dahlia had the *secret* part down. The *surprise* was how much he wanted what they had to be permanent. The *mystery* was how she'd managed to change his mind about relationships and…maybe even marriage. That last one was tricky. Maybe she was changing his mind, or maybe he was conflicted because of his father's sudden dive into this wedding of his.

"I'm getting used to seeing you in suits." Dahlia stopped at his side with a bright smile. "It's a good look." She nodded toward the courthouse steps. "Are you ready for this?"

"I don't think Dad cares if I'm ready. It's *his* wedding."

"You know what I mean," she answered, putting her arm through his. "Have you accepted it, in your heart?" She patted his chest. It was a surprising show of affection in the middle of town on a sunny late-August afternoon. She seemed to come to the same conclusion, stepping back and releasing his arm. "I forgot, we're just friends. How *did* you explain my presence here to your father and JoAnn?"

He grimaced. "I…uh…didn't."

Her eyes went round. "Oh my God, you didn't tell them I'm coming? I'd better wait out here—"

"No! Look, you asked how I'm dealing with this, and the truth is, I'm still struggling. I need you here. I trust you to keep me from doing or saying something stupid."

Her eyes softened, making his chest feel warm. He loved it when she let down her guard with him. It felt like a gift, and she'd been doing it more and more lately.

"I'm happy to help, but what do we say when your dad sees me with you?"

"Nothing. He…uh…he knows. I'm guessing JoAnn does, too."

She hesitated, and he thought she was going to blast

him for telling anyone. But then she shrugged. "Okay. Let's go, then."

"You're not angry?"

"I told two of my sisters and my mom. I can hardly fault you for telling *one* family member. Come on, we shouldn't keep them waiting."

He wasn't sure who this new, mellow Dahlia was, but she was nice to be around.

The wedding was quick and charming. Dad was in his best suit. JoAnn wore a pale blue lace dress and carried a small bouquet of black-eyed Susans. They were beaming at each other, and Rawlston found himself smiling, too. He hadn't seen his father this genuinely happy in years. If JoAnn could do that, then he would welcome her to the family wholeheartedly. Neither seemed surprised to see Dahlia with Rawlston, and they'd warmly welcomed her as their second witness.

They were leaving immediately for Boston, where his father would meet his bride's family. Rawlston wondered what they'd think about meeting him *after* the wedding, but JoAnn had insisted they only wanted her to be happy. Dad was taking JoAnn to Europe in the fall for the official honeymoon.

And just like that, in less than an hour, he and Dahlia were standing together on the sidewalk again, waving goodbye to his father and JoAnn—his new stepmother.

"This is weird," he said as their car drove away. "I'm okay with it, but it's still weird."

She touched his side lightly, not wanting to make a public spectacle. The brief touch was enough to let him know she cared, but, as always, it left him wanting more.

"This all happened pretty quickly. Why don't you come to the house early today? We can take a ride together before dinner to clear your head."

He nodded as they started walking. "A lot of things are happening quickly lately."

"I know. It's been one thing after another for you and me both." She gave him a strange sideways glance. "But that's not always a bad thing, is it? Sometimes surprises can turn out pretty well."

There was more meaning to her words than she was letting on…and he was about to ask for an explanation when a tall, blond-haired man walked up in front of them. Rawlston bristled, stepping ahead of Dahlia, but, being Dahlia, she shoved him to the side.

"Sorry to bother you," the man said, "but I'm new here and I'm looking for someone. Do either of you know a woman with the last name Perry? Actually, I think there's three women here who might have that name." He must have seen the caution on both of their faces, because he held his hands up in innocence. "I'm Heath Blackwood. I promise I'm not here to cause any trouble. I just have… business with the Perrys."

Rawlston started to tell the guy to get lost, but Dahlia put her hand on his arm to stop him. She was studying Heath intently, then she smiled and took the hand he'd held out.

"Hi, Heath." She introduced herself and Rawlston. The usually cynical Miss Fortune was Miss Chatty all of a sudden. "All three of the Perry triplets live in the area, but they don't have the last name *Perry* anymore. One of them is a good friend of mine." She checked her watch. "I'm sure you'll find Haley Perry at the newspaper office this time of day." She gave him directions and sent him on his way.

Before Rawlston could ask what was going on, she turned to him, excitement written on her face. "Did you see his eyes? Just like the triplets'! I think he might be the Perry's mystery brother."

"Wait. The triplets are actually quads?" He was confused. "I've heard his name before, but it was about business, not the Perrys." Rawlston was pretty sure Blackwood did something in tech. "His *business* with them is probably just that."

Dahlia wasn't convinced. "Maybe. They're not sure a brother even exists. But there is a rumor and they're trying to track it down."

She told him about the hazy claim that there'd been a boy, possibly born with the girls, or possibly not. Rawlston couldn't deny a family resemblance, but the odds that Blackwood was that long-lost sibling were mighty low. He didn't want to diminish Dahlia's enthusiasm though. It was a wild story, but then again, things had been wild around Chatelaine for a while now. He looked at this tall, caring, incredible woman in front of him.

Ever since Dahlia Windham Fortune *Ames* came to town.

DAHLIA STARED AT her twin in shock. "You got the same invitation?"

They were sitting on the veranda at Fortune's castle, staring at the two embossed ivory wedding invitations sitting on the table. She'd come to ask their mother if she knew anything about the strange invitation, but she wasn't there. The young woman at the front desk—the spa was having a soft opening that week—said Wendy Fortune was going to be spending a few days in San Antonio, visiting a spa that was owned by a friend there.

Just as Dahlia had turned to leave, Sabrina walked up the steps to the castle, so they'd decided to have a glass of tea together. She'd told Sabrina about the invitation, putting hers on the table, and Sabrina had pulled out an identical invitation.

The gold-stamped invitations read:

You are cordially invited to attend
a very special wedding
to be held at the Chatelaine Courthouse.
More details will follow, but please
save the date.
You won't want to miss it!

Sabrina tapped her invitation. "The date is in January, but it says nothing about who is getting married. And it's not just you and me. We *all* got them—Jade, Ridge, Arlo and Nash. I don't know, maybe the whole town got them. Maybe it's some sort of annual Chatelaine ritual or a PR trick for some company."

Dahlia shrugged. "I was going to ask Mom if she might have heard something about it. You know how plugged in she is with what's happening in Chatelaine. She has her fingers on all the gossip."

Sabrina snorted. "That's exactly why I drove over. But she's not answering her phone."

"I guess she's on a business trip to San Antonio, so that might be why she's not answering. Something about a friend who owns a spa there?"

Sabrina thought for a moment. "She did mention a college classmate who has some sort of day spa. It could be in San Antonio." She slumped back in her chair. "Well, damn. Who's going to give us the gossip now?"

They laughed, and changed the subject, tucking the mystery invitations in their bags. Sabrina was right—it was probably something silly like a publicity stunt. '

She stopped at GreatStore to pick up some groceries for dinner that night. Rawlston was coming over, of course, but tonight would be different. Tonight she was going to tell him she loved him. That he made her feel the way no other man had made her feel. Respected. Accepted. Cherished. Possibly even…loved?

She suspected he felt the same way she did, but he hadn't said anything. Maybe because of all her rules to keep things casual, where either one of them could just walk away without a word. At the time, she'd thought it best. But she'd had no idea she was going to fall in love with the man.

"Dahlia!" A woman's voice called out from behind her. She turned to see Haley, her cart loaded to overflowing with baby food and paper products. Her friend gestured at the cart. "Sure, you're carrying everything in a basket, and I'm going to need a second cart pretty soon! I'm helping Tabitha and West restock. Their twins both have tummy bugs, and everyone in that house is exhausted. What do you have in there?" She peeked in the basket, then started to laugh. "If I didn't know better, I'd say that's a date night in the making. Shrimp, steaks, veggies, wine and…oh, is that tiramisu cake?"

Dahlia froze. "Just…um…a friend coming into town from Dallas." She forced a laugh. "Nothing scandalous, I promise."

It wasn't a lie. There was nothing scandalous about her having dinner with her husband. And telling him how much she loved him. She suddenly remembered crossing paths with the man in town who looked so much like Haley.

"Oh! How did your meeting go the other day with that guy?" She couldn't remember his name off the top of her head. "I sent him to the office."

Haley stared at her blankly. "What guy?"

"His name was Heath. He didn't…?" She stopped. If Blackwood didn't introduce himself to Haley, he may have had a good reason. Maybe Rawlston had been right, and

Heath was just here on business. Perhaps Haley hadn't been there, or he'd talked to Tabitha or Lily instead. Or maybe she'd spoil his surprise if she said any more. All she knew for sure was that this was one Fortune family drama she didn't need to be in the middle of. "Oh, never mind. I must have misunderstood. When did the twins get sick…?"

She and Haley chatted for a few more minutes, then she headed toward checkout. Her nerves were jumping with anticipation of tonight with Rawlston. She didn't know how he would react to her confession of love, but there was no way she could hold it inside any longer.

CHAPTER SEVENTEEN

"So your dad and JoAnn get back from their honeymoon tomorrow?" Dahlia set a glass of dark beer by Rawlston's seat. They were on the deck, watching the sun set low over the lake. He took the beer with a nod of thanks. He enjoyed their evenings out here, after a nice meal as the air began to cool.

Who was he kidding? He enjoyed any time he spent with Dahlia. In fact, he was beginning to despise any time he spent *away* from her. His world had shifted to revolve around his wife. And that was okay. Which was the biggest surprise of all. He was not only okay with it, he was loving it. Loving *her*. Things were great between them. They spent nearly every night together, usually at her place. They'd fallen into an easy routine around each other. It was comfortable. Which had him feeling suddenly vulnerable.

"Yeah," he answered. "It wasn't really a honeymoon, though. Just a quick trip to meet her children. Dad said it went well."

He'd spoken to his father a few hours ago, and it sounded as though their trip to Boston to meet JoAnn's family had been a success. They'd been introduced over brunch on the first day there, and were all going to a nice seafood restaurant tonight before Dad and JoAnn headed back to Texas.

Dahlia sat next to him on the upholstered outdoor

sectional, her wineglass in her hand. "Remember what I said…"

"I know, I know. It's a marriage, whether it happens in a judge's chambers, a church or…" he winked at her "…a Vegas chapel."

It was a risk, bringing that up. They'd *both* stopped mentioning the wedding or their current state of matrimony. But they couldn't ignore it forever. They were legally husband and wife. The annulment papers were sitting in a folder on the kitchen island, but she hadn't mentioned them once since they'd started sleeping together. Maybe she didn't want the annulment anymore. Or was she thinking this was just a fling between them?

Dahlia had gone still at his side, her glass in her hand, staring out across the water. She finally took a sip, and he had a feeling she was measuring her words carefully.

"Yes, it's a marriage no matter what. And the location doesn't determine the success of that marriage. I think your dad and JoAnn are going to be good together. They seem to truly care for each other, you know?"

So she was still avoiding the topic of *their* marriage. He went along with it.

"I guess so. I'm still not sure why they needed to make it official so quickly, but Dad said they were both determined not to just live together. As if that's so bad. Everyone does it these days. I don't think there'd be any scandal about it."

"I've never thought of your dad as the old-fashioned type, to be worried about that. But I don't know about JoAnn." She moved in closer to his side, and he slid his arm around her shoulder. She looked up at him. "I think being married shows how committed they are to the relationship."

"Being married is just a piece of paper, Dolly. We're living proof of that."

There. He'd thrown the topic of their marriage out there again. She blinked and looked away.

"Keith and JoAnn didn't get drunk and wander into a wedding chapel," she said. "They made a conscious decision to commit to their love for each other. I know Lana burned you, but you can't possibly think *all* marriages are bad because of that one experience. Your parents were happily married for decades."

He considered that for a moment as he drank his beer.

"Don't you think people learn the most from their own experience?" he asked. "Sure, I've observed people being happy in a marriage, but just because I've seen my dad fly a plane doesn't mean I know to fly one. Maybe the issue is that I don't think *I'm* cut out for a successful marriage, because I haven't experienced one."

"Well, that's just…sad." She sighed, resting her head on his shoulder. "Have you given up all hope, then?"

"I don't know about *all* hope, but I've been highly skeptical about the idea."

Except with her. He might have some hope of happiness in a marriage with Dahlia. A *real* marriage. He frowned, yearning for something more than what they had now, with both of them refusing to talk about what was next. It didn't have to be tonight, but sooner or later, they were going to have to discuss their future.

He'd seen Arlo Fortune yesterday at the feedstore, and Dahlia's brother had mentioned that Carter Powers was due back any day now. Carter was another one of those topics that had been carefully avoided between Dahlia and Rawlston. And he sure as hell wasn't going to bring that one up. He rested his cheek on the top of her head.

They stayed like that, relaxed and snuggled together, for a while, watching the Texas sky turn shades of coral and pink, then deep purple as the sun disappeared below the horizon. They both sipped from their drinks, content to just…be. Then Dahlia gave a quick laugh, sitting up to look at him, her eyes bright with humor.

"What?" he asked, smiling in return.

"It's so ironic that you have all these feelings about the institution of marriage, but I couldn't convince you to end ours, no matter how hard I tried. Why were you so stubborn about it?"

She hadn't mentioned if she *still* wanted to end the marriage. She was talking about it being a thing of the past. But more importantly, she was point-blank asking him why he'd stalled the annulment. And he couldn't lie to her anymore.

He hesitated long enough that Dahlia noticed. But her smile was still in place as she playfully nudged his ribs with her elbow.

"Seriously, what made you so determined to avoid it? I never did believe your 'lucky pen' story, and I know you spilled that tea on purpose. You probably fibbed about your printer, too, right?"

He nodded, wishing he didn't have to tell her, but knowing he had no choice. Dahlia's smile began to fade as she studied his face.

"Rawlston?"

"Look," he started, trying to think of a way to soften the blow. But he knew her so much better now. She was fiercely self-reliant, and she probably wasn't going to appreciate his good intentions. "Every time I thought about you being with Carter Powers, it just…frustrated me."

Her forehead furrowed. "You were jealous?"

"What? God, no!" Not at the time, anyway. He hadn't known then that she would steal his heart and own his soul. "But he's…he's not who you think he is, Dahlia. You deserve so much better than a sleazeball like Carter."

She sat up straighter, shrugged out of his embrace.

"Yes." She spoke carefully. "I agree with you. But what did Carter have to do with you not signing the annulment? You've made it pretty clear you don't believe in marriage."

"I don't. At least… I didn't. It's not like we intended to end up married to each other. But you'd said something about Carter proposing to you when he came back from his trip, and—" He paused. Had she just agreed that she deserved better than Carter? So maybe he didn't need to confess… *No.* If there was any chance of a forever between Dahlia and him, he had to tell her the truth. "You said yourself you couldn't do that if we were legally married. I wanted you to have time to see him for who he really is. The guy isn't just ambitious, Dahlia. He's unethical—he doesn't care who he hurts to get what he wants. He cost my dad nearly a quarter million dollars in one of his schemes."

There was a long beat of heavy silence before Dahlia stood and began to pace back and forth on the deck. Even then, it was a while before she spoke.

"So let me understand this…" Her words were slow and deliberate, and she wouldn't even look at him. He had a feeling this was very bad. She paced some more. "You didn't sign the annulment papers because you wanted to block me from marrying Carter…by forcing me to remain married to you."

"*Forcing* is putting it harshly, I think."

She came to an abrupt halt, staring at him in disbelief. "Tell me how I'm wrong, Rawlston. You made every excuse not to sign. I thought maybe it was something cute, like…you *liked* me, or something."

He more than liked her. He was in love with the furious woman standing in front of him, hands resting on her hips, clenched into tight, angry fists.

"Dahlia, I *do* li—"

"Eh-eh!" She held up one hand, opening then pinching her thumb and fingers together in the universal signal to shut the hell up. "Didn't you just tell me you didn't sign because you didn't want me to marry Carter?"

"Well—"

"Never mind. I know what you said. You didn't talk to me about it. You didn't say, *Hey, you might want to rethink your plans and here's why.* You never told me your dad lost all that money with Carter. You just manipulated me to keep me from doing something you thought I wanted to do."

She'd nailed it, laying out exactly what he'd done. He had no defense, but he had to try.

"I know it sounds bad, but I really was trying to protect you."

"From what? My own judgment? You knew better than me, huh? I... God, I can't even look at you right now." She spun to stare out at the darkening lake. "You should go."

He stood and walked up behind her, knowing better than to touch her. "Dahlia, I'm sorry. I told Jade it was a bad idea—"

Her shoulders went even stiffer. "This was my *sister's* idea?"

"No! No, I swear this is all on me. But she said you'd told her about Vegas, and she...supported my plan." He had a feeling he'd just made things worse by mentioning Jade. He was still speaking to Dahlia's back, talking faster to say as much as possible before she forced him to leave. "It was a stupid idea. At first it was more about Carter. He's a jackass who doesn't deserve you. And then...then we spent more time together and I started falling for you. I hated the thought of you being with him. And then..."

He gently rested his hands on her shoulders. She didn't relax into his touch the way she usually did, but she didn't pull away, either. "And then we kissed, and made love, and I was in too deep, babe. It became all about me not wanting to lose you—to him or anyone else. *Ever*. And as you and I became more serious, I didn't know how to explain all of this to you—"

She turned and faced him, her large eyes shining with tears. It felt like a razor blade was being run across his heart.

"You should have told me the truth."

"I just *did* tell you the truth, and I've gotta be honest—this is not going all that great for me." If he'd hoped his attempt at lightness would help, he was wrong. Her eyes narrowed.

"It hasn't been great for me, either. It's bad enough that you thought you had the right to manipulate me and keep me from making a decision about Carter *myself*. That's worse than bad, actually. It's…downright awful. But then, even after we started being…" she gestured vaguely "…I don't know—intimate? Serious? In a relationship? What *have* we been doing?" She pulled away from him, as if she could no longer tolerate his touch. "Whatever it was, I damn sure deserved to know the truth a lot sooner than this. How am I supposed to trust you now, Rawlston?"

She stomped toward the house, and he followed automatically. He wasn't sure how he was able to move, because he'd felt his heart stop when she said she couldn't trust him. She headed for the front of the house, ushering him out of her home, and possibly out of her life. He had no idea how to defend himself without making things even worse. Dahlia stopped near the front door, and gave a bitter, humorless laugh.

"My sisters didn't want me with Carter because they said he was so much like our father. But *you're* the one who tried to gaslight me, which is *exactly* what Dad would do when he didn't like my decisions. So, really, what is the difference between the two of you?"

"The difference is I love you." Saying it wasn't planned, but she needed to know it. "You wanted the truth, and that's it. I love you, Dahlia."

SHE TRIED TO corral her emotions, but they refused to be tamed. This whole conversation had spun out of control, and now he was saying *this*? Did he think she was going to just forget everything else? Forget that he'd lied to her? Manipulated her? And worse…tried to take away her ability to make her own decisions?

"Seriously? You think *now* is the time to tell me you love me?" She folded her arms on her chest, mainly to keep him from seeing how her hands were trembling. "How am I supposed to believe you?"

"Look, I screwed up. It was a stupid plan I cooked up weeks ago. I didn't know what would happen between us. I didn't know I was going to fall madly in love with you." He put his hands on her shoulders, but she quickly pulled away, shaking her head to warn him not to try that again. His hands fell to his sides. "Yes, I made up a few stories about lucky pens and my printer not working. It was bad, but I swear on my mother's grave those are the only lies I've told. Everything else between us has been genuine. Including my love—"

"Stop *saying* that!" Her raised voice echoed off the walls. His claims of loving her hurt more than his duplicity about their annulment. "Saying *I love you* isn't a get-out-of-jail-free card. The more you insist on saying it, the more I wonder about the convenient timing of this sudden revelation." Why did he look so confused? How could he not get this? "Rawlston, I don't believe you. I don't know if I'll ever believe you again. You didn't trust me to make the right choice about Carter, so you played games with my heart… Hell, you played games with the rest of my *life*."

He jammed his fingers through his hair, his face going red. "Damn it to hell, Dolly, if you think I'm the kind of man who would toss around the L-word lightly, you don't know me at all."

"I didn't think you'd lie to me, either," she answered hotly. "But here we are. I clearly *don't* know you."

"I'm the same man that you made love to last night!" His volume rose. "I'm the guy you ride with. The guy you dine with. The man who held you in his arms by the firepit and listened to all the crap your dad did, and the man who understood why you still mourned his death."

That had happened two nights ago. She'd had a bout of melancholy over her father's death and their complicated relationship. How she'd spent her teen years working so hard to please him, and then her adult years blatantly de-fying every so-called *suggestion* Dad had for her life—personally and professionally. She and her father hadn't argued as much as they'd continually danced around his constant disappointment in her and her quiet but deter-mined defiance of him. And yet…

Her father was dead. And since his death, it sometimes felt as if the family was rushing headlong to change *every-thing* about their lives. Moving to Chatelaine. Changing jobs. Changing *names*. The experience sometimes left her feeling conflicted. The man had never seemed satisfied with her, but she still mourned his loss. It was confusing and frustrating.

That had been when Rawlston had moved over to her chaise by the firepit and pulled her onto his lap, holding her like a child against his chest while she'd cried. He'd whispered words of comfort to her, telling her that noth-ing she was feeling was wrong. That it was natural, and she should embrace her feelings instead of bottling them up. God, how she'd wept at that. How she'd *loved* this man.

But her anger burned bright and hot right now. Perhaps even more so. Him being so good then made his betrayal all the worse.

"This isn't a negotiation. You can't pay off your mistakes by listing good things you've done. It doesn't erase anything. You *hurt* me, Rawlston." She put her hand over her heart. "I can't… I can't deal with you right now. Please go."

He looked as shattered as she felt, but she didn't have it in her to feel sympathetic. The pain was too sharp and hot. His eyes glistened with unshed tears.

"Dahlia, the last thing I wanted was to hurt you." His voice cracked with emotion. "I'll do whatever you want. You want the papers signed? I'll do it. I'll give you whatever you want."

CHAPTER EIGHTEEN

"WAIT." JADE LEANED forward to take Dahlia's hand. "He *signed* the annulment papers? Just like that?"

"It was *his* idea." Dahlia sniffed, trying to stop crying after doing it for three long nights. How could she miss someone she was so damn *mad* at?

"It sounds like he was desperate, sis." Sabrina was next to Jade. They were on the veranda at Fortune's Castle. Their mother was sitting at Dahlia's side, but she hadn't said much yet.

"Of course he was desperate," Dahlia snapped. "He did the one thing that's a deal breaker for me—he tried to make a decision *for* me."

"But it was the *right* decision," Jade pointed out. "Even you agree that Carter was all wrong for you. God, I wish I could have been a fly on the wall, or on a tree, for that wedding proposal. Did Carter really have an arbor of yellow roses in the shape of Texas?"

Dahlia buried her face in her hands. "Don't remind me. I tried to stop him, but he wouldn't listen. I said we needed to talk, and he insisted we were 'late' and had to get to the park. I should have just sent him a Dear John email two weeks ago, but I felt like I owed him an explanation in person. Just like everything else this week, it was a disaster."

She and Carter had arrived at the historic gardens outside Austin two days ago. Carter had led her to a giant, rose-covered arbor in the shape of Texas, with the sun setting behind them, making the roses glow. It was lovely, but as usual with Carter, it was…too much. The thing had to be seven feet high, and had a banner on top that spelled out T-e-x-a-s, just in case anyone was confused. It was more appropriate for a campaign photo than a proposal setting.

When she'd spotted the photographer setting up a tripod, she'd realized that's exactly what Carter intended. He was planning to use their engagement in his political campaign. *Look at me, I married a pretty blonde Fortune girl from Texas!* She'd dug her heels in and physically tried to stop him, but he'd had her hand in his and would not slow down. He muttered something about "don't be nervous" and "we're losing the light," never thinking she was about to dump him. On camera.

The one blessing was that the cameraman was the only witness, hired by Carter. He had staged this to *look* intimate and private…but conveniently captured on film by a professional photographer to be shared later. Carter had dropped to one knee and opened that box to display an enormous diamond-encrusted ring, with a three-carat round diamond set high above the rest. It was gaudy and completely impractical for a rancher like her.

All she could think about as she stared at the ring was the one Rawlston had given her in Vegas. Their gold and platinum wedding bands had matched, but he'd bought her a diamond, too. A simple square pillow cut stone in a low gold setting that would protect it. It had been perfect for her. And she'd made him return it the next morning.

She'd turned Carter down as gently as possible, aware of the photographer videotaping every word. She told him she didn't love him, and wouldn't pretend to in order to help his campaign. The truth was, she didn't want to be a politician's wife. Didn't want to live in Austin. Didn't want to marry him. She wanted to raise sheep in Chatelaine. With Rawlston…but she didn't say that last bit to Carter. No need to rub salt in the wound. Besides, a future with Rawlston was highly in doubt right now. They hadn't spoken in days, and she was still working through her feelings about what he'd done.

Carter had been stunned at first, then quickly angry. After sending the photographer away, he'd told Dahlia how she'd humiliated him, how she was making the "biggest mistake of her life," how much she'd regret it one day. She'd let him rant, knowing he was already recalculating a solution in his mind. After he'd settled down, he gave her one last, dismissive look.

"It's just as well. You'd have made a lousy campaign wife anyway. You'd rather chase around after a bunch of stupid sheep." He'd turned away. "You'll end up married to some dirt-poor rancher, watching me on television and wondering where it all went wrong."

She hadn't answered, letting him walk away and leave her there in front of the giant rose map of Texas. She'd gone from two men in her life to none. But at least *she'd* controlled both situations. She turned to Jade.

"Yes, I realized Carter was wrong for me," she answered. "But *I* decided that, for *myself.* It wasn't Rawlston's choice to make. And it wasn't *yours,* either. I can't believe you encouraged him."

"Because I *care*," Jade replied. "Sometimes you get so bullheaded that you refuse to listen to anyone, even if they're trying to help. You met a guy just like Dad, one you know Dad would have approved of, and you dug your heels in." Jade squeezed her hands. "You define the phrase 'cut off your nose to spite your face,' girl. We thought if Rawlston could give you some time to slow your roll, it would just…help you make your own decision. We weren't trying to make it *for* you."

Wendy Fortune shook her head with a sad smile. "I love you, my darling daughters, but what you two and Rawlston did to your sister was wrong. Well-intentioned? Yes. But wrong."

"Thank you, Mom." Dahlia pulled her hands from Jade's, but she did it gently. Her hot rage from the other night had faded to a dull hurt and sadness that weighed on her.

"Don't thank me yet, young lady." Mom turned to face her. "Because Jade is right—sometimes making your *own* choice is more important to you than making the *right* choice."

"But—"

"I'm not finished," Mom interrupted. "I *love* you, Dahlia. I love your fierceness and your independence. They are gifts that make you uniquely you. But sometimes you hide behind them to protect yourself, and you end up missing out. The question is, are you doing that now?"

"I…" Dahlia slumped back in her chair. "I don't know, Mom. Rawlston really hurt me. He lied to me. How am I supposed to forgive that?"

"Do you love him?"

"Yes." She didn't hesitate with her answer. "And I miss him. Everything feels all wrong without him in my life. But what he *did* was wrong, too."

Sabrina sighed. "It sounds like you're trying to do my thing, creating some sort of balance sheet to sum up what he did versus what you did and what he'd have to do to make you 'even' or something. I'm no expert—" Sabrina laughed softly "—but I don't think that's how relationships work. You're two humans, which means you're both going to screw up. One of you will be right and the other will be wrong, or maybe—just maybe—you'll *both* be wrong. Like now."

Dahlia bristled. "How are we *both* wrong? He lied. He manipulated. He signed the damn annulment papers."

"Honey," Jade said, "he lied about having a lucky pen. It's not like he lied about hiding some secret love child or something scandalous like that. And yes, I see why you say he manipulated you, but...that started before you two were in a relationship."

"We were *married.*"

"Give me a break," Sabrina scoffed. "You stumbled into a chapel while drunk and you didn't even remember it the next morning. That is *not* a relationship. The relationship came after you got back to Chatelaine. And he didn't lock you in a basement somewhere. He just didn't sign the paperwork."

"Until he *did* sign it."

Sabrina threw her hands up in frustration. "Because that's what you'd wanted all along! You can't be mad at him for *not* signing *and* for signing."

"Girls." Their mother's voice was soft but firm. "We've all had a chance to share our views about Rawlston, but your sister needs to make this decision on her own." She spoke directly to Dahlia. "You said you love him, and I believe you. He told you he loves you, too, and I think that's true. Love has a way of sneaking up on you like that, out of the blue. And when it does, you have to grab it." Mom paused, a soft smile appearing and quickly disappearing again. "You're hurt and angry right now, but are you willing to give him up forever? Or are you willing to forgive him? You two had an unconventional start, but that doesn't mean you don't have a path forward if you're willing to work at it. Have you talked at all?"

Dahlia shook her head. Rawlston had certainly tried. He'd called and texted over and over, begging forgiveness. Asking to talk. He'd even come to the ranch, but Sabrina had sent him home at Dahlia's request. She furrowed her brow, remembering how he'd left a voicemail just that morning. His voice had sounded muffled, as if he'd been drinking. But that couldn't be, not at that hour.

She wanted to forgive him, but she was afraid. Dahlia had thought he was the one guy who was different from other men in her life. She'd thought he was her safe place. That she could trust him. What he did, and the fact that he hadn't told her, had shaken that trust.

Wendy Fortune sat up, checking her watch. "I'm sorry, but I have a potential corporate client coming in to tour the castle as a possible work retreat location. I'll call you later, sweetheart." Their mother stood and kissed each of them, staying longer over Dahlia, before heading back inside. There was a beat of silence around the table.

"So…" Jade began. "Any more news on those wedding invitations?"

Sabrina embraced the topic change with a loud, animated laugh. "No! And it's making me crazy. The invitations were expensive, so I guess that's a clue, but not much of one. Dahlia, do you have any ideas?"

She knew what they were doing—distracting her from Rawlston. She smiled. It was a little shaky, but it was her first in a few days. And that gave her just a glimmer of hope. She was going to get through this, no matter what happened. Because she had a family who would always be there for her. She gave them an exaggerated shrug, with her hands in the air.

"I've got nothing. I asked Haley if there'd ever been a mysterious event like this in Chatelaine before, but she doesn't know any more than we do." She couldn't help herself. "It must be nice to be able to plan a wedding instead of waking up married to a guy who won't even fight to keep you."

"Technically, Rawlston *did* fight to keep you by not signing the annulment," Sabrina pointed out. "But Mom wants us to keep our opinions to ourselves so that you can do this on your own, so forget I said anything." She made a motion with her hand as if locking her lips with a key. "You're on your own, twinsie."

And that was the problem.

Bottom line? She had to listen to her heart. And her heart was telling her that Rawlston was still her safe place.

RAWLSTON KNOCKED BACK a shot of whiskey on the patio behind his house. It was ten o'clock in the morning, but he figured the drink was medicinal. If you wanted to cure a hangover, you were supposed to drink something, right? Hair of the dog and all that. He grabbed the bottle at his side and refilled the shot glass. At least he wasn't drinking straight from the bottle, like he'd done the first couple of days.

It wasn't like him to drown his sorrows. But he'd never had a sorrow this deep before. A sorrow he couldn't see a way out of. And a love that apparently wasn't returned. Or that had been shattered by his foolish attempt to protect her. He downed another shot with a grimace. The whiskey wasn't hitting his empty stomach well at all.

Dahlia hadn't needed his so-called protection. As much as he wanted to deny it, the real reason he'd delayed signing those papers was because he'd wanted her to be with him. To stay married. Which was ridiculous, because he *hated* marriage. And, as it turned out, he'd been right all along—marriage didn't work for him. Dahlia had proven it. After all they'd shared with each other, and after all the intimacy and passion they'd experienced together, after he'd confessed he *loved* her…she'd let him sign those damn papers anyway. He was refilling the shot glass when he heard footsteps behind him.

"Is this pity party a solo gig, or can I join in?" His father came out of the house and set another shot glass on the table. Rawlston filled it and nodded toward the empty chair.

"Suit yourself, but I'll warn you—I'm lousy company."

"Yeah, I figured that when I saw you sucking down whiskey this early in the day." Dad sat with a heavy sigh, staring out at the range. "Is it working?"

"Is *what* working?"

"Soaking yourself in booze. Is it dulling the pain? Has it solved any problems?" His father's tone was light and conversational, as if he was asking if Rawlston thought it might rain today.

"Not yet," he answered, downing the third shot and giving a satisfied sigh. "But I still have hope."

"Hope is good." Dad downed his shot, too, but slid the bottle out of Rawlston's reach to avoid an immediate refill. Then he set his shot glass down with a thunk. "But this isn't the way to get your girl back."

"I think that ship has sailed, Dad." He paused, confused. He hadn't talked to anyone since Dahlia watched him sign the papers that ended their marriage. "Wait…how did you know about Dahlia and me? You just got home."

His father was still staring out into the distance, watching Tripp chase a rabbit into a pile of brush. Happy with the thrill of the chase, the dog emerged from the brush without a rabbit, but with a happy bounce to his gait as his stubby tail wagged. Some of the cattle had come closer to the barns last night as a storm rolled through. Spotting the nearby cattle, Tripp trotted over, going under the fence and casually bringing the cows together in a group, working back and forth slowly. It was like he was practicing his herding skills without really trying to move the cattle.

Keith Ames gave a small shrug. "One person tells a friend who tells another friend who tells me. It's how small towns work, son."

Rawlston frowned. Who would have told a friend of Dad's? How many people knew, not only about their argument, but about their marriage? He thought about his conversation with Beau Weatherly at the reception. How Beau had just randomly brought up the topic of sheep and cattle grazing together. Rawlston didn't know how Beau had found out about him and Dahlia, but it was clear he had. And he *was* Dad's best friend.

"Marriage and me just don't get along, Dad. Never have, never will."

"That's a load of bull. Marriage, even the good ones, take work, son. You don't quit the first time you hit a speed bump. Not if you love each other. And I've got a hunch you two love each other quite a bit."

"I love her completely. I thought she felt the same way, but…well, I hurt her, and now she doesn't trust me. I've apologized over and over. I call. I text. Hell, I even sent her emails. I went to her house, but she wouldn't talk to me. She sent her twin out to tell me to leave. I left another voicemail just this morning. I even sent her roses…twice."

His father turned to stare at him, looking dumbfounded. "That sounds a touch desperate, don't you think? Give the woman time to think without you pestering her every hour."

Rawlston shook his head sharply, and immediately regretted it when everything went blurry. Maybe whiskey wasn't the solution after all. He swallowed hard, clearing his throat and trying to clear his head.

"I *am* desperate, Dad. She ended the marriage, and if I

give her too much time, she might just end *us* for good. I can't sit back and let that happen. I have to *do* something." He slapped his hand on the table, making the empty shot glasses jump. "Why can't you see that? I have to do something, or I might lose everything that matters to me."

"It was *doing something* that got you in trouble in the first place. Dahlia Fortune is an independent woman, maybe too much so, but that's who she is. That's who you fell in love with. Do you really think browbeating her is going to be effective? Is she the type of woman who responds to being nagged?"

"I'm not nagging her. I'm just… I'm being persistent." He winced. That was the same as nagging, and they both knew it. "But isn't that persistence proving to her that I want her back?"

"Maybe." Dad nodded thoughtfully. "Or maybe it's proving that you want to control her decisions. Isn't that why she got upset in the first place? Because you tried to take away her ability to make her own choices for herself?"

"That's not what…" His voice faded. "Oh, hell, that *is* what it probably feels like to her. I'm making the same mistake all over again. I'm making her hate me."

His father chuckled. "Slow down, boy. Let's not leap to extremes here. If she loves you, it'll be damn tough to turn that into hate. But you gotta give her time to breathe. You're worried that she doesn't trust you, but you have to trust *her* a little, too."

Tripp gave a light yip out beyond the fence. A cow and her calf had decided to leave the group, and Tripp dropped his head low and went to work to bring them back. He didn't charge at them. He got beyond them and started crossing back and forth, easing them in the direction he wanted.

"Look at that dog," Dad said. "Look how he's moving them, but without chasing them or stressing them out. He's left them an opening, and he's just hanging out, giving them a chance to *take* that opening. Instinctively, he trusts that old cow to know she and her baby belong with the herd. And watch, there she goes." The cow and calf trotted toward the others, with Tripp quietly zigzagging behind them. "That's what you need to do with Dahlia."

"I need to *herd* her?" Rawlston was teasing, and realized it felt good to laugh a little. It felt normal. Hopeful. His dad just rolled his eyes.

"No, you lunkhead. You just need to give her an open path back to you, then shut up and trust her to take it. Have some faith in the woman. If she loves you, she'll come around, once she nurses that hurt for a while." Dad took the whiskey bottle, but he only filled the shot glasses halfway. He held his up in a mock toast, and Rawlston returned the gesture as his father made his point. "Let her come back without being pushed, son."

An opening. The words rolled around in his head a few times, until an idea was born. He drank the whiskey, knowing that sip would be his last for a few days. He had work to do. He grinned at his father.

"Dad, you're a genius."

CHAPTER NINETEEN

DAHLIA WAS SITTING with Hope and little Evie when she checked her phone and noticed she'd missed a text from Rawlston. They were on the shaded portion of Ridge's deck, after Dahlia had brought over a breakfast casserole to share. Hope still hadn't remembered much about her past, other than knowing that she'd been running from danger of some sort. But Dahlia had stopped by a few times, as Ridge suggested, and he was right about her liking the quiet woman and her sweet infant girl once she'd gotten to know them.

Her brother had gone to the ranch office after breakfast, and the women had decided to enjoy some fresh air while the temperatures were still on the cooler side. Evie was sound asleep in the baby carrier Ridge had bought for her.

"Is everything okay?" Hope asked, frowning at the phone in Dahlia's hand. "Is that bad news?"

"I'm not really sure *what* it is."

It had been two days since Rawlston's last text, where he'd promised to back off and give her time. That he'd be waiting for as long as it took, but he wouldn't bother her anymore. She couldn't help wondering who had talked to him about his barrage of messages after their argument. Whoever it was, she was grateful to them. It had been easier to think without him trying so hard. But here he was, texting again. He wasn't asking her to do anything this time, though. Not talk to him. Not forgive him. He was just telling her something that made no sense.

I'll be up by the cottonwood tree this morning working on a project you might want to see. If you'd rather see it alone, I'll be done around noontime.

Was he asking to meet her? If so, why was he so careful to let her know when he *wouldn't* be there? Her pulse jumped. Rawlston did it because he wanted to give her options. He was opening the door, but not forcing his way through it. Not pulling her through, either.

She bit down on her lower lip, still mulling it over. What *project* was he working on up there? Had the sheep gotten through his fence again? Maybe he'd added the lower strand of wire he'd mentioned to keep them out, despite his concern that they'd crawl under it anyway. Why was he making it a mystery?

Then Dahlia smiled. Fortunes loved their mysteries. He was teasing her with just enough information to make her curious. He knew her so well. Her smile deepening, she checked her watch. He'd sent this text an hour ago, but she'd set her phone aside while they were eating breakfast and hadn't seen it.

"Um, Hope, I'm sorry, but—"

"You have to go." Hope nodded. "I figured from that big smile on your face that I haven't seen much this week. Go on. We'll catch up later."

They hugged and Dahlia hurried to her golf cart, then down to her stables. She was in capris and canvas flats with a ruffled gauzy top—not exactly riding clothes. She didn't even have a hat. She wasn't going to take the time to change.

Once she'd made the decision to try to meet with Rawlston, her heart was thumping so hard in her chest that she could almost hear it pounding out *Hurry! Hurry!* She pulled Rebel from his stall, forcing herself to slow enough that she wouldn't upset the stallion. Meanwhile, the clock was ticking in her head. It was almost noon.

Rawlston had put the invitation out there, and she was finally ready to make the move toward a future together. He'd made a mistake. A couple of them, actually. But once her sense of betrayal had cooled, she'd realized her mother was right. She was clinging to her anger to protect herself from being hurt again, without considering that he was sincerely remorseful and deserved a second chance. She'd want one from him if she'd been the one to make a mistake.

If they loved each other, they'd probably be giving each other lots of second chances through the years. She felt a warm thrill at the thought of years together with Rawlston. It was worth risking occasional hot tempers if it meant spending a lifetime with the man. They could handle it. *Love* could handle it.

Luckily, it was overcast, keeping the air cool enough that she didn't have to worry about stressing her horse physically. Once he was saddled, Rebel was ready for a run. She made him wait until they were in the main range before giving him his head. The stallion actually hesitated for a moment, unsure what to do. She'd very rarely just let him run. Once he realized she meant it, he took off like a bullet, racing across the meadow. She spotted the sheep on the far side of the hill, and, even though they were far away, they still scattered at the sight of the big horse charging toward them.

Rawlston was there. Or at least, *Malloy* was there, grazing under the wide cottonwood. So Rawlston had to be nearby. She reined in Rebel as they approached the summit. He was blowing hard, prancing sideways and snorting as Malloy raised his head and let out a whinny. That's when Rawlston straightened over near the gate.

Wait. Where did that *gate* come from? The only gate between their properties was down at the bottom of the far side of the hill. She and Rawlston had joked about adding a gate that would make his rides to her house shorter. He watched as she pulled up and slid off Rebel. He arched a brow at her shoes.

"Not exactly safe footwear for riding—especially *that* kind of riding." He watched as she patted Rebel's neck. "You gave the big boy a good run. In a hurry to get somewhere?"

He still hadn't moved from his spot by the gate. What was he waiting for? He'd given her the opportunity, but now she realized it was up to her to make the final move. She tucked her horse's reins through her belt loop. With these linen capris, it wouldn't take more than Rebel shaking his head to rip the loop loose, but his training held. The stallion wasn't interested in testing her today. Trusting her, the same way Rawlston was.

Seeing him so close was all she needed to chase away any remaining doubts. Tall, sweaty, handsome. Eyes full of worry and love. He took off his hat and wiped his brow with his handkerchief. Watching her. Waiting for her to come to him. She led Rebel forward a few steps so she could move into Rawlston's arms. He wrapped her in an embrace so tight it almost took her breath away, and they stood like that for a long time, just clinging to each other. It had only been days, but it felt like years since he'd held her. Kissed her, like he was doing now. Hard. Deep. Desperate.

When he finally pulled away, they were both breathing heavily. He turned slightly and gestured toward the gate.

"I was an idiot, Dahlia. I should have fought for you instead of signing those damn papers. And then I kept pressuring you instead of trusting you. I love you, sweetheart, and I'm opening my heart, just like I've opened this fence line. No more fear. No more doubt. No more lies, I promise. Never again…"

"No more lies," Dahlia repeated, kissing the corner of his mouth. "No more fear. No doubts. I like the sound of that." She moved to kiss him again, but he stepped back.

She was confused until he gestured to the other change he'd made to the fence. The sections on either side of the gate had been reconfigured. He hadn't added a third strand to block the sheep. Instead, he'd raised the second strand right in the middle, so there was now plenty of room for her sheep to walk through to his range.

"I don't understand," she said. "I thought the idea was to keep sheep *out*. Aren't you worried about your cattle?"

"Turns out I was wrong about more things than just marriage. I've since been educated on the facts about sheep and cattle sharing ranges. And it actually can work. We'll just have to check to be sure your whole herd doesn't cross over. Kinda like marriage, it requires the right balance." He pulled her in for another kiss. "A little cooperation." He kissed her again. "A little compromise." Another kiss. "Patience."

She chuckled. "You'll probably need that patience more than me."

He nodded and kissed her again. They were both so hungry for each other. "That's okay. I'm sure there are things you'll have to be patient about, too." He stepped back, then dropped to one knee, reaching for his pocket.

What. Is. Happening?

He pulled out a small box and opened it.

"Marry me, Dahlia. Again. For real."

Inside the box were two familiar wedding bands and a diamond ring. The rings from Las Vegas. He gave her a bright grin, his eyes shining, with only the slightest touch of guilt showing.

"I couldn't return them, babe. Somehow, I already knew that our marriage was for keeps." He shrugged. "Well, maybe not *that* marriage, since we annulled it, but—"

She dropped to her knees in front of him, ignoring his surprise. Her hands clutched his fingers, which were holding the box and rings between the two of them. She was laughing, giddy with relief and joy.

"You're not the only one with a confession to make." His forehead furrowed, and she placed her hand on his cheek. "I never sent those silly papers to the attorneys. I shredded them the day after we argued. No matter what happened, I wanted us to make the decision about our future calmly, not in anger. And frankly, I knew in my heart that I didn't want our marriage to be over, either."

He stared, then took her hand from his face and kissed her palm, smiling against her skin. "So it appears neither one of us can be trusted to end this marriage."

She nodded. They were still on their knees, facing each other. "Something else we have in common. Loving each other."

He leaned forward, looking deep into her eyes until she felt him touching her soul. "I will love you forever, Dahlia. With all my heart. I don't ever *not* want to be married to you." He slid the band and the diamond onto her finger, then watched as she put his wedding band on his hand. The rings looked like they belonged there. "I'll be a real husband this time, and no more secrets. All that drama is for Fortunes, and you're an Ames now. I can't wait to tell the world."

"I love you, too, Rawlston. With all my heart. Maybe it was fate that made that bratty kid pour so much vodka in our fruit punch that night."

He laughed, kissed her again, then looked over her shoulder. "Uh, your killer horse seems to be bored with us."

She looked back in surprise. Rebel must have pulled his rein from her belt loop without her even noticing. Or maybe it came free by itself when she dropped to her knees with Rawlston. Either way, the paint horse was grazing calmly about ten feet away, between them and Malloy. Neither horse seemed the least bit interested in each other or their humans.

She and Rawlston stood slowly, and she moved closer to Rebel until she was able to take up the reins. He lifted his head and bumped it against her, then went back to grazing.

"Well, I'll be. A good gallop was exactly what he needed," she said, patting his shoulder.

Rawlston walked up and slid his arms around her. "Or maybe he's a romantic at heart, and we charmed him."

She leaned back against his chest, laughing softly. "I think my theory is more likely."

A few of the sheep had wandered closer, and Rawlston gave a short command. She hadn't even noticed Tripp sleeping in the tall grass by the tree. He was awake now, watching the sheep intently. But he didn't move.

"That poor dog's going to be very confused when he can't chase sheep anymore."

"He's a quick learner. Besides, maybe we'll put him to use herding sheep on *your* side of the fence."

"You mean *our* side." She pulled away, but held on to his hand. "We're married for real now, so there is no more yours and mine. Which means…" She tapped under his chin with her fingers teasingly. "That *you* are now a sheep farmer."

"And you—" he tugged her close "—are the prettiest damn cattle rancher in Texas." He nipped at her ear, his words sending shivers across her skin. "A cattle rancher

I really want to make love to right now. I've missed having you in my arms."

"My place is…" She grinned. "I mean, *our* lake house is closer."

He chuckled. "The attorneys are going to have fun with all of this, aren't they? But I agree that heading to the lake house is a good idea. *Right now.*"

They both mounted and headed down the hill, hand in hand. Rebel had pinned his ears at Malloy's closeness at first, but then begrudgingly settled into walking at his side. The ride was slow and easy. Comfortable.

Dahlia could picture them making this same ride thirty, forty, maybe fifty years from now. Coming down the hill to their home together. The barns were in sight when Rawlston spoke again.

"I know we're legally already married, but I want to give you a real wedding and a reception. Pick a date… maybe in the spring when everything is in bloom. It's my favorite time of the year in Texas. We'll renew our vows and party like we're still in high school."

"Spring sounds perfect," she agreed, remembering one more thing. "And I know exactly what my 'something old' will be." She waited until he looked over at her before she continued. "I just happen to have a long, sparkly wedding veil that lights up, if you can believe it. I'm sure it's a style that will be all the rage in Texas by next spring." He barked out a laugh as she continued. "It was something else I couldn't part with from Vegas."

He was still laughing as he leaned toward her, making Rebel unhappy enough to pin his ears again. Rawlston paid him no mind.

"Am I also something that you won't part with from Vegas?"

"You were by far the best thing I got on my trip to Las Vegas, Mr. Ames. I'm not about to give you up."

"That's good news, Mrs. Ames, because I feel the same way. Vegas was very good to us."

"I agree." They reined in the horses at the stable, dismounting and quickly moving into each other's arms. He traced a trail of kisses down her neck until she sighed. "If I had to wake up married to someone in Las Vegas," she whispered in his ear, "I'm very glad that someone was you."

* * * * *

Don't miss the stories in this mini series!

THE FORTUNES OF TEXAS: FORTUNE'S SECRET CHILD

Follow the lives and loves of a complex family with a rich history and deep ties in the Lone Star State.

Fortune's Secret Marriage
JO MCNALLY
July 2024

Nine Months To A Fortune
ELIZABETH BEVARLY
August 2024

Fortune's Faux Engagement
CARRIE NICHOLS
September 2024

MILLS & BOON

Home To Her Cowboy
Sasha Summers

MILLS & BOON

Sasha Summers grew up surrounded by books. Her passions have always been storytelling, romance and travel—passions she's used to write more than twenty romance novels and novellas. Now a bestselling and award-winning author, Sasha continues to fall a little in love with each hero she writes. From easy-on-the-eyes cowboys to sexy alpha-male werewolves to heroes of truly mythic proportions, she believes that everyone should have their happily-ever-after—in fiction and real life.

Sasha lives in the suburbs of the Texas Hill Country with her amazing family. She looks forward to hearing from fans and hopes you'll visit her online: on Facebook at sashasummersauthor, on Twitter @sashawrites or email her at sashasummersauthor@gmail.com.

Visit the Author Profile page
at millsandboon.com.au for more titles.

Dear Reader,

It's been a while since our last visit to Garrison, Texas—and I'm so happy to be back. We've had engagements and babies and weddings and festivals, and we're just getting started.

Mike Woodard has his hands full. One of the only EMTs in the county, Mike balances his time between work, volunteering as a rodeo pickup rider and caring for his father.

Eloise Green is still trying to find her footing in Garrison, and she worries over her children. Her daughter, Kirby, is an upbeat, precocious five-year-old, while seven-year-old Archie is often tense and anxious.

When she's reunited with the boy—now a ridiculously handsome cowboy—who betrayed her trust and shattered her heart, she's surprised by how raw those wounds still are. She can be neighborly, as is expected in a small town, but she won't befriend him. No matter how many times they're thrown together, how much the kids love his dog, or how kind and loving he is with his father, she'll keep her guard up. At least she'll try.

Until our next Garrison adventure, stay well and read happy!

Sasha Summers

DEDICATION

Dedicated to my precious mother, Jeannie,
who supports everything I do (and write)!
I love you so!

CHAPTER ONE

ELOISE TUCKED A strand of wavy brown hair behind her ear and offered the blue-and-white stoneware bowl to her five-year-old daughter, Kirby—and held her breath. Her daughter's resistance to eating anything green had become a nightly battle. "One spoonful."

"Peas." Kirby wrinkled up her little freckled nose and leaned back in her chair, crossing her arms over her chest. "Peas are icky. And squishy. And gross."

"They *are* mushy, Mom." Archie, her seven-year-old son, nodded. "They also look like rabbit poop." He announced this lovely tidbit of information without breaking a grin.

Really? Where did he come up with this stuff? Eloise stifled a smile and ignored her grandfather's muffled laugh. Archie was hysterical—which made it hard to stand her ground on important things like eating vegetables, bedtimes, and not harassing Grandpa Quincy's sweet cat, Dandelion.

"Rabbit poop?" Kirby squeaked and pushed her plate away. *"Ew."* This word was drawn out—for full effect.

"Yep. A spoonful of peas is like a little pile of poop," Archie went on. "But rabbit poop isn't green." He paused, pushing his glasses up on his nose. "Is it?"

"Archie." Eloise tried to sound stern. "Let's not talk about rabbit poop at the dinner table."

Archie nodded, scooping mashed potatoes onto his fork then pausing to ask, "What about whale poop?"

Grandpa Quincy didn't cover his laugh this time. He had a big, booming laugh that was impossible to resist. Archie started to giggle. Then Kirby. Even though she wasn't thrilled over why they were laughing, she loved the sound of it.

When they'd quieted down, Eloise said, "No." She eyed the peas and set the bowl aside. "No poop talk, of any kind, at the dinner table."

"It's okay if you don't like 'em, Freckles. I do." Grandpa Quincy reached for the bowl. "I'll take a big ol' helping of peas."

Eloise smiled and handed over the bowl. "There's plenty."

Kirby sat, slouched in her chair, staring at her plate. Her big mossy green eyes—the same color as Eloise's—narrowed as her frown grew.

"Come on, Freckles." Grandpa Quincy used his most encouraging tone. "Eat up those yummy mashed taters and your momma's crispy fried chicken. If you do, I might have a pink cupcake for dessert."

As much as she appreciated her grandfather's support, offering them sugar this close to bedtime guaranteed chaos.

Kirby perked up, her brown ponytails swinging. "With sprinkles?"

"Yup." Grandpa Quincy winked. "Pink *and* white ones."

Kirby clapped her hands.

"All you have to do is eat up your dinner first." He pointed at her plate with his fork.

Kirby's nose wrinkled again but she picked up her fork, scooped up some potatoes, then let them fall—splat—back onto her plate.

"She doesn't like mashed potatoes." Archie took a big bite of mashed potatoes.

Surprise. Since they'd moved in with Grandpa Quincy, her daughter's list of food she would eat continued to shrink. Kirby had always been on the slight side. Her lack of caloric intake was something Eloise worried over—on top of all the other things she worried over. She wouldn't push the mashed potatoes, but Kirby had to eat *something.* Other than cupcakes, that is.

"Your fried chicken is like one big chicken nugget." Eloise hoped Kirby would buy her sales pitch. Chicken nuggets were still one of the things Kirby would always eat. "Here." She pulled Kirby's plate closer, cut the fried chicken breast into small pieces, and slid the plate back in front of her daughter. "See? Now it's just like homemade chicken nuggets."

Kirby's eyes narrowed and she sucked in her cheeks as she leaned forward to inspect her mother's handiwork.

Eloise—Grandpa Quincy and Archie, too—waited to see what happened next.

"'Kay." Kirby speared a piece of chicken and ate it. Then another piece. "Yum. This is so good, Momma." She chewed with enthusiasm. "Yum-yum-yum." She murmured around her mouthful of food.

"Right? It is good chicken." Unlike his sister, Archie would eat almost anything.

Grandpa Quincy nodded. "Your momma is a good cook. If she cooks it, I'm going to eat it."

Eloise had always enjoyed cooking. Growing up, she'd spent some holidays and one week every summer here with her grandparents. She'd helped out with countless meals in Gramma Beryl's kitchen. Cooking had been her gramma's love language and she'd had a lot of love to give. When Eloise had been too young to cook, Gramma Beryl sat her on a stool to snap beans or shuck corn and watch and learn. When she was a little older, she'd been allowed to peel potatoes or pound the steak until it was the perfect thickness to batter and fry. Later, she'd mastered perfect cream gravy, smooth-as-silk mashed potatoes, flaky and sweet pie crust, and iced tea.

"We've got a big wedding coming up this weekend. Your momma gets to work her magic and make beautiful flower arrangements for the ceremony and the bride." Grandpa Quincy owned Garrison Gardens, the only flower shop in Garrison. "Warden Hattie Carmichael is marrying Forrest Briscoe. I remember when she was a little thing, all braces and red hair and freckles—"

"Freckles like Kirby?" Archie asked.

Kirby was very proud of her freckles.

"Only Kirby doesn't have red hair. She has brown hair. Like me and mom."

"No one has freckles like our Kirby." Grandpa Quincy grinned. "They're good people. The both of them. Truth be told, I can't imagine a better matched pair. It's nice when good things happen to good people."

Grandpa Quincy, a lifelong Garrison resident, knew everyone and everything about his hometown. She was still learning the names and faces of Garrison, but she'd managed to piece together some things from her childhood visits. She knew the Briscoe and Crawley families owned the two largest cattle ranches in these parts—and had a lot of influence in town. The Schneiders owned Garrison Family Grocer's and were, in Grandpa Quincy's words, good folk. Garrison even had its own celebrity in retired country singer Buck Williams—now owner of Buck's Bar and Honky-Tonk.

Grandpa Quincy had warned her about one group in particular. According to him, the Garrison Ladies Guild were a bunch of gossipy do-gooders "with too much time on their hands." He'd gone on to say their leader, Miss Martha Zeigler, was apparently prickly, opinionated, and "entirely too much."

Eloise had yet to do much exploring for herself. Between the kids, sorting through the mess of paperwork her ex-husband had left for her to deal with, and working at Garrison Gardens with her grandfather, it was hard to carve out an hour for herself beyond her early morning walk.

"Will the bride wear a big white dress?" Kirby asked, looking hopeful.

"Hattie?" Grandpa Quincy chuckled. "She's not one for dress wearing but…maybe. I guess we'll see, won't we?"

Fortunately—or unfortunately—their family had received an invitation to the event. Which meant she'd have to keep an eye on the kids while she and her grandfather set up the flowers for the ceremony *and* she'd have to hope they'd behave through the ceremony and reception.

The good news was the ceremony was outdoors. Both the wedding and the reception were to be held under Garrison's beloved legendary tree, erste Baum. The tree, sometimes called the First Tree, was purported to be the oldest in Texas. Seeing it firsthand, Eloise could believe it. The tree's canopy was massive, providing shade for a large gathering—like the wedding that would be taking place this weekend.

"Need help, Momma?" Kirby loved flowers. "I can help."

"Of course you can, Freckles." Grandpa Quincy nodded.

Kirby smiled broadly, then ate the last bite of chicken.

Grandpa Quincy pointed at her plate. "You did good, Freckles. Ate all your chicken up."

"Can I have more, Momma?" Kirby asked, holding out her plate.

More? "Of course." Eloise slid another chicken breast onto her daughter's plate, cut it into small pieces, then slid the plate back to Kirby.

"Momma... I need you to sign a paper from Miss Ramirez." Archie pushed his glasses up and glanced her way.

She knew that expression. It was his I'm-in-trouble-please-don't-be-too-mad face. "Oh?" Miss Ramirez was Archie's second-grade teacher. Since kindergarten, Archie's talkative and inquisitive nature had him sitting right next to his teacher's desk. By the end of the year, Eloise knew his teachers well. He wasn't a bad kid; it was the opposite. He was charming and well-liked—just like his father—but he was a talker. "What about?"

"Well...you know." He shrugged, shoving an extra-large forkful of mashed potatoes into his mouth.

Eloise exchanged a look with her grandfather.

"He was talking," Kirby said, devouring her chicken. "Again. Lots and lots."

"Archie." Eloise set her fork down. "We've covered this, hon. There's a time and a place for talking, right?"

He nodded.

"I know it's hard and you're still making friends, but you have to listen to your teacher. It's disrespectful to talk over her—or interrupt during lessons. When it's free time or you're on the playground, talk all you want." Eloise stopped then. The kids, like her, were still adjusting to their surroundings. And, so far, they were doing well. Archie was talking too much, but it could be worse. At least he was being himself—not clamming up or acting out in a destructive way. It was, in a weird way, a relief that he was his chatty self. "Bring me the paper after dinner and I'll sign it, okay?"

"Yes, ma'am." Archie had lost one of his front teeth, giving him a jack-o'-lantern grin. "It's so hard. Words just sort of…come out. But I'll try harder, Momma, I promise."

"Thank you." She couldn't resist that grin of his. "Everyone done?" She waited for them to nod. "Archie, go on and pick out your clothes for tomorrow. Kirby, get your nightie and I'll be in the bathroom to get your bath started in a sec."

The kids scurried from the room, and Eloise started to clear the table.

"You look tired, El." Grandpa Quincy stood, helping her carry the plates and cups into the kitchen. "You worry too much. Kirby and Archie are happy little things. You're doing real good with them, you hear? Just breathe."

Grandpa Quincy always saw the bright side of things. She tended to be a realist. "Thanks, Grandpa."

"I swear, little Kirby looks so much like you did at that age." He kissed her temple. "And I like peas—even if they do look like rabbit poop." He chuckled, stacking the plates by the sink. "I got this. You go on and get them tucked in and we can watch the news together. Maybe some of that game show, too."

She smiled up at her grandfather. Grandpa Quincy's evening routine meant watching the nightly news and the latest episode of *Wheel of Fortune* that he recorded daily. Now that was her nightly routine, too. "You're sure?"

He nodded.

"Okay, thanks." She headed down the hallway to the bathroom. The door was closed but she heard Kirby's squeal, Archie mumble something, and a cabinet door slam. The two of them were up to something, she just knew it. She took a deep breath and pushed the door wide.

There, on the bathroom floor, was a towel and an empty bottle of Benadryl. A bottle that had been mostly full and should have been locked in the medicine cabinet… Kirby and Archie both spun to face her, their hands behind their backs.

She eyed the empty bottle. "Guys. What happened to the medicine?"

Archie and Kirby exchanged looks. *Guilty* looks.

Her lungs went tight. "Archie?" she repeated, panic welling.

"I… I drank it." Kirby spoke quickly. "I did it."

"You what?" Eloise's heart slammed to a stop, then kicked into overdrive. This was bad. This was really bad. Kirby was so tiny… "Grandpa," she called out, crossing to her daughter. "Grandpa, call 911. Tell them to hurry. Kirby drank an entire bottle of Benadryl." She squatted on the floor, terrified, and tugged her daughter into her arms. *Please, hurry. Please.*

THERE WAS NOTHING Mike Woodard dreaded more than a call concerning children. Nothing. Now he had pulled up in front of Quincy Green's garden-like front yard, preparing for the worst. He grabbed his bag, jumped from the ambulance, and ran to the open front door.

"I'm right behind you." Terri, Mike's partner, called after him.

Mike nodded, the protocol for an overdose scrolling through his mind. Luckily, it didn't happen all that often around these parts. But this, a little kid, didn't always have a happy ending. Adrenaline was coursing through his veins, preparing him for what was to come.

"Mikey." Quincy Green stood in the open front door. "Bathroom." He pointed down the hall, his expression taut and his pallor gray.

He nodded and ran in the direction Quincy indicated. "EMT." He pulled on a pair of gloves as he scanned the room.

A young boy sat on the bathroom floor, his face covered with his hands. A young girl was quietly crying while a woman—mom, most likely—wiped the girl's face with a washcloth.

"She drank a bottle of Benadryl." The woman didn't look at him as she held out the bottle. From the rigid posture to the waver in her voice, it was clear the woman was barely holding on. "It was almost full."

A *whole* bottle? "How long ago?" Mike moved closer, taking the little girl's pulse and flashing a penlight in her eyes. So far, all the girl's vitals were normal.

"Maybe seven minutes?" The woman eased her hold on the little girl. "Her name is Kirby."

"Kirby." Mike offered up a smile. "Hey there. I'm here to help you."

Kirby wasn't buying it. She leaned into her mother and shook her head. "Momma."

"It's okay, Kirby." The woman patted her back. "We need to do whatever he says, okay? That medicine could make you really sick."

If this little girl had ingested an entire bottle of Benadryl, things were more dire than that. There was no time to waste.

"But medicine is supposed to make you better." Kirby's lower lip wobbled.

"It does." Mike nodded. "But only when you're sick. And only a little bit." He pulled open his bag.

"What do we do?" the woman asked. "What do I do?"

Now wasn't the time to assign blame to the woman. *But* he couldn't help wondering how the kids had access to the medicine. A parent's top priority should be keeping their

children safe. "We need to go for a ride in the ambulance."
He glanced behind him to find his partner, Terri, waiting
outside the bathroom with the gurney.

"Of course." The woman stood, lifting Kirby. "And
then?"

Terri headed into the room. "We'll pump her stomach—"

"Pump my stomach?" Kirby squeaked. "Pump?" The
little girl stared at her brother, panicking. "Archie!"

"I did it." The boy jumped up. "Not Kirby."

"You did what? *You* drank the medicine?" Their mother
turned, her forehead creasing. "Archie." Her voice broke.
"You have to tell the truth." She looked back and forth between them. "Both of you. *Now.*"

Mike frowned. "Kids, this is serious. We need to know
exactly what happened. We can't afford to waste time." He
and Terri exchanged looks.

"I thought it was shampoo." Archie pointed at the bottle on the counter. "And Grandpa Quincy said he needed
to give Dandelion a bath with his special cat medicine
shampoo." He looked over at his sister. "So, me and Kirby
wanted to be nice and give Dandelion a bath for Grandpa
and we used the medicine to give him a bath."

Mike was lost.

"We need to get her to the hospital." Terri was right.

"Let's go." Mike gestured to the gurney.

"Wait." Archie, the boy, grabbed his arm. "Kirby didn't
drink it. Really. Me, neither." He ran across the room and
opened a bathroom cabinet. "See. She doesn't need to get
pumped. She doesn't."

"I don't," Kirby wailed. "I really don't."

Inside the cabinet was the most pathetic-looking cat
he'd ever seen. The poor thing was shivering, it's gray-
and-white fur covered in goopy, purple liquid.

Mike frowned, processing the boy's words. "You washed the cat in Benadryl?" He scratched the back of his neck. This was a first.

The cat let out a pitiful meow.

"It's medicine." Kirby sniffled. "Dandelion needs medicine shampoo."

"Poor Dandelion," Quincy Green said, peering around the doorframe.

It might have been Mike's imagination but it sounded like Quincy Green was trying not to laugh.

"You didn't drink any of it? You're sure?" Terri asked, hesitant.

"No." Archie shook his head. "I didn't. My sister didn't. We didn't. Really. We're sure, aren't we, Kirby?"

"No way. It tastes nasty." Kirby stuck out her tongue.

From the puddle of purple-stickiness the cat was sitting in and how saturated the feline was, Mike believed them.

The kids' mother slumped against the bathroom counter, looking stunned, as tears started streaming down her cheeks. "You two..." All the color drained from her face as she let Kirby go.

"I'm sorry, Momma." Archie did *look* sorry.

"Me, too." Kirby sniffed. "Do I have to have my tummy pumped?"

"Not if you didn't drink it?" Mike had to be sure.

"Not one drop." Kirby nodded.

"This isn't funny. It's serious business," the kids' mom added, her voice breaking.

Both children nodded.

"Promise we didn't do it, Momma." Kirby hugged the woman's leg. "I'm sorry."

"I'd say they're telling the truth." Terri squatted by the open cabinet and was studying the cat. "Might want to give your veterinarian a call, Quincy. Make sure the cat's going to be okay."

"Will do. Best see what we can do for Dandelion." Quincy came into the bathroom. "Come here, sweet girl." He reached into the cabinet and lifted the cat. Strands of the congealed medicine dripped from the cat to the interior of the cabinet. "You definitely need a bath now."

Dandelion offered up another pathetic meow.

"We're sorry, Grandpa," Archie mumbled.

"You two are going to help Grandpa." Archie's mom said. "And clean this up."

"Yes, Momma." Archie followed his grandfather from the bathroom.

"Me, too. Me, too. Poor, poor Dandelion." Kirby ran after them.

"Well…" Mike wasn't sure what to say. To say he was relieved was an understatement. But it was more than that. Times like this challenged his professionalism. What could have happened tightened his stomach… Snatches of his own childhood surfaced and made things ten times worse. Which didn't help. He took a deep breath. Tonight had a happy ending. That was a win. That's what he needed to focus on.

"I'll put the gurney up and start the paperwork." Terri was smiling as she pushed the wheeled bed back down the hall.

"I'm sorry to have caused a fuss over nothing." The woman ran a shaking hand over her face. "I… I panicked."

"Calling was the right thing to do." It was. But none of this should have happened to begin with. "I've got some papers for you to sign. And…a few pamphlets on how to safely store medicine and poisons in the house so your children won't have access to it." He pulled off his gloves.

For the first time, her gaze focused. "Excuse me?"

There was something familiar about the woman—something he couldn't quite pinpoint. "Well, ma'am." He paused, trying to keep his voice even and calm. "The best thing to do is take steps to stop these sorts of things from happening." He chose his words with care. If he started laying blame at her feet, she'd get defensive and stop listening. But his job wasn't just to provide life-saving measures, it was also to educate folk. As much as he'd like to think tonight's scare was lesson enough, he wasn't going to count on that.

"These sorts of things?" She blinked, her words tight. "You have a pamphlet that prevents kids from washing a cat with Benadryl?"

"No." He was amused, in spite of himself. "Mostly, it's about prevention. Accidents can happen, of course, but there are things we can do to reduce the chances."

There was a moment of strained silence before she said, "I can assure you this has never happened before and it won't happen again, Mr…"

He'd give her the benefit of the doubt—this time. But he was still leaving the brochures. "Woodard." He held his hand out. "Mike Woodard."

Her gaze widened, fixed on his face, before she blinked, drew a deep breath, then shook his hand. "Eloise… Green." It was a mere whisper. "I—I appreciate your quick response."

"Eloise?" He swallowed. *Little El Bell?* He hadn't thought about her in years… That was after the years it had taken to get over the hurt she'd caused. Now, here she was. And he was reeling.

"Yes… Hi…" She ran a hand over her thick, brown hair. "As you can see, this was all a misunderstanding."

Right. Business. What had *almost* happened here tonight. He cleared his throat and said, "I'm glad it played out the way it did." The kids were fine, that was what mattered most.

Eloise's kids. He was still trying to wrap his mind around the fact that this was Eloise. The last time he'd seen her, there'd been tears and heartbreak and now... she was here. And he didn't know how to feel about it. He shouldn't *feel* anything—period.

Her gaze, a mossy green he remembered so well, swept over his face. "I do know that this is my fault. And, clearly, you feel the same way. I can see it." She pointed at his face, her posture stiffening. "Thank you for not denying it."

She was calling him out? And he was speechless. But, if memory served, she'd always been on the sassy side. In fact, that's what Quincy had called her back then. *Sassy.*

"You mentioned something about papers?" Eloise asked, brushing past him and heading down the hall to the front door. "I'm sure you have other people to help... And judge." She crossed her arms over her chest and stared up at him, eyes flashing.

It had been years, but hearing her accuse him of being judgy was like the pot calling the kettle black. All he could do was stare back at her.

"Mikey." Quincy came down the hall. "Hold up." He held out his hand. "Thanks for helping out."

"No problem." He shook the older man's hand. "How's Dandelion?" His gaze darted back to Eloise, who was looking everywhere but him.

"Vet said to keep an eye on her. If she gets groggy, to call again." He shook his head. "She's clean—the kids are drying her off. They feel pretty bad. But I know they meant well." He cleared his throat then. "I feel terrible, El. I thought I'd locked that bottle up. I told you I would and I forgot."

"Grandpa." Eloise placed a hand on his arm. "It's all okay."

"No, now, it's not." Quincy took an unsteady breath. "It's not. You put in all those locks and hooks and such to keep them safe and I... Well, I need to be more careful with the kids around."

"It's okay, Grandpa. Having us underfoot is a big adjustment." Eloise hugged him. "Tonight was tough for all of us."

And just like that, Mike felt lower than dirt. Quincy's words offered a very different viewpoint on the evening's events. Eloise *had* done her due diligence as a parent *and* she was giving her grandfather grace and forgiveness for what could have been a potentially tragic evening.

He'd been quick to pin it all on Eloise, and it left a bad taste in his mouth and a knot in his gut. Immediately blaming her had nothing to do with what happened here tonight and everything to do with his own childhood. Assuming anyone—even Eloise—was like his mother was just plain wrong.

Quincy squeezed her shoulder as he let her go, glancing between Mike and his granddaughter. "I'm guessing you two remember each other?"

Eloise didn't look his way. "Vaguely."

Vaguely? If the edge to her voice hadn't rubbed him the wrong way, he'd have laughed.

Quincy chuckled. "It has been a while. I'd say ten or more years? A lot has happened between then and now."

It was closer to fifteen years, but he only said, "Isn't that the truth."

"Eloise and her kids—my great-grandkids—Kirby and Archie are living with me now." Quincy beamed as he said this, draping an arm around Eloise's shoulders. "I've got a full house again."

Mike had heard something about Quincy taking in his

grandkids. People in a small town liked to talk—especially about new arrivals. It hadn't occurred to him that it was Eloise and her kids. He couldn't help but notice Quincy hadn't mentioned anything about the kids' father. Not that it mattered one way or the other. "Welcome *back* to Garrison."

She seemed to ignore his greeting. "I'm sure you're regretting the invitation, Grandpa."

Quincy chuckled. "Oh now, El. You wouldn't believe the chaos your mother and uncles got into growing up. Let me tell you, this is nothing."

"Here." Terri arrived, a clipboard in hand. "We just need a few signatures." She handed the clipboard to Eloise, flipping the page for more signatures. "And here." She flipped to another page. "We're out of poison control pamphlets, Mike—I looked." She took the clipboard Eloise offered. With a nod, she headed back to the ambulance.

He didn't miss the narrow-eyed glare Eloise sent his way.

Quincy scratched his chin. "How about you bring your pamphlets by tomorrow afternoon? Sit on the porch, have some tea, and talk a spell? El, here, makes perfect iced tea."

Mike heard the slight hiss of Eloise's indrawn breath. If there'd been any doubt of the woman's displeasure at her grandfather's suggestion, one look at her pinched face cleared that right up. But once Quincy Green looked her way, she was all smiles. And what a smile.

Eloise Green had been a pretty girl and now she was a fine-looking woman. "Tomorrow?" Mike found himself nodding. Why was he saying yes? She didn't want him here. He didn't want to be here, either. "I should have time to drop them by."

"Good." Quincy clapped him on the shoulder. "Maybe you'll have time for tea, too."

There was no denying the flash in Eloise's eyes. "Can't wait."

He'd been a jerk tonight, that was true, but any apology stuck in his throat. "I'll see you then." Mike gave her a tight smile and headed back to the ambulance. Tomorrow, he'd force himself to apologize and leave well enough alone. Now that he knew Eloise Green was back in Garrison, he could do his best to make sure their paths wouldn't cross. He was already bracing himself for tomorrow's visit.

CHAPTER TWO

Eloise kept up her rapid pace as she rounded the corner and headed back up Main Street. The sun was just up, the birds were singing, and cars were beginning to park in front of the Buttermilk Pie Café for breakfast. She scanned the shop windows, reading about sales and upcoming events until one flyer caught her eye.

Hill Country Dance Studio was advertising a Ladies Only Stretch and Yoga class. It sounded like the perfect stress reliever. And, maybe, a way to make friends. She loved her kids and her grandfather, but she was lonely. Not that she had the time—or money to pay for it.

Since her ex-husband, Ted, had been incarcerated, Eloise had lost all of her friends. Not that she could blame them. Ted had managed to get most of their friends and family to invest in his *business*. When the Texas Criminal Investigations Division got involved and Ted's not-so-legit company led to fraud and embezzlement charges, those friends and family lost thousands of dollars, retirement capital, summer homes, and kids' college education funds.

While Eloise had been oblivious to Ted's dealings, not everyone believed that. How could they? She and Ted had seemed so devoted—so in sync with each other. Eloise had thought so, too, until she learned he had a mistress. That was why she'd divorced him. And that was months before everything else came out and he was arrested.

What a joke.

When it came to deceit, Ted's mistress had only been the tip of the iceberg.

No matter what anyone else said, the only thing she was truly guilty of was believing her husband.

No, that's not entirely true. She'd known better but she'd still given Ted her trust. She'd wanted to believe he loved her. That he'd be there for her and support her, no matter what. But wanting something didn't make it real. That's how she'd ended up here—with no one to blame except herself.

Then last night happened… What could have happened turned her blood cold.

She *was* guilty. It was her fault. Thanks to Mike and his big blue I'm-judging-you eyes, it was indelibly etched on her brain. She'd messed up and there was no forgiving herself. If her father and Ted had taught her anything, it was not to trust anyone—Grandpa Quincy included.

Mike Woodard. It was hard to reconcile the sharp-eyed giant of a man with the big-hearted, fun-loving little Mikey she'd believed him to be. There was a time she'd thought he was special. She was wrong, of course. And that wake-up call had pulverized her heart.

It had been an insult to injury that he'd been the one to come in to save the day—and he was bringing her pamphlets to hold her accountable. As if her guilt wasn't real and heavy enough.

"Good morning." A woman stood at the door of the dance studio, keys jangling in her hand. With her long blond hair and sunny smile, she was one of those women who was effortlessly beautiful.

"Morning." Eloise was very aware of her too-big shirt, sloppy bun, and the twenty pounds she'd put on over the last six months. She'd never been eye-catching. Average was more like it and she was okay with that. No, it took effort for Eloise to feel attractive—effort she hadn't put in to go on her morning walk.

"I'm Gretta Williams." The woman introduced herself.

"Nice to meet you. I'm Eloise Green." She ran a hand over her off-center bun.

"I couldn't help but notice—are you interested in the new class?" Gretta shifted the strap of her canvas tote and slid the key in the lock.

"I am." But Eloise wasn't going to get her hopes up. "It's just… I have kids."

"I get it." Gretta laughed. "I have one and he's more than enough. Between running this place and keeping up with him, it's hard to practice self-care."

Eloise smiled. *Self-care? What's that?*

"I'm trying to figure out some sort of a day-care option. I mean, I figure moms would benefit the most." Gretta pulled the door open. "Want to come in? I can make some coffee?"

As much as she wanted to, one look at her watch told her she was running out of time. "I wish but the kids will be up soon. They're a lot for my grandpa to handle on his own."

"Gotcha." Gretta paused. "Single mom, too? It's hard. My dad tries to help but… Well, it's hard."

Too? Meaning this gorgeous woman was a single mom? Eloise probably shouldn't be so excited by this information, but she was. "Yes. It is. Yes."

"Well, now, I really have to figure out a babysitter option and let you know."

She laughed.

"How can I reach you?" Gretta smiled.

"Garrison Gardens. That's my grandpa's flower shop. And me, now." She shrugged.

"That's right around the corner. That's great. I'll definitely let you know." She waved. "Have a great day, Eloise."

"You, too. It was really nice to meet you, Gretta." Eloise waved and headed toward home, an extra spring in
her step. She and the kids had been here for almost two
months now and this was her first interaction with an adult
that hadn't centered around a flower order, the kids, or
making sure the cashier applied all the coupons the kids
and Grandpa Quincy cut out of every Sunday morning
newspaper.

She'd almost reached the corner when she spied Mike
Woodard. He came out of the Old Towne Books and Coffee shop with a pastry box in one hand. After a full body
stretch and yawn, he adjusted his straw cowboy hat on his
head. He looked every inch the cowboy. A giant bear of
a cowboy, maybe. His black T-shirt clung just enough to
emphasize his broad shoulders.

Not that I care about his shoulders.

She didn't. And she didn't want him to see her there—
not caring—so she realized she'd better get a move on—

But he turned and saw her.

Why am I frozen? Even from here, she saw him hesitate.
Then he… What? He smiled? And it was infuriating. He
might not know it but he'd poked at her biggest insecurity:
that she was a bad mom.

He lifted a hand in acknowledgment and took a step
in her direction.

No. No way. Her morning had gone from sunny and
hopeful to irritated and tense, and it was all thanks to him.
She spun on her heel and headed, double-time, around the
corner and as far away from Mike Woodard as possible.
Her near-jog pace had her home in record time—and gasp-
ing for breath.

"Momma?" Kirby called out, running down the hall to
greet her at the front door. "You're all red."

"I'm fine," she said, panting.

Kirby took her hand. "You're hot and sweaty, too."

"Sorry." It was possible she'd overreacted. And was out of shape.

"It's okay. Come on." Kirby tugged her down the hall to the kitchen. "Look."

There, on the round kitchen table, was one of her mother's china platters covered in a pile of waffles. There was a bowl of fresh fruit, four cups of orange juice, and a steaming mug of coffee by her usual chair.

"What's all this?" she asked, still breathing hard.

"Land sakes, El, you're as red as a beet." Grandpa Quincy looked alarmed. "Take a seat, won't you?"

"I told her." Kirby nodded. "She's so, *so* red."

Archie came over to assess her. "Wow, Momma. Are you sick?"

"No." She took a deep breath, willing her breathing into a pseudo-normal pattern. "But I need to exercise more."

There was a knock on the front door and Eloise froze.

He would not *have followed her. Surely not.*

There was another knock followed by the telltale squeak of the front door's hinges. "Quincy? It's Mike." His voice rang down the hall. A strong, slightly amused voice.

"Come on in," her grandpa called out.

He would and he had.

"Morning, Mikey." Grandpa Quincy headed to the door. "Come on down. El here might need your medical attention."

She was mortified. "Grandpa." Here she was, a red-faced, heaving, sweaty mess, about to face the man she'd literally panicked over and run away from.

"Is that so?" His voice was closer, the sound of his boots on the wooden floor louder and louder. Until he was standing in the kitchen door—a large red dog at his side. "Good morning. I'm happy to be of service."

Good was not how she'd describe her current state of mind. She stared at the toes of her neon green walking shoes.

"Dad heard about what happened and wanted me to bring over some pastries." There was something warm about Mike's voice.

"Well, that was mighty neighborly," Grandpa Quincy said. "Why not have a seat and have some breakfast?"

"We made Momma an 'I'm sorry' breakfast." Kirby studied Mike for a minute before asking, "Are you a cowboy and a doctor man?"

"I guess I am." Mike was smiling, she could hear it in his voice.

"Is your name Mr. Mike or Mr. Mikey?" Kirby asked.

"Mr. Mike. Only old folk like me and his daddy still call him Mikey." Quincy chuckled.

"And my brother." Mike shook his head. "He gets a real kick out of it."

"Is that your dog?" Archie loved dogs. "Can I pet him? What's his name? What kind of dog is he?" He took a deep breath. "Is it a boy or a girl? Does he like waffles 'cuz we have lots of waffles."

"Archie." She reached out and took her son's hand. "One thing at a time."

Archie shoved his glasses up on his nose. "Sorry, Mr. Mike, sir. I like dogs."

"No apologies necessary. I like dogs, too." Mike chuckled. "His name is Clifford—"

"Like the big red dog?" Kirby was ecstatic. She loved the *Clifford the Big Red Dog* books.

Eloise made the mistake of glancing Mike's way.

"Yup." He patted the dog on the head, his handsome face was animated as he spoke. "He's a big red dog so I figured it fit. He's a golden retriever and, as far as I know, Clifford would enjoy a waffle. Did I answer them all?"

Archie was too entranced by the dog to care.

"You did." Kirby nodded. "Wow. 'Cuz that was a lot."

Mike chuckled again.

Eloise tore her gaze away. It was hard to be mad at someone who was being nice to her kids. She ran a hand over her hair—her sweat-dampened hair—and pulled the "Books are better than people" shirt away from where it was clinging to her chest.

Grandpa Quincy put a glass of water on the table and pushed it toward her.

"Thank you," she whispered, taking a long drink.

"Can we pet him, Momma? Can we?" Archie was practically shaking with excitement.

"You'll have to ask Mr. Woodard, Archie." She squeezed his hand. "Be gentle. And extra patient." Archie struggled with patience.

Archie nodded. "Yes, ma'am."

"Clifford." Mike squatted and scratched the big dog behind the ear. "You get to make some new friends. This is Kirby and Archie."

Clifford's great plume of a tail swayed rapidly.

"Hi, Clifford." Kirby waved at the dog, then hugged herself. "He's so pretty." This was whispered. "He'd look even prettier with some bows in his fur."

"He doesn't want bows." Archie held his hand out for Clifford's inspection.

Clifford's enthusiastic tail-wagging led to a big, wet doggie kiss on Archie's hand.

Archie giggled, which made Clifford wiggle and move closer to her son.

"I don't know about bows, Kirby." Mike watched the kids with his dog, a crooked grin on his handsome face.

"Clifford has a lot of energy, and he'll play fetch for hours. I'm afraid he might lose any you'd give to him."

Before Eloise knew it, the kids were sitting on the kitchen floor giving Clifford a tummy rub. She wasn't sure who was happier, her kids or Clifford. There was no way she could resist their gleeful smiles and free laughter. She didn't want to. Nothing was better than seeing the two of them this way.

Mike shook his head at the contented groan Clifford made, his eyes bouncing her way. His smile tight as he said, "All I wanted to do was leave those." His gaze held hers but he nodded at the box Grandpa Quincy had put on the kitchen counter. "I didn't mean to intrude."

He was not *serious.* She stared at him, incredulous. There was no way he could have misinterpreted her mad dash to get away from him. And yet, here he was. Very much intruding. He knew it—and he was smiling about it.

"Dad's idea but, I guess, they're also a peace offering of sorts."

Eloise sat back in her chair, curious.

"Peace?" Grandpa Quincy's brow furrowed.

"I might owe El an apology."

For last night. Not for the devastation he'd caused her all those years ago—not for doing the one thing he knew she couldn't accept or forgive.

Where did that come from? Why was she thinking about something that doesn't matter? Why was he still smiling at her? And why had he called her El? El was reserved for her family. Her closest friends. Not…him. He needed to stop smiling, stop looking so…like he did. She needed a shower. But mostly, she needed him to leave so she could get on with her day. A day that, with any luck, wouldn't include any more time with Mike Woodard, his smile, tight black shirt, big blue non-judgy eyes, or the pain-filled and anger-laden memories his appearance had stirred up.

IF HIS DAD hadn't threatened to do this pastry delivery himself, Mike wouldn't be here. His dad didn't care about his doctor's orders to rest—or that he wasn't supposed to be driving. That's how Mike ended up here, on the receiving end of El's frigid glare, wishing he was just about anyplace else.

He'd been headed to the Greens' place to appease his father when he'd spied her on the street. When she hadn't waved back, he'd headed over to get it over with, give her the pastries and get on with his day. By the time he'd crossed the street, she was a speck in the distance.

Eloise was fast. Like fast, fast.

He didn't know if her red cheeks were from her sprint home or if she was just that mad he was here. It's not like he was thrilled about it, either.

"Is that so? An apology?" Grandpa Quincy asked. "Did I miss something? It wouldn't have been the first time."

"You were doing your job." Eloise was avoiding eye contact—and she wasn't exactly being subtle about it. "We need to eat and get ready for school, kids."

He got the hint. He was all too happy to hit the road.

"But, Momma…" Archie's disappointment was almost comical. "Clifford is here."

"And he's so, so soft," Kirby added, continuing to rub Clifford's stomach.

"I'm sure Clifford will understand." Eloise's mom voice was impressive.

With sighs and groans, the kids returned to their seats at the table.

"I'll get another plate." Quincy pulled a plate from the cabinet.

"I appreciate the offer, sir, but I've got to open up the hardware shop this morning. As Dad says, Old Towne Hardware and Appliances won't operate itself." He stifled a yawn. "Until Doc Johnston gives him the *all clear*, my brother and I are running the place." Between his EMT shifts, working with the high school rodeo team, and helping out at the shop while his dad recuperates, he was plumb tuckered out.

"I hope he's listening to doctor's orders." Quincy's brow creased with concern. "You tell him poker night wasn't the same without him."

"I'll tell him. You know how he is, Quincy. But Rusty and I are keeping a close eye on him." He chuckled. He and his brother had their work cut out for them. "We keep reminding him he was just released from the hospital a week ago."

Two weeks ago, life had been very different. He'd been in final job negotiations with the National Rodeo League. In the industry, Mike was well-respected, well-liked and both an experienced pick-up rider and an EMT. He was beyond flattered that they'd come to him. And the offer had been too good to refuse. He'd always wanted to see more of the country so, with his father's and brother's full support, he'd accepted. Sure, it'd keep him on the road for more than half the year, but he'd make sure to spend as much time back home as he could.

Then his dad had a stroke, the world had tipped, and his plans had come to a hard stop. He'd fully expected the NRL to withdraw the job offer when he explained his situation and that he couldn't consider leaving for at least a month. Instead, they'd given him their total understanding. They'd told him to take the month, more if he needed it. As grateful as he was for their flexibility, he was no longer sure about taking the job. His father, his family, came first.

"May I ask what happened to your father?" Eloise's question interrupted his mental musings.

"He had a stroke a couple of weeks ago. A small one." Thankfully, his father hadn't been left with any lingering maladies or side effects. "Good thing he's strong and stubborn—both attributes will work in his favor."

"I'm glad to hear he's recovering." For the first time, Eloise's expression softened.

"Thank you. Me, too." Seeing his father in a hospital bed had hit him hard. The man was his rock.

"He's determined to be back in fighting shape for Founder's Day. You know how involved he gets with the festivals. But that's his favorite. He loves dressing up and being one of the Founding Fathers." He broke off, chuckling. "Rusty and I are hoping the doc gives him the okay or we're going to be fighting Dad *and* Miss Martha."

"I don't envy you that. Just because she can push around the members of the Ladies Guild, she thinks she can go ordering everyone else around. Not me. I see her coming, I'll duck and cover." Quincy opened the pastry box. "My goodness, muffins and donuts and more. Looks like you cleared out the place."

"I didn't know what the kids would like." Mike watched as Archie stealthily slipped Clifford a bite of waffle.

Clifford gobbled up the waffle and sat, ears perked, all alert, hoping for more.

"I like donuts." Kirby frowned at her plate. "I like donuts more than waffles."

"Kirby is a picky eater." Archie pushed up his glasses. "*Very* picky."

"She likes sugar," Eloise murmured. "Eat up your waffle and fruit and I'll save you a donut for an after-school snack."

Kirby's sigh was pitiful. "'Kay, Momma." She speared

a strawberry, put it in her mouth, and chewed slowly. "Will Clifford be here after school?"

"No, sweetie. I'm sure Clifford and Mr. Woodard have lots to do today—just like you and Archie." Eloise blew a strand of hair from her forehead.

She'd always had thick chestnut hair. Soft, too. Mike frowned.

"Oh." Kirby looked and sounded heartbroken.

"Don't fret, Freckles." Quincy placed a hand on the little girl's shoulder. "I bet we can stop by and visit Clifford sometime." He paused, sitting back in his chair. "Maybe, if you think it wouldn't be too much for him, we could stop by and visit your pa tonight, Mikey? I'll get him a new crossword book."

"I'd be obliged." His father would enjoy seeing his buddy—and the kids, too. Of course, having the kids in the mix might backfire. His dad was already on him and Rusty about needing to get married and have kids. He said it was high time for him to have grandkids to spoil. *Like it was easy to find someone you could trust for a lifetime.* "And Clifford would, too."

"I can take him for a walk. Or a run. I can run real fast." Archie sat up on his knees. "Or we can play fetch. Dad says I can throw the ball really far. My dad's always right. He says I should play softball. Right, Momma?"

Eloise's smile was forced. "We'll make sure to get you signed up for softball this year."

"Dad will come see me play." Archie was all smiles. "I bet he will."

"We'll see," Eloise murmured.

Eloise's response struck Mike as unusual. Why wouldn't the boy's father come watch his son play? If he had a son, he'd be at every game—cheering him on and likely embarrassing his boy to the high heavens.

"Okay." Archie dropped another piece of waffle on the floor. "Can I play with Clifford later?"

"I'd be mighty grateful, Archie. Clifford here is still a puppy. Sometimes I tire out before he does." Quincy was always welcome at his place and the kids were pretty darn cute, so, for his dad's sake, he'd make peace with her tagging along. "Only when your momma says it's convenient, of course." He glanced at Eloise.

Eloise propped her elbow on the table and rested her chin, her eyes meeting his. "We'll be there. Something tells me they'll both get their chores and homework done tonight without arguing."

He couldn't tell if he'd gotten her feathers ruffled again or not.

"No arguing." Kirby pretended to lock her lips. "Tell her, Archie," she whispered.

"Nope. Not from me." Archie adjusted his glasses. "I never argue."

"Glad to hear it." Mike saw Quincy roll his eyes—followed by Eloise—and grinned.

"Dad says respect…" Archie paused, thinking. "Respect makes a man." Archie fed Clifford another piece of waffle. "I don't know what respect is, but it's important."

Mike didn't miss the way Eloise's lips thinned. So, things between Eloise and the kids' father weren't…great. For one thing, Eloise and the kids were living here without the man. Then there was the other thing. A quick look at her hand showed she wasn't wearing a wedding ring.

She caught the look. Her hands slipped off the table and into her lap. "Finish up. We've got…" She glanced at the big sunshine-shaped clock on the wall. "Ten minutes until we need to head to school." With that, she stood, glanced around the table, then hesitated.

"I've got this." Quincy sat between the kids and sipped his coffee. "You go and take a shower."

"You're still all sweaty, Momma," Kirby pointed out. "Ew."

Eloise's cheeks, which had almost returned to a normal hue, flared red again. And yet, she lingered.

"You know, I've got a few minutes before I need to get to the shop. If that offer of a cup of coffee's still good, I'd be mighty appreciative, Quincy. I've got a long day ahead of me." He wasn't offering to help Eloise, he was helping *Quincy*. Kirby and Archie were a hoot. Plus, Clifford was all too content eating waffles and being spoiled.

"Make yourself at home and help yourself, Mikey. And get yourself something to eat, too. You brought enough to feed an army." Quincy waved him to the cabinet. "See now, El, you go on. Clifford, Mikey, and I are on the job."

With a sigh, Eloise held up her hands. "Okay. I'll be quick." Not that she looked happy about it. With that, she headed out of the kitchen and down the hall.

"Poor Momma." Kirby shook her head, working her way through her waffle. "She's so, so, *so* tired."

"Yeah." Archie served himself another waffle, cut it into bites, and fed a piece to Clifford. "Dad says we have to go easy on her—since he can't be here."

Mike returned to the table with a blueberry muffin and a full mug of coffee. He didn't ask any of the questions he had, but he'd be lying if he said he wasn't curious about the man that *can't* be here for his kids.

Quincy took another sip of his coffee. "Little things like not talking in class—" Quincy glanced at Archie "—and eating up the food on your plate—" he looked at Kirby now "—go a long way for your sweet momma."

Mike took a sip of coffee to hide his grin. It was easy to imagine Archie talking in class. He was precocious and, he suspected, full of energy. Growing up, Mike had been a lot like the boy.

"Dad also said we'll be going on a vacation soon. The mountains or the beach with a big water slide and swimming with the dolphins." Archie said this to Kirby, then took another bite. "And he said Momma can go to a spa for ladies."

"He said that, did he?" Quincy's expression was further affirmation that things weren't right with the kids' father. Instead of wearing a big, excited smile, the older man looked concerned—maybe even upset.

"Something like that." Archie shrugged. "Maybe. Sort of."

"Hmm." Quincy sighed. "It's likely to be a while. You know that, Archie. Don't you?"

Archie sighed heavily, then nodded.

Mike wasn't sure what to make of it.

"What's a spa?" Kirby asked around her mouthful of waffle. "Can Momma go spa-ing here?" Kirby glanced at him, dropped a big piece of waffle on the floor, then giggled as Clifford gobbled it up.

"Hmm." Mike scratched the back of his head. "Not that I know of. I'll ask around, see if there's one hereabouts?"

Kirby nodded. "Yes, please."

"Will do." He took a bite of muffin—which elicited a mumbled groan from Clifford. "No, sir. I know better. You're not starving. I'm pretty sure Archie's fed you a whole waffle—and then some. Don't go giving me those sad eyes." He reached over and gave the dog a pat. "You lay down and rest a while."

Clifford yawned, stretched, then flopped on the tile floor.

"Good boy," Kirby said. "Good, good boy."

"Dogs can understand a hundred words." Archie pushed

his glasses up on his nose. "I bet Clifford can understand a hundred and one."

"A hundred?" Mike glanced down at his snoozing dog. "I didn't know that."

"Archie knows lots and lots." Kirby ate the last strawberry from her plate, put her fork down, and held her hands up. "Done. I'll go get dressed, Grandpa."

"You do that, sweetheart." Quincy smiled. "Make sure to wash your face—"

"And brush my teeth." Kirby gave him a thumbs-up and slid from her chair. "Be right back, Clifford." And she ran from the room.

"I'm done, too." Archie took a last bite—a bite so big it should have been two or three bites.

Mike watched, stunned at the amount of food the boy managed to fit into his mouth.

"Chew, son. Slow down. It's not a race." Quincy shook his head. "I guess it's a good thing Mikey is here. He can give you the Heimlich if you choke."

The older man was joking but Mike found himself holding his breath.

"Okay." Archie chewed and chewed—then swallowed. "Done."

Crisis averted. Mike went back to eating his muffin.

"All right." Quincy chuckled. "You go on and get yourself ready."

"Yessir." Archie paused by Clifford. "I'll be back, too. I bet you understand that, don't you?"

Clifford wagged his tail.

"See." Archie was grinning from ear to ear. "He does." Then he ran from the room, yelling, "Don't squeeze out all the toothpaste, Kirby."

"There's been some big changes since I last visited you."

Mike held out his mug when Quincy carried the coffeepot to the table and offered him a refill.

"You could say that again." Quincy filled his cup, put the coffeepot back, and returned to his seat. "Having El and the kids here has been a jolt to the system. A good kind. I like seeing them every day. I like feeling useful and helping out." He smiled. "They're full of spirit, those kids. After the mess they've been through, I'm glad that hasn't changed. I only wish I could say the same about El. She's not my Sassy anymore. Some spark is…missing." His smile faded and he shook his head. "I can't blame her, though. That big heart of hers has taken a beating—makes sense she's got her guard up." He shrugged and took a sip of coffee. "I guess you're chomping at the bit to get started on your new job?"

But Mike was still mulling over Quincy's words. It was on the tip of his tongue to ask what sort of mess Quincy was alluding to when Kirby reappeared. Her brown plaid dress was inside out and her shoes didn't match, but she flopped down next to Clifford without a care in the world.

"Wanna read, Clifford?" She pulled a book from her backpack and opened it. "This book is about Harvey." She pointed at a picture. "He's a squirrel."

Clifford was on his feet then. His ears perked up and his tail wagged at frenzied speed as he barked and spun in a circle.

Kirby watched, then glanced at Mike. "What's he doing?"

"You said the magic word." Mike patted the dog on the back. "You can't say the 's' word or Clifford wants to chase it."

"The 's' word?" Kirby cocked her head to one side. "What's the 's' word?" she whispered.

Mike pointed at her book. "What kind of animal is Harvey?"

"A squir—" Kirby broke off the second she understood what he was saying. *"Ooh."* She nodded. "Oops."

"Are we ready?" Eloise appeared in the kitchen door. "Kirby, sweetie." She sighed. "Come on, let's fix your dress." She held her hand out. "And shoes. And your hair."

Kirby's long-suffering sigh implied she wasn't thrilled with this announcement. "Okay, Momma."

Archie appeared, immediately at Clifford's side. "Your dress is wrong-side out, Kirby." He pointed at his sister. "And your shoes don't match. But I'm ready."

Kirby shrugged. "Clifford doesn't care. Me neither." She took Eloise's hand and followed her mother from the room.

Quincy's house phone started ringing. Like the Woodard home, there was still a landline in the Green house. Mike believed it was a generational thing—as most of his father's friends had the same.

"I bet that's Dad." Archie ran to the phone.

Quincy headed for the phone. "He normally calls on weekends, Arch."

"Yeah, but it might be him." He waited, smiling, as Quincy answered.

"Quincy Green here." He glanced at Archie and shook his head. "Morning, morning. I heard about the meeting. I'll be there."

If the boy was upset, Clifford's presence seemed to buoy Archie's mood. "Dad's real important," he explained to the dog. "He's real busy. All the time. He travels for work."

The boy looked at Mike then. "But he calls lots. He likes to hear about our day and school and stuff."

"My dad likes hearing that stuff, too—from me and my brother." No matter what the circumstances were, it was obvious the boy adored his father.

"Now we're ready." Eloise re-entered the kitchen with properly dressed and matching Kirby. "Ready, Archie?"

Archie pointed at the phone. "It's not Dad."

For a split second, Eloise's brow creased and her jaw flexed tight. "No, probably not today, sweetie." Her gaze bounced from Archie to Kirby to Clifford. "Now, give Grandpa a hug and I'll get you two to school."

"Yes, ma'am." They spoke in unison.

He watched as the kids hugged their grandpa, hugged Clifford, then hugged him, too. "That's a surprise." He patted Kirby's back.

"Momma says sharing kindness and hugs will make the world a better place." Kirby beamed up at him.

"Except strangers. We don't talk to strangers. Or hug them." Archie pushed his glasses up. "But we can talk to and hug people we know. Or Momma knows. Or Grandpa knows."

"That's a good rule." Mike saw the way Eloise smiled at her kids—there was so much love and pride on her face his heart ached. His father had always loved them unconditionally and, for the most part, that was enough. But there was a piece of him that had yet to heal over his mother's abandonment. Most of the time, he accepted her leaving was the best thing for him, Rusty, and their father. Most of the time, the hurt didn't gnaw at his insides and make him ponder "what-ifs." This wasn't one of those times.

He'd heard what had been said this morning. As much as he wanted to keep his distance, he was sorry to hear she'd been through tough times and it had taken a toll on her. Life wasn't always fair. He knew that firsthand. But the support of family, friends, and time to heal could make a world of difference. That being said, they weren't family, he no longer considered her a friend, and his time here was limited. All he could do was wish her well and hope that Garrison gave her the fresh start she and her kids needed.

CHAPTER THREE

"FOUNDER'S DAY?" Eloise asked, snipping the ends off the stems of six perfect pink roses. "It's a big deal?"

"Any festival in Garrison is a big deal, El." Her grandfather chuckled. "Small towns rely on those sorts of things to keep the community strong and bring in some tourism dollars. This year is extra special. Not only has it been one hundred and seventy-five years since Garrison was founded, it's also been a year since the whole county rallied to save erste Baum." He glanced over the rim of his reading glasses. "Some smooth talker came into town trying to buy up erste Baum Park and build one of those big-box store chains. You can imagine how that went over. It was a big to-do, El. The whole town was in an uproar. Newspapers and reporters from all over showed up. Big news—for these parts, anyways. You and the kids missed it by a couple of months."

Thank goodness. Eloise had had enough of newspapers and reporters to last a lifetime.

While Garrison was rallying to save their beloved tree, her world had been completely falling apart. She'd been making ends meet, barely. Her credit card debt had skyrocketed but, after selling her little flower and tea shop, she'd been managing to make payments and keep food in the house.

Things would have been okay if their house had sold. But the five-thousand-square-foot monstrosity, with fifteen-foot ceilings that cost a small fortune to heat and cool, had been on the market for almost six months and there hadn't been a single offer.

She'd thought waking up to find her minivan had been repossessed in the middle of the night was bad. But bringing the kids home after school to find the locks changed on the house—while their neighbors watched from their front yards and windows—had subjected her to abject humiliation. She'd had no idea they were months behind on the mortgage. Thanks to Ted. It was only when the bank foreclosed on the house that she learned he'd managed to sweet-talk their banker, a friend and investor in Ted's scam, into giving them extension after extension.

"That's why Miss Martha Bossy-pants Zeigler has declared this Founder's Day Festival will be the biggest one yet." Grandpa Quincy seemed blissfully unaware that her thoughts had drifted—for which she was thankful. "I don't know what sort of changes she's thinking, but it's a little too late to overhaul the whole dang thing. And, if she's got all sorts of harebrained ideas, I've a mind to tell her just that."

"That sounds exciting." She tried to imagine her sweet grandfather taking on the town's battle-ax but couldn't do it. "Any idea what she's thinking?" She tucked one rose into the green glass vase, adding a sprig of white-tufted baby's breath, then another rose.

"We'll find out at tomorrow night's planning meeting." He paused, glancing her way. "It'll give you a chance to get to know some of our Main Street neighbors."

She met his gaze. He meant well, he did, but she was still processing the shame of…everything. Meeting new people was nerve-racking.

"I know things have been real tough, El, but no one knows about Ted's…shenanigans in these parts. You don't have to worry about that." He shook his head. "And, even if they did, why would anyone hold it against you?"

They might not hold it against her but they'd *know*, and knowing meant long, curious looks, whispers, and, eventually, an interrogation. Once her dirty laundry was aired, she was forever linked to the pain and embarrassment she'd like to leave in the past.

"You're too young to wall yourself up with just me and the kids. Besides, those young 'uns need to meet folk and make friends, too." He cleared his throat. "Hattie's in charge of the Junior Rangers—I think I've mentioned them a time or two? Anyhow, Kirby and Archie would probably enjoy it. Being outdoors, learning stuff, doing projects, and spending time with other kids."

She wanted them to have friends—for Garrison to feel like home. "I'm not against it, Grandpa. I'd need to know the details—"

"I was getting to that. It just so happens there's a Junior Ranger meeting the same time Martha Zeigler's set for the festival planning meeting. Archie and Kirby can have fun and you'll have a whole hour to yourself." He chuckled.

Junior Rangers was a good idea; it was this planning meeting she wasn't so sure about. But her grandfather asked so little of her, there was no way she could refuse. With a sigh, she tucked the last rose in, stepped back to see her handiwork, then added another sprig of baby's breath.

"More like an hour with me and all the Main Street business owners, that is. And since you are part-owner of the shop now, you should be there." He pushed through the swinging doors that separated the workroom from the shop front.

Working at Garrison Gardens was a comfort. She and her grandfather both shared a deep love of all things green and flowering, but she sensed he was tired. That was why she took the phone orders and put together the bouquets and arrangements in the workroom and Grandpa Quincy manned the front. Besides creating two birthday flower arrangements she'd have to deliver later that afternoon, it was a slow morning. That was the way of things in Garrison—slow and steady. After the nonstop stress of the last eight months, it was a relief.

About noon, she heard the doorbell chime.

"Morning, Mr. Green."

"Morning, Miss Gretta," her grandfather answered. "What can we do for you today?"

"Actually, I thought I'd stop by with lunch. For you, me, and Eloise."

Eloise wiped her hands on the green apron she wore and pushed through the swinging doors. "Hey, Gretta."

"Hi." Gretta held two brown paper bags. "I come bearing food. From the Buttermilk Pie Café fall menu. Apple and pecan salad, chicken and dumplings, and yummy yeast rolls."

"That sounds like a feast." Her grandfather patted his stomach. "That's mighty kind of you, Gretta." He flipped the sign on the door from Open to Closed. "I've learned never to say no to a meal—especially when it comes with good company."

"There's plenty of room in the back." Eloise waved them both through the swinging doors. "Let me clean off one of the tables." She moved the ribbons, wires, and bud vases aside, then wiped down the metal surface with a disinfecting wipe.

"I've never been back here before." Gretta set the bags on the table, staring around the room.

"El's done a lot of work since arriving." Her grandfather sat in one of the chairs. "I didn't have these, what do you call them? Vision boards? Those and scraps and clip-pings and stuff all over."

"They're for inspiration, Grandpa." She winked at her grandfather. "And it was a little dark and dreary." She helped Gretta unpack the bags.

"Without windows, you have to do something to brighten the place up." Gretta passed out the individual packets of plastic utensils. "I like the vision boards." She scanned El's handiwork. "They're gorgeous. I love that one." She pointed at one with a variety of blues and bits of lace. "If I do ever get married again, I'll let you do the decorations. Not that it's likely to happen anytime soon—I haven't been on a date in a couple of years." She shud-dered. "Dating. Ugh."

Eloise laughed. "My thoughts exactly." The very idea of dating turned her stomach.

"I don't know what's wrong with men these days." Her grandfather shook his head, dismayed. "There should be a line of fine suitors wrapped around the block for the both of you."

"Can I be honest with you, Mr. Green?" Gretta sat, opening her salad.

"Please do." He waited.

"I don't want a line of suitors. I'd be happy with one. One good man with infinite patience and a great sense of humor." Gretta's sigh was wistful.

Grandpa Quincy was frowning. "I can come up with a half-dozen men that fit that description."

"What about you, Eloise?" Gretta poured salad dress-ing on her salad. "What's on your wish list?"

Eloise took a bite of salad, pondering the question as she chewed, then swallowed. "I don't have a list but honesty is a must—like my number one." She shrugged. "That's all I've got, for now. But I think I'm going to steal yours,

Gretta. A sense of humor and patience are both necessary qualities."

Gretta tucked a long strand of blond hair behind her ear. "I think so."

Grandpa Quincy wiped his mouth with his napkin. "Well, I've got a few names for both of you—"

"Since we are being honest—" she gave her grandfather a long look "—I'm not interested in dating. Not a bit. Zero."

Her grandfather's sigh was all disappointment, making Eloise and Gretta laugh.

"I'm a strong, independent woman, Grandpa." She was a long way from independent but she was trying. "I don't need a man. Well, other than you." She reached over and patted his hand. "I don't know what we'd have done—would do—without you. You're the only knight in shining armor me and the kids need."

"Knight in shining armor, huh? I like that." He speared some lettuce with his fork before asking, "Gretta, your boy is a Junior Ranger, isn't he?"

"He is. And Hattie Carmichael is a saint, that's all I can say." Gretta took a sip of her tea. "I love my son, dearly, but he's…a lot."

"Oh, I get it. How old is he?" Eloise took a bite of the yeast roll and regretted it. Carbs were her weakness. Bread, pasta, cakes, cookies… The pastry box Mike had delivered was pure temptation. If she didn't get rid of it, she'd likely eat them all and add to the extra pounds that now resided on her not-so-toned thighs and tummy.

"Levi likes to say he's almost seven. But he's six. First grade." Gretta finished off her salad. "I regularly send thank-you notes to his teacher. And cookies or candy or gift cards or whatever I think might help. He tends to get into mischief." She held her hand up. "His teacher says he has an abundance of curiosity."

Grandpa Quincy chuckled. "Sounds like he and Archie would get on just fine."

"Oh?" Gretta perked up. "Really?"

"Archie is in second grade." Eloise smiled. "He's seven and a talker. He likes to tell stories—and embellish them. I had to explain to his teacher that Archie's father was not starting a polar bear farm in Antarctica. Only that his father had seen a polar bear when he was on a cruise in the arctic—Alaska, specifically." A trend seemed to be developing as most of her son's embellishments revolved around his father.

"Aw, now. There's no harm meant. He's good at storytelling." Grandpa Quincy set aside his salad container and reached for his soup. "Maybe, one day, he'll grow up and be a writer."

"Maybe. But, for now, there's a fine line between storytelling and lying, Grandpa. It's important he knows the difference." It wasn't Archie's fault. Ted had been the same—he loved adding dramatic flair to his stories for the kids. In the end, Eloise wasn't sure there was a hint of truth to anything Ted had said. "You're the one who taught me a man's only as good as his word."

"But he's just a boy, El." Her grandfather was loyal to her kids—to a fault. "I've been tellin' El that Archie and Kirby might make some new friends at Junior Rangers." He blew on his soup. "And, with the Founder's Day meeting coming up, I figured it was as good a time as any for them to give it a try."

"Oh, yes. The Founder's Day Festival." Gretta shook her head. "So far, we're doing a clogging extravaganza and a line dance, too."

"So far?"

"Miss Martha hasn't weighed in yet. In case no one's told you, she's sort of the boss of…everything. Somehow." Gretta chuckled. "She always has something more in mind."

"I'm getting that. She sounds…interesting." Eloise reached for her soup bowl. "Clogging and line dancing sound fun. My daughter, Kirby, was in dance back… Well, Kirby used to be in dance." Eloise opened her soup container and stirred the creamy contents. She had fond memories of her little girl in glittery tutus, spinning on the stage and smiling with pride.

"There'd be room for her if she wants to join one of my classes."

"That's sweet of you." Too bad Eloise was trying to keep a tight rein on their spending.

Grandpa Quincy wasn't asking for rent or help with any of the bills. Instead, he'd insisted on making her co-owner of the shop and paying her for her work there. He said he was getting forgetful and tired so having her and the kids was a help to him, but she knew better. Yes, his memory wasn't what it used to be, but he was still more than capable of living on his own.

Since they'd invaded his home, his life had been turned upside down. Her kids were constant noise and chaos, including that scary visit from the local EMTs. He said they gave him a renewed sense of purpose but what else could he say? He knew she had no place else to go. It was painful but true.

After Ted, she hadn't wanted to be reliant on anyone ever again… Now she was entirely reliant on her grandfather's kindness and generosity. In time, she hoped, somehow, in some way, she could repay him for all he'd done for them.

"I haven't eaten so well in a long time." Grandpa Quincy

sat back with a sigh. "First Mikey's delivery and now this."
He patted his stomach. "At this rate, I could play Santa
come Christmastime."

And there he was. Mike Woodard popping up, again.
This morning had been a catastrophe. Seeing him, running
from him, and him following her? How had he not gotten
the hint? She hadn't wanted to see him or talk to him. She
certainly hadn't wanted him in the kitchen while she was
red-faced and dripping sweat. Then he'd had to go and be
handsome and charming and handsome. She frowned. He
wasn't that handsome.

He had been awfully sweet to Archie and Kirby, en-
chanting them with his dog and the promise of more Clifford playtime. *Why had I agreed to that?*

"Santa? We have to get past the Founder's Day Festival
before I can start thinking about Christmas, Mr. Green."
Gretta wiped her hands on her napkin. "Believe me, I start
rehearsing for our Christmas Jamboree the day after we
wrap up the Founder's Day show." She started collecting
her trash. "And, Eloise, not that you asked me, but you
should let the kids go to Junior Rangers this week. The
high school football team will be there to help them make
paper chain streamers to decorate erste Baum for the festival. There will be lots of helping hands and less for you
to worry about."

Gretta was easy to talk to. The two of them were chatting and laughing the entire time they cleaned up.

"Thanks for the lunch. It was fun." Eloise walked Gretta
to the front door.

"Kirby is welcome to come visit the studio—no obliga-
tion," Gretta said on her way out of the shop.

After Eloise turned the Closed sign back to Open, she
was feeling the tiniest bit hopeful. Sure, the day wasn't
over and there was still a chance she'd get a call about Ar-

chie from the school—and she'd have to deal with Mike this evening… But she'd had an entire conversation without Ted or the path of ruin he'd left in his wake coming up. And it felt good.

"Is YOUR DADDY getting better, Mr. Mike? I miss him. He's funny." Little Samantha Crawley was one of his father's favorite clients at their family's hardware and appliance shop. Well, her father, Jensen Crawley, was the client. But Samantha went everywhere he did so the little girl was a frequent visitor. His father said she was a ray of sunshine that always made his day bright. "He told me about his pet dragon, Bongo."

"He did?" Mike typed in the price on the tools on the register. "You know, my dad told me a little something about you." He reached under the counter for the glass jar his father kept full of lollipops. "He said you liked lollipops. Red ones." He pulled one out and offered it to the little girl.

"He 'membered." Samantha's smile was oh-so-sweet as she took the lollipop. "Thank you, Mr. Mike. And thank Mr. Nolan, too."

"You're welcome. And I'll tell my dad, too."

"'Kay." Samantha pulled off the wrapper and put the lollipop in her mouth.

"Anything else?" he asked Jensen. "What's all this for?"

"Microwave." Jensen sighed. "I'm going to try to fix it this time." He ran a hand along the back of his neck. "But chances are I'll be in here next week ordering a new one."

Samantha took the lollipop out of her mouth. "Another new one. Aunt Twyla always breaks them."

"Is that so?" Mike chuckled. "Well, that happens, I hear."

Jensen slid his credit card across the counter. "Four microwaves in less than two years?"

Samantha tugged on her dad's sleeve. "But this one didn't explode, Daddy."

"That's something, I guess." Mike was laughing as he bagged up Jensen's purchases and handed over his credit card and the brown paper bag of supplies. "Good luck."

"Thank you." Jensen took the bag. "Give your father our best, please."

"Will do. Y'all have a good night." Mike followed them to the front door, all too happy to turn off the illuminated Open sign and lock the front door.

He was tired. "And it's only Monday." Then again, it had been a long Monday. He made his way to the back of the store, flipping off lights as he went. After locking up Old Towne Hardware and Appliances, he climbed into his truck and headed to his dad's little place a couple of blocks off Main Street. He had an old farmhouse with some acreage he'd been fixing up, but since his father's stroke, he'd been spending most of his nights on his father's couch.

As soon as he parked, he heard Clifford's bark hello and smiled. The dog had been intended to be their father's companion. Instead, the dog stuck to him like glue, and Mike was pretty attached to the dog. Thankfully, his father was content with his bearded dragon, Bongo, and his aquarium full of fish.

He was halfway up the path when he heard voices— kid voices. Archie and Kirby? Already? Meaning, Eloise was likely here, too.

Eloise. He paused, running a hand along the back of his neck. His father's hardware shop always had steady customers but, during downtime, his conversation with Quincy and the odd exchanges about the kids' father tugged at his brain. He didn't like it but Eloise had been weighing on his mind. And now... He'd had no right to look her up online but that's exactly what he'd done. After a few minutes, he'd learned more than he wanted. He'd closed down the browser and walked away from the computer.

Eloise had been married to Ted Barnes. The man came from old Highland Park money and had more connections than most politicians. Apparently, he was good-looking and smooth-talking enough to get a whole lot of people to hand over a whole lot of their money and "invest." But not long after he and Eloise divorced, the man was arrested for his not-so-legit investments. Mike didn't linger over the headlines of Ted's trial and conviction or the stricken images of Eloise; they had made his stomach churn.

The truth was the man was serving time for first-degree felony fraud and embezzlement charges. But since Archie and Kirby thought their father was traveling for work, they must not know.

Then again, how would you go about explaining all that to your kids?

Still, Ted Barnes wasn't a complete fool. There's no way the man could have gotten away with his scheme for so long if he'd been dim-witted. And he'd had the good sense to marry Eloise.

Mike scrubbed a hand over his face but he couldn't scrub the images or the knowledge from his brain. It ate at him.

The last few times she'd visited, she'd told him how tough things had become with her father. His drinking and his unpredictable moods—and his temper... It was her father's addiction that had driven them, forcefully, apart.

Then she marries some charming, sweet-talking yahoo who'd rather con people than do an honest day's work.

She had every reason to be standoffish and prickly. Yes, he'd gotten her back up that first night but her hostility toward him for doing his job and assessing the situation had seemed…extreme. Could her attitude be colored by the big blow-up that ended their relationship? For the most part, he'd moved on. But if he thought about the things they'd said to each other, it still stung something fierce.

He was reading too much into it. Eloise had more things to worry about than dwelling on long-ago hateful words and teen heartbreak—his internet search results had said as much.

The thing is, his search hadn't been out of idle curiosity. This wasn't some stranger—this was Eloise. Before that awful fight, she'd been…well, she'd been everything. He'd lain awake for most of last night, sifting through memories he'd locked up years ago.

Clifford's mumbled groan was audible through the door. When he pulled it open, Archie, Kirby, and Clifford all poured out onto the front porch.

"Good evening." He smiled down at them.

"Evening." Kirby hopped up and down. "We're here to see Clifford."

"So, I see." He tipped his cowboy hat back on his head. "You three having fun?"

Archie stood, pushing his glasses up on his nose. "Yep. But Momma said I can't take him for a walk."

"'Cuz he got in trouble for talking." Kirby crossed her arms over her chest and gave her brother a disapproving face. She looked a whole lot like her momma when she did that. "Momma said we should be happy we got to visit Clifford at all."

"I know." Archie sighed. "I can't help it." He shrugged. "I…talk."

Mike did his best not to smile or chuckle at that.

"You're letting all the bought air out." His father sat in his leather recliner. "Come on in and tell me about your day."

"He means, tell him what happened at the store." Rusty sat on the couch beside Quincy Green but there was no sign of Eloise.

Mike pulled the front door closed, stepped over the kids and dog, and headed into the front parlor. "Not much to tell. The place is still standing, if that's what you're worried about." He winked at his father.

"I didn't think I had to worry about that." His father wasn't amused.

"You don't." He gave his father's shoulder a squeeze. "How're you feeling?"

"Fed up and tired over people asking me how I'm feeling." His father sighed. "Other than that, I can't complain. I've got Quincy here filling me in on what I'm missing and these kids here to put a smile on my face."

Mike glanced back to see Clifford, on his back, with Archie and Kirby smoothing his fur and giving him a belly rub. "I don't think a dog could get much happier."

"Ain't that the truth?" Quincy chuckled.

"Did you see the flowers they brought?" His father pointed at the buffet table against the wall. "Sunflowers. And those pretty blue flowers there. What are those?"

"Delphinium. They're one of my favorite flowers." Eloise carried a refreshment tray into the parlor. "A snack and some tea." She set the tray on the coffee table, smiling.

Mike found himself lingering over how her green shirt made her eyes seem even bigger—greener. He tore his gaze from her and stared at the tray she'd brought in. He was pretty sure the contents of this morning's pastry box had been artfully arranged on one of his mother's serving platters, but he didn't say as much.

"It looks like we're one glass short." She headed into the kitchen before he could argue.

He wasn't sure what he was doing or why he was doing

it but he followed her. "I appreciate that but you don't have to wait on me, Eloise."

She opened the refrigerator and pulled out his mother's glass tea pitcher. "I appreciate you letting the kids smother your poor dog with affection." Her gaze bounced from his to the tea.

"Clifford's happy as a clam." He nodded his thanks as she filled up a glass for him.

"Well, we won't stay too much longer. The kids have school tomorrow and I like to keep them on a routine." She put the tea back in the refrigerator and closed the door.

"I get that." Mike sipped his tea and tried not to study the woman before him.

Did she really only have *vague* memories of him? It was a hard pill to swallow. Once upon a time, Eloise had a hold of his heart. Each one of her visits to Garrison had only deepened his affection for her. So much so that he'd married her beneath the sprawling branches of erste Baum. He might have been fourteen but, at the time, he'd been certain it would last forever. Instead, it was the last time he saw her—before their fight.

He realized he was staring and, for a second, she stared right back. "You...you and your grandfather going to the meeting tomorrow night?"

"It would appear so. Grandpa keeps telling me it's a big deal." She crossed her arms over her chest.

Mike grinned. "Garrison's a small town that values its traditions. Do you remember the egg hunts at Easter? The caroling along Main Street at Christmas. Or watching the fireworks in the summertime?" Holding hands during a hayride? Sharing a kiss under erste Baum?

"Vaguely." There was a ghost of a smile on her face.

That word again. "That's what makes this place special. It's about the memories you make and the community you forge. I'm sure it's a mite different than Highland Park, but it's a good place to raise a family."

Her eyes locked with his, searching. "That's why I'm here. For the kids."

"For Quincy, too, I'm thinking." He leaned against the kitchen counter. "He's perked up since you got here."

She rubbed her upper arms. "I don't know about that."

"I do." He sipped his tea. "It's good you're here, El-Eloise." The nickname almost slipped out.

For a split second, he thought she was going to say something. Then her lips pressed tight and she focused on the window over the kitchen sink.

"Momma, Momma." Kirby came running into the kitchen, with Archie on her heels. "Clifford shook. He did. He shook my hand."

Eloise squatted beside her daughter, all smiles. "He did?"

"He has a big paw." Kirby held up her hands for scale. "Mr. Nolan said it's 'cuz he's going to get bigger and bigger."

"He didn't shake with me." From the looks of it, Archie was pretty devastated.

Something about the boy reminded him of Rusty when he was young: a little high-strung and sensitive. He didn't like seeing his little brother upset then—he didn't like seeing Archie upset now. "He didn't, huh?" He scrambled to come up with a reason. When it came to tricks, Clifford was pretty treat-driven. "Remember what I said about Clifford being a puppy?"

Archie nodded, his frown too much for Mike.

"He's still learning things—like shake." He put his glass on the counter. "I bet I can get him to shake with you, too." He headed out of the kitchen, waving Archie after him.

Archie followed, dragging his feet and sighing heavily.

Clifford was sound asleep on the floor.

"I don't want to wake him up." Archie rubbed his nose with the back of his arm. "Momma says sleep is important."

"Amen to that," Mike's father sounded off. "But I'm pretty sure he'd rather play with you two while you're here."

"Are you sure?" The boy looked to be on the verge of tears.

"Yup." Mike opened the closet and, before he could pull the treats out, Clifford was wide awake. "All he has to do is hear that door open and he knows it means food."

"He's just like you, Archie." Eloise laughed. "Once you're awake, you're awake and wanting breakfast."

Mike handed Archie a treat. "Now, don't give him that until he shakes. Okay?"

"Okay." Archie stood in front of Clifford, uncertain. "Hi, Clifford. Shake?"

Clifford's tail was wagging but he didn't lift a paw.

Mike squatted behind the boy. "Almost. Use a strong, firm voice and I bet he'll do it."

"Okay." Archie cleared his throat. "Clifford. Shake."

Clifford lifted his paw.

Archie shook the dog's paw. "Good boy." He fed the dog his treat. "He's not like me, Momma. He's like Kirby. She'll do almost anything for a cupcake." He paused. "Except eat salad or peas or green things."

Mike was laughing then. And so was everyone else. His father's big booming laugh had been so absent, it was a joy to hear. From the looks of it, Rusty felt the same.

Then another laugh grabbed his attention. A high, free breeze of a laugh he recognized in an instant. There she was. El-Bell. She was sitting on the floor, with her kids in her lap, hugging them close while they giggled—carefree and happy and beautiful. Entirely present in the moment.

After everything he'd learned, he agreed wholeheartedly with what Quincy had said this morning. She deserved better. She deserved this.

Mike drew in a slow breath, pushing against the sudden pressure in his chest. He wasn't some naïve sixteen-year-old anymore, but he was having a sudden rush of his sixteen-year-old self's feelings. He didn't know what to do with that but he'd get over it. Like Eloise, he had too much going on in his life to add further complications. Something told him El-Bell and her sweet kids would be one big complication.

CHAPTER FOUR

"You're sure?" Eloise stood outside a jam-packed classroom of the Garrison Community Center. It wasn't the noise or crowd that got to her, it was the realization that this was the first time she'd leave her kids since they'd moved to Garrison. Other than school, of course. She couldn't help it, she worried—all the time. *A little too much, maybe?*

"I'm sure." Archie's enthusiasm was obvious.

"Look, Momma, there's Samantha. She's in my class." Kirby was almost jumping up and down with excitement as she pointed out a little girl with curly hair. "She's nice and she never gets in trouble."

"Hi, there. I don't suppose you're Eloise Green?" A woman wearing a khaki Game Warden uniform and baseball cap approached her.

"Yes, that's me." Eloise nodded, reading the woman's name badge. Carmichael.

"I'm Hattie Carmichael. Gretta mentioned you might be stopping by." She shook her hand. "I think we've spoken on the phone a time or two about the big to-do this weekend."

"Of course." Hattie Carmichael was the one getting married this weekend. It was nice to put a face with a voice. "It's so nice to meet you. Are you getting excited?"

"Not really—but don't tell anyone." Hattie had an infectious laugh. Even more so when a snort slipped out. "Forrest and I would be fine getting hitched down at City Hall." She shrugged. "But our families wanted to be involved so we sort of let them take the lead. That's how we ended up with a guest list that included all of Garrison and having our ceremony and reception under erste Baum."

There was something instantly likable about the woman.

Hattie tipped her cap back and put her hands on her hips. "I'm guessing these two fine young people belong to you?"

"Yes. Archie and Kirby. Say hello to… Warden Carmichael." She smiled at Kirby's wide eyes and slightly starstruck reaction to the woman.

"Are you a police person?" Kirby asked.

"What's a warden?" Archie pushed his glasses up, inspecting Hattie's uniform with interest.

Hattie nodded. "Well, Archie. I'm a Game Warden for the state of Texas. My main job is to make sure the animals and land in these parts are respected and looked after. But I'm also a licensed police officer, so I can arrest someone if the need arises."

"Wow." Kirby was impressed. "You're like a superhero."

"She doesn't have a cape." Archie pointed.

"Capes are dangerous, Archie." Kirby shook her head. "'Member in the movie? It showed that capes could get all tangled up and so it was better for superheroes not to have them?"

"Right." Archie nodded. "Are game wardens superheroes?"

About that time, a very tall, very handsome cowboy joined them. "I'd say so. I've seen Hattie here rescue baby deer, turtles, even an alligator once."

"An alligator?" Even Archie was impressed now.

"This is Forrest Briscoe." Hattie smiled up at the man. "He might be a little biased."

Eloise smiled. "I should hope so, you are getting married on Saturday. I'm Eloise, I have the great privilege of putting together your wedding flowers." She held her hand out. "It's nice to meet you, Mr. Briscoe."

"Forrest, please. It's a pleasure." He shook her hand. "Looks like we've got two new recruits?"

"Can we, Momma?" Archie asked. "Warden Carmichael is here and she'll make sure nothing bad happens. And if I act up, she can arrest me."

Hattie laughed at that. Forrest, however, looked slightly concerned.

"He talks a lot. His teacher sends notes to Momma all the time," Kirby explained. "Can he get arrested for that?"

Forrest relaxed now, grinning. "As long as he doesn't talk when Warden Carmichael does, we should be okay."

"Can you do that, Archie?" Eloise crossed her arms over her chest. "Because if you can't, you can just come along with me to the meeting—"

"I can. I can." Archie nodded, then pretended to lock his mouth shut.

"All righty, then let's find you a partner." Forrest ushered the kids into the room.

Eloise lingered, watching as Kirby took a seat by Samantha. Samantha squealed with glee, they hugged, and the two of them started chatting. Archie sat where Forrest indicated, beside a boy who appeared close in age. They looked at each other, nodded, then started talking.

"There you have it." Hattie smiled. "If only it was that easy for adults."

"Isn't that the truth." Eloise shook her head. "I appreciate this. I'm right down the hall if there's a problem."

Hattie glanced at Kirby, then Archie. "There won't be. You go on to your meeting and take notes so you can fill me in on what's happening." She grinned. "I'm sure there will be something to tell, there always is."

Eloise left the classroom, headed down the hall and turned left, into the main hall of the Community Center. It, like the classroom, was packed but with adults instead of children. She couldn't help the unease that settled over her. For almost a year, social outings included pushy photographers or tabloid journalists shouting questions about every detail of her old life. But that was over now and she was here. Besides, Ted's antics were old news for the rest of the world. He'd been incarcerated for over a year now.

"You look so pretty, Eloise. I mean, you look like a deer in headlights—but a pretty deer." Gretta placed a hand on her arm. "I felt exactly the same when I attended my first planning meeting."

"I wasn't expecting so many people. I thought this meeting was for the Main Street Association?" Surely, all of Garrison was here. She let Gretta steer her into the room.

"Technically." Gretta gave her a reassuring smile. "But Miss Martha made some calls. I guess it makes sense for everyone involved in the Founder's Day Festival to be here—it cuts down on the number of meetings, anyway. Now, let me introduce you to some folk."

She could do this. This was her home now, she couldn't keep hiding in her grandfather's house. She had to engage and network and, hopefully, have a life again. She'd dressed up, put on a light dusting of makeup, and done her hair—wanting to make an overall good impression. Grandpa Quincy had said she shined up prettier than a new copper penny. Kirby said she looked pretty. Archie, on the other hand, had no comment on her appearance.

But despite her best efforts, she still felt off-balance. All she could do was dig deep and paste on her hostess smile. It was one of the things she'd perfected when she'd been unknowingly helping Ted schmooze and swindle potential investors. She knew how to be just the right amount of gracious and engaging—things that had also helped her little flower and tea shop be successful.

"This is my father, Buck Williams." Gretta introduced a dashingly handsome older man. "Daddy, this is Eloise Green."

"I've been hearing quite a bit about you." Buck had a mischievous sparkle to his eye that reminded her a bit of Archie. "All good things, of course."

"Oh." Quite a bit? About what? From who? "That's nice to know."

"Making the rounds, Daddy." Gretta steered her on before anything else could be said.

"Eloise Green, this is Brooke Briscoe, Mabel Briscoe, and Kitty and Twyla Crawley."

"Brooke?" Eloise smiled. Brooke Young, now Briscoe, hadn't changed much. Except for the very round, very pregnant stomach, that is.

"Eloise? Oh, my goodness." Brooke hugged her. "It's been forever since I saw you last."

Gretta and Brooke introduced Eloise to a group of women close to her age. It was exciting and terrifying at the same time.

"Don't worry, the only one who bites here is my sister, Twyla, and she's on her best behavior." Kitty Crawley smiled at her.

Twyla shot her sister a narrow-eyed look. "I haven't bitten anyone since first grade. And RJ Malloy deserved it." She turned a guarded smile toward Eloise. "As long as you don't go putting gum in my hair, we will get along just fine."

"I promise," Eloise assured the woman.

"I can't believe you're here. It's been years." Brooke squeezed her hand. "Christmas, I think?"

Brooke had been a part of a lot of Eloise's adventures

3 SASHA SUMMERS   65

in Garrison. Not as much as Mike, but almost. "That was
a long time ago."

"Time flies. Now I own the town beauty shop, Young's
Beauty Salon. Kitty and Twyla own the Calico Pig bou-
tique." She pointed at Mabel. "Mabel doesn't have a Main
Street storefront."

"I'm here for moral support." Mabel had a warm, curious gaze. "And because I figure I have to represent the
Briscoe family. Not to imply you're not a Briscoe, Brooke."
She glanced down at Brooke's belly. "You are one. And
you're carrying one, too."

"Congratulations." Eloise had loved being pregnant.
She'd been lucky to breeze through both of her pregnancies. "Your first?"

"We have a daughter through adoption but, yes, first
pregnancy. Though, Audy is already talking about the next
four." Brooke shook her head. "He said something about
having our own basketball team."

"He doesn't even like basketball." Mabel looked confused.

"I might be married to him but that doesn't mean I
understand the way he thinks." Brooke arched back and
placed a hand in the middle of her back.

"You should sit." That was one thing Eloise did remember, backaches.

"I won't argue." Brooke rolled her shoulders.

"Watch out, move aside." Twyla had no problem making space. "Lady with a baby."

Not only did people make room for them, several folk
offered up chairs and refreshment to Brooke.

"That's why Garrison is special," Gretta said for her
ears alone. "When my father is getting on my last nerve
and I'm dying to go watch a professional ballet in a real
performance hall with a live orchestra, I have to remind

myself that this sweet little town would rally around me, my son, or my father in a heartbeat. It makes the two-hour-plus drive into any place with a decent ballet company worth it."

Once they'd all found seats at one of the large round tables, Eloise found herself searching the room for her grandfather.

"They're over there." Mabel looked toward the far wall. "My uncle Felix calls it the Old Cowboys club. Where there's one, the rest are soon to gather."

Sure enough, her grandfather was wedged in among a group of white-and silver-haired men seated along the edge of the room.

"Now that handsome fella there is my uncle." Mabel pointed. "You met Gretta's father, Buck?"

Eloise nodded.

"Then you've got Nolan Woodard—it's so good to see him out and about—and Doc Johnson. He's been practicing medicine since I was little." She went on. "Dickie Schneider is one of the young ones, but they tolerate him. He and his wife own the grocery store. That one is Earl Ellis. He owns the feedstore in town. And there's Bart Carmichael. He's Hattie's daddy and a real sweetheart." Mabel listed off a few more, offering up a tidbit of information about each one.

Eloise listened but there was no way she was going to keep everyone straight. She'd reached her limit and the meeting had yet to start. People were still milling around the refreshments table, clustered together and talking, with no hint of urgency. She glanced at her watch. Junior Rangers only lasted an hour.

It was only when a gray-haired woman came through the doors that the commotion died down a little. A distinguished older man trailed behind her, using a wooden cane for balance.

"Daddy came," Kitty whispered to Twyla. "I can't believe it."

But Twyla was smiling. "Good for Miss Martha."

"Miss Martha Zeigler and Dwight Crawley are quite the pair," Gretta whispered. "No one could have imagined it but…love finds a way."

As nice as that sounded, Eloise wasn't the romantic she once was.

"I think it's sweet." Mabel's smile indicated she *was* a romantic. "It's never too late to find the right person."

That part might be true. She liked the idea of finding the right person eventually. Way, way down the road. Now? No. She wasn't ready to open herself up for more disillusionment and pain.

From the corner of her eye, she saw Grandpa Quincy wave.

She turned and waved back.

But, between where she was and where Grandpa Quincy was sitting, stood a group she hadn't noticed before. A group Mike Woodard happened to be a part of. Fine. She could be neighborly. That's what being in a small town was all about. She'd set aside the hostility and whatever else his blue eyes might stir up and focused on the meeting.

"Oh, Eloise, how's that been going? Seeing Mike?" Brooke leaned forward to rest her elbows on the table. "Tough? That was a long time ago."

It had been years ago. Her father had her sent to Garrison under the guise of giving her a normal Christmas but that wasn't true. Her mother had been recovering from her first heart attack and her father was drinking more than ever to cope. If it wasn't for the alcohol, her father never would have hit her. But he had—and it forever changed their relationship. He'd had a hard time looking at her and she'd been wary of him. That was why her father had sent her to Garrison.

As soon as she'd arrived, she'd gone looking for Mike. She needed him, needed his gentle words and strong embrace. When she'd found Mike drunk with his friends, the betrayal was more than she could bear. He'd *known* how her father's alcoholism made her feel and how anti-drinking she was. The unexpected death of Gene Briscoe, the oldest Briscoe boy, had rocked the small town. Grieving was to be expected but drinking? Getting drunk? That's what her father had done. And, if her father could hit her, there was no guarantee Mike wouldn't do the same. It scared her. That had been *the* fight—the one that got heated and mean and ended it all.

When her mother had suffered a second heart attack and died a few days later, she'd been called back home. Her whole world had collapsed—taking all sense of security in the process.

She and her father never talked about what happened, how to grieve her mother, or how to heal. In fact, they never talked about much of anything. Instead, her father married Eloise's first stepmother and moved them halfway across the country from her home, friends, and family. After two more moves and two more stepmothers, she'd become pretty good at bottling things up.

"All of that is ancient history." And Eloise wanted to leave it that way.

"Mike Woodard is such a sweetheart." Mabel's gaze bounced between Eloise and Mike. "I can't believe he's single. He's quite a catch."

"That wasn't subtle. At all." Kitty Crawley patted Mabel's hand.

"That was painful." Twyla sighed, shaking her head.

Eloise would have agreed but she found herself laughing instead. Laughter was good. She needed more of it. So, she was going to enjoy herself, listen to what the formidable Martha Zeigler had to say and what was decided about Founder's Day, and ignore the odd looks Mike Woodard seemed to be sending her way.

"You KNOW, growing up, Dad said it was rude to stare." Rusty nudged his elbow.

The nudge almost had Mike dropping his cup. Instead, he splashed a good portion of his tea on his long-sleeve button-up.

"See." Rusty shook his head. "If you'd been paying less attention to her and more attention to what you're doing, you wouldn't have tea staining the shirt you spent thirty minutes ironing."

Mike shot his brother a look.

Rusty smiled back. "What?"

"Sometimes I wonder what it'd be like to be an only child." He used napkins to blot his shirt.

"Lonely." Rusty was unfazed. "Sad." He shrugged. "You couldn't make it without me."

Mike sighed. "Probably not."

"What's going on over there?" Tyson Ellis joined them, his gaze trained on the table where Eloise sat—the table Mike had been staring at. "You seem awfully concerned about whatever's happening over there, Mike."

"Told ya," Rusty murmured. "People are gonna notice."

"Wait." Tyson moved to Mike's other side. "Oh. I get it."

Don't ask. Don't say a word.

"Get what?" Rusty was grinning.

Tyson leveled a long, assessing look Mike's way. "That's Mike's El-Bell, isn't it? That's answer enough."

El-Bell was his nickname for Eloise. His and only his.

Everyone who'd known them back then knew that and how devoted he'd been to her. Especially Rusty and Tyson.

Growing up, the three of them had always been getting into trouble and covering for each other. The point both Rusty and Tyson were trying, miserably, to make was his present behavior was going to lead to a whole lot of embarrassment and poking and prodding at old wounds.

"I don't know what you're talking about." Mike turned his back on Eloise. "What are you doing here, Tyson? How'd Martha Zeigler drag you into this?"

Tyson tipped his hat back on his head. "Something about a Founder's Day rodeo."

"A rodeo?" Mike knew the woman was ambitious but to organize a rodeo in two weeks' time was impossible. "She's serious?"

"It would seem so." Tyson took a cookie from the expansive refreshments table. "I'll hear her out but I'm not promising a thing."

"I'd say it can't happen but Miss Zeigler does have a way of making the impossible, possible." Rusty reached for a cookie, too.

"I think that's the nicest compliment I've ever received, Rusty Woodard." Martha Zeigler stood behind them, a white baker's box in her hands. "I came to add my contribution."

Out of habit, all three of them froze. Over the years, Martha Zeigler had doled out many a deserved punishment for their youthful shenanigans. Whether it was riding their bikes through her flower beds, setting off firecrackers under her porch, or crashing the golf cart Tyson had borrowed, without his father's permission, into her white picket fence, she'd made them work hard to repair the damage and teach them respect. At the time, Mike hadn't appreciated the way she'd handled it. Now, he did.

"Allow me." Mike took the box.

"I appreciate that, Mr. Woodard." The woman glanced between the three of them. "I declare, you three are acting mighty guilty."

"Guilty?" Tyson's chuckle was forced. "No, ma'am."

"We're just talking, is all." Rusty's cheeks were red.

"Uh-huh." She gave them each a long, assessing look. "I'm keeping my eyes on you all so you'd best behave."

Mike had always admired her ability to put someone in their place with a look. She didn't have to raise her voice or carry on. Nope, one look, and that was the end of it.

"I see your sweet father is here." Her tone softened. "I'm glad he's on the mend." She pointed at the box. "You add those to that tray and don't eat them all yourself." And with that, she headed for the podium at the front of the room.

"Every time." Rusty shook his head. "Every time I see her, I feel like I've been caught with my hand in the cookie jar."

Tyson chuckled. "Don't I know it."

Mike chuckled as he put the box on the table, using the serving tongs to move the cookies from the box to the serving tray. He'd just finished when the crackling static of the microphone brought the room to absolute silence.

"Good evening, everyone." Martha Zeigler took a moment to look over the room.

Mike could almost imagine her taking note of those who hadn't attended.

"We have a lot to discuss and not a lot of time to do it, so let's begin." She lifted a yellow-paged legal tablet from the podium and turned the top page.

Mike was impressed with the woman's efficiency. The celebrations started with dawn's chuck-wagon breakfast and ended with fireworks at the fairgrounds. Somehow, she managed to convince all the Main Street shop owners to wear frontier attire, arrange for a farmer's market on the courthouse lawn, and have interactive historical booths and activities for children in the park around erste Baum. There would be hayrides from the main square to erste Baum and back, and a cattle drive down Main Street to the fairgrounds, and more.

By the time the meeting was all over, he had his phone out and was making notes.

"At least you don't have to put together a rodeo." Rusty sat back in his chair.

Tyson's brows rose. "Nope, just make sure there's no fire concerns and that the cattle are out of there before the fireworks start." He ran a hand over his face. "That's all."

"I'll help." Rusty slapped Tyson on the arm. "I'm sure the Briscoes will help out, too. And Jensen."

As much as Mike would have liked to lend a hand, he knew that he'd have to work. Big crowds meant a high risk for injury and a high need for EMT services. In all of Colton County, there were only four ambulances, a half-dozen certified paramedics, and a handful more of volunteer firefighters and medical professionals that could help out in an emergency. A festival wouldn't classify as an emergency, so he and Terri would be on duty.

All this was assuming he'd still be here. And that was up to his father. Until his father was hale and hearty, Mike wasn't going anywhere. He scanned the room and saw his father making his way toward them. And, from the looks of it, he was tuckered out. Quincy was walking along with him but if Dad went down, Quincy would probably go down, too. He headed that way but Eloise beat him.

"Is that the way these planning meetings always go?" Eloise asked. "I'm not sure I managed to process everything Miss Zeigler said."

A smile creased his father's face when Eloise hooked

her arm through his. "That's understandable. It's taken me years to figure out how to sift through everything and find that piece of her grand design that's my responsibility."

When Eloise smiled up at his father, Mike's throat went dry. She was beautiful. Her hair was free, a glossy chestnut wave that rested on her shoulders. Her lips were a bold red—the same as her dress. A wide leather belt encircled her waist, showing off curves that had him tongue-tied and admiring.

"Ahem." Rusty nudged him in the side. He coughed, cleared his throat, and nudged him again.

"Yeah, yeah. I get it." Mike tore his gaze from Eloise.

Rusty and Tyson were laughing so hard, there was no way his father, Eloise, and Quincy could miss it.

"What's so funny?" Quincy Green was already smiling.

"Mike," Tyson managed, then started laughing again.

"What about him?" His father shot Mike a curious look.

"Nothing. You know how these two get." Mike sighed, hoping that would be the end of it.

"Eloise, you remember Tyson Ellis? He was always running around with the Woodard boys when you'd come to visit. And, for the most part, he's still running around with them." Quincy patted Tyson on the shoulder.

"Nice to see you, Tyson. I admit, after that—" Eloise pointed at the podium "—my brain's short-circuiting."

"Understandable." Tyson touched the brim of his hat. "I remember you. You still scared of spiders?"

Eloise blinked, her mouth opening, then closing. All of a sudden, her gaze shifted and locked with Mike's. Was she thinking about that time a huge tarantula went crawling into their path and she'd climbed up onto his back—making Tyson and Rusty laugh so hard they had tears running down their cheeks? He sure was.

"You have a seat, Nolan." Quincy pulled out a chair as

he spoke. "No need taxing yourself while the young folk converse a spell."

When his old man didn't argue and sat, Mike knew it was time to head home. He poured a glass of tea, grabbed a napkin, and took two gingersnap cookies off the tray. "Have a little snack. Keep your blood sugar up." He set the cookies on the napkin before his father and handed over the drink.

"I'm fine." But his father took a long sip of tea and nibbled on the cookie.

"I'll bring the truck around." Mike waited for Rusty's nod. "It was nice seeing you all." He tipped his hat at Eloise and forced himself across the room and down the hall to the front door.

He'd almost reached it when he saw Brooke leaning against a column and fanning herself. He paused. "You okay?"

"I'm great. I'd be better if everyone stopped looking at me like a ticking time bomb. I know I'm huge but I still have another six weeks." She patted his arm, then folded her hands across her pregnant belly. "Leaving?"

"I think Dad's done in for the night." He paused, giving her a nod.

She glanced around, then stepped closer. "You doing okay?"

"Good. With Dad on the mend, I've got no complaints."

"I'm glad he's getting better—we all are." There was a pause. "You know I'm not a fan of gossiping, Mike, but Eloise's grandpa's been worrying out loud." She was whispering now. "All about how hard she is on herself, how closed off she is around folk, and not reaching out to old friends." She hesitated, then added, "I figure that stings a little, all things considered."

It did, but he wasn't going to say as much. "Considering how things were left, it's no surprise."

"Mr. Mike, Mr. Mike. I'm a Junior Ranger." Kirby came running toward him. "We made all sorts of stuff for the Founding Day festival. And I got to sit with Samantha. She likes horses and princesses. I like horses and princesses, too."

"Sounds like you had quite an evening, Kirby." He smiled down at the little girl. "Did you have fun?"

"Yes. It was the bestest time." She looked as delighted as she sounded. "Was your meeting fun?"

Mike chuckled. "It was…something. We didn't make anything but there were snacks."

"Any cupcakes?" Kirby asked.

"Mr. Mike." Archie arrived, turning this way and that as if he were searching for something, with Hattie Carmichael trailing behind him. "Is Clifford here? Can I say hi?"

"Clifford's still tuckered out from your visit last night." Mike winked at the boy. "But I'll be sure to give him an extra treat from you."

"Okay." Archie's disappointment was obvious. "I hope he won't forget us. I hope Momma lets us visit again."

"Let's go find your momma and find out." Hattie waved as she led the kids down the hall. "Night, y'all."

"Cute kids. Who do they belong to?" Brooke asked, watching them go.

"Eloise."

Brooke arched her back. "They sure seem to like you."

"They like my dog." He laughed. "If you'll excuse me, I'm going to bring the truck up for Dad. You put your feet up and take it easy—let that husband of yours wait on you."

"Oh, he does." She pointed. "See."

Audy had pulled his truck right up to the front door of

the Community Center. He was grinning from ear to ear when he reached Brooke's side. "There's my wife."

"I'm so big, it's impossible to miss me." But Brooke melted into his embrace.

"You're not big, you're perfect. My boy needs room to grow." Audy kissed her nose.

"Your boy? What if it turns out to be your girl?" Brooke asked.

"She needs room to grow, too." Audy turned. "Mike, didn't see you there. Too blinded by my wife's beauty."

Mike was still laughing when he reached his truck. It was a wonder the way things worked out sometimes. Not all that long ago, Brooke and Audy couldn't stand each other. Now, they seemed about as well suited as a couple could be. And he was happy for them.

He pulled up and parked in the spot Audy had vacated. When his father and Rusty didn't come right out, he went in to find his dad sitting in the same chair. He was smiling at something Archie was saying, but there was a definite droop to his shoulders. Tonight had been too much, too soon.

He didn't realize Eloise had come to stand by him until she spoke. "I think he'll need a hand getting to the truck."

Mike nodded.

"Is there anything I can do?" The concern on her face touched him.

"I appreciate that, El." He shook his head, then paused. "Your visit last night sure lifted his spirits. If you have the time, you and the kids are welcome."

She glanced his way. "I'm sure Grandpa would be happy to bring them."

His eyes met hers. "I'm pretty sure he enjoyed your company, too."

"*He* did?" She'd turned to face him.

Okay, if they were being honest—he hadn't exactly hated her being there. But he didn't say as much.

"It's best if they come with my grandfather." She took a deep breath. "I don't want people talking about me. Or me and you. With our history, I don't want people thinking we're pursuing…" She faltered.

Pursuing what? What was she getting at? "Friendship?" He frowned.

"I don't see how that's possible." Her full lips pressed tight.

"Maybe not." He cleared his throat. "But we were pretty good friends, once."

Her gaze was hard and her tone was brittle as she said, "Friends don't treat each other the way we did."

"We were both hurting. Both young." When he looked back on their fight, he felt as wounded and betrayed as he had the day it happened. They'd both been grieving and raw—too caught up in their own suffering to see how much they needed each other. And that grief broke them. He cleared his throat again, eager to leave. "I'd best get my father home to rest. I'm sure I'll see you around, El-Bell. You take care of yourself." He touched the brim of his hat only to find her staring up at him.

But she didn't say anything. Just stared at him with those big, wary eyes.

Even after he'd gotten his father home and into bed, he couldn't help thinking about that look. Had he done something? Said something? Did it even matter? She'd made it plain she had no interest in having anything to do with him. It was probably for the best. He'd follow her lead, leave the past in the past, and leave well enough alone.

CHAPTER FIVE

ELOISE BACKED IN the front door, a full grocery bag in each hand. "I'm back," she called out, only to find her grandfather and both kids sitting on the couch. "What are you three up to?" She pushed the door shut behind her.

"I'm showing them a little about Garrison and a little bit about you when you'd come visit." He smiled up at her.

"Grandpa says you're about my age in this picture." Kirby pointed at one of the pictures.

"How about I get some help putting everything away and then I'll come look at the pictures with you?"

"Now that's a plan." Her grandfather stood, took a bag, and headed for the kitchen.

Archie did the same, while Kirby skipped along beside her down the hall.

"The pictures Grandpa was showing us were real old." Archie started unpacking the bag onto the counter.

Eloise had to laugh at Archie's announcement. "I thought you were looking at pictures of me when I was young?"

"Yep." Archie pushed his glasses up on his nose. "Grandpa said you took your first hayride at the Founder's Day Festival. Me and Kirby will, too."

"That's true." She put the milk and orange juice in the refrigerator.

"Is it scary?" Kirby asked, taking the eggs from Grandpa Quincy and carrying them, with extreme care, to Eloise. "Archie says the wagon is pulled by horses and sometimes, horses can take off running for no reason. They can buck and bite and be wild."

Eloise paused, glancing at her son. "Where did you hear that?"

"Levi told me." Archie shrugged. "He's a real cowboy and he lives on a real ranch so he knows about horses and cows—cattle—and stuff."

"Who is Levi?" When had Archie been talking to a cowboy?

"He's so cool. He was at Junior Rangers. He knew all sorts of stuff."

"He was a helper?" Eloise had a hard time imagining Hattie being okay with one of the helpers telling the kids something like that.

"No, he's a Junior Ranger." Archie folded up the shopping bag.

"Levi Williams." Grandpa Quincy nodded. "Gretta's boy."

"Oh." Eloise put the yogurt in the refrigerator and closed the door. "I don't live on a real ranch *but* I know the horses pulling the wagon for the hayride will be gentle and won't take off running, Kirby."

"You promise?" Kirby didn't look convinced.

"I do." Eloise smiled. "I learned how important Founder's Day is at that meeting Grandpa and I went to. They wouldn't want anyone to get hurt. They will only pick the most gentle and best wagon-pulling horses around."

"Okay." Kirby relaxed. "Then can we go on the hayride?"

She nodded.

"Yay!" Kirby clapped and jumped up and down. "Samantha is going on the hayride, too."

"She keeps talking about Samantha." Archie rolled his eyes.

"She's nice. Levi's not." Kirby crossed her arms over her chest. "He said girls are stinky."

"I told him you didn't stink." Archie sighed.

"I think we're all done in here." Grandpa Quincy took the recyclable shopping bag from Archie and stored it away. "How about we go look at more pictures?" He waved the kids down the hall and smiled at her. "That Levi is a handful. From what Doc was saying, that boy tells tall tales that might just rival our Archie."

"Great." Just what Archie needed—a co-conspirator. She flipped off the kitchen light and followed her grandfather back down the hall to the living room.

Once they were all comfortable, Grandpa Quincy lifted the oversized album off the top of the stack. "Your great-grandmother used to get so much joy putting these things together." He ran his hand over the fabric cover. "She had some sort of subscription that sent her stickers and fancy scissors and stencils and such. I can't tell you how many stories we shared while she was making these books."

Eloise draped an arm along the back of the sofa so she could give her grandfather's shoulder a squeeze.

"She'd be tickled pink to know her great-grandchildren were looking at them." He chuckled. "Now, let's see." He flipped a few pages. "Here we go." He tapped one photo. "That's your momma. She was about six here. It was Founder's Day."

Eloise studied the picture. Another lifetime. A happy one—before her mother died.

Her memories of Garrison were warm and real and comforting. That's why she'd brought the kids here. She wanted them to grow up feeling connected and seen. And, maybe, she wanted that for herself, too.

"And that's your great-grandmother," her grandpa was saying. "There's always something fun happening.

You'll see. Your momma always had a real good time when she visited."

"Did you, Momma?" Kirby stared up at her, waiting for her answer.

"I did, Freckles."

"What about Dad? Did Dad ever come here?" Archie went from concerned to panicked. "Wait, will Dad know how to find us?"

"He has the address. I know, when he's able, he'll come see you both." She gave him a reassuring smile. Her sweet boy had always been anxious. The divorce didn't help. Ted "traveling" didn't help. But Archie's counselor thought that explanation would cause Archie less stress and anxiety than knowing his father was in prison. Prison was a scary and dangerous place—and, for the time being, too much for Archie's fragile psyche. Ted had, of course, been on board with this recommendation.

"Do you think he will move here, too?" Archie flipped the page. "He should."

"I don't know, sweetie. That will be his decision." Eloise couldn't imagine her ex settling here. "I know he'll do his best to be close to you and see you whenever he can." She hoped that would be the end of it.

"What's that?" Kirby was all too happy to get back to the pictures.

"That was a World Hat Day party." Grandpa Quincy shook his head. "Something the Garrison Ladies Guild put together one year."

Eloise smiled over the pictures of her grandparents. "Gramma Beryl looks so glamorous."

"She always was a looker." He smiled at the picture. "But your momma wasn't here for that so..." He flipped a few pages. "Here we go. Christmas."

The picture was like stepping back in time. "We were

caroling." She ran a finger along the edge of the photo. "I was trying to sing. But I'd been practicing so much that my voice was almost gone." Caroling was one of her favorite parts of Christmas and she'd been so sad.

"You sounded like a rooster trying to crow." Her grandfather chuckled. "If I recall correctly, the other kids sang off-key and real loud to make you feel better."

He was right, they had—at Mike's suggestion.

"Who's that?" Archie leaned forward to frown at the picture.

"That's Mike Woodard and your momma." Grandpa Quincy shook his head. "I'd say that boy's done some growing."

"*That's* Mr. Mike?" Kirby giggled. "He's little. Was he your friend, Momma?"

"Why does he have his arm around you?" Archie wasn't happy.

"He and your momma were sweethearts." Grandpa Quincy chuckled.

Archie crossed his arms over his chest, displeasure lining his face.

"I was cold." She hurried to explain, surprised by Archie's reaction. "He let me wear his coat but my teeth were chattering."

"That's a good friend." Kirby patted the picture. "I like Mr. Mike. And Clifford."

We were friends once.

Yes, they were. There were plenty of pictures of them together to prove that. Page after page of the holidays and festivals she'd spent here. Whether it'd been a Fourth of July picnic, hunting for Easter eggs, or caroling along Main Street, Mike always found her and—just like that—things were more fun. He'd included her in the shenanigans he and his brother got into and she'd loved laughing at all of his bad jokes and silly faces. He'd been sweet and funny and the person she'd looked forward to seeing most when she visited her grandparents.

Later, he'd been so much more than her friend. She'd loved him—really loved him. She'd loved the way her hand fit in his. She'd loved the way his arms had felt around her and how breathless she'd get from his kisses. He'd loved her, too. At least, she thought he had. She'd honestly thought he'd always be there for her. That he understood and respected her.

I was so naïve. He'd hurt her. A lot.

Grandpa Quincy was her mother's father. When her mother died, her father couldn't bear to have contact with anyone associated with her. Which meant Eloise lost contact, too. In a way it had been good—she hadn't known how she'd face Mike after what happened.

"I'm hungry." Archie was still frowning at the picture. "What's for dinner?"

"Chicken Alfredo." Eloise pushed off the couch. "Which I should start cooking."

"Do you need any help?" Archie stood, too. "I'm done looking at pictures."

"I'm not." Kirby leaned against Grandpa Quincy's side. "Show me more, Grandpa."

"You bet, Freckles."

Eloise waited until they reached the kitchen to ask, "Is everything okay? You seem kind of glum."

"Fine." He sat at the kitchen table, draped his arms across the surface, and rested his chin on the tabletop. Clearly, he wasn't fine.

"Bad day at school?" She filled the large stainless steel pot with water and put it on the stove burner. "Or something else?" With a turn of the knob, the blue fire of the gas range started. "Talking will help." She wanted to make sure her kids felt safe enough to talk and share their emotions—even when it was hard.

"I got another note," he mumbled.

She didn't want to be upset but she was tired of having the same conversation with her son. "What happened?"

"Some kid said we were poor and that's why we're living with Grandpa Quincy. I told him to shut up." He pushed his glasses up, then looked at her. "Are we poor? Is that why we live with Grandpa Quincy? But we can't be poor since Dad's always working so much."

Oh boy. Eloise walked over and knelt beside him. "We live with Grandpa Quincy because we're helping each other out. I help him at the shop and he helps us by letting us live here. It's what family does, you know? Look out for one another."

"Then why is Dad gone all the time? He should be looking out for me and Kirby."

She rested her hand on his back. "Your father loves you and your sister more than anything in the whole world. Don't you ever forget that." That was the one thing she never doubted about Ted: his love for his children. "Sometimes, being a grown-up is hard."

"Some dads have jobs that let them stay home. Why can't he have one of those jobs? Why, Momma?" He sniffed, rubbing his nose with the back of his arm. "I miss him."

"I know you do, sweetie." She leaned forward and drew him into a big, long hug. Archie wrapped his arms around her neck and held on tight. Her heart ached for him. As a mother, she wanted to take away her son's hurt. But this was one of those times where that was impossible. "I'm sorry about what happened in class today." She held him away from her and tried to smile. The tip of his nose was red and there were tears on his cheeks. "What can I do to cheer you up?" She wiped away the tears.

He was quiet for a while. "Can we have pizza for dinner?"

She was pretty sure there wasn't a pizza delivery place in Garrison. "Let's go ask Grandpa Quincy if there's someplace to get pizza."

"Okay. I'll go ask." Archie perked up a little. "Kirby likes pizza." He hopped down from the chair and ran down the hall into the family room.

"She does." Eloise turned off the burner. Surely there was someplace with pizza in Garrison. It would be nice to have a night out and not have to clean up the kitchen. And she could make chicken Alfredo tomorrow.

"Yay!" Archie's excited voice carried down the hallway.

She grabbed her purse and headed down the hall. "Are we going to get pizza?"

It took a good five minutes to find Kirby's shoes, but then they were on the sidewalk making the short walk to Main Street.

"I like walking, Momma." Kirby held her hand, skipping at her side. "My teacher Miss Rowe says that's one of the things she likes best about living here."

"I agree. I love that we don't have to drive everywhere." Garrison was such a pretty little town. Her grandfather's neighborhood was neat as a pin. It didn't matter if it was the grandest house on the block or one an eighth that size, people took pride in their homes. Yards were neatly mowed, sidewalks swept clean—there was even the occasional white picket fence. "And I love the trees." The town was full of tall oak trees that provided shade even on the hottest days.

"Erste Baum is even bigger. Miss Rowe says it's the biggest tree ever." Kirby kept on skipping. "In Garrison."

"It is." Grandpa Quincy was walking with Archie right behind them. "You'll get to see just how big it is this weekend at the wedding. And I bet you'll get to see some of your school friends, too. From the sounds of it, the whole town will be there."

"Do you think Mr. Mike will bring Clifford?" For the first time since earlier, Archie sounded happy.

"Well, now, I don't know about that. But I was thinking of stopping in on Nolan tomorrow, anyway. Seeing how he's feeling." Grandpa Quincy was close to Nolan Woodard. "I'm sure he'd be happy to see you all. I'll tell you a secret."

"What, Grandpa?" Kirby stopped and turned to face them. "I'm a good secret keeper."

"Me, too." Archie stared up at his grandfather, waiting.

"Well, maybe it's not a secret. More like life advice." He chuckled. "When you get as old as I am, you learn how important the little things are. Like making time for your friends and family. Nothing, I mean nothing, says you care or lifts a person's spirits as much as spending time with them."

It sounded so simple. Most of the people she'd loved hadn't wanted her time or her company, they'd wanted something from her or her compliance. It wasn't about *her*. But that was a different time and place. If she was truly going to make Garrison her home, she couldn't be so jaded. She had to give this place and these people a chance. She'd even try, for the kids and her grandfather, to get along with Mike Woodard. She'd try. But there was no guarantee.

MIKE'S HORSE, CHUCK, snorted and pawed at the dirt of the arena. "Yeah, I'm ready to go home, too." He patted the horse on the shoulder. "Not too much longer." He tipped his hat forward to shield the setting sun from his eyes.

From the stands, Tyson waved.

He nodded back, stifling a yawn.

He wasn't worrying over his father tonight—thanks to the Garrison Ladies Guild. Patsy Monahan had called the shop to tell Rusty the whole guild was coming to his father's place to lend a hand. According to Rusty, they were going to cook and clean and who knows what else. Unfortunately, Mike's plan to head home and turn in early had been foiled when Audy Briscoe had texted him a reminder about the high school rodeo teams' practice. Being an EMT and a pick-up rider, the team relied on him to keep everyone safe. Most of the time he enjoyed it. There was nothing like seeing a kid have a good ride or set a new personal best record and get a confidence boost. But he was dragging and it was only Wednesday.

"Good." Audy Briscoe called out to the teen on horseback. "Keep a hold of that rein, Hans." He rode closer to Martha Zeigler's grandson and adjusted the boy's grip on the thick braided material of the reins. "Believe me, you'll need to keep a hold. It might be eight seconds, but it'll feel a whole lot longer."

"Yes, sir." The boy nodded, listening as Audy gave him some more pointers.

With a light squeeze, Mike steered Chuck to the pipe fence that surrounded the entire arena.

Tyson walked down the bleacher stairs, a clipboard hanging from one hand. "How'd you get wrangled into this? Don't you have enough going on?"

He chuckled. "I gave my word I'd be at all the practices."

"I'm sure Audy and the kids appreciate it. Looks like the Zeigler boy has some talent." He nodded at the boy working with Audy.

"Yep. And Audy's a good coach." He yawned again. "What are you working on?"

"Making a list of repairs. That row needs replacing." Tyson lifted the top page. "The whole place could use an overhaul but we don't have the budget."

"Put Miss Martha on it. She'll put together some fund-raiser and you'll have all the money you need—and then some." Mike was only partly kidding.

Audy whistled, catching Mike's attention, and signaled they were wrapping things up.

"You eaten yet? I'm hungry." Tyson glanced at his watch. "You can turn Chuck loose in one of the corrals and come back and get him after we eat."

Mike rested his hands on the pommel of the saddle and looked at his friend. "You buying?"

Tyson laughed. "I didn't say that."

Twenty minutes later, he and Tyson were walking into the Buttermilk Pie Café.

"Evenings, boys." Miss Lucille waved from behind the counter. "You go on and find yourself a table and we'll get you taken care of."

"I'm gonna go wash up." Mike headed for the bathroom. He needed to splash some cold water on his face or he'd fall asleep at the table. On the way out of the restroom, he heard an excited squeal.

"Mr. Mike, Mr. Mike." Kirby came running and hugged him around the knees. "Are you here to have pizza, too?"

"Oh. Kirby, honey." Eloise reached for her daughter's hand. "I'm sorry," she said to him.

He wasn't. Kirby's cheery disposition perked him right up. "It's not very often I get such an enthusiastic greeting." He grinned down at Kirby. "Pizza, huh?"

"Uh-huh. I like pizza."

"It might be waiting for us at the table." Eloise wiggled her daughter's arm. "We should go wash our hands."

"Okay. You have to wash your hands to stay healthy." Kirby pulled against her mother. "Oh, and it's important to eat breakfast, lunch, and dinner. Miss Rowe says it's how you keep your brain and body healthy and strong." The little girl paused. "Miss Rowe is my teacher."

"Sounds like she's pretty smart." Mike got tired just thinking about corralling a classroom full of bouncy, curious five-year-olds.

"She's a teacher. Teachers are smart." The little girl nodded.

"Come on, Kirby. I'm sure Mr. Mike is as eager for his dinner as you are for yours." Eloise steered her daughter to the ladies' restroom.

Before the door closed, Kirby waved at him.

He was still smiling when he joined Tyson at their booth.

"What's that about?" Tyson glanced up from his menu. "That smile?"

"Can't a man smile?" Mike set his menu aside. He was so hungry, he knew exactly what he wanted.

"Hey, hey now. Someone's sounding hangry." Tyson cocked an eyebrow.

"Hangry, huh? I think you've been hanging around with the rodeo club kids too much." He hung his hat on the hook Lucille had added to the outside of each booth. She knew her clientele well.

"It means angry and hungry."

"I know what it means." Mike shook his head, chuckling. "I just never thought I'd hear you say it."

"What can I get you two?" Myrna Ingells stood at the end of their booth, a pad in hand.

"Hey, Myrna. When did you start working here?" Tyson set his menu down. "Things slowing down at the salon?"

Myrna was one of the beauticians that rented booth space in Brooke's salon. She'd been there as long as Mike could remember, long before the place was Brooke's—so seeing her waitressing was a first.

"Slowing down?" Myrna's snort was dismissive. "No, sir. I'm picking up some shifts. Trying to help my little sister finish college."

"That's mighty nice of you." Mike meant it. "What's she studying again?"

"She's going to be a nurse practitioner, whatever that means exactly." Myrna shrugged. "All I know is she's helping sick people get better and I'm proud to help her do that. So, you two know what you'd like?"

"Hamburger special. And a chocolate shake. And tea." Tyson handed over his menu.

"I think I'm hungry enough to go for it." Mike handed her the menu. "I'll take the Texas-sized chicken fried steak dinner. And a tea."

Myrna blinked. "You sure about that?"

"I'm sure." He smiled.

"Okay. It's your heartburn." Myrna took the menus and walked to the counter to put in their orders.

"Think your dad's surviving with the ladies?" Tyson asked, his gaze wandering around the restaurant.

"Oh, he's probably enjoying having a houseful of women taking care of him." He paused, thinking. "But he'll be just as happy when they go home."

"Uh-huh." Tyson's attention returned to him. "I see why you were smiling."

"Can we talk about anything else?" Mike heard Kirby's infectious laugh from somewhere behind him but didn't turn around. He did, however, smile.

"You wanna tell me why we're not talking about…that."
Tyson pointed at his face.

"There's nothing to tell." Mike wasn't smiling now.
"Whatever happened was fifteen years ago—it doesn't
mean a thing now."

Tyson's eyes narrowed and his mouth tightened, like he
was holding something back.

"Go on and say it." He propped himself up on one
elbow. "You're going to anyway."

"For something that doesn't mean a thing, you're awful
riled up about it." Tyson smiled his thanks as Myrna put
their drinks on the table.

"Riled up about what?" Myrna asked.

Mike glared at Tyson. If the man opened his mouth,
he'd kick him in the shin—but good.

"Oh, you know how it is. Your friends start getting married and people start asking you when you're going to get
married, that sort of thing." Tyson grinned up at Myrna.

"Wait a few years and people will stop asking." Myrna
tucked her pencil behind her ear. "You reach a certain
age and you're past your prime. Believe me, I know. And,
boy howdy, am I grateful." She laughed. "There's nothing
wrong with being your own person."

"That's what I was telling Mike. He shouldn't cave to
any pressure." Tyson's smile meant trouble. "You see, he's
always been a ladies' man. A heartbreaker. Not the marrying type." Tyson was having way too much fun. Mike was
no ladies' man and they both knew it. Tyson liked to give
him grief for being too nice—saying that's why Mike always ended up stuck in the friend zone. "A no-count love-
'em-and-leave-'em sort of man, that's him. Starting back,
oh, in high school, I'd say."

"Well, Mike Woodard, I'm surprised." Myrna's brows
rose high.

Mike opened his mouth to contradict Tyson's load of horse pucky but his friend cut him off.

"Oh, he is. Believe me." Tyson was near laughing now. "Not me, though. People say I'm too nice for my own good. I didn't think a person could be too nice."

Which is what Mike would say to him when Tyson would throw the whole "too nice" thing in his face.

"You can't be too nice." Eloise's brittle voice came out of nowhere.

And, just like that, things were no longer funny.

He leaned forward to see Eloise and her kids standing around the side of the booth.

"What's a ladies' man?" Kirby asked. "Or a heart-breaker? Doesn't sound very nice."

"I'm going to go check on your food." Myrna made a beeline for the kitchen.

Tyson was no help; he'd gone as still as a statue.

Now's a fine time to stop talking. Mike took a deep breath. "Tyson was teasing—even though it's not funny."

"Why is he teasing?" Kirby looked confused. For that matter, so did Eloise. Archie, on the other hand, looked upset.

"Well." He swallowed. "Sometimes friends do that." Which sounded pretty pathetic.

"That's not nice." The little girl shook her head. "Or friendly."

Mike turned to Tyson, silently pleading for help.

"You're right," Tyson managed, pulling at the neck of his shirt. "I'm sorry, Mike. I shouldn't have said that… Sorry." He took a sip of tea.

"Archie had something he wanted to tell you." Eloise nodded at her son, barely glancing Mike's way as she said, "Hurry up, before our pizza comes."

But Archie didn't say a word. Mike had never been on

the receiving end of such anger. But it was rolling off the boy—at him.

"Go on, Archie." Kirby patted her brother. "Don't be mad."

"Why do you love 'em and leave 'em?" Archie crossed his arms over his chest. "If you love someone, you shouldn't leave." Then the boy burst into angry tears. "You should stay. You should take care of them. That's what love means."

It didn't matter that every person in the restaurant heard the boy's outburst, Mike *felt* it. Every one of the boy's words was a cut to his heart. He knew that kind of anger. He knew that kind of hurt. It'd taken years to grow and heal before he could let it go. "You're right, Archie. I'm sorry. I'm so sorry." He didn't know what to do or say, but he had to do something.

Before he could move, Eloise had dropped to her knees beside her son and pulled him into her arms. "It's okay, sweetie." She ran a hand over his hair. "It's okay."

"I wanna go home, Momma." Archie's words were muffled against her shoulder. "I want to go *now*."

"Okay." Her arms stayed tight around the boy. "Kirby, please go tell Grandpa we want to take our pizza home, okay, sweetie?"

"Is Archie going to be okay, Momma?" Kirby was on the verge of tears now.

"He will be just fine." She managed a reassuring smile. "Don't you worry."

"'Kay. I'll go tell Grandpa." Kirby ran across the restaurant, too upset to keep her voice down. "Grandpa, we need to take the pizza home in a pizza box because Archie's crying."

"I don't want to go back to Grandpa's." Archie pulled

back enough to see his mother. "I want to go to our real home. I want my old friends. I—I want Daddy."

Eloise blinked rapidly, the muscle in her jaw tight. "I know, Archie. I know you do. Change is hard." She smoothed the hair from his forehead. "It's okay to be upset. I'm so proud of you for telling me what you're feeling. If there was a way I could give you everything you want, I would. But, I promise you, we'll figure this out together. Me and you and Kirby. And Grandpa Quincy, too. Okay?"

Mike was in awe of the woman. She didn't hush her son or get embarrassed over his outburst or care about the stares and whispers of the restaurant patrons. Her son hurt and that was all that mattered to her.

And Mike felt lower than dirt that he'd been the one to trigger such pain.

"Okay." Archie sniffed and wiped his nose.

"Okay." She smiled, squeezing his shoulders.

"I wanted to tell you that we walked here and I saw your brother walking Clifford so we said hi." Archie barely looked at him. "That's all."

Eloise stood and said, "You two have a nice evening." She kept her eyes on her son as they walked away.

He sat, trying to figure out what to do now. What to say. He couldn't just leave things this way. That boy… He swallowed hard against the jagged lump in his throat.

"Well, I hope you're hungry." Myrna slid his platter-sized plate in front of him. "You know the deal. If you eat it all, it's free." She eyed the plate and shook her head. "And your burger special." She glanced over her shoulder. "Oh, they're leaving." She sighed. "That poor boy. And his sweet momma. I don't know much about that family but something tells me they've been through a world of hurt." She patted the end of the table. "Let me know if y'all need anything."

Mike stared down at the mountain of food he'd been starving for not ten minutes ago. His appetite was long gone.

"I am sorry, man." Tyson groaned. "I didn't think... How was I to know... I'm sorry."

Mike nodded. It had been an accident. There was no way to know Archie had heard them, let alone how he'd react. But it didn't matter. The boy had heard. And his reaction would haunt Mike for the rest of his days. He couldn't let the boy think the worst of him. He had to fix it.

CHAPTER SIX

SATURDAY WAS A perfect outdoor wedding day. The sun was out, the clouds were fluffy and white, and there was enough chill in the air to keep things comfortable. Eloise hoped this was a good indicator for the day ahead of them.

"Where do these go?" Grandpa Quincy held a large white wicker basket overflowing with dahlias, hydrangea, lily of the valley, and white roses.

"I'll weave them into the arch." She pointed at the large wooden arch wrapped in green and brown vines. "But I can get it, Grandpa." As much as he refused to admit it, she knew lifting and carrying things was a struggle for him.

"Of course you can," he grumbled. "But so can I. That's what my cart is for." He set the basket in his collapsible red wagon. "There's no shame in making life a little easier."

"No, sir, there is not." She smiled. "Archie, would you and Kirby pick up all the flowers that fell inside the van and put them in Grandpa's wagon? Then you can blow bubbles all you want."

She stood back to assess her work so far. Each of the white folding chairs had a swath of tulle across the back. The end of each row had a distressed metal milk churn ready and waiting for the arrangements Eloise had waiting in the truck—along with the dozen flower balls to hang from the canopy-like branches of erste Baum.

She stared up at the tree overhead, marveling at its size. She'd never seen a tree this big before. It had seemed huge when she was little but children often see things as bigger than they are. Erste Baum was the exception to this. It really was huge. Kirby said it was big enough for a whole village of elves to live in. Eloise agreed.

"Ready for the ladder?" Her grandfather headed back to the van.

"Sure." While she climbed up to tie each of the flower balls to a branch, Grandpa Quincy held the ladder steady. "How does it look?" she asked, staying on the ladder in case she needed to adjust the twine length.

"I'd say it's just about perfect." Grandpa Quincy shook his head. "You're a creative one, Eloise Green."

She climbed down the ladder and smiled at him. "I'd say we're a pretty good team."

"Isn't that the truth?" He chuckled. "What else?"

She put Grandpa Quincy in charge of placing the aisle arrangements, made sure the kids were okay, then started on the arch. It was a painstaking process. Making sure each flower was visible while ensuring the cascade pattern hung in just the right way.

She was halfway through when she heard voices.

"Holy cow. This…this is incredible." Hattie Carmichael stood at the end of what would be the aisle with Mabel, Brooke, and Gretta.

"Oh, Eloise." Mabel placed a hand over her heart. "It's beautiful. It's like the flowers just sort of bloomed here— like they belong."

It always thrilled her to hear her work praised. "I was told to make it glamorous rustic." Which was a term she'd never heard before. "I hope this works."

"I don't know what you'd call it, but it's beautiful." Brooke was taking everything in, turning slowly.

"It's settled, if I ever do get married again, you're doing

my flowers." Gretta stared up at the hanging flower balls. "*Just* like this."

"Can we help?" Hattie asked.

"Um…" Eloise wasn't sure she was serious. "You're the bride."

"Don't I know it." Hattie shrugged. "I can't see Forrest. I don't want to get into that dress until I have to. My parents keep giving me these teary-eyed looks… Something you should know about me, I like to do things. I'm a doer. I can't just sit and wait or watch others do."

There was no way Eloise was going to let them help with the arch—she had a very particular layout. But her grandpa did seem to be slowing down. "If you're sure?" She waited for Hattie to nod. "Grandpa, you can go play with the kids, if you want?"

"I don't mind if I do." He grinned. "I'll leave you ladies to it."

It was only when the four women started helping that Eloise realized how quiet things had been. Now, the chatter and laughter made the work feel less like work and more like fun. She stayed busy, kneeling and crouching and bending to get the flowers onto the arch just right, while listening in on the conversation.

"I can't believe you're not nervous, Hattie," Gretta said.

"I didn't say that." Hattie's sigh was long and drawn out. "I'm nervous. I could trip in that big ol' poofy dress."

Eloise smiled, tucking a white rose and a cluster of baby's breath into the vines of the arch.

"That's not what I meant." But Gretta was laughing.

"I wasn't nervous when I married Audy." Brooke was sitting in a chair close to Eloise, her hands resting on her stomach. "I was…happy."

"And as long as I make it down the aisle without tripping, I'll be happy, too." Clearly, Hattie was worried about her wedding dress.

"You won't trip." Brooke laughed. "Go slow. One step at a time."

Archie came running up. "Momma, we're out of bubble juice."

"Already?" Eloise stopped working and sat back on her heels. "There's a big jug in the van. But let Grandpa pour it, okay? If you get some on your hands and wipe your eyes, it'll make your eyes burn."

"Yes, ma'am." He ran over and climbed into the van. "Hey, Warden Carmichael."

"Hey, Archie. You looking for this?" She handed over the jug.

"Thank you." He held the bottle close. "Are you getting married in that?"

Hattie looked down at her jeans and too big T-shirt. "I wish."

"It's all right by me." Archie shrugged, jumped out of the van, and ran back into the field where Kirby and Grandpa Quincy were waiting.

"Maybe I will get married in this." Hattie slid from the van, holding the last of the vases. "Then I wouldn't worry about tripping."

"You know Forrest won't care." Mabel came over to Eloise's side and sat on the grass next to where she was working. "My brother still gets tongue-tied whenever you wear a dress. He'll probably pass out when he sees you in your wedding dress."

Hattie dropped down in the grass beside Mabel, then lay flat. "I do kind of want to see his face when he sees me."

"That's the look." Brooke nodded. "That look that tells you he loves you more than anything and he's proud that you're his."

"Audy's always looking at you like that." Hattie groaned. "And Jensen's all googly-eyed as soon as he sees you, Mabel." She looked at Eloise. "I think we owe it to Eloise and Gretta to find them men who'll look at them like that."

"Oh, let's." Mabel perked up a little too much for Eloise's liking.

"You two sound like a younger version of the Garrison Ladies Guild." At least Brooke didn't sound excited. "Of course, if *we* don't find them their perfect men, then the Garrison Ladies Guild will hound them until they're satisfied."

Eloise paused, a lily in her hands. "That sounds ominous."

"Have you met them?" Mabel wrinkled up her nose.

"Grandpa Quincy told me to stay out of their way. He said they loved to stir up gossip and spread it all over everyone." Eloise glanced into the field where the kids were chasing bubbles.

"Your grandpa is a smart man." Hattie rolled onto her side. "I'm sure he'd agree with what Mabel and I are proposing."

"Oh, I'm sure he would, too." Eloise went back to work. "But I've made it clear that I'm not interested in dating—or finding the perfect man. Even if he does give me the look."

"Same." Gretta held up her hand. "No, thank you. I've got my hands full with Levi and the studio. I'm supposed to add dating?"

The rumble of a truck engine drew all eyes.

"It's not Forrest, is it?" Hattie hid behind Mabel. "He can't see me."

"It's not," Mabel assured her. "It's Audy and the Woodard brothers."

The Woodard brothers. And she'd been having such a nice morning. When she was being rational, she knew that the conversation hadn't been meant for her children's ears. But the overprotective, irrational part of her didn't care. She also didn't care if Mike was or was not some cowboy Casanova. What she did care about was her kids and how upset Archie had been.

"What are you all doing here?" Brooke tried to stand.

"Checking on you. You stay just like that, Brooke Briscoe." Audy hopped over one of the chairs to get to her. "How's my gorgeous wife?" He kissed her forehead.

"Pregnant." She sighed. "Very pregnant."

"What?" Audy jumped back. "When did this happen?"

They all laughed then. Audy Briscoe was a character. His open adoration for Brooke suggested things like love and commitment might still mean something.

"We were on the way out to the ranch and wanted to see if you needed help with anything." Rusty Woodard paused. "Did you do all this, Eloise?"

"I had some help." Eloise tucked the last bud into the arch and stood, dusting off her green overalls. "Let's see how it turned out."

She walked down the aisle, stopped at the end, and turned to take it all in.

Everyone but Brooke and Audy followed suit, standing alongside her.

Rusty gave a long, slow whistle. "It looks *good*."

"It looks beautiful." Mabel grabbed Eloise's arm. "I don't think erste Baum has ever looked so grand."

This was punctuated by a bark.

"Sounds like Clifford agrees." Mike scratched the dog behind the ear. "This is…something." He turned in a slow circle, then shook his head. "You've done it now."

"Done what?" She tucked a strand of hair behind her ear but refused to make eye contact. He had nice eyes—

warm and likable—and she really didn't want to like him at the moment.

"When Miss Martha gets a load of this, you're going to get put on every decorating committee for every festival for the rest of your life." Mike scratched his jaw.

"That's not at all dramatic." Eloise laughed, then realized no one else was laughing.

"Oh, Eloise." Mabel frowned. "He's right. It's too good."

"I'm so sorry." Hattie ran a hand over her curly hair. "Forrest and I should have eloped—that's what we wanted to do anyway."

"Hattie Carmichael." Eloise put a hand on Hattie's shoulder. "I forbid you to be anything but happy today. I did this for you and Forrest and your families and no one else. If you're happy, that's all that matters." She paused. "I can handle Miss Martha so don't you worry about that."

"Oh, I'm happy. I didn't know it could be this perfect." She smiled. "Now I definitely can't trip on my dress."

Clifford barked again, whimpering at the sight of the kids.

"Is it okay if he says hello?" Mike asked.

She nodded, but continued not to make eye contact.

"Let's go." Mike released Clifford from his leash and the dog ran toward the kids. "I think he's excited."

She watched, smiling as Archie and Kirby saw the dog and cried out, "Clifford!" in unison. If only they didn't love the dog. She sighed, her gaze accidentally tangling up on Mike's. If only he wasn't such a handsome…ladies' man? Heartbreaker? It was possible. After fifteen years, she couldn't claim to know Mike Woodard. Not that she cared, she didn't. She paid an inordinate amount of attention to an imaginary speck of dust on the front of her overalls. "I guess we're all done here."

"I can't thank you enough, Eloise." Hattie hugged her. "You should know, I don't hug people."

"I'm glad you think this is hug worthy." Eloise laughed and hugged her back. "I should get the kids so we can clean up."

"I'll walk with you." Mike waited. "I was hoping to talk to Archie."

She didn't slow for him but he matched her stride soon enough. If he thought her pace was brisk, he didn't comment. When she glanced his way, his waiting smile was a little too warm and a little too genuine to be a love-'em-and-leave-'em type.

Come on, Eloise. Just because she wanted everything she'd heard to be a joke didn't make it so. Wait. No. When it came to Mike Woodard, she didn't want anything. Well, that wasn't entirely true. "It's no secret Archie was upset the other night."

"I understand what he's feeling." He ran a hand along the back of his neck. "I was sixteen when my mom left us—I knew she was gone and not coming back. I was angry from the time I woke up until the time I went to bed." His gaze wandered to where the kids and Clifford were playing. "My dad tried but he never said anything like what you said to Archie. You keep talking to him like that, letting him get his feelings out, letting him be angry and sitting with him through it, and he'll be okay." He paused, then added, "It's good he knows you're on his side. Always. Even if it's hard, even though he's young, it matters now—and it will years from now."

And before Eloise could think of a single thing to say, Mike left her standing in the middle of the field and headed for her kids.

Mike's mom had left him? She'd lost her mother but her mother hadn't chosen to go. Mike's mom had. That was a pain she couldn't wrap her head around. And yet, it was his reality. It also offered up some explanation as to why Mike would be a player—assuming Tyson hadn't been teasing. And even though it was none of her business and she didn't care, she hoped Tyson had been teasing.

"MR. MIKE." Kirby greeted Mike with her usual exuberance, giving him an around-the-knee hug and a big grin. "You're here. And you brought Clifford."

"I knew he'd want to see you." He nodded at the dog, running around them in a circle. "He's so excited, he can't sit still."

"He's silly." Kirby giggled and ran after the dog.

"Quincy." Mike nodded in his direction.

"It'll be interesting to see who wears who out." The older man stood with his hand on his hips, watching Kirby and Clifford running.

But Mike was on a mission. "Hey, Archie." He cleared his throat. "I was hoping I could talk to you for a second? Man to man?"

Archie pushed his glasses up on his nose and nodded. "Okay."

He tipped his cowboy hat back on his head. "What you heard Tyson say about me sounded bad. Horrible, even."

Archie nodded.

"And I got to thinking, if I were in your shoes, I'd have been upset, too." He shook his head. "Tyson was teasing me—making up stuff to make me sound…"

"Like a jerk?" Archie shoved his hands into his pockets.

"Yep." Mike smiled. "He thought it was funny because everything he said was the opposite of who I am."

Archie's brow creased and he cocked his head to one side, like he was thinking.

"Kinda like if you or your grandpa said Kirby doesn't

like donuts or cupcakes." He was pretty sure he was going about this all wrong. "It'd be funny to you because you know it's not true."

"She loves donuts and cupcakes." Archie nodded slowly.

"Exactly." He took a deep breath. "I wanted to set the record straight. None of that stuff was true. I'd never leave someone I love—not if I could help it. Not ever." He couldn't help the gruffness of his tone.

"Grandpa said you and Momma were sweethearts in high school. Did you break her heart?" He crossed his arms over his chest.

Mike swallowed. "I don't think so." If anything, she'd broken his.

Archie was silent for a long time. "Mr. Mike, if someone does leave, does that mean they don't love you anymore?"

There it was, Archie's fear laid bare. And it was a knife to the heart.

Mike squatted by the boy and looked him in the eyes. "No, sir. Not at all. My daddy loved us but he had to leave when he was a soldier. He went off to do his duty to the Army but he still loved us and he came back just as soon as he could."

Archie thought about this for a moment, then nodded. "Okay." And he took off after Kirby and Clifford.

"I guess that's that." Mike chuckled and stood up—to find he had an audience. Quincy, Eloise, and Rusty stood, each of them wearing a very different expression. He took off his hat and ran his fingers through his hair. Had he messed up? Again?

Quincy came forward and clapped him on the shoulder. "You took a load off that boy's shoulders. And I thank you for that."

"That was some heavy stuff." Rusty ran a hand along the back of his neck. "I get the feeling I missed something."

"Tyson…being Tyson." Mike broke off, his gaze shifting to Eloise.

There was a smile on her face as she watched her kids running and playing and laughing with Clifford. When she smiled, it was easy to remember the girl he'd once adored. Time had passed, but she hadn't changed much. With her hair up in a ponytail and her green overalls, she didn't look old enough to be a mother. But the love she had for Kirby and Archie was all over her face.

"Anyway, we should be heading out. Gotta get back to the groom and all." Rusty shook his head. "I still can't believe Forrest's getting hitched." Forrest and Rusty had been team roping together since high school. While Forrest was pleased as punch to be marrying Hattie, Rusty was having a surprisingly hard time with it.

"It happens." Mike chuckled. "It's not like the world's coming to an end, Rusty. I hear some people even like being married."

Rusty's snort was answer enough.

Surprisingly, Eloise laughed. "I'm with Rusty on this one. Marriage isn't for everyone."

"Now, Eloise." Quincy shook his head. "You can't let one bad apple ruin the whole bunch. No man, or woman, is meant to be alone."

"Oh, really? What about you, Grandpa Quincy?" Eloise hooked her arm though his. "You've been single for a long time now."

"That's different. What me and your grandmother had gave me enough love and happiness to last the rest of my life." He patted her hand.

Eloise rested her head on his shoulder. "That's the sweetest thing I've ever heard." There was just a hint of wistfulness in her voice. "Well, I've got Archie and Kirby.

And you. So I'm not alone. What else could I need or want?" She smiled up at him.

"A man." Her grandfather answered so quickly, they all laughed. "A good man. One who'll treat you right and love those kids and—"

"That was a rhetorical question." She hugged his arm.

Quincy sighed as he let her go. "I'll tell you one thing, Eloise Lynn Green. You're as stubborn as your grandmother."

"Considering how much you adored her, I'll take that as a compliment." She released him and headed across the field. "I'll get the kids. If you're really set on coming to the wedding, I'm going to need time to get them ready—then myself."

"I want to show off my great-grandchildren and my talented granddaughter. Of course we're coming." He was frowning, his hands on his hips as he turned around.

"Whatever I did, I'm sorry." Rusty held up his hands.

"I'm not mad at you, boy. You didn't do a thing," Quincy muttered, his voice low and gruff. "You didn't have to. It started with her selfish father dragging her all over and taking her away from family. And that no good, lying, cheating, waste of a space she was married to made good and sure she'd never trust again. That's why she won't find the right fella. And it chaps my hide something fierce."

Mike and Rusty exchanged a look. Their whole life, Quincy Green had always been a generous and even-tempered man. It was a bit of a shock to hear him insult someone with such vigor—even if it sounded like the insults were deserved.

This new bit of information sparked Mike's temper.

Bad things had happened to the carefree, fun-loving El-Bell he'd pledged his heart to under erste Baum so many years ago. She'd had her heart stomped on over and over. Her father. Ted. *And me.*

He glanced across the field to where El was. She was talking to the kids, pointing at something in the sky, her ponytail blowing in the morning breeze. She was more than just a strong, beautiful woman. She was a loving mother and granddaughter and an accomplished business-woman. If she was happy, that was all that mattered.

"I shouldn't have run my mouth." Quincy's agitation was obvious. "Do me a favor and forget I said all that, will ya? I'd no right. El would never forgive me for airing her dirty laundry that way. It was wrong. I just... I—"

"We won't say a thing, Quincy." Mike rested a hand on the older man's shoulder. "I imagine I'd have a few choice words to say myself, if I were in your shoes."

"What my brother said, Quincy." Rusty nodded, his expression grave. "She's lucky to have you in her corner."

"I'm the only one." Quincy shook his head.

"She's in Garrison now, Quincy. It won't be too long be-fore she has the whole town watching her back." Mike hur-ried to offer Quincy reassurance. After his father's stroke, he was all too aware of what stress could do to a person.

"I know you're leaving soon, Mike, but..." Quincy gave each of them a long, hard look. "I'd be mighty grateful to you both if you'd help with that. I know she's prickly and stubborn and likely won't take too kindly to—"

"I will." Mike answered before he'd thought about what he was saying. Quincy was asking him to do the very thing Eloise had asked him not to do.

Quincy's posture relaxed and he took a deep breath. "Good. Good. I knew I could count on you, Mike."

"I'm not the only one." That last comment seemed a little too pointed. "Seems like she's made friends with Gretta. Hattie and Brooke, too." He ignored the way his brother was looking at him but suspected he'd get an earful later.

Clifford was panting when he reached them, turning every so often to make sure Eloise and the kids were still following.

"You keeping an eye on them?" Mike asked, giving the dog a scratch behind the ear.

Clifford's tail wagged.

"We have to get ready to go to the wedding," Kirby announced. "Momma says we have to use our manners."

"You always do, Freckles." Quincy chuckled.

"I've never been to a wedding before." Kirby shrugged. "I hope there's dancing. I like to dance."

"There is." Rusty nodded, smiling at the little girl.

"You know what else there is?" Mike crouched. "It's something I think you'll really like."

"What is it?" Kirby waited, her hands clasped in front of her as she leaned forward to hear him.

"There will be cake. A gigantic one, too." Mike held his hands apart.

"That big?" Kirby was impressed.

"What's that big?" Archie asked, only now reaching them.

"The cake." Kirby jumped up and down. "There's gonna be cake, Momma. And lots of it." She grabbed Eloise's hand and tugged. "Come on, Momma, we need to get ready."

"I'm coming." Eloise laughed and tucked a strand of hair behind her ear. "Say your good-byes and thank Mr. Mike for letting you play with Clifford."

"Thank you, Mr. Mike." Kirby gave him a big hug.

He was getting awfully fond of the little girl's hugs.

"All right, let's go. I guess we'll see you later." Eloise's gaze wasn't frigid—it was warm and clear when she glanced his way.

He nodded, touching the brim of his hat. "Yes, ma'am."

She smiled at that, then steered the kids—with Quincy bringing up the rear—back across the field to where the van was parked. Clifford ran after them, accepting more hugs and pats before they climbed into the van, then ran to Audy.

"You done staring?" Rusty adjusted his hat. "Or should I give you a minute?"

He glared at his brother and started walking. "Let's go."

The Garrison Gardens van pulled away and Clifford trotted back to them, staying by his side. "Get all that running out." He smiled down at his dog. "You get tired enough, maybe you won't chew up any more of the couch while I'm at the wedding." Not that Mike was overly upset about the couch—it was years past needing to be replaced.

"What was that?" Rusty fell in step beside him. "With the kid?"

"I know he's a kid and it might not make much sense to you." He glanced at his brother. "Didn't want him thinking ill of me, is all."

"Okay." Rusty looked like he was holding back a smile, but he let it be.

They made their way back to Audy without another word being said.

"I have to go." Gretta held up her phone. "Dad texted. Levi's asking if he can help cook and Dad said yes. I hope the fire extinguisher works." She all but ran down the path to her car.

"Mike." Hattie's tone suggested something was awry. And Mabel and Hattie were both wearing the oddest expression.

He stopped. "Something tells me I'm not going to want to hear what you two have to say."

"Oh, trust me, it's good." Audy chuckled.

"Behave." Brooke shook her head and said, "This is all Hattie and Mabel. Just so you know."

Rusty tipped his hat back, smiling. "This *will* be good."

"You know how the Garrison Ladies Guild is always tending to other peoples' business? Well, we were thinking, this time, it might be better if we interceded." Mabel glanced at Hattie, who nodded.

"That'd be kind of you." Mike knew Eloise would appreciate it, too.

"It's just you know they'll hound Eloise until they've got her paired up and married." Hattie put her hands on her hips. "Like they're trying to do with Gretta."

"With Gretta? Who are they pairing her up with?" Rusty's brows rose. "I haven't heard anything."

"Then you're not listening." Hattie rolled her eyes. "They're convinced she and Fritz Koch were a match made in heaven. He's got little Abigail. She's got Levi."

"Fritz? The high school teacher? Isn't he a little old for her?" Rusty scratched his stubbled jaw.

"Not really. And he's a nice man. But poor Abigail cries all the time." Mabel shook her head. "And Levi loves to make her cry. That alone is reason enough for them to find someone else for her."

"What does this have to do with me?" Mike had a sinking suspicion.

"You and Eloise." Hattie, being Hattie, cut to the chase.

"No." He crossed his arms over his chest.

"But it's you." Mabel acted like this explained everything. "I mean, Brooke and Audy filled me in—"

"Then you should know why it's impossible." Mike leveled a hard look at Audy. He couldn't bring himself to do the same to Brooke. "Besides, as soon as my dad is back on his feet, I'm leaving."

"You're really going to take that job?" Hattie was stunned.

"It's a good job." Rusty jumped to his defense. "He'll get to see more of the country, do what he loves, and get really paid for it. Why wouldn't he take the job?"

"Because we're all here." Hattie shook her head.

Mike saw the way they were watching him then. Except Rusty. Rusty was staring at his boots, his jaw clenched tight. When he'd told them about the job offer, they'd all been excited for him. He took a deep breath. "Back to Eloise." He adjusted his hat, antsy. "I think it's best if we respect what she wants. Friends. Not dating. That sort of thing." He didn't pause too long before he said, "We need to go. Forrest is waiting and, if I recall correctly, there's a wedding in less than three hours." With that, he headed to Audy's truck feeling uneasy. Today wasn't the day to second-guess his career choices or worry about Hattie and Mabel pairing Eloise up with someone else in town. Today, two of his best friends were getting married and he wanted to celebrate that.

CHAPTER SEVEN

"DID YOU WEAR a big white dress when you and Daddy got married, Momma?" Kirby sat on the stool in front of the antique vanity in Eloise's room. She was swinging her legs, chattering away, while Eloise braided her hair.

"I did." Her wedding had been quite a production. Big and over-the-top in every way. She didn't want to think about how much money it'd cost—or where the money had come from. Thinking back, she had so many questions about her life with Ted. But she was pretty sure she wouldn't like any of the answers.

"Was the dress poofy like a cloud?" Kirby picked up one of Eloise's makeup brushes.

"It was. It was so big it was hard to dance at the reception."

That made Kirby smile. "What's a reception?"

"The party after the wedding." She used a hair tie to secure the braid that hung halfway down her daughter's back. "All done."

Kirby looked in the mirror. "I like it. Thank you, Momma." She turned on her stool. "Mr. Mike said there will be dancing. I want to dance."

"We will." Eloise started pulling the hot rollers from her hair and frowned. Her hair was hopeless. It was mousy brown, too thick, and had no natural curl. It went frizzy when it rained or was too humid. No matter what she tried to do with it, it didn't work—like now. The few curls that had set were too tight. Out of habit, she pulled some bobby pins from the jar on the vanity and picked up her brush. She'd worn her hair up every day in Highland Park, but now she paused.

She put the bobby pins away and ran a brush through it, pondering options. The headband she'd bought for Kirby, which her daughter refused to wear, hung on the necklace stand on the vanity top. She reached for it and slid it into her hair and sat back. Was she too old for headbands?

"You look pretty, Momma." Kirby smiled up at her. "You do."

"Thank you, sweetie." Kirby approved and that was enough. "I think we're ready."

"Yay. Time for cake and dancing. And cake." Kirby clapped her hands and ran from Eloise's bedroom.

Her grandfather and Archie were in the family room. Eloise had picked up a puzzle the last time she was at the store and it had been a hit for the whole family. The coffee table was now the puzzle table. Archie sat on the floor with a puzzle piece in his hand. Grandpa Quincy perched on the edge of the sofa, sorting through a pile of pieces. They were both too focused to notice their arrival.

"No fair." Kirby ran to the coffee table. "We're supposed to work on it together."

"I was only sorting through the piles here, Freckles." Her grandfather stood. "My, my, aren't I the luckiest man in town? I get to escort the two loveliest women in all of Garrison."

Eloise rolled her eyes but Kirby was all smiles as she spun in her pink dress with tiny blue flowers.

"You do look nice." Archie stood, shoving his hands into his pockets. "Momma, do I have to dance? Levi said you get cooties from dancing with girls."

Eloise managed not to smile. "Cooties?" The fear of cooties had been around since she was a kid.

"Levi said it'll make you sick. Your hands turn green and you throw up and your eyes bulge out." And Archie believed every word of it. "He said he wouldn't dance with anyone. Not even his mom."

Poor Gretta.

"Didn't you get the kids their cootie vaccine when they had their last doctor visit, Eloise?" Grandpa Quincy asked, his expression grave. "You got some shots, didn't you?"

She was impressed that her grandfather managed to keep a straight face.

Archie thought for a minute. "Yes."

"And they hurt." Kirby rubbed her upper arm like she was still sore.

"Well, there you go." Grandpa Quincy nodded. "You don't need to worry about cooties. You can dance all you want."

Archie relaxed. "Okay, then. You should tell Levi's mom so he can get one, too."

"We need to scoot or we'll be late." Grandpa Quincy led them to the front door, giving her a wink.

Sometimes her grandfather was almost as mischievous as her kids. Maybe Archie didn't get all of his storytelling abilities from his father after all.

The kids chattered about weddings the whole way to erste Baum Park. Archie was set on having his wedding in outer space. He wanted aliens to shoot firework laser guns and his guests would all bring bubbles. Kirby said she wanted to get married underwater with mermaids and sea turtles. Then she would ride off on a pink dolphin. They were still talking about it when they parked in the nearly full parking lot.

"But I want bubbles, too," Kirby said, waiting for her mother to unbuckle her from her booster seat.

"Copycat." Archie jumped out of the back seat of Grandpa Quincy's car.

"Archie." Eloise used her mom voice. "Remember what I said about today?"

"I need to be on my best behavior." Archie nodded. "Sorry, Kirby."

"It's okay. I was copycatting. I like bubbles, like you." Kirby grinned at her brother.

Archie smiled back.

This was one of those rare moments where Eloise was content.

Grandpa Quincy took Kirby's hand and Eloise held Archie's before the four of them walked the long path from the parking lot to the shade of erste Baum.

"Hattie wasn't kidding." Eloise was stunned at the number of people. "This has to be the whole town."

"Looks like it." Her grandfather nodded. "And all of them are going to be tickled pink by what you did for Hattie and Forrest's wedding."

"*We* did."

Grandpa Quincy snorted. "You came up with the plans, El. I just did what you told me to do."

"I'm sorry. I didn't mean to take over—"

"Hold up, now. I wasn't complaining. Not one bit. I kinda liked it." He patted her shoulder. "I'm not as creative as I once was. You've got more creativity in your little finger than...well, I do." He chuckled.

"You're sure?" The last thing she'd ever want to do is run ramrod over her precious grandfather. "You'd tell me if I stepped on your toes?"

"Why would you step on Grandpa's toes?" Kirby asked.

"That hurts." Archie looked up at her.

"It's an expression." Grandpa Quincy was laughing now. "Your momma would never step on my toes. Your momma wouldn't hurt a fly." He paused. "That's another expression. It means she's nice to everyone."

"Oh." Kirby's expression was pure confusion.

"I see Levi." Archie tugged on her hand. "He's right there."

Eloise glanced in the direction he was pointing. Sure enough, there was Gretta and her father. The little boy in the too-big cowboy hat sitting between them had to be Levi.

"And there's Samantha." Kirby's squeal was pure delight.

Samantha sat at the end of one row, a big bow in her curly hair. She'd seen Kirby and was waving excitedly.

Kirby waved back.

"Let's go find us some seats before there aren't any." Grandpa Quincy led them down the rest of the hill to the rows of chairs Eloise had decorated earlier.

"Quincy." The voice was commanding. "I have a bone to pick with you."

Eloise recognized Martha Zeigler but not the handful of women following in her wake. Was this the dreaded Garrison Ladies Guild?

"And a good afternoon to you, Martha." Her grandfather smiled at the woman.

"Why didn't you tell me what your granddaughter was capable of?" The woman turned and gave Eloise a head-to-toe inspection. Her gaze was shrewd, assessing. "This is…well, this is… I mean to say… This is a wonder."

"Thank you?" Eloise glanced at her grandfather for translation.

"No, no, thank you." Martha Zeigler was openly studying her. "I'm so glad you've moved to Garrison."

The way she said it made Eloise nervous. "Thank you." She swallowed.

A woman with fire-engine-red hair joined them. "Brooke was telling me all about you." She rested a hand against her bountiful chest. "We're the Garrison Ladies Guild. I'm sure your grandpa has told you all about us?"

If they only knew what her grandpa had said about them. Eloise only smiled and nodded.

"Well, I'm Miss Patsy. That's Dorris Kaye—watch out, she's a bit of a gossip." She pointed at the woman wearing a bold flower-print dress. "That tall string bean over there is Pearl Johnston. Don't let that face fool you, she's got a wicked sense of humor. And somewhere around here is Barbara Eldridge."

"The service is about to start, but I'll find you during the reception." Miss Martha continued to study her. "I have a proposition for you."

And just like that, the ladies left.

"There they go, waddling off all proud-like," her grandpa whispered.

"They're not that bad." She glanced his way, saw the look on his face, and asked, "Are they?"

He shrugged. "Let's find our seats."

It took time and a little maneuvering to get four chairs together but, finally, they were seated. Not ten seconds later, the groom and his groomsmen took their place on the right side of the arch.

Forrest Briscoe stood proud and tall, his eyes fixed on the path of rose petals serving as the aisle. His groomsmen, Audy and Rusty, were at his side. Of all of them, Rusty seemed nervous—shifting from foot to foot while his gaze never stopped moving.

"That's Mr. Forrest," Kirby whispered loudly. "He was at Junior Rangers."

Eloise nodded and patted her daughter's leg.

The strum of a guitar echoed from the back and Eloise turned to see who was playing.

Mike. He sat on a stool, one leg kicked up, playing the strings of his classic acoustic guitar with ease. Like the groomsmen, he wore black jeans, a starched white button down, black boots, and a black felt cowboy hat. Only, on Mike, it was more...he was more... He was the very definition of a handsome, manly man.

Eloise swallowed hard. She'd heard every word he'd said to Archie. While he'd cleared the air with Archie, he'd left her more confounded than ever. Did he believe what he'd said? That he hadn't broken her heart?

Everyone stood, blocking Eloise's view and making her acutely aware of how distracted she'd been by the man.

"I can't see, Momma." Kirby tugged on her arm.

Eloise lifted Kirby onto her hip. "Better?"

Kirby nodded, staring with wide, curious eyes. "She looks so pretty."

But Eloise didn't look at Hattie, not yet. Instead, she waited to see Forrest's reaction. And when he looked up, Eloise felt tears stinging the corners of her eyes. To see such a big, brawny man gasp was powerful. He shook his head, one hand covering his mouth—struggling to control his emotions.

Eloise wasn't a romantic anymore, but this... It was hard not to be when faced with such love.

When she turned her attention to Hattie, her eyes burned all the more. Hattie Carmichael was a beautiful bride. Yes, her dress was big and poofy, but she needn't have worried about tripping. With her father's help, she was gliding down the aisle—solely focused on the man waiting for her.

"Why are you crying, Momma?" Kirby whispered.

"They're happy tears," Eloise whispered back. "I'm so happy for them."

Kirby didn't say a thing, she just hugged her tight and rested her head on Eloise's shoulder.

Eloise pressed a kiss to the top of her daughter's head and, with the rest of the guests, sat when Hattie reached her groom. Kirby crawled back into her seat and sat up on her knees, transfixed.

The service was short and sweet. Hattie and Forrest were oblivious to everyone else. Mabel and Brooke, Hattie's bridesmaids, cried. Audy spent most of the time staring at his wife while Rusty pulled at his collar. When Hattie and Forrest kissed, the crowd erupted and that was that.

"Ew. They kissed." Archie's wrinkled-up nose was all disgust.

"That's how you seal the deal." Grandpa Quincy chuckled. "One day, you won't mind kissing so much."

Archie stuck his tongue out. "No way, Grandpa. Now what?"

"Now, we move the chairs to those tables over there and we get the dance floor set up." He paused, smiling. "Nolan made it."

"You can go keep him company, Grandpa. I'm sure Rusty and Mike would appreciate someone keeping an eye on him—so he doesn't get overtired." It wouldn't hurt for her grandfather to sit a while, either.

"If you're sure?" He waited for her nod, then patted her on the cheek and headed toward his friend.

"Are we supposed to help?" Kirby was already trying to pick up her chair.

"I can do it." Archie lifted his. "See?"

"And you're doing a good job, too." Eloise's words

trailed off as Mike approached. Why was he heading their way? And why did he have to smile that way?

"Need a hand?" He reached for Kirby's chair.

"I can do it." Kirby's arms shook beneath the weight of the chair.

"I believe it." He crouched. "But I'm a gentleman, Kirby. That means I like to do chivalrous things. Like opening doors for ladies. Or carrying their chairs for them."

"Oh." Kirby seemed to think about this for a second, then offered him the chair. "Thank you, Mr. Mike."

He smiled and stood, those warm eyes of his locking with hers. "Eloise."

She swallowed, hard. "Mike."

"You're beautiful." He cleared his throat, then said, "You and Kirby both…are. Let's move these chairs, Archie." And with that, he folded and carried four chairs while Archie carried one.

Eloise tried not to notice what a fine figure he made as he walked and talked to her son. She tried not to think about the sweetness of his awkward compliment or what a truly handsome man he was. She tried. But it didn't work.

HE'D MADE A deal with Quincy and he'd honor it. He'd be Eloise's friend. That's all. Friends helped each other out and gave each other compliments. Friends didn't get tongue-tied and doe-eyed over each other. He was pretty sure he'd just done both.

It'd help if she wasn't the prettiest woman here. But she was. Seeing her under erste Baum, with tears in her eyes and a gentle smile on her lips, had dragged him back to the last time he'd seen her here, all those years ago. He'd been so caught off guard, he'd played the wrong notes. No one noticed. At least, he hoped no one had.

He had to stop this. The staring was bad enough. But

getting sentimental over things best left in the past was asking for trouble. She was his first love and, for that reason, she'd always be special to him. But no one met their soulmate when they were nine years old. It was ridiculous to even think it.

"Mr. Mike?" Archie was staring at him. "You okay?"

Mike realized he'd been standing next to a table, holding the chairs, and staring off into space. *Not at all conspicuous.* "I am." He started setting up chairs. "How's your day been going, Archie?"

"Okay, I guess." He shrugged. "I'm kinda bored. And my stomach hurts a little."

"You okay?" A quick inspection showed the boy's color was normal, he wasn't sweating, and there was no labored breathing or signs of distress.

"Yeah." He sighed. "Too bad you didn't bring Clifford."

"I didn't want him eating the wedding cake before the bride and groom cut it." Mike set up the last chair. "And, believe me, he would have. He's fast and sneaky. That cake wouldn't have stood a chance."

That had Archie smiling. "You should take him a piece."

"I don't know. He's got enough energy without giving him sugar." He glanced back in the direction they'd come.

Eloise was talking with Mabel while Samantha and Kirby were going row by row, smelling the bouquets at each end.

"Should we get some more chairs?" Archie tugged on his arm, glancing back and forth between Mike and Eloise.

"How about we get your grandpa and my dad to come sit over here first?" He pointed out where the old men sat. "Then maybe get some punch?"

"I like punch." Archie walked with him. "Do you think you'll get married, Mr. Mike?"

"Oh, maybe someday." If his father had it his way, it would be sooner rather than later. "Why are you asking?"

"Will you kiss her?" Archie's disgusted expression had Mike swallowing down his laughter.

"Well, now…" He paused, nodding slowly. "I guess I will."

"You will?" Archie shuddered. "If I ever get married, I'm not kissing her. No way."

Mike couldn't help but laugh then. He'd have to check in with Archie in another eight or nine years and see how the boy felt then.

Mike stayed busy. Once he got his father and Quincy set up at a table with Archie, he went back to moving chairs. When that was done, he helped set up the dance floor. If there was something that needed doing, he volunteered. But, through it all, he was acutely aware of Eloise. Her voice. Her laugh. The way she'd run her fingers through her hair or tuck a strand behind her ear.

He forced himself to focus on Hattie and Forrest as they cut the wedding cake.

"Be nice." Hattie shot Forrest a warning look as he prepared to feed her a bite of cake.

"I'm always nice." True to his word, Forrest was careful.

Hattie, on the other hand, got great joy out of smearing frosting across Forrest's chin.

"You knew she was going to do that." Tyson gave Mike a firm nudge in the ribs.

"Ow." He rubbed his side. "Forrest doesn't seem to mind."

Forrest had pulled Hattie into his arms and was kissing her, making sure she wasn't frosting-free before it was all over.

"Your brother holding up? He looked like he was going to hyperventilate up there."

"I don't think I realized how much Rusty hates weddings until today." He and his brother had both been affected by their mother's desertion. "Unless something changes, I don't see him walking down an aisle any time soon." Or ever.

"I'm not saying it would have been funny if he'd passed out but... I'd have laughed." Tyson shrugged and headed toward the giant six-layer wedding cake. "I'm getting some cake."

Mike followed. He and his brother tried to limit their heart-to-heart talks, but this might be one of those times. Mike struggled with the wounds his mother had caused, but he was pretty sure it wouldn't interfere with him having a future—a family. With Rusty, he wasn't so sure.

He got enough plates for his father and Quincy and reached the table to find it occupied with all of his father's cronies. "Sorry. I only brought two." He put a plate in front of his father and Quincy.

There was a lot of general grumbling and some heckling, but Mike brushed it off.

"There's a chair over here." Brooke waved him over. "And I won't be mad at you for not getting me cake."

Mike paused, taking in the other occupants at the table. Mabel. Gretta. And Eloise. "I can get you cake."

"Audy is." She smiled up at him. "But you're a sweetheart for offering."

"Anyone else?" He glanced around the table, hoping one of them would send him on his way.

"Nope." Mabel shook her head.

"Already had some." Gretta smiled. "But it's nice of you to ask."

"No cake for me." Eloise sighed. "Not if I'm ever going to fit into my jeans again."

Mike frowned. Was that some sort of dig at her weight?

As far as he was concerned, she was perfect. Any less and she'd be too skinny. But nobody asked him and he was doing his best not to offer up his opinion unsolicited.

"It's bad luck." Gretta turned to Eloise.

"That's birthday cake. Everyone has to have a bite for good luck. Not weddings." Eloise smiled, then paused. "Isn't it?"

"Don't ask me." Brooke shrugged. "Mike?"

"As a general rule, if there's cake, I eat it." He loved to hear Eloise laugh. Too much. "So, no cake?"

"Now I'm worried." Eloise stood. "But I can get it myself, thank you. And I should probably check on Archie."

He hadn't intended to watch her walk away.

"Mike Woodard." Brooke hissed. "Sit down, right now."

He sat.

"You should ask her to dance." Mabel propped her elbow on the table and rested her chin in her hand.

"No, he should not." Brooke sighed. "You should dance with anyone except Eloise."

Mabel huffed. "But Brooke—"

"Mabel, Dorris Kaye already asked if Eloise was the little girl Mike used to follow around like a puppy. And Pearl Johnston said something about first loves lasting forever. Then Nolan said something about her being Mike's first love." Brooke shook her head. "Mike's not interested. He needs to be careful."

Mike seriously regretted sitting down. "Where's Audy?" If Audy were here, this conversation wouldn't be happening.

"He's coming." Brooke's forehead smoothed. "With the biggest piece of cake I've ever seen." But she was smiling.

When Audy sat, Mike sighed in relief.

"These ladies grilling you?" Audy asked. "You were panicking." He scooped up a bite of Brooke's cake with a fork. "Not as bad as Rusty was earlier—but I'm not sure I've ever seen someone that uneasy."

"Poor Rusty." Brooke took a bite of cake. "Oh, this is too good."

Audy nodded. "Where'd he run off to? Rusty, I mean?"

Mike hadn't realized his brother had left. He scanned the crowd, but no Rusty. Now he was concerned. "I'm not sure. But I think I'll go find out." He stood. "If you'll excuse me."

"You want some help?" Gretta's concern was sincere.

"I don't think so." He touched the brim of his hat. "But I'll let you know if that changes." He did his best to be casual about his search, making small talk as he worked through the tables and doing his best to fly under the radar. But he made the mistake of standing too close to a table he should have avoided altogether.

"Mike Woodard." It was Martha Zeigler. "You've been running around like a chicken with its head cut off all afternoon. Come, sit a spell, won't you?"

It was only Martha and Dorris Kaye, but that was enough to make him scramble for an excuse not to sit. Since he couldn't come up with one, he sat.

"A little bird told me you're leaving Garrison." Martha's brows drew close together. "This was news to me."

"I'm not leaving. I'll just be on the road six months out of the year." He shrugged. "Garrison is my home. It always will be."

"What are we going to do without you?" Dorris Kaye was downright indignant. "I don't trust any of the EMTs but you." Unfortunately, Dorris Kaye called 911 enough to know all the EMTs in the county. From bad heartburn to sciatica to hiccups that wouldn't go away, Dorris seemed to prefer having the paramedics come to her versus her going to a doctor. "That Terri is never nice to me—but you are."

"She's a good EMT, Miss Kaye. She's the only partner I'd want with me in an emergency." He couldn't exactly blame Terri for being brusque with the older woman. So far, none of her calls had been real emergencies.

"What about the high school rodeo team?" Martha's tone was sharper now. "My grandson is on that team. I can't, in good conscience, let him participate if his safety is in question."

"My brother Rusty is taking my place." He didn't appreciate her tone, but he did respect her concern. Her grandson was her pride and joy—and the only family she hadn't chased off with her less than cordial ways.

"Rusty?" Martha's brows rose high but she didn't say anything for a long minute. "And your father?"

"I'm not leaving until after the Founder's Day Festival, Miss Martha." He ran a hand along the back of his neck. "By then, Dad will be back to his normal self. He and Rusty both support my decision."

"All any parent wants is for their child to be happy. Even at the cost of their own happiness." Martha patted the edge of the table. "Now, if you'll excuse me. Dwight is here and I have some dancing to do." She stood, staring down at him. "But, Mike Woodard, you listen to me. Garrison needs you. Your daddy and brother need you. I'm not sure what itch you're hoping to scratch with this new job, but you might want to think about that before you go running off."

They left and he sat, alone, at the table. How two women could make a person feel so shell-shocked he didn't know. Somehow, those two women had managed just that.

"Mr. Mike?" Kirby patted him on the arm.

"Hey, Kirby." It was impossible to be angry when this little girl was smiling up at him. "Having fun?"

"I am." She patted her tummy. "I ate cake. And it was yummy."

"It was."

"And I was having fun with Samantha but now she's dancing with her daddy." She pointed at the dance floor. "Archie won't dance with me. Grandpa Quincy's friends are scary so I can't ask him."

"Would you dance with me, Kirby?" He couldn't think of a better way to shake off his foul mood. And after, he'd go back to looking for Rusty.

"Oh, yes, please." She bounced on her feet. "Thank you."

"My pleasure, Kirby." He stood and took her hand.

On the dance floor, he soon realized he was too tall. He tried to hunch over but it wasn't working.

"You can pick me up. That's what Samantha's daddy did." Kirby held out her arms. "I don't mind."

Mike chuckled and scooped her up. "That's better." He two-stepped along with the music, spinning them once—and making Kirby giggle.

"You're really tall." She stared up at the tree branches overhead. "I'm almost as tall as the tree."

"That tall, huh?" He spun them again and was rewarded with another giggle. Funny how a little girl laughing could ease all his stress and worry. Instead of letting people get in his head until he was doubting himself, he needed to do this. Take it day by day, minute by minute. And enjoy all the giggles he could.

He was smiling when the music came to an end. He was smiling when he walked Kirby off the dance floor to where Eloise was waiting. Eloise. Looking so beautiful it put a knot in his throat.

"Now it's Momma's turn," Kirby said, grabbing her mother's hand and putting it in his. "Go on, Momma. Mr. Mike's a good dancer."

"Shall we?" he asked, his stomach a ball of nerves. All at once, he was aware of every little thing. The feel of her silky-smooth hand against his calloused palms. The way her hair lifted and moved in the fall breeze. The tiny specks of gold in her mossy green eyes. And the way her full lips tilted up in a smile.

"Sure."

One word and he was happy. Mike led her onto the dance floor knowing full well people were watching and not caring one bit. People would talk. Whether they danced together or not wouldn't change that. He'd been wanting to dance with Eloise for the last fifteen years. Now he had the chance and he was going to savor every last second.

CHAPTER EIGHT

WHAT AM I DOING? She tried not to stiffen as Mike's arm slipped around her waist. He didn't pull her against him or hold her too close—but that didn't stop her heart from picking up or her breath from growing uneven.

"You've got one sweet little girl." Mike's voice was deep and low.

She stared at his chest. "She is that. You made her day." Her eyes darted up to his far too handsome face. "Thank you for that." Her words were a whisper.

"Until now, it was the high point of my day." His eyes trailed slowly over her face.

She swallowed hard. "Mike." But that's all she could say. He was so close, smiling a smile that rattled her to the core, and all she could think about was how good it felt to be in his arms.

"It's just a dance, El-Bell." He shook his head. "Nothing more. Neither of us wants more."

He was right. But, instead of being relieved, she was… disappointed. Because she knew, deep down, that there was something between them. There always had been a connection. In every one of their pictures together, she'd been lit up from the inside. And he…well, he was looking at her like he was right now. Why was it so hard to breathe?

"You know, one of the last times I saw you was right here." The muscle in his jaw tightened.

She stared up at him, memories rushing in on her. Good

memories. "It was the summer before my mother died," she managed, the words tight. "Before Dad..." *Got lost in drink and depression.* She shook her head, trying to smile. "Well, that was when the world still made sense. It had been a good summer. The best summer."

Because of Mike. All at once, she was wrapped up in images so vivid she could feel them. His sweet smiles. Holding his hand. Sweet, stolen kisses. She'd been in love with Mike Woodard. Real, true love. So much so that she'd "married" him, right here, beneath the very tree they were now dancing under.

"El." The hand holding hers tightened. "The last time I saw you..." He broke off, the muscle in his jaw going tight. "I didn't know about your mom or what was happening until I came looking for you." His voice was gruff as he added, "All I knew was you were gone."

She wasn't sure she was breathing at all now. "You came looking for me?" After their fight, she'd assumed he'd never want to see her again.

His brow furrowed and his jaw clenched tighter. "Of course I did, El." Mike's hand squeezed hers. "I looked for you for years—hoping I'd get the chance to tell you I was sorry about your mom. And for what I said to you." He cleared his throat. "Telling you your problems were nothing compared to losing Gene was pretty heartless. So was telling you that you needed to learn to pull yourself up by your own bootstraps and stop making everything about you. You were losing your mom and, thanks to drinking, your dad, too. I'm sorry. It might not matter to you anymore, but it does to me." The space between them seemed to spark and compress. "I drank most of a bottle of whiskey before that night was over." The corner of his mouth kicked up. "If it makes you feel any better, I threw up all night and could barely move for two days after."

"Maybe. A little." His words eased some of the hurt she'd been holding on to all these years. "I was so mean to you, Mike. You'd lost a dear friend and I came in there yelling at you because you were drinking." She took a deep breath. "It scared me. You… My dad was my dad but, when he drank, he wasn't. He got mean and aggressive and…"

"And what?" His hand pressed against her back.

"Nothing." She sucked in a deep breath. "Thinking of you that way scared me. But I had no right to call you selfish or heartless. Or a liar."

"That part was true." His eyes held hers. "I'd promised you I wouldn't drink. Then I did."

"Because you were grieving and trying to cope—"

"It was still a lie, El. And I'm sorry for that." He sighed. "We were too young to know what we were doing—or what we were throwing away."

"You did break my heart." She was horrified. That had been the last thing she'd meant to say.

"No, ma'am." His voice was a soft whisper. "You broke mine."

Something inside her seemed to thaw and shift. Something warm and alive, sparking in her stomach and rising up into her chest. "Was Tyson really teasing you?" She hadn't meant to ask him but…

"I'm the one that's *too nice*." He was smiling now.

"You always have been." And it had been one of the things she'd loved about him. Her heart thumped a little harder, a little faster.

"Interesting that's still weighing on you, though." There was a sparkle in his eye.

Interesting? Or concerning? But it had been weighing on her. The longer they danced, the harder it became to deny the growing pull between them. It was familiar. And disconcerting. More so when his thumb ran along the back of her hand. *Enough.* She scrambled to find a safer topic. "Hattie didn't trip on her dress."

He nodded. "She didn't. Forrest was worried he'd cry. He didn't—but it was close."

"How's your brother?" She couldn't have been the only one who noticed Rusty's discomfort during the ceremony.

"To be honest, I'm not sure. He seems to have disappeared." And Mike's tone implied he was worried about him. "Our mother leaving… Well, he has commitment issues. I didn't realize how much until today."

Her heart hurt for the man. "Parenting is a tricky business. Some of them don't realize that what they say and do will forever impact their kids."

"Or they don't care." His words were hard.

"Or that." It was her turn to squeeze his hand.

"You don't have to worry about that, El-Bell. You're a good mother." His thumb stroked along her back and, for a second, his gaze dipped to her mouth.

Thankfully, the music stopped and Mike led her off the dance floor. Any minute now, she'd find her footing and things would go back to normal. Any second.

"Thanks for the dance." He let go of her hand, that muscle in his jaw tightening again.

"I'm glad Kirby forced us." The spot on her back felt cold now that his hand was gone. She felt colder.

"Forced?" He chuckled. "No, ma'am." He touched the brim of his hat and took one step away—

"Mike." She swallowed. What now?

He waited, watching her intently.

"I… I'm glad we had a chance to talk." Which was a pretty pathetic reason to stop him.

"That it had to happen after so long makes me sad." His gaze fell from hers.

What was she doing? Her heart had no business reacting to this man. But it did and the realization was more than a little shocking.

"I should probably go find my brother. Enjoy yourself." And with that, he walked into the crowd and away from her.

"Momma." Kirby grabbed her hand. "Archie's sick."

"What?" She frowned. "Where is he?" She'd left him with Gretta and Levi to check on Kirby—then ended up dancing with Mike.

"He's over there." She pointed out into the field. "He says his tummy hurts real bad."

"Probably ate too much cake." She took Kirby's hand. "Let's go check on him." Sure enough, Archie was crumpled up on the grass beside Levi Williams. His face was red and his legs were drawn up and into his chest.

"Archie, honey, are you okay?" She knelt in the grass beside him.

"He's not." Levi shook his head. "He's been moaning and groaning. I think he's real sick." The boy pushed his too-big cowboy hat back. "I figured I should stay with him."

"Thank you, Levi." Eloise pressed a hand to Archie's forehead. "You're hot." Not too much cake, then. "I think I need to get you home."

"Momma." His voice was a croak. "It hurts." He pressed his hands against the right side of his stomach.

"Okay, sweetie." She scooped him up in her arms. "We'll get you some medicine and let you rest."

Levi hopped up. "I'll go get my mom." And he ran across the field to the tables before Eloise could stop him.

"Is Archie going to be okay?" Kirby's chin trembled and her eyes welled up with tears.

"He will be." She cradled Archie close as she started for the parking lot. Unlike Kirby, he was heavy.

Archie's moan worried her. He'd never made that sound before.

"Eloise." Gretta waved her down. "What can I do?"

"I think he'll be okay. I just need to get him home." She kept walking. "Can you get my grandfather?"

"Of course." She pressed a hand to Eloise's arm. "Call me if you need anything. It's no fun when they get sick."

"Thanks, Gretta." Archie wasn't getting any lighter but she couldn't bring herself to put him down.

The path to the parking lot stretched out before her, ten times as long as it had been when they'd arrived. With every step, Archie's noises became more distressing. *Maybe we should go to the hospital.*

Mike. She kept walking but glanced back, searching the sea of people for him. The one time she'd needed him to pop up and he's nowhere to be found.

It seemed like forever until her grandfather reached them. By then, she had sweat running down her back and her arms were shaking. "He's really sick, Grandpa. I think we need to take him to the hospital."

Grandpa Quincy gave Archie a long look, then nodded. "Then let's go."

He buckled Kirby in while Eloise wedged herself beside her daughter's booster seat and let Archie lay across her lap. Every bump and bounce along the road had Archie crying out—and there was nothing she could do. She smoothed his forehead and murmured words of comfort, but he was sobbing by the time they reached the small emergency clinic.

From there, things picked up.

A gurney was wheeled out and, finally, a familiar face.

"Terri." Eloise almost hugged the woman. "He was fine and then he wasn't. It's his stomach."

Terri gave her a reassuring pat. "Don't you fret. Let the doc look him over and we'll see what's ailing him."

Eloise left Kirby with her grandfather, then went into the ER with Archie. She held his hand, hating how helpless she felt. The tears streaming down his cheeks broke her heart. But seeing him ball up in pain was terrifying.

"It'll be okay, sweetie." She ran her hand across his forehead, smoothing the sweat-slicked hair back. "The doctor will find out what's wrong and fix it."

Archie's nod was slight.

She stood, holding his hand, watching the second hand on the clock tick by. It was taking too long. Her son was in pain. He needed help. It's not like there were wall-to-wall patients. As far as she could tell, they were the only ones here.

What if it was something serious? Was the Colton County Emergency Center and Hospital equipped to handle whatever Archie was struggling with? And, if they weren't, what happened then?

Finally, the curtain moved aside and a middle-aged woman came to the side of Archie's bed. "Hi, Archie. Miss Green. I'm Dr. Rowe." She was already zeroed in on Archie. "I hear your stomach is bothering you?" She put on her stethoscope and leaned forward. "I'm going to listen to your stomach, okay? I'll try to be extra careful."

Archie turned his face into the pillow.

"Did he eat anything unusual?" Dr. Rowe lifted Archie's shirt.

"No. Some wedding cake, maybe. But nothing else out of the ordinary." She saw the way Archie flinched away from the stethoscope.

"How long has he been in pain?" Dr. Rowe rested her hand on the right side of his stomach.

"Not long." Eloise racked her brain for any signs of distress earlier in the day. "He never said anything about it—until ten minutes or so ago. He was crumpled up like this." She took a deep breath. "He's in a lot of pain."

Dr. Rowe nodded. "I think we're dealing with appendicitis. But we need to get a CT scan of his stomach to confirm that." The woman met Eloise's gaze. "Once we get that done, we'll know exactly what we're dealing with and how to treat it."

Eloise nodded. "Can he... Will he be able to be treated here?"

"Yes, ma'am. Now, let's get this CT done." She typed something into the computer on the stand next to Archie's bed. "Order's in." She offered Eloise a smile. "I'll be back to check on him soon."

Eloise went with him to get his CT. He was in too much pain to care what was happening. Instead of taking him back to the ER, Dr. Rowe met them in the hall outside the radiology department.

"The CT confirmed it. Archie is going to need his appendix taken out." Dr. Rowe spoke calmly. "It's a quick surgery—an hour or so."

Surgery. She nodded. If Archie heard he was headed for surgery, she couldn't tell. He lay on the gurney, curled on his side, hugging the pillow.

"All right?" Dr. Rowe asked.

She nodded again.

"We are going to go to pre-op and get an IV started and give him some antibiotics." She started walking, but kept talking. "Then our anesthesiologist will come in and sedate him. He'll sleep through the whole thing."

Eloise followed, keeping a hold of Archie's hand as a nurse pushed the gurney. He'd be okay. In an hour, he'd be out of pain and feeling better. Until then, she had to be strong. For Kirby and her grandfather and Archie, too. They were all counting on her and she wouldn't let them down.

For the first time in a long time, she felt completely alone. There was no shoulder for her to cry on and no one to offer her strength or comfort. She'd get through this on her own, but it would be nice if she didn't have to.

JUST ABOUT THE time Mike had given up on finding Rusty, he found him. He'd climbed up one of the large rock outcroppings and sat on the edge, his legs hanging over the side.

"You sure didn't want to be found," Mike called, searching for the best way up.

"Which begs the question, why are you here?" His tone was all irritation.

"I'm your brother. It's my job to irritate you." Mike climbed up the least treacherous side and stood on the relatively flat top. "Not an easy climb in boots."

Other than a sigh, Rusty didn't acknowledge him.

Rusty wasn't happy he was here, he got that. But something was bothering his little brother and Mike couldn't just sit by and do nothing. He'd never given up on his brother, and he wasn't going to start now. He sat beside Rusty, draping his legs over the edge as well.

"Nice view." It was, too. A clear view of the park below, erste Baum, and the wedding festivities still taking place.

Rusty stayed silent.

"You try the cake?" Mike took off his hat and ran a hand through his hair. "I brought you a piece but dropped the plate. I'm sure there's still plenty, though."

Rusty glanced his way.

"Whenever you're ready." Mike shut up then. He wasn't going to badger his brother. If he sat with him long enough, he'd start talking.

For the next fifteen minutes, Mike watched Hattie and Forrest dance and enjoy their special day. He was too far away to make out their features, but the laughter echoed so loud he could hear them up here.

"I don't get any of this," Rusty muttered. "The vows. The whole 'death do us part' thing doesn't mean a thing. They're just words."

Mike held his peace. He wanted Rusty to get it all out in the open so they could face it together.

"Forrest and Hattie are our friends and it's gonna hurt something fierce when it falls apart. You know that." Rusty glanced his way.

"What if they make it work?" Mike kept his tone casual.

"That's a pretty big if. An 'if' that impacts all of us." He ran his hands along the top of his thighs. "Sure, everything's fine now but it won't last."

"It might." He looked at his brother then.

"Mom left after twenty years, Mike." And Rusty was still angry. "She had a life and kids and a good husband and that didn't stop her from going. Why is Hattie any different? Or Audy?"

"Because Hattie is Hattie. And Audy couldn't survive without Brooke." He took a steadying breath. "Mom might have been there physically all that time but she'd tapped out mentally years before she finally left. You know that." How many times had she left them alone when their father had been working? How many times had Mike made peanut butter and jelly sandwiches because the one time he'd tried to use the stove Rusty had burned his little hand? It was his mother's fault for leaving them alone but he was the one that let his brother get hurt and it had gutted him.

"If it's not a lie, if they all stay married and happy, then the only other explanation is us." Rusty gripped the edge of the rock. "We're the reason she left. Not Dad—

she could have left before we were born—but you and me. *We* made our mother want to go." He paused to look at Mike. "If that's the truth then why should we think anyone else would stay? If our mother doesn't want us, who else would?" He broke off, staring blindly ahead of him. "Whether it's all a lie or it's just us, we're not getting a happy ending."

Mike shook his head. All this time and she was still hurting them. "This hit you while you were standing up with Forrest?"

Rusty didn't respond.

"That's an awful lot to contemplate while your best friend is getting married." Mike nudged his brother. "You ever stop to think it was her? That something inside of her snapped—"

"Because of us."

"Because of the way she was wired. We've both wasted too many years trying to make sense of what happened. Who knows why she chose to leave when she did, Rusty? We'll never know. And, to be honest, I don't care." He managed a smile. "Don't let what she did stop you from living a full life. She's got no right to stand in your way— don't you dare let her."

Rusty was quiet for a long time. They both were. Besides the noises from the wedding below and the occasional gust of wind, it was silent.

"I made a fool out of myself down there, didn't I? I'm sure people were laughing." His brother turned to face him.

"No." Mike rested a hand on his brother's shoulder. "You had some people worried after you—because they care. Nobody was laughing."

Rusty nodded. "I guess we should go back?"

"Probably. If for no other reason than to check on Dad."

He stood, offered Rusty his hand, and pulled his brother to his feet.

Conversation was easier on the way back. Mike suggested they try to get their dad to go part-time at the shop once Doc Johnston cleared him to go back to work.

"He'll probably argue." Rusty laughed, following the path down to erste Baum. "That shop is his baby."

"I know it. But it's not like you won't take care of it. You know the place like the back of your hand." Mike paused, watching his brother as he asked, "It's still what you want? To take over the shop? You're not just saying that to make me or Dad feel better?"

"It is." Rusty nodded. "Dad said I have a good eye and a good ear. I can normally see problems before they happen or I can figure out what the problem is by the sound it makes." He shrugged. "I guess that's a good thing."

Mike chuckled. "I'd think so."

"You need to do what makes you happy, too." Rusty stopped before they reached the celebration. "This job." He adjusted his hat, his eyes shifting to the ground before meeting his. "I figure you've got some concerns about leaving—with Dad and all. But you staying here won't stop life from happening. Nothing will. If this job is what you want, if it lights a fire in you, then don't let this opportunity slip away." He didn't wait for Mike to answer. "That's all I wanted to say."

"You're the second person today to give me an earful about this job." Though Martha Zeigler had been a little less supportive than his brother.

"Let me guess, Eloise Green?" Rusty grinned, elbowing his brother.

"No." Mike shook his head. "Why would you think… No. Martha Zeigler."

Rusty's eyes widened. "How'd that go?"

"Not so great." Mike sighed. "She meant well. I think."

Conversation stopped when Audy jogged to them. "Mike. Eloise took Archie to the hospital."

"What?" Mike froze. "What happened?"

"Something about his stomach bothering him? Gretta said he was curled up, moaning. He was hurting something fierce, Mike." Audy was rarely serious—like he was now. "I— We figured you'd want to know."

Every instinct told him to go. It wasn't his place. She'd have Quincy and Kirby and Archie to look after. Who'd be looking after her? Mike glanced at his brother, scanned the field for his father, then turned back to Rusty. "You got Dad?"

"You go." Rusty nodded. "We'll be fine."

Mike nodded, already heading for the parking lot.

"Call if you need anything," Audy called out.

Mike was a careful driver. He'd seen one too many accidents caused by distracted or speeding drivers. It took every ounce of his self-control not to step on the gas and fly to the Colton County Emergency Center and Hospital. He was kicking himself all the way there. Archie had mentioned his stomach was hurting and Mike hadn't thought much of it.

He tried to stay positive and not focus on the worst-case scenarios. Archie was right where he needed to be.

He spotted Quincy and Kirby as soon as he walked into the waiting room.

"Mike." Quincy stood, shaking his hand. "You get called in or something?"

"I heard about Archie." And he'd come running.

"Thank you, son." Quincy's face crumpled. "El's in the back with him."

Mike didn't hesitate to pull the older man in for a hug.

"It'll be fine, Quincy. Archie's young and strong. They'll take care of him, you'll see."

"You're right. Of course you are." Quincy sniffed, a tired smile on his face. "She's worrying mightily over her brother."

Kirby's knees were drawn up and her face was buried in the fabric of her dress. If she knew he was there, she didn't acknowledge him.

"Hey, Kirby." He sat in the chair beside her. "You feeling scared?"

She nodded but kept her face covered.

"About Archie?"

Another nod.

"Your momma is with him. So is the doctor. They're taking good care of Archie." He waited, searching for something to make the little girl feel better.

"He's not going to die?" she whispered.

Mike frowned.

"Levi said one of their horses got a bad tummy ache and he died." Kirby's voice was thick and wavering.

That explained why she was so upset. "Oh, Kirby." Mike reached over and put his arm around the little girl.

Kirby turned toward him, wrapped her arms around his neck, and started to sob.

"Hey, hey." He pulled her into his lap. "Your grandpa and I are right here, Kirby." He rocked her, looking to Quincy for guidance.

The old man shrugged, concern and a hint of panic on his well-lined face.

Mike's shirtfront was wet with tears when Eloise pushed through the doors leading to the ER. She was pale but composed. A smile was in place, but he saw how badly her hands were shaking.

"Kirby, Archie's with the doctor getting fixed up right

now." She scooped up Kirby and gave her a squeeze. "That's a good hug."

"Hugs help, Momma." Kirby gave her another tight hug.

"That's perfect. Can you give Grandpa Quincy a hug? I think he needs one, too." She offered her daughter a tired smile.

"Do you, Grandpa?" Kirby sniffed.

"I do, Freckles." Quincy sat and gathered the little girl into his lap.

Mike hesitated. He didn't want to overstep but… Since he was here, he was pretty sure it was too late. No going back now. He was at her side before he could change his mind. "El?"

She blinked, staring up at him. "Mike?"

"How's Archie?" He resisted the urge to take her hand or wrap his arms around her.

"You know… That's why you're here?" She swallowed hard, her smile faltering.

He took her hand and gave it a squeeze.

"He… It's his appendix." She took a deep breath. "He's gone back for surgery now."

"That's good, El-Bell. Great news." He sighed. "He's going to be okay."

"He is." But it sounded more like a question than a statement.

He gave her hand another squeeze. "Are you okay?" He kept his voice low and soothing. "What can I do?"

"Stay?" Then she shook her head. "You don't—"

"I'm not going anywhere." No way, no how was he going to leave her side. She was strong, no denying that. But she'd weathered too much on her own. Not this time. This was where he needed to be. And even though she might not know it yet, this was where she might need him to be.

CHAPTER NINE

ELOISE SIPPED THE tea Mike had gotten her and tried not to worry. Mike was confident everything was going to be fine. Since he was an EMT and had medical training, Eloise believed him. She had to. She'd been in shock since she'd found Archie in the field. Seeing her boy that way… Nothing had prepared her for the panic and terror that threatened to pull her under.

But now Archie was in surgery, Mike had Terri keeping tabs on things, and there was nothing to be done except wait.

In the span of thirty minutes, Mabel had arrived with a care package. She'd packed a snack basket with wedding cake, peanut butter crackers, apples, and punch. But the biggest treat was an oversized coloring book and crayons for Kirby. Grandpa Quincy, Kirby, and Samantha were currently sitting around one of the waiting room's tables coloring away.

"I can't thank you enough." Eloise turned the paper cup in her hands. "As soon as you and Samantha walked in, Kirby's tears stopped."

"Samantha was worried about her friend. And I was worried about mine." Mabel's smile was warm. "Samantha might be my future stepdaughter but I love her as if she were my own. When she gets sick, it's horrible. I feel so helpless. I'm sure this is ten times worse."

Eloise nodded.

"Thank goodness he's going to be okay."

"Mike said an appendectomy is a pretty common childhood surgery." Eloise glanced at the man sitting on the opposite side of the waiting room. He was here—nodding at something Jensen Crawley said—as if he somehow belonged here.

Technically, he did. He worked at the hospital. But he wasn't working today. He'd come for Archie—and for her.

"He would know." Mabel glanced at the men. "He took off running before I knew what was going on. Once Gretta and Samantha filled me in, we knew we had to do something. Gretta and Brooke are already planning to bring some meals over. You shouldn't have to worry about cooking and all that."

"Oh, Mabel, that's not necessary."

"Necessary or not, it's happening." She patted Eloise's hand. "I think it makes people feel better to help and do something in times of upheaval versus sit and do nothing. So let us do, please."

Eloise's phone started ringing. Ted. She stared at the screen. She'd called and updated Ted's prison warden but hadn't expected Ted to call back. He was the last person she wanted to talk to. "If you'll excuse me." She stood, walked down the hall to the cafeteria, and pressed accept on the screen. "Ted?"

"Eloise? What's going on? Is Archie okay? What happened?" He was frantic.

"He's in surgery. His appendix. The doctor says it's a routine procedure and he'll recover in a couple of weeks." Which is what she'd told the warden. She leaned against the wall, staring up at the fluorescent lights overhead.

"Routine? He's in surgery." His muttered curse was pure frustration. "I should be there."

She pressed her other hand to her forehead.

"I know he's in good hands. You'll handle this better than I ever could. And I'm grateful that my boy has you." His voice broke. "Oh, Eloise, I'm so sorry. I left you alone to carry the weight of the world on your shoulders all this time—"

She didn't want more empty apologies. "I have Grandpa Quincy and my friends here, with me." From the corner of her eye, she saw Mike feeding coins into the vending machine. "Good people who care about me and the kids. I'm not alone." She took a deep breath. "I'll tell Archie you called when he gets out of surgery. I know it would mean the world to him if you call him tomorrow."

"I will. Don't you worry about that." His voice wavered again. "I'll make sure he knows I love him—even if I can't be there in person."

"That will make him happy, Ted."

"Benny, the guard, said he'd pass along any messages you leave." He sniffed. "I'd appreciate you keeping me updated. If you can?"

"I will."

"Thank you, Eloise. Thank you for calling me." He sighed. "You're a good woman—a good person. And I'm the fool that let you go."

She shook her head. Every time she talked to him, he'd say something along these lines. She couldn't decide if he wanted her forgiveness or a second chance but now wasn't the time for either conversation. "Ted, I should let you go. Kirby—"

"Is Freckles around? Can I talk to her? For just a minute?"

While she understood he was missing the kids, she had to put their well-being first. Kirby was understandably fragile. Talking to her father and then saying good-bye would upset her all over again. "She cried for over an hour—she's just calmed down. I don't want to upset her all over again. They have a hard enough time saying goodbye after your weekly talk. It would be too much for her."

"Every time I hang up, it's like having my heart cut out all over again. I just want to talk to my little girl, Eloise." There was an edge to his words. "She *needs* me. You're telling me I can't talk to her? It's not right."

"Ted—"

"I never expected you to be so cruel." He was definitely angry.

"Cruel?" That hurt. "I'm their mother. I have to do what I think is right, even if you don't agree."

"I don't agree. And I'm their father." His voice rose. "But there's nothing I can do, is there? I don't have any say-so in any decisions in here. Or out there. You're making sure of that."

"I'm doing the best I can." She was exhausted. Scared. Frustrated. Hurt and angry. "I'm trying to be a good mother. Sometimes that means telling half-truths to protect my hypersensitive son and daughter, sometimes it means screening who they talk to when they're vulnerable. That's the way it is—whether or not you agree or think it's fair, Ted."

The silence stretched out until she thought they'd been disconnected.

"I'm sorry. I got angry and I shouldn't have snapped at you. I *am* sorry, Eloise." He cleared his voice. "I'll reach out tomorrow and talk to Archie. You have a lot on your plate, I know. But things will be different—better—soon."

She didn't have the energy to argue.

"You'll tell them that I love them? That I'll be there to hug them just as soon as I can?" He said something, muffled, to someone in the room with him. "I've gotta go. Just… I am sorry, Eloise. For everything. I don't know what I'd do without you. I promise, I'm going to make it up to you." And the line went dead.

She tucked her phone into the pocket of her dress and ran a hand over her face.

"Here." Mike handed her an orange soda. "I don't know if it's still your favorite but the sugar will do you some good."

"It is." She took the can.

"You are a good mother, El-Bell." The way he said her name flooded her with warmth. "You love those kids more than anything."

Did he mean that? Or was he trying to make her feel better? Her gaze met his and she knew. He meant it. For a second, she wanted nothing more than to be wrapped in his big, strong arms—for him to hold her until she was calm. "Did you listen to the entire conversation?"

"I figured… Maybe…" He shrugged, his brown eyes searching hers. "Yeah. I wanted to make sure you were okay."

Oh, Mike. He'd always looked out for her. She could always count on him. Something told her she still could.

No. Now she was letting her emotions get the better of her. It had been a long, hard day, that's all. Nothing would make sense or be right until Archie was safe and sound. "We should get back."

He nodded but didn't move. "If you ever need to talk, I'm a good listener."

"I know." But it would be stupid to start relying on him when he was leaving soon. Without another word, she edged around him and headed for the waiting room.

"Momma." Kirby was standing in the middle of the room with tears running down her cheeks. "Where did you go?" she wailed.

"Oh, baby." She scooped up her daughter. "I had a

phone call. I was right there, in the hall. Mike got me an orange soda."

"That's your favorite." Kirby sniffed, wiping at her eyes.

"Want a sip?" Eloise offered her the can.

"Really?" Kirby was surprised. "Sodas are for parties."

"Normally, yes." She hugged her daughter close. "Today is an exception." She carried Kirby back to the table where they'd been coloring. "Show me your picture."

Time ticked away at a snail's pace. Grandpa Quincy dozed in one of the waiting room chairs. Mabel, Samantha, and Jensen said they'd come back to visit Archie later. Mike checked in with Terri but there was no update. Gretta called to check up on things and then Rusty and Nolan Woodard walked into the waiting room with balloons, flowers, and a large gift bag.

"How's the patient?" Mr. Woodard gave her a hug. "How's the patient's mother?"

"He's still in surgery." She tried to smile. "I'm coloring and drinking soda and trying to stay positive."

"That sounds like a plan." Mr. Woodard sat beside her grandfather. "We figured we'd keep you company while you wait."

"You don't have to—"

"You won't talk him out of it." Rusty grinned. "Hey, Kirby. Whatcha doin'?"

"Coloring." She pushed the box of crayons toward him. "You can color this zebra unicorn if you want to?"

Rusty nodded and sat. "Are zebra unicorns a specific color?"

"No." Kirby giggled. "Any color you want."

"Whew." Rusty pulled a crayon from the box. "That's a relief."

"Miss Green?" Dr. Rowe pushed through the doors leading back to the emergency room. "We just finished up."

Eloise hurried to the woman. "How did it go?"

"Archie did great. He's in recovery right now. The nurse will come get you and take you to him in a few minutes. I'm sure he'd like you to be there when he wakes up."

"Yes." Eloise felt the tears starting. "Oh, thank you."

A cheer went up in the waiting room and Kirby clapped and jumped up and down.

"You're welcome." Dr. Rowe smiled. "He'll be staying overnight so I'll see you later." And with that, the doctor went back through the swinging doors.

She'd been so scared. More scared than she realized. "He's okay." Even though she was relieved and happy, she was crying.

"El?" Poor Grandpa Quincy was flustered by her tears. "Oh, Sassy, it's all right now."

She nodded, but they wouldn't stop. "I—I know."

"It scared the daylights out of her," Mr. Woodard murmured. "Of course it would."

"Holding it together for everyone else is hard work." Mike stood beside her. "You take all the time you need—"

She wrapped her arms around his waist and buried her face against his chest. Those big, warm arms of his held her tight against him. Later, she might regret this, but now? This was what she needed. A minute where she didn't have to be strong because Mike would be strong for her.

"Hey, now," he murmured against her ear. "It's all right, El-Bell."

She nodded against his chest.

His hands pressed against her back to anchor her in place. She was safe. Protected. Supported. Because Mike was Mike. It was highly improbable that this handsome bear of a man still had the same heart of gold he'd had fifteen years ago. Too much time had passed... And yet, no matter how long it had been between visits, they'd al-

ways picked up right where they'd left off. He'd been true
blue, always.

He'd given her his Easter candy. He'd comforted her
when she'd fallen and skinned her knee. He'd handed over
his coat when it was freezing and never once complained.
He'd listened to her dreams and told her to go after them.
He'd kissed her once and forever ruined any other kisses
she'd have in the future. He'd been constant and loyal,
kind and loving.

That boy was not this man.

But what if he was? Was it possible the man currently
giving her the comfort she so desperately needed was the
same Mike she'd known and loved?

It didn't matter, did it? He was leaving. She wasn't stupid enough to open herself up for certain heartache.

Her emotions were all over the place, that's all this
was. She was a mess. Period. And she was making a fool
of herself. She pushed out of his arms. "I'm so sorry." She
wiped at her face. "I don't know where that came from."

"It's okay, Momma. Sometimes a hug can make things
better." Kirby took her hand and smiled up at her. "Mr.
Mike gives good hugs."

He gave the *best* hugs. It had felt so good. "But you
give the best hugs." She picked up Kirby and hugged her
tight. "You and Archie." She glanced toward the emergency room doors, willing the nurse to come and get her.
She needed to see Archie with her own two eyes and know
he was okay. Once that happened, this day would be over
and things could get back to being relatively stable and
calm. Her emotions, too.

A RESTLESS NIGHT on his dad's sofa had left him with a crick
in his neck, a headache, and a bad attitude. He'd had two
cups of coffee, but it hadn't perked him up the way he'd

hoped. But he had a shift starting in an hour so he'd drink the whole pot if he had to. Until then, he'd do his best to wear Clifford out before he had to go.

"His battery never runs out." His father sat in his old wicker rocking chair on the front porch.

"No, sir." Mike smiled at Clifford—who was happily chasing a butterfly. "I could use a little of that energy today."

"Couldn't we all?" His father chuckled, rocking away.

Rusty came out the front door, a coffee cup in his hands. "What are you talking about, Dad? You'll be running circles around the two of us again in no time." He sipped his coffee, then set his cup on the railing and joined Mike on the lawn. "It almost feels like fall."

Texas wasn't known for having much in the way of seasons. It was hot for most of the year. The few months when the sun wasn't making the air ripple were a treat. Especially for Clifford.

"What's on the agenda for today?" Rusty picked up Clifford's ball and tossed it back and forth between his hands.

"I'm in the rig today." And he was grateful. When he was working, he put everything else aside. That's what he needed—to take a break from his own thoughts.

"If you get a chance to check in on Archie this afternoon, will you?" His father kept on rocking. "Yesterday was tough on that whole family. I'm sure they could use a friendly face. Only wait a bit. Quincy sent me a text that the whole Garrison Ladies Guild was in Archie's room."

As if Eloise needed more difficult personalities to deal with. Like her ex-husband.

Yesterday had been a roller-coaster ride for El. Just about the time she'd seemed calm, her ex had called. And that call had upset her something fierce. Not that Mike blamed her. He only heard her side of the conversation, but it'd been enough. Not only did the man have the nerve to pick a fight with El, he'd said something that made her feel the need to defend herself and her mothering style.

Mike hoped he never came face-to-face with Ted what's-his-name. If he did, they were going to have words. For the first time in his life, Mike disliked someone he'd never even met.

"You good?" Rusty asked.

"Fine." He hadn't meant to snap.

"You can go back now, you know?" Rusty threw the ball and Clifford went tearing across the yard after it.

No. He couldn't. "The Garrison Ladies Guild would love that." He took the ball Clifford brought to him. He'd already spent more time at the hospital than anyone that wasn't family. That alone was sure to cause talk.

"Fair point." His brother sighed. "Why am I the one throwing the ball and you're the one he brings it back to?"

"I'm his favorite." Mike crouched and gave Clifford a good back scratch. "Aren't I?"

Clifford flopped and rolled onto his back. The dog had always preferred tummy rubs to back scratches.

"I know." Mike chuckled and rubbed the dog's stomach. "You're not the least bit spoiled. Are you?"

Clifford's tongue lolled out the side of his mouth.

Mike's phone pinged so he pulled it out of his pocket. It was Audy. The high school rodeo team would be practicing twice this week—to help out with the cattle drive for Founder's Day. "You free tonight?"

"No hot date yet." Rusty grinned.

"Good. Audy needs a hand." He held up his phone so Rusty could read the message.

"Can do."

Mike texted, We'll be there, and hit Send. "Dad, you've got your poker game tonight?"

"You bet I do." And he was tickled pink. "I can't wait to take their money and run."

"How about you take their money and *walk* this time?" Mike put his hands on his hips and faced his father. "Please."

"Oh, fine." His father sighed heavily. "You two act like I'm some porcelain doll or something. I'm not. I won't break."

Mike and Rusty exchanged a long look of understanding. The chances of either of them forgetting just how breakable their father had seemed in that hospital bed were slim to none.

"But I'll be good. Besides, Doc Johnston's playing tonight so, technically, I'll be under medical supervision." He chuckled again.

"Is that how it works?" Rusty scratched the back of his head.

After another cup of coffee, Mike got ready for work. He buttoned up his pale blue shirt with Colton County EMT stitched across the back before tugging on his pants and checking the two large multi-compartment pockets.

He paused on the front porch, buttoning the cuffs on his shirt, and asked, "You sure you're up to going to the shop today, Dad?"

"I don't see why you're worried. I'm only staying until noon." He frowned up at Mike.

"I love you, Dad." Mike leaned forward to drop a kiss on his father's head. "I kinda want to keep you around. Okay?"

His father smiled and nodded. "All right, son. You go save people that need saving."

"Yes, sir." He walked down the steps. "You keep an

eye on Dad while I'm gone." He scratched Clifford behind the ear. "I'm counting on you. Now, Clifford, shake."
He held his hand out and Clifford put his paw in Mike's
palm. "Good boy." He fed the dog a treat. "Good boy,"
he repeated and gave the dog a final pat on the head before leaving.

He walked to his truck, started the ignition, and pulled
out onto the road. He glanced up to see Clifford sitting inside the gate, watching him. Once Archie was home, he'd
ask Eloise if he could bring Clifford by.

"Or not," he murmured, as he turned onto Main Street
and headed out of town.

Before he let himself get any further invested in Eloise's
family, he had to stop and think things through. Rusty was
right. Instead of charging into things—this job or his feelings for Eloise and her kids—he had to determine what
he wanted. And why.

He pulled into the parking lot of the Colton County
Emergency Center and Hospital, parked around back, and
entered through the staff door.

"Right on time." Terri stood at the nurses' station inside.
"Always."

Terri's brows rose and she narrowed her eyes as she
gave him a once-over. "Need some coffee?" She cocked
her head to one side. "I'm thinking someone woke up on
the wrong side of the bed."

"Couch." He scrubbed a hand over his face.

"Stay at your dad's place?" She nodded. "He doing all
right?"

"Yep. Getting feistier by the day." He signed in on the
clipboard. "We got any calls or is it all paperwork?"

Terri exchanged a quick smile with the nurse at the
nurses' station. "You don't need to, I don't know, make a
stop real quick? Check on a certain patient?"

He almost groaned. "Nope." Why was she surprised?

"All righty, then." She shrugged. "Don't go biting my head off."

After a quick inventory of the rig's interior and restocking as needed, the two of them headed inside to their office. In a small county with limited resources, they didn't drive around all day waiting for a call. They waited here, centrally located, for any emergency that might come in.

He was working. He needed to keep his mind clear and focused. In his line of work, there was no room for mistakes—even on paperwork. And, boy, was there a lot of paperwork to catch up on. By noon, he'd finished and offered to help inventory the supply closet.

At one, he and Terri ate lunch in the cafeteria. Besides the two of them, there were a few surgical techs and a doctor. Nobody else.

At two, he wandered down the empty hall to get a snack.

At two thirty, he gave up and headed upstairs to check on Archie. His dad had asked him to check in on the boy. Plus, he wanted to make sure the kid was doing better. Eloise, too.

Mike lingered in the doorway to get a read on the room. Archie had two huge balloon bouquets on either side of his bed. He was propped up with several comic books spread out over his lap. From where he stood, the boy's color was good. That was the thing about kids. They bounced back pretty quickly. A fact he was thankful for.

Kirby sat on the foot of the hospital bed listening as Archie read aloud.

Quincy occupied one of the two chairs in the room. The television was on with the sound turned off and the captions on. The old man was all wrapped up in some sort of fishing show.

There was no sign of Eloise.

"Mike?" Patsy Monahan tapped on his shoulder, then edged into Archie's hospital room. "You come to check up on the patient?"

"Yes, ma'am."

"I've heard all about how sweet you've been with those kids in there. Aren't they the cutest?" She didn't wait for him to answer. "Their poor momma was so tired out, Quincy and I sent her home for a quick shower. Seems like the doc is keeping Archie here another night."

Which was unusual. "Oh?"

"Mike." Quincy saw him. "Come in, come in."

Mike stepped inside the room and headed to Archie's bedside. "I was in the neighborhood and figured I'd check in." He smiled at the boy. "How are you feeling?"

"Fine. Until I sneeze or laugh or cough." Archie held up a pillow. "Then I have to hug this 'cuz my stomach hurts bad."

"Worse than yesterday?" Mike didn't like that Archie was being kept a second night.

"No." Archie shook his head. "Better."

"I'm glad to hear it. Looks like you've got something to read." He nodded at the comic books.

"Levi brought them." Archie held one up. "It's about robot aliens."

"They're scary." Kirby wrinkled up her nose. "They suck people's brains out with their straw mouth."

Which didn't exactly sound like kid-friendly reading.

"They're bad robot aliens." Archie said this like it explained everything. "Levi said they all explode and die."

"They die?" Kirby pushed the comic books away. "I don't like this story."

Mike was acutely aware of the way Patsy Monahan was watching the exchange. It made him nervous.

"You don't have to read them, Freckles. How about

we find you something to watch. There's that talking dog show? Or the singing, flying ponies you like?"

"Ponies." Kirby turned so she was able to look at the TV. "Samantha likes ponies and I do, too."

"Well, I like robot aliens." Archie went back to reading his comic books.

"Kids." Patsy smiled. "If you come back in a while, Eloise will be back. She'd love to see you."

Would she? They'd had quite a talk on the dance floor—one that left him hoping. But then she'd pushed out of his arms yesterday and he was more confused than ever. Did she still want him to leave her alone? Did she want him with her? And, if so, as a friend? Or more? Now wasn't the time to ply her with questions—not until Archie was better, anyway. With Patsy watching his every expression, he shouldn't even be thinking about such things. He'd do his best to shut down the talk before it got too out of hand. "That's okay. Now that I see Archie's doing so well, I'll get back to work."

"I'll tell Eloise you stopped by. I'm sure she'll call you." Patsy was determined.

"I don't think she has my number." He shook his head.

This wasn't the news Patsy wanted to hear—but the woman rallied. "I can pass it along to her."

"That's kind of you, Miss Patsy, but Quincy knows how to reach me. If something comes up, that is." He had to bite back a smile when Quincy rolled his eyes. Poor Quincy. "You all have a good day."

"Bye, Mr. Mike." Kirby smiled at him. "I can't hug you. The bed's too high."

"That's all right. Next time." He winked at her. "Enjoy those robot aliens, Archie."

"Okay." Archie nodded, his gaze glued to the pages.

With that, Mike left and headed back downstairs. It was

good to see Archie was on the mend, but there was a reason Dr. Rowe was keeping him. And, before Mike could get on with his day, he needed to find out what that was.

CHAPTER TEN

"THESE ARE AWFUL." Eloise skimmed one of the comic books, horrified. "Where did you get these?"

"Levi brought them." Archie fanned out the stack of comic books, all smiles. "He and his grandpa came to visit. They brought these and a water gun and a whole bag of bubble gum."

"Was Levi's mom with them?" She had a hard time believing Gretta would be okay picking these comic books out for a seven-year-old.

"No." Archie shook his head.

"She and Mabel are down cleaning up after the wedding." Grandpa Quincy nodded at the comic books. "I don't think she had any idea. Still, I should have checked myself."

She turned the page to find one gruesome scene of death and dismemberment and shut the book. "I'm sorry, hon, but these are too grown up for you."

"But, Momma, they're a gift from Levi." Archie held the comic books close.

"I know they are, sweetie. He's a good friend to come and see you—but I don't feel comfortable with you reading about this." Giant lizards with laser-beam eyes that melted their opponents, leaving only the bones behind? Absolutely not.

"The robot aliens suck out people's brains, too, Momma." Kirby shook her head. "I did not like that."

"Archie." She held out her hand.

"You can't throw them away, Momma." He handed over the comic books and drooped back against the pillows.

"I'll put them away—for now." Eloise shoved them into her bag. "What else have you been up to?"

"Miss Patsy kept asking Grandpa questions." Kirby shrugged. "And she tried to braid my hair. Oh, and she had candy in her purse."

"But we only had one piece." Archie huffed. "Only one."

"That's probably for the best, Archie. Too much sugar might make you sick to your stomach. We don't want that." She pushed the hair off his forehead and pressed a kiss there.

He sighed. "You're right, Momma." He lifted the extra-firm pillow the nurse had brought him to hug when his stomach hurt. "It hurts to sneeze. I don't wanna throw up."

"Ew." Kirby stuck her tongue out in distaste. "Gross." She patted her brother's foot. "We can watch that wild animal show you like since you can't read your comics."

"Okay. Thanks, Kirby."

Grandpa Quincy changed the TV channel and stood, stretching.

"You should go home, Grandpa. Get some rest." Eloise lowered her voice. "The antibiotics are working so we should be discharged early in the morning."

"I know, I know. But he's my boy, too. I don't like him having an infection." He glanced at Archie. "I can't help but worry. I'd rather worry here, where I can see him, than sit at home alone."

"I can't argue with that." She smiled at him. "Thank you for putting up with us. I know it's been a lot."

"Aw, El, stop worrying about that, will you?" His hands rested on her shoulders. "I'm happy to have you back in my life, Sassy. I'd do just about anything to help you and these kids out."

"You're the best grandpa. Ever." She felt her phone vibrating in her pocket and pulled it out. "It's Ted," she whispered. "For the kids."

Grandpa Quincy sighed. "That's good. It's good he's consistent on that front. A kid needs to be able to rely on their parents."

"I agree." She answered the phone. "Hello?"

"Eloise. How's Archie doing?"

She turned away and whispered, "He has an infection so we're staying another night. Other than that, he's doing well. Feeling more like his old self."

"Is this infection cause for concern?" He sounded worried.

"No. Dr. Rowe said she wanted to watch him overnight and make sure he was responding to the antibiotics before sending him home." She ran a hand over her hair. "I'd rather be cautious, too."

"Of course. Of course. So he'll still be in the hospital tomorrow?"

"Until Dr. Rowe says he's ready to go, yes. That's it." She turned back to the kids. "Guess who's on the phone?" She infused as much enthusiasm into her voice as she could muster.

"Daddy?" Kirby asked, all smiles.

"Is it? Is it Dad?" Archie was reaching for the phone. "Can I talk to him first?"

"You go first. You're sick." Kirby patted his foot.

"That's very sweet of you, Kirby." Eloise handed the phone to Archie.

"Dad?" Archie's excitement was almost too much for Eloise to bear. She loved that her son loved his father. It was the way it should be. But every week, the lie seemed bigger and heavier than the week before. "Good." Archie put one of his pillows across his lap and played with the tag on the edge of the pillow. "I didn't cry." Another pause. "Yep. I'm a big kid now."

Eloise nodded.

"Momma said they didn't keep it." Archie sighed heavily. "I wanted to. In a jar. Kirby said that would be gross."

She hadn't been disappointed when Dr. Rowe said they had disposed of his appendix. As interesting as the idea was, she didn't relish keeping her son's discarded organ in a glass jar for visitors to appreciate. Though, it would have been a conversation starter.

She sat in the chair beside Archie's bed. It was a habit. When the kids talked to Ted on the phone, she listened in. It wasn't meant as eavesdropping—more like staying informed. If something was said that she needed to handle, she'd rather take care of it immediately versus letting them get upset. They were still so young.

"No. Momma and Grandpa Quincy drove me." He paused. "Or I bet Mr. Mike would take me in the ambulance. He's Momma's friend and he drives an ambulance." Another pause. "He was friends with Momma when she was little, too. I like him a lot, too." This pause lasted longer than the others. Archie's gaze shifted to her, widened, then went back to the tag on the pillow. He took a very deep breath and said, "Okay."

Eloise sat forward. Archie sounded...off. "Everything okay?"

Archie nodded but didn't look at her. "She's asking me if everything is okay," he said into the phone.

Eloise frowned.

"Everything is great, Momma." Archie gave her a thumbs-up. "Okay." He smiled. "I love you, too. Okay. Here's Kirby." He handed the phone to his sister.

"Hi, Daddy." Kirby held the phone with both hands. "He's fine. He has a hug pillow in case his tummy hurts." She was nodding. "Yep. He's super brave."

Eloise's eyes shifted to Archie. He was fidgeting with the pillow tag, his whole body tense. "Archie, sweetie. Is everything okay?"

"Uh-huh." Archie shrugged. "We were just talking about stuff." For a kid who loved to tell every detail of every conversation, he was too quiet. Almost like he was hiding something.

"I'm glad. What sort of stuff?" She moved to sit on the side of the bed.

"Daddy said…" Archie finally looked at her. "Dad said he'll see us real soon." He was practically radiating with excitement.

Eloise, on the other hand, was dismayed. Why would he say such a thing? All he was doing was getting the kids' hopes up—only to disappoint them. Soon? Ted had been sentenced to two years—he'd only served, what, a year? Twelve months was an eternity to a seven-year-old. *Not soon.*

"My new friend Samantha likes ponies. And I have a dog friend named Clifford. He's big and red just like Clifford in the books." She stopped talking and took a breath. "He belongs to Mr. Mike. Yes, Momma's friend." Another pause. "Clifford came to Grandpa's house and we went to Clifford's house and he helped set up the wedding, too." She nodded. "Yes, with Mr. Mike. And Mr. Mike stayed with us yesterday but he didn't bring Clifford to the hospital." She shrugged. "He's nice. He gives good hugs, too." Another pause. "Me and Archie and Mommy."

Eloise's patience was running out.

"Okay, Daddy. I love you more." Kirby giggled. "More

and more." She giggled again. "Even more. The most." She nodded. "Okay, bye." Kirby handed her the phone.

Eloise went into the hall. "Ted?" The line was dead. She stared at the phone, grappling with her mounting frustration. "What is he thinking? What is he up to?"

"El?" Gretta was walking down the hall. "You okay?" She reached her and frowned. "You're mad at me, aren't you? I'm so sorry about the comic books. I came to replace them. I was hoping Archie hadn't read them yet."

"He did. But—"

"You have every right to be mad. I can't believe Dad thought his old comic books were okay for the boys." She was so upset. "I'm so sorry. Truly."

"I'm not mad at you, Gretta." She gave her a quick hug. "I figured you didn't know about the comic books." The comic books didn't seem like such a big deal now. "It's…"

"What?" Gretta's brow dipped. "What's happened? Archie's okay?"

"Yes. He's fine." Eloise hesitated. As much as she'd like to keep Ted out of Garrison, it couldn't last. The man would always be a part of the kids' lives. And, through them, her life, too. "My ex," she murmured.

"Oh." Gretta sighed. "Exes are the worst. Is yours a champion gaslighter? Mine misses his visitation days and then shows up when he wants, expecting Levi and I to adjust accordingly." She broke off. "Sorry. Too much?" She frowned. "What did yours do?"

Gretta's rant was exactly what Eloise needed to hear. If anyone would understand how she felt, it was Gretta. "He told Archie he'd see him soon. Which isn't possible because he's…in jail. But the kids don't know that because Archie is hypersensitive and his father being in jail would cause him constant stress." She paused. "Too much?"

"Oh." Gretta blinked. "No. Not at all." She frowned.

"Why on earth would he say that? Is he normally careless with their feelings?"

"Not really." Eloise didn't like the knot in her stomach. "He is the best version of himself with them. They adore him, especially Archie. I don't want them disappointed, you know?"

"I do." Gretta looked as confused and upset as Eloise felt. "I'm here for you. I mean it. Being a single mom... You're single *but* your ex is still around for your kid. A kid that you try to shelter from the bad side of their father. But you understand—I mean, you *really* understand."

"Boy, do I." Eloise smiled. "It's exhausting."

Gretta squeezed her arm. "And you've just been through this scare with Archie, too. How are you holding up? Really?" She paused. "I heard Mike's been watching over you. That's nice, isn't it? He's one of the good guys, you know? Taking care of his dad. Working as an EMT and a pick-up rider. He's the protect-and-shelter type." She shrugged. "If he wasn't moving, I'd say Mike Woodard was someone you could consider dating."

"But he *is* moving." It was hard picturing the place without Mike.

Gretta paused. "Last I heard, that was the plan. Some really good job with one of the national rodeo companies, too. Then his dad had a stroke and he delayed his start date to take care of him." Her smile was almost sad. "Like I said, he really is one of the good guys, isn't he?"

"Yes." He was. Her chest seemed to collapse in on itself, compressing her heart to the point of rupture.

But if he left, this intense *thing* between them would go, too. Wouldn't it? He'd go on to bigger and better things and so would she. They'd both be happy.

But...was it impossible for them to be happy together? The truth was he was *still* her Mikey. Knowing that, could they do what they always did? Pick up where they left off. Together.

Stop it. He was leaving. She was staying and she had no right to ask him to give up this opportunity and stay here, too.

This whole time, Gretta had been watching and waiting for her reaction.

Eloise pinned on her hostess smile. "He deserves only good things." That much was true.

MIKE SPLASHED COLD water on his face. Yesterday's paperwork had been mind-numbingly boring. But today had made up for that. He ran a hand along his forehead, the surge of adrenaline that had carried him through the afternoon's accident beginning to wane. Nothing like a multicar pileup along Interstate 10 to keep things tense and focused. Luckily, there'd been no fatalities. There had been, however, a number of injuries.

He wiped his hands on a paper towel and pushed out of the staff bathroom and into the locker room.

"I don't know about you but I'm thinking a nice long shower and a tall, cold beer is in order." Terri opened her locker and pulled out her bag. "Jimmy texted to tell me the brisket he's been slow roasting should be ready for dinner. Tonight's looking good."

"I would say so." Last night, he'd gone straight from the hospital to the stockyards arena to help out with the high school rodeo team. His plans for this evening were low-key. Check in on his father, go home, play catch with Clifford, and go to bed early. "I'm tempted to invite myself over."

"You don't need an invitation, Mike." Terri's snort was dismissive. "You're basically family. Our door is always open. But, knowing Jimmy, he might be stingy with his brisket."

"I understand. The man's a legend." Mike appreciated how proud Terri was of her longtime boyfriend's barbecue awards. He'd won several local competitions and had even placed at the state rodeo barbecue competition two years back. "Anything he cooks is a work of art."

"I won't tell him you said that." Terri shot him a look. "The man's ego is already two sizes too big." She slung her duffel bag over her shoulder.

"Next time, I'll be there." Brisket sounded good but he was too bone-tired to enjoy it.

"Sounds good. See you next week."

"Yep." He nodded as she walked out, then stowed his personal stethoscope and supplies in his locker, and stopped by the nurses' station long enough to sign out.

He was halfway down the hall before he realized where he was going. To the elevator—to Archie's room. Dr. Rowe assured him the boy was responding to antibiotics but Mike wanted to check on him all the same. Besides, his dad would want a report.

He got in the elevator and pressed the button.

"Hold the elevator, please," a man called out, the large balloon bouquet and cellophane-wrapped gift basket in his arms covering most of his chest and face.

"Got it," Mike answered, not wanting the man to trip over the dozen or more ribbons trailing on the ground. "You need a hand?"

"No, no, but thank you." The man entered the elevator.

"Going to see someone special?" He eyed the balloons and the basket. It was a lot.

"I am." The man set the basket on the floor. "My son. I haven't seen him in a while."

"Oh." Mike tried not to stare but… Were his eyes playing a trick on him or was this Eloise's ex-husband? Ted Barnes was here?

"I feel like a kid on Christmas morning." He ran a hand over his pressed shirt, then his hair. "But also like a man who's facing the most important job interview of his life."

"Is that so?" It was a good thing Mike was so tired or he'd have a hard time keeping his temper in check. There were so many things he wanted to say to this man and not one of them was nice. *Not that Ted Barnes is any of my business*.

"It is." He nodded. "You have kids?"

Mike shook his head. But if he did, he'd do everything in his power to be there for them. Things like not breaking the law so he didn't go to jail and that sort of thing.

"It's the best thing I ever did with my life." Ted shook his head. "Believe me, I have a lot of things to make up for. But today is a fresh start and, from here on out, I want to be that dad, you know? The one that embarrasses his kids because he's always there? Making them pancakes for breakfast or cheering them on at a school event. That's going to be me."

Mike nodded but didn't say a word. Hopefully, Ted Barnes meant everything he was saying. Archie and Kirby deserved a reliable, loving father—every child did.

The elevator arrived on the third floor and they both stepped out.

"Time to go surprise them." Ted picked up the basket and headed out of the elevator.

Surprise them? They didn't know he was coming? Mike was torn. Should he head back downstairs and let Ted surprise his family? Or should he be there, in case the surprise didn't go as well as Ted was counting on. Eloise was in for a shock.

He couldn't leave. With a sigh, he headed down the hall, a few steps behind Ted.

Ted was practically jogging, and the balloons bounced

and the ribbons swerved back and forth along the lino-
leum floor.

There was no denying the man was excited. But would
the kids—and Eloise—feel the same way? Mike's discomfort grew the closer they got to Archie's room. He
was overstepping—again. But when they reached room
319, it was empty. Good news for Archie. Not so good for
Ted Barnes.

"Mike?" Dr. Rowe came out of one of the other rooms.
"Are you looking for Archie?"

Mike and Ted exchanged a quick look.

"I am." He nodded. "Guess those antibiotics took care
of the infection."

"They did. He went home about an hour ago." Dr. Rowe
nodded. "Sweet kid. Sweet family." She glanced at Ted.

"Dr. Rowe, I'm Archie's father. Ted Barnes." Ted was
all smiles as he shook the doctor's hand. He turned to Mike
and raised an eyebrow.

"Mike Woodard." He shook the man's hand.

Ted's grip was unnecessarily strong. "I just arrived in
town and was hoping to surprise him."

"It's nice to meet you. I'm sure he'll be happy to see
you." Dr. Rowe glanced back and forth between the two
of them. "I should get back to checking on my patients."

"Thanks, Dr. Rowe."

"Yes, thank you for taking care of my son." Ted Barnes
waited until the doctor had walked away before saying,
"This is awkward. Are you the Mr. Mike I've heard so
much about?"

Mike couldn't have been more surprised. "I guess so."

"Mr. Mike and Clifford?" Ted gave him an assessing
once-over. "Eloise's childhood friend? It seems like you've
made an impression on my children."

More like, they've made an impression on me. Eloise

and her kids mattered to him—more than that, they'd taken up residence in his heart. And this man showing up had Mike's defenses on the rise.

"Maybe you can help me." The man was dead serious.

For a minute, Mike was too stunned to say a word. "I'm not sure how."

"You've been friends with Eloise for a long time, so you know she's not big on second chances. Once you mess up, that's it." He gave Mike a long, narrow-eyed look.

"Is that so?" What was the man fishing for exactly?

"I don't know what she has told you about us. Or me." Ted cleared his throat.

Us? Mike shook his head. "We don't talk much about the past."

"No?" He didn't seem too pleased by that. "Why would she? I messed everything up." He looked Mike in the eye, his posture slightly defensive. "I've got a lot to make up for. A lot. But that's what I'm going to do. They are all that matter to me. My family." The muscle in his jaw clenched. "That's why I'm here to stay."

The sinking feeling in Mike's stomach was hard and fast. More like the floor falling out from under him. "You're moving here? To Garrison?" Archie and Kirby might be happy about it, but would Eloise? Quincy? For a man who wanted to fix things, this seemed like an awfully bold first move.

"The kids miss me. I miss them. I'm hoping, maybe, Eloise misses me, too." He paused, almost like he was waiting for some sort of reaction. "We were a happy family not too long ago. I want to be part of their lives again."

He couldn't stop himself from asking, "Have you talked to Eloise about this?"

"I know what her answer would be. No. She's… It'll take time to win back her trust but, lucky for me, I've got nothing but time." He went on, an edge to his voice. "I want a second chance. I'll do whatever I have to in order to get my family back."

If he was trying to intimidate Mike, it wasn't working. Irritate, yes. He was ready to wrap this up. Should he try to give Eloise a heads-up or mind his own business—something he'd had a hard time doing when it came to Eloise and her kids. "There's nothing I can do to help with that."

"That's not what I need help with. I was hoping you could give me the inside scoop on Earl Ellis. I'm going to be working for him."

Mike ran a hand along the back of his neck. He didn't want to talk about Earl with Ted. He didn't want Ted anywhere near Earl Ellis. Earl was a friend of his father's—Tyson's father. "Good man. Hard worker. Expects his employees to do the same."

"I'm a hard worker. He won't find anyone more motivated than I am." Ted tugged at the collar of his shirt. "Anything else I should know?"

He didn't want to stand in the hospital hallway and help Ted Barnes figure out a way to make a living in Garrison. Selfishly, he didn't want Ted Barnes living here. Especially since Mike was leaving. "He's a good man."

"My parole officer, Wilson Newcomb, said as much. I'm staying in his garage apartment until I can get my own place."

"Wilson Newcomb?" As far as Mike knew, Wilson was the only parole officer in the county.

Ted nodded. "You know him?"

"Small town. You know pretty much everyone." He eyed the balloons and gift basket, his frustration welling up until there was no holding back what he had to say. "You don't know me from Adam but I need to speak my piece." He took a deep breath. "You have every right to a relationship with your kids. It's good you're here for *them*." Now came the tricky part. "I've known El since she was about Archie's age. We were close growing up. She's special— she always has been. I…care about her." *I always have and I always will.* "I wasn't around when things got tough for her, but I'm here now. She's been let down a lot. Too much. If you're here to win her back, you better mean it."

Ted seemed to be contemplating what Mike had said. "Or what?"

"Or you'll jeopardize the relationship you want with your kids. Don't put them in a situation where they have to pick sides." He ran his fingers through his hair.

"You're saying all this because you're worried about my kids?" His brows rose. "Not because you *care* about Eloise?" He didn't sound angry so much as curious.

Mike didn't answer. He didn't owe Ted Barnes any explanations.

"I respect what you said. And that you care about the kids and Eloise." Ted shifted the gift basket. "It's certainly been interesting meeting you, Mike Woodard. I have a feeling we'll be seeing more of each other. Like you said, it's a small town."

Mike watched the man walk down the hall and get back into the elevator. Ted Barnes wasn't the out-and-out villain he'd imagined—but he still didn't like him. How could he? He'd shaken up Eloise's world. And he was about to do it again. Mike sighed. Soon, Ted would be showing up on Quincy's front porch for his big surprise!

It wasn't right. Eloise deserved a heads-up. He pulled his phone from his pocket and called Quincy.

"Mike?" Quincy answered right away. "Everything okay with your dad?"

"He's fine." He stared into Archie's now empty hospital room. "But… I figured I should call and let you know that Ted Barnes is here."

"He what now?" Quincy barked out.

"He showed up at the hospital with balloons and presents for Archie. Almost talked my ear off, too." He ran a hand along the back of his neck. "I didn't think you and Eloise would appreciate him surprising you—I figured you'd want some time to prepare."

"You figured right." Quincy grumbled. "That would have been some surprise. And not a good one, either."

Which was exactly what Mike had been thinking. "Can I do anything?"

"Well, now, that's a good question." The older man sighed. "How about I call you in a bit. A visit from Clifford might be just the distraction the kids will need—once he's gone." He muttered an expletive. "Might help El, too. She's going to be fit to be tied."

"I'll wait for you to call." It'd be one of the hardest things he'd ever done, but he'd wait.

"I can't thank you enough for calling, son." Quincy's voice was thick. "You know, I always thought the two of you would end up together. You'd never pull anything like this, that's for sure." Another sigh. "I'll let you know how it goes." And he disconnected.

He left the hospital and headed straight for his father's house. At this rate, he might be spending another night on his dad's lumpy couch. That way, if Quincy called, it wouldn't take long to get to Eloise and the kids.

CHAPTER ELEVEN

ELOISE LAUGHED. "Don't let it fall." They were all gathered around the coffee table, watching the wooden block Jenga stack wobbling just a smidge as Archie slowly pulled a piece free.

"Whew." Archie sat the piece down. "That was close."

"You're good at this, Archie." Kirby sat on the edge of the couch. She didn't want to play Jenga because it scared her when the tower toppled over, but she didn't mind watching and cheering them on. She was a very good cheerleader.

Today had been a good day. Archie was healing and home. Gretta and Levi had come over after school with a stack of age-appropriate comic books. Kirby and Grandpa Quincy had made cupcakes that they were all enjoying. Brooke had dropped off a pizza for dinner that was devoured in minutes. It'd be bedtime soon and then she might enjoy a glass of the wine Brooke had brought over with the pizza. It was the first time in a long time she felt relaxed.

"Eloise." Her grandfather stood in the hallway. "Give me a hand?"

"Sure." She stood and followed her grandfather down the hall and into the kitchen. "What can I do?"

"I got a call from Mike." He sat, heavily, in one of the kitchen chairs. "We're going to have a visitor."

"Mike's coming over?" It shouldn't make her this

happy. "Is he bringing Clifford? Archie will be happy to see them both."

"No." He glanced down the hall. "Not Mike. Ted."

Eloise blinked, staring at her grandfather. "What?" She sat in the opposite chair.

"He turned up at the hospital—wanting to surprise everyone, Mike said." He shrugged. "Talk about a surprise."

"But he…" She swallowed. "It's too early for parole?" Wasn't it? "Wouldn't he have known about this for a while?" He had to have known. Why hadn't he told her? What was he up to? In seconds, her muscles were tense and knotted and a dull ache settled at the base of her neck.

"I'm grateful Mike called." He reached across the table and took her hand.

Eloise was, too. If Ted had shown up out of the blue, shock was more likely than surprise. She couldn't wrap her mind around how that would have gone.

Grandpa Quincy gave her hand a squeeze, then let it go. "Now, what do you want to do about this?"

Throw up? She swallowed. "What can I do? He is their father."

"I have a few other choice words to describe the man." He stood, hands on his hips, and stared down the hallway. "I'm not all that happy to have him under my roof."

"I'm sorry, Grandpa." She rested her elbows on the table and covered her face.

"You have nothing to apologize for." He rested a hand on her shoulder. "He's the disrespectful one—springing this on you and the kids. I'm not sure how he thinks showing up like this is a good idea."

"I hate seeing you upset." Eloise stood and went to hug him.

"Well, now…" He sighed, patting her back. "I'll stop

my blustering. No point to it, anyway, is there? Might as well make the best of it."

The best of it? "The kids will be so happy." Until he left. Was he leaving? What was his plan?

"Momma, it's your turn," Kirby called down the hall-way.

"You good, Sassy?" Her grandfather held her by the shoulders.

She had to be—for the kids. "I'm good." She pinned on a smile. "It's my turn." She took a deep breath and headed back to the family room. "My turn?" Her hands were shaking so when she went to pull out her piece, the whole tower came tumbling down.

"Poor Momma." Kirby hugged her. "It's okay."

"Wanna try again?" Archie asked, propped on his side with his hug pillow tucked under his arm. "Or play something else?"

"Let's play again." Levi sat up on his knees.

Kirby crawled around on the floor, picking up pieces and gave them to Gretta. Gretta handed them to Levi, who was stacking up the tower.

"Excellent teamwork." Grandpa Quincy sat in his recliner, his gaze turning to the front window every few seconds.

Every creak of the floorboard or old-house noise made Eloise startle. The kids didn't notice the new tension flooding the room, but Gretta did. There was no preventing the stretching of Eloise's nerves—and patience. Being reunited after a year was bound to be emotional. And after the reunion? Then what?

They made it three rounds before the inevitable knock on the door.

"I'll get it." She stood, rubbed her hands together, and

took a deep breath. She grabbed the doorknob and yanked the door open.

There he was. Ted. With balloons and a huge gift basket full of who knows what. It didn't matter really. Because it *was* Ted.

He smiled. "Hi." His smile wavered. "I… Um, surprise."

"Hi." She swallowed. "Yes. You're…*here*." And he looked exactly the same way he had the last time she'd seen him.

There was an awkward pause as he took inventory of her appearance.

She pulled at her T-shirt. She did not look the same. She'd let her hair go back to its natural color, sold off all of her couture and name-brand clothing, and there was the extra weight.

"I… I was hoping to see the kids. I've got something for Archie." He shifted from foot to foot. "And Kirby. Are they here? Can I see them?"

If she sent him away, the kids would never forgive her. That's all that mattered right now. The kids. "Sure." She stepped inside, then whispered, "Just remember, Archie needs to be pretty still for now."

"Of course." He took a deep breath and followed her into the house.

Everything seemed to move in slow motion. Ted set the basket and balloons down, then hurried to Archie's side. Archie was ecstatic. His happy smile tore at her heart—right before it was replaced by a flood of tears.

"Oh, Archie." Ted cupped his son's face. "Don't cry. Please, don't." He was at a loss, looking to her.

Eloise stepped forward, sat at the foot of the couch, and squeezed Archie's foot. "He's here to see how you're feeling. Don't cry, sweetie. You don't want to irritate your stomach."

"Hug your pillow," Levi said, looking mighty suspicious of Ted. "Who are you, mister?"

"That's my daddy," Kirby whispered but didn't move. She stared at Ted with saucer-like eyes, frozen in place. "Mommy and Daddy are divorced and Daddy has to travel lots and lots."

Eloise was having a hard time not crying herself.

"Hi, Freckles." Ted held out a hand for her.

Kirby blinked, glanced at Archie, then back at Ted. Her chin crumpled and her lower lip wobbled. "Daddy?"

"I'm here." Ted's struggle was real. Archie had a grip on one hand but Kirby wouldn't get close enough for him to reach her. "I've missed you two so much."

Kirby nodded, took one step, then another—until she took his hand.

Eloise watched the whole thing with a knot in her throat and her lungs fighting for air. When he pulled them both in for a hug, it was easier to breathe. She blinked rapidly, staring at the ceiling overhead until the threat of tears had passed.

"You're here?" Kirby leaned back and rested a hand along the side of his face. "You're real."

"I am." He pressed a kiss to her temple. "I couldn't wait to see you. Hug you. See your smile—and your freckles, too."

Kirby pointed at her face. "They are still there."

"I'm glad." He chuckled and pulled her in for another hug.

"Are you done traveling?" Archie asked. "Can you stay with us for a while?"

"I'm done, Archie." Ted smoothed his son's hair from his forehead.

That answered that. If Ted was on parole, what was

his plan? She might not want to know, but she needed to know. For the kids.

"Really?" Archie hugged his pillow. "You're staying here?"

Ted nodded. "I am." He glanced at her. "We'll talk about all that later. Now, tell me what you've been up to."

"Lots." Archie paused. "This is my friend, Levi. And his mom."

"Nice to meet you." Ted always had a charming smile.

"Gretta Williams." But Gretta's smile was cautious and her posture was standoffish.

"You remember my grandfather, Quincy Green? From our wedding." Which felt like another life.

Grandpa Quincy didn't bother with a smile. Disapproval was written all over his face. "Oh, I remember. You can call me Mr. Green." He didn't stand or extend a hand. "Quite a bit has happened since the last time I saw you, Mr. Barnes."

"Yes, sir." The muscle in Ted's jaw tightened, but he nodded. "I appreciate you taking care of the kids and Eloise—"

"That's what family does," her grandfather interrupted. "No thanks needed."

Eloise managed to catch her grandpa's attention. She shot him a long, pointed look. He was upset, she got that. But being angry at Ted wouldn't change this new reality. If anything, the kids might get upset with their great-grandfather for not being nice to their newly returned father.

Luckily, her grandfather seemed to get the message. He took a deep breath and tried to relax his hold on the arms of his recliner.

"Did you go anywhere exciting when you were traveling, Dad?" Archie was all wide-eyed and curious. "What was it like?"

"Did you go to Paris?" Kirby asked. "I don't know where that is. Is it far? My friend Samantha's mom and dad are going there after they get married."

"Are they? That's a good place for a honeymoon." Gretta smiled at Kirby. "It is very far away. So far, you have to ride in an airplane for hours."

"That far?" Kirby appeared impressed.

"Did you go there, Dad?" Archie wasn't going to let up. "Africa with the lions or Egypt and the pyramids?"

Ted looked extremely uncomfortable—and unsure of what to do or say.

"Why don't you see what your dad brought you." Eloise pushed the large gift basket forward. "Afterward, we'll need to start getting ready for bed."

"But, Momma." Archie's mouth dropped open. "I'm not going to school tomorrow. Do I *have* to go to bed?"

"You do." She nodded. "I'll be getting your school-work from your teacher. You're not going to be watching TV all day."

Archie sighed heavily and crossed his arms over his chest.

"I can come back tomorrow." Ted pulled the gift closer. "If that's okay?" He glanced at Eloise, then Grandpa Quincy.

Her grandfather snorted.

"After school," Kirby asserted. "I don't want to miss anything."

"That sounds fair." Eloise faced Ted. "Does that work for you? Around four."

"That's perfect." Ted directed their attention to the contents of the basket.

The kids "oohed" and "aahed" over every item as if they'd never seen anything so amazing. Crayons, action figures, a dog puzzle, coloring books, and more. Ted didn't seem to realize the gift wasn't what was in the basket, it was him—being here.

Every few minutes, Gretta would send a sympathetic smile her way, but Eloise was okay. All things considered, everything was going well. She didn't relish the one-on-one conversation she and Ted were going to have to have, but it wasn't going to happen tonight.

When the basket was empty, Gretta made a big production out of stretching and yawning. "We should get home, Levi. You do have to go to school tomorrow."

"Aw, Mom." Levi huffed. "I can stay home and keep Archie company. He's going to be bored. *So* bored."

"That's a kind offer, Levi. You're a good friend." After seeing the two boys together, it was clear they were fast friends. Eloise might have a few concerns about Levi being older and prone to more aggressive storytelling, but she could work with that.

"But you're going to school." Gretta stood and held out her hand. "Come on."

Levi huffed and groaned and made sure everyone knew he wasn't happy.

"Thank you for coming." Eloise accepted Gretta's hug. "And for staying," she whispered for her ears alone.

Gretta's hold tightened. "I'll call you later."

"I guess I'll head out, too." Ted ruffled Archie's hair and gave Kirby a wink. "But I need more hugs, first."

"But you'll be back tomorrow?" Archie asked. "You promise? You're not going away?"

"I promise." Ted gave him a gentle hug. "I'll be here at four."

"Okay." Archie toyed with one of the action figures Ted had brought. "I'm glad."

"Me, too." Kirby gave him a big hug. "I'm going to tell

everyone in my class that you're here. I bet Samantha will be so, so happy for me."

Ted accepted a second hug from Kirby and stood. "Night, Eloise. Good night, Mr. Green."

"Night." Eloise opened the front door for everyone. "Thank you for coming." As soon as she closed the door, Kirby and Archie started talking. They were both thrilled that their father was here and staying and coming back tomorrow. Eloise only nodded, unwilling to say too much until she knew what, exactly, Ted's plans were. "It's been a good evening. Let's get you ready for bed and tucked in so tomorrow can get here even faster, okay?" And once they were tucked in, she'd take three cupcakes to the Woodard house. Mike's phone call was the only reason the evening hadn't turned into a nightmare and she wanted him to know how very grateful she was.

MIKE SAT ON the front steps of his father's porch. He'd been sitting there for an hour or more—long enough for the sky to go from blue to violet to the deep purple it was now. At some point, his father had turned on the porch light so he wasn't sitting in the dark. The solar lights lining the flower beds glowed warmly, giving enough light for Clifford to sniff out and snap at a moth or cricket.

"You tired?" he asked when Clifford climbed the steps and slid flat beside him, his big head in Mike's lap.

Clifford yawned.

Mike chuckled and gave the dog a thorough head and neck scratch.

Clifford went from relaxed and sprawling to sitting up with his ears perked up. The dog stared down the street, head turning one way, then the other.

"What's up?" Mike looked in the same direction but didn't see anything. "A raccoon or something?" Hopefully it wasn't another skunk. Clifford's attempt to befriend the varmint hadn't ended well. After two tomato baths and a haircut, the poor dog was allowed back into the house—but not on the furniture.

Clifford trotted down the steps and across the yard. He barked once, his fluffy tail swaying slowly, then faster.

"Hey, Clifford." It was Eloise.

Mike pushed off the porch. "El?" It was almost like he'd willed her here with his worrying. But she was here and his chest was the slightest bit lighter.

"Hi." She raised one hand in a little salute and held a tinfoil-covered plate in the other. "I wanted to stop by. I hope it's not too late."

"No, it's not too late." He was so relieved to see her. The last couple of hours had been all stressing and pacing and hoping she and the kids were okay. He opened the front gate. "Come on in."

She did, laughing when Clifford circled her several times. "Are you saying hello, too? I'm sorry I didn't bring anything for you, Clifford. I don't know what I was thinking."

He loved that laugh more than any other. "Oh, believe me, he's been spoiled plenty today. Dad's a little too generous with the treats." He glanced at her as they walked, slowly, to the front porch. "You want something to drink? A lemonade or tea or something?"

"No, thank you. If it's okay, can I sit? It's so peaceful." She followed him up the steps of the porch.

She wanted to stay? He drew in an easy breath. "Anytime." He took the plate she held out to him. "What's this?"

"Cupcakes. 'Thank you' cupcakes."

"Thank you? For what?"

She shot him a disbelieving look and sat in one of the wicker rockers. "Calling Grandpa. If you hadn't, he probably would have had a heart attack and I…well, I don't know what I'd have done." She glanced up at him. "Thanks to you, it went smoothly. As smoothly as one could expect, all things considered."

He sat in the other rocking chair, placing the plate on the small circular table between the chairs. As much as he wanted to know more, he wasn't going to push. She seemed okay, that was enough.

"It's a nice night. Cool. It's almost fall-like." She leaned back in the chair.

"A rarity." Made better by the fact that he was enjoying it with her.

She sat for a while, one leg tucked beneath her, the other kept the rocking chair rocking. "The kids are thrilled he's here." She turned her head and met his gaze.

"He is their father. It's good they're happy." He paused. "Isn't it?"

She took a deep breath. "I think so… Yes." She shook her head. "I don't know, honestly. I'm still processing *everything*." She stopped rocking. "I should be mad, Grandpa Quincy sure is, but I can't be. I have to…" She stopped talking and shook her head again.

"Go on. Let it out." He leaned forward, resting his knees on his elbows.

The way she was studying him—she seemed to be searching for something.

His gaze held hers. "I mean it. I honestly can't imagine what you're thinking or feeling. It's probably all over the place. I'm on the outside looking in and I'm hot one minute, cold the next."

There was a hint of sadness to her smile. "I'm… I'm so tired of being mature and keeping it together." She pushed out of the chair. "I haven't had a choice in so long." She paced the length of the porch, then came back, turning to him. "It's not just Ted. It started years before Ted." She leaned against the wooden porch railing. "My mind is sort of spinning and spinning, you know? I'm trying to sort it out."

He sat back. "You talk. I'll listen."

"Why, Mike?" She swallowed. "I know you're a great guy. I know you've always been here for me... I just don't understand why."

Because, fool that I am, I still love you. He cocked an eyebrow, doing his best to keep his tone light. "Too nice, remember? Go on."

She swallowed again. "When Mom died, Dad sort of... broke. He'd been drinking, you know that, but I wanted to stay close to Mom after that first heart attack. Then he got *really* drunk and he hit me. I think it shocked him as much as it shocked me—that's why I wound up here that Christmas. That one thing changed my whole life." She shrugged.

He ran a hand over his face, his heart twisting and a huge lump in his throat. Her own father had struck her? Not hugged her or comforted her or given her the love she needed. No, he'd hurt her mentally and physically.

And then she'd come to him—to find him fall-down drunk... No wonder she'd been so upset. If he could go back, leave that bottle of whiskey untouched, and hold her, he would.

"Dad's drinking stole the security I needed." Her gaze locked with his. "And everything good and stable was buried with my mother. Dad couldn't talk about her—wouldn't talk about her—or he'd drink. Obviously, I stopped talking about her. I never got a chance to really grieve her."

He hadn't let her grieve? For her own mother? He swallowed against the knot in his throat.

"We moved a lot, Dad got married and divorced a lot,

and I felt more trapped with each passing day. Once I was accepted to university, I left and severed all ties with my father." She ran a hand over her hair. "College was the first time I was on my own. It was pretty great. And I met Ted. He was this life force. So…so kind and funny. He didn't drink." She shook her head. "I'd talk and he'd listen. Fast-forward a couple of years to graduation, the kids, I got a little flower and tea shop and his business was taking off." She laughed. "You should have seen some of the big dinner parties and events I'd organize to help grow his business." She shuddered. "I didn't know what he was doing." She glanced at him. "I didn't know a lot of things until after we divorced. Like his mistress."

Mike was stunned. "I thought the man couldn't be a total fool since he married you…"

She was smiling. She'd just told him all she'd told him and she was smiling?

"Why are you smiling?"

She stood. "Because… You're *you*." Her cheeks flushed. What did that mean?

"The memories I have of here, growing up… It's one of the reasons I brought the kids here." She laughed. "Well, and because I had no place else to go."

He could study her face for hours. "Most of our memories together were…special to me."

"Me, too." Her hand rested on his arm. "Thank you for today."

All he could do was stare at her. If he spoke, he'd say something that he'd regret.

"I'm sorry if I hurt you. Then and now." She squeezed his arm, then rested her hand on the railing between them. "Time has passed and things change and here we are. I'm trying to start over and you will be soon, too."

He blinked. "How's that?"

"Your job." She pushed off the railing and sat in the rocking chair once again. "When do you go?"

"After Founder's Day." He ran a hand along the back of his neck. "I don't trust Dad to take it easy." Not that that would change after he left. And that worried him.

"You're a good son." She smiled. "And you're a good friend, too. I'd really like to be your friend again, Mike."

There were so many things he wanted to say but all he managed was, "Done." She'd just shared years of upheaval and hurt with him.

"Tell me about this job?" She sat forward as Clifford sat at her knees, waiting. "I hear you'll be traveling?" She scratched behind Clifford's ear.

"It's with the National Rodeo League. Doing what I do here, only there." He smiled. "Pick-up man and EMT."

"Always the protector." She said this in a baby voice, totally besotted by Clifford's floppy-tongued smile. "Isn't he? Your daddy is taking care of everyone."

Clifford's tail thumped against the wooden-planked deck.

"I don't know about that." He chuckled. "But it's what I'm trained to do."

"More like what you're wired to do." She sat back, smiling when Clifford rested his head in her lap. "Even when we were younger, you were that way."

"I was?" He sat back in the rocker. "Do tell."

"Okay. One example?" She peered at him.

"You have more than one?" It felt good to be sharing stories with her. There were so many happy ones.

"Oh, Mike. I have so many." She shook her head. "How about Easter. I'd just reached for a golden egg—which, if I recall correctly, was a big deal—and that boy tripped me, took the golden egg, and started picking up all the eggs that had spilled out of my basket." She paused. "What was his name? RJ something?"

"Malloy." Mike chuckled. "RJ Malloy. He's still causing trouble."

"You know what they say, if you love what you do, you'll never work a day in your life. He did love getting into mischief."

Mike laughed—and so did she. "He did and he does."

"Anyway, you came over and told him to make it right or else." She glanced at him. "What would the 'or else' scenario have looked like?"

"I never found out. I was always just that much bigger than everyone else that no one tried to test me." He grinned. "It's a good thing, too, because I don't have much of a stomach for fighting."

She was doing that thing again—like she was looking for something. "RJ not only handed over all the eggs I'd dropped but the golden egg, too."

He nodded. "I *do* remember that."

"Fourth of July. I was really young." She kept rubbing Clifford's head. "I'd never been that close to fireworks before and it was so loud. It felt like the ground was shaking, too. You told Rusty to stay with me and you ran off. When you came back, you had those safety headphones for me to wear. So, I sat there, wearing those too-big earphones, watching the fireworks." She smiled at him. "It wasn't just me, though. You took care of all your friends."

He listened as she regaled him with tales of bandaging up Rusty's leg after he'd fallen out of a tree—into a cactus. Another time, he'd crawled under Brooke's grandma's house to get an entire litter of kittens out before the impending flash-flooding put the little felines in danger.

"I was covered in mud." He chuckled. "I remember my mother's face when I stood on the front porch. She made

Rusty hose me off in the backyard, while it was pouring rain, before she let me into the mudroom."

Eloise laughed, too. "Rusty probably loved that."

"He did. My little brother never passed up a chance to torment me. Come to think of it, that hasn't changed all that much." He shook his head.

"He idolized you."

"That part has changed." He laughed, loving that she was laughing along with him.

"When I first met you two, I was so jealous. You were so close and, being an only child, I'd never had that sort of connection. But you included me, in everything, and I felt like part of the family." She sighed. "Coming to Garrison was always...special."

He nodded. "It's a good little town."

There was another stretch of silence.

"Won't you miss it?" she asked, her voice soft.

"I'm not leaving, not really. I'll be on the road part of the year, is all." But the more he thought about it, the less enthusiastic he became.

"So really, the best of both worlds?" She doubled her pats at Clifford's grumble-moan.

"I guess." His mind wandered, circling back around to where this all started. "You and the kids are going to be okay? With Ted here, I mean?"

She nodded. "I think so. I want to believe it will be. We have some details to work through but we will. If he's going to stay in Garrison, I'm going to be the one to set the terms."

"Good." He liked hearing the resolve in her voice. "That's as it should be, El."

"I'll have to stay vigilant until Ted accepts that." She shook her head, her jaw tightening. "I hate giving the man any more of my time, but it's what I have to do until I know he's on the same page as I am. Right? It's worth it for the kids?"

Ted Barnes didn't deserve the thought and consideration she was giving him. He'd hurt her and disappointed her and the kids over and over. Yet, here she was, figuring out how to fit him back into their lives. If the man hurt them...

Mike gripped the arms of the rocking chair and took a slow, deep breath. She was smart and tough and he trusted she could handle this. It was Ted he didn't trust. El needed his support, not to be burdened with his concerns. "For the kids." He nodded.

"I'm their mom. They come first. And they're counting on me to protect them." She glanced at him. "You know all about that."

"You're a good mother, El-Bell. They don't know how lucky they are to have you as their mom." He swallowed the lump in his throat. "Just remember you've got a whole team of folk here that will support you—and be on standby for you and the kids. I know what you've been through but things are different now. You're not alone, you hear me? People care." *I care.* He cleared his throat, the warmth in her eyes pressing in on him. "And if good ol' Ted gets out of line, let me know and I'll come 'or else' him."

She was laughing again, her whole beautiful face alive and happy. This was how she should always be. El-Bell deserved nothing less than a life of laughter and love—surrounded by people who'd offer her nothing but the same. Now that he had her friendship again, he'd be one of them. She was his first and only true love and he'd always love her. That was fact. But that didn't mean he had to act on it. She'd come to him as a friend. His fool heart would just have to accept that her friendship was more than enough.

CHAPTER TWELVE

AFTER A SOLID night's sleep, Eloise had woken with the sun. Her talk with Mike had given her a sense of calm and purpose. She could do this. She would do this. And she didn't have to do it alone. Her morning walk had only confirmed what Mike had told her. People did care. Not only had the sweet couple from Old Towne Books and Coffee come out with a box of freshly baked blueberry muffins and to ask after Archie, she'd come home to find Miss Patsy Monahan—with her fire-engine red hair—waiting on the front porch with two casseroles and a coloring book.

"How is sweet Archie?" she asked.

"He's doing well." Eloise opened the front door. "Would you like to come in?"

"Oh, no, I wouldn't want to intrude." She hesitated. "But, well, we heard about your unexpected visitor last night and we, the Ladies Guild, wanted you to know that we are one phone call away." She handed an envelope to her. "We girls have to stick together. This is *your* home now, Eloise Green, you and those kids."

Eloise wasn't sure how to respond.

"My own late husband was a no-count excuse of a man that spent more of our marriage in jail than out. When he dropped dead in his cell, it was a relief. I'm not saying the same is true for your ex-husband, I'm simply saying we'll be keeping an eye on him." She patted Eloise on the cheek. "I'm sure we won't be the only ones."

She wasn't about to feel sorry for Ted but…things were certainly going to be interesting.

"That's all I wanted to say." She offered over the two casserole trays and the coloring book. "We'll stop by in a day or two to see what we can do to lend a hand around the house. Your grandfather relies on you at the shop. We might not be able to work magic with flowers like you can, but there's not a one of us in the guild that hasn't raised at least one child." And with that, she spun on her heel and left.

She wasn't going to ignore her grandfather's warning about the guild, but she couldn't help but be touched by Patsy Monahan's confession.

Miss Patsy wasn't the only one who had left care packages. Her grandfather had said it was all part of small-town living but it touched Eloise deeply. She was smiling as she packed Kirby's lunch box, kissed her cheek, and said goodbye to her little girl and her grandfather.

"What are we going to do today?" Archie asked, walking oh so slowly from his bedroom to the couch. He sat, his pillow pressed to his abdomen.

"Rest, rest, and more rest. Doctor's orders. With a little bit more walking each day. How are you feeling?" She sat beside him. "How's your tummy?"

"Better than yesterday." He gave her a thumbs-up.

"That's great news." She smoothed his curls from his forehead. "Make sure you tell me if that changes, okay?"

He nodded. "I'm really hungry."

"I just happen to have some breakfast for you." She smiled. "Blueberry muffins or donuts from Mr. Woodard. Lucille from the café sent a breakfast pizza."

"What's breakfast pizza?"

"Lots of sugar." She chuckled. From the looks of it, it was all cinnamon sugar and a cream-cheese topping.

"Can I have some of that?" He rubbed his hands together.

"A sliver." She nodded. "But you have to eat an egg, too."

"Yes ma'am." He grinned.

"This is for you." She handed him the activity workbooks Miss Patsy had brought with her. "Crosswords and word searches, hidden object pictures, all that sort of stuff. Good exercise for your brain." She helped him get comfortable against the pillows and placed his hugging pillow along his side.

"I don't want my brain to get bored." He opened the book.

"Me neither." She handed him a pencil. "I'll get breakfast going."

"Thanks, Momma." He was already working on the first page.

Eloise turned on the radio, then pulled the eggs from the refrigerator. Her son was recovering from surgery and her ex-husband had showed up in town, but she was surprisingly upbeat. She put a skillet on the stovetop, turned on the gas burner, and added a touch of butter to the skillet.

The house phone rang so she reached for it. "Hello?"

"Eloise? It's Nolan Woodard. I wanted to check in on you and the boy."

"Archie's doing really well, thank you. I'm doing well, too. And thank you for the donuts, too." She cracked an egg into the ceramic mixing bowl.

"Mike said Miss Kirby liked donuts so I was hoping Archie did, too." He chuckled. "You think Clifford and I could come over and visit for a spell later on this afternoon? I was thinking around two or so?"

Would Mike come, too? No, he had a job. Jobs. "Oh, Mr. Woodard, that sounds wonderful." She added another egg.

"Well, you let me know if you need anything before then. I know you've got your hands full. You have a good morning."

"You, too, Mr. Woodard." She hung up and reached for

a whisk—when the phone rang again. He must have forgotten something. "Mr. Woodard?"

"No. Mr. Barnes." Ted chuckled. "Good morning."

Great. Okay. We're doing this already. "Morning."

"I thought you'd like to get together and talk things through." He paused, waiting.

She let him wait.

"Now that I'm here, we can set up some sort of visitation schedule that accommodates your work and *social* life." There was a smile in his voice.

What did that mean? She whisked the eggs before dumping them into the skillet. "It's best if we take it a day at a time."

"Eloise—"

"I'm happy for you to arrange visits here, for now." She wasn't going to budge on this.

"Fair enough." He sighed. "I have a garage apartment at my parole officer's place a few blocks from you."

"Your plan is to stay here?" she asked. He'd yet to say that outright.

"Yes. You and the kids are here. This is where home is." He paused. "I've got a job lined up at Ellis's Feed Store or something or other."

"Oh?" It was Garrison. From what Grandpa said last night, Ted was going to have a hard time finding a job without a local vouching for him.

"Parole officer set it up. Your friend Mike said Earl Ellis was a good man."

Eloise frowned. Mike and Ted had talked? How had that gone? "If Mike says he's a good man, then he is."

"Mike's a decent guy."

Decent? That was almost offensive. Mike was so much more than that. Not only had he listened to her long-winded rant last night but he'd talked to Ted about his new job and reassured Ted about his new boss? Decent didn't do him justice.

"He's very fond of you and the kids." He cleared his throat. "Sounds like he's been a good friend to you for a while so... I guess I need to find a way to like the guy."

She frowned, grabbed a spatula and flipped the eggs. She was not going to talk about Mike with Ted.

"You hold the keys to the kingdom here, Eloise. I just want to be part of your lives again."

"The kids want that, too." She turned off the burner.

"What about us?" He cleared his throat. "No chance—"

"No." She closed her eyes and pinched the bridge of her nose. "No chance. If that's part of your master plan here, this isn't going to work. I need you to understand that. I'm not playing hard to get. I mean it. There is *no* chance of the two of us *ever* getting back together."

"Message received."

"I hope you'll respect my decision." She pulled two plates from the cabinet and divided the eggs between the two. "Can you?"

"I can and I will, Eloise. You can't blame me for asking, though. Once upon a time, we had a good thing."

"I'm going to hold you to that. Respecting what I say, that is. The rest doesn't matter. That part of our lives is over." Ted having a mistress was a deal-breaker for her. There was no recovering or coming back from that. "We will see you at four?"

"I'll be there." He hung up the phone.

She added a piece of dessert pizza to Archie's plate and carried it into the family room. "Breakfast is served."

Archie didn't look up from his workbook. "Almost done."

She smiled and sat the plate on the table. "It's right here waiting, when you're ready."

The day consisted of reviewing the online queries for the Garrison Gardens website—a project she'd taken on when she'd first arrived in Garrison.

The Carmichael-Briscoe wedding had caused all sorts of chatter. There were three serious inquiries. She had to look up where, exactly, Jasperton and Holsom were in relation to Garrison but it might be worth the drive. She'd have to discuss that with Grandpa Quincy.

And, possibly, bringing on some part-time help. Her grandfather had happily been working shorter days since they'd moved. He was seventy-six, so he'd earned it. While she hoped there wouldn't be a lot of days like this in her future, it would be nice to have someone that could cover for both of them so he could rest and she could be with the kids—as needed.

When Mr. Woodard and Clifford showed up, Archie was ecstatic. Clifford happily laid alongside Archie on the couch while Mr. Woodard read to them about King Arthur, Lancelot, and Merlin. Eloise listened in while making raspberry thumbprint cookies for later.

Gretta showed up a little after three with Kirby, homework for Archie, and Levi. Her grandfather walking in ten minutes later was a surprise.

"It was a slow day," he explained, standing in the middle of the kitchen. "I put a sign on the door. It's not like people don't know how to reach me." He sighed. "Besides, I wanted to check in on Archie."

"Aww, that's so sweet." Gretta nodded. "He's right, Eloise. Everyone knows what happened with Archie."

Eloise poured out four glasses of tea. "You being here early doesn't have anything to do with Ted coming for a visit?"

He shrugged.

"I love you." She smiled at him. "You go sit with Mr. Woodard. I'll bring you some refreshments."

"Will do." He grabbed a cookie and popped it into his mouth. "Mmm-mmm."

"He is precious." Gretta stacked cookies onto a plate.

"He is. But don't let him fool you. He and Mr. Woodard are here for Archie—*and* Ted. You just watch." She eyed the cookie plate. "How about I chop up some apples for the kids, too?"

At three thirty, Mabel and Samantha arrived. At three forty-five, Brooke and Audy showed up with a set of miniature cowboys and horses—that all four kids immediately started to play with.

When Ted knocked at four, conversation came to a stop and all eyes turned his way.

"Hello?" He stepped inside the front door Eloise held open for him, shifting from foot to foot. "Ted Barnes."

"He's our daddy." Kirby jumped up and gave him a quick hug. "We're playing cowboys, Daddy." She sat on the floor, holding up the cowboy and his horse for him to see.

"Hi, Dad." Archie patted the couch beside him. "Come meet Clifford. And everyone."

Introductions were awkward, but Ted managed not to shy away from Audy's very direct eye contact and Mr. Woodard's rather tight-jawed nod of acknowledgment. Once he'd settled on the floor with the kids, Eloise decided it was safe to clean up the mess she'd made in the kitchen.

"Goodness. Did you use every bowl and pan in the house?" Brooke sat in one of the kitchen chairs at the table.

"Almost." Eloise smiled. "Here." She slid another chair around. "For your feet. I don't know about you, but my ankles got lost toward the end of my pregnancies."

"Same." Brooke pointed at her ankles.

Mabel tied on one of the aprons. "I can't wait to have babies."

"Babies?" Gretta laughed. "How many babies are you and Jensen planning to have?"

"Oh, I don't know. Lots, I hope." Mabel grinned.

"You do not have to help clean up, but you can keep me company." Eloise filled the sink with soap and water and got to work.

"How is *this* going?" Mabel pointed at the hallway. "When Gretta told me he'd just showed up, I couldn't believe it."

"Me, neither." Brooke shook her head. "Rusty told Audy. He also said Mike was pretty upset last night."

Eloise stopped scrubbing long enough to look at her pregnant friend. "He seemed okay when I saw him." If she could rewind the last ten seconds, she wouldn't have said those words.

But she had and all three of the women in the kitchen were studying her.

"You saw Mike last night?" Brooke asked, her brows high.

Gretta and Mabel seemed equally expectant.

"I... I wanted to thank him for warning us so I took him some cupcakes." She finished scrubbing the pan. "That's all."

"That was nice of you, Eloise." Mabel took the wet pan and dried it with a clean kitchen towel.

"He's still sweet on you." Brooke said it so matter-of-factly that Eloise turned to face her. "What's that look for?"

"We're friends. That's all." Eloise's chest was heavy.

"I think he wants more than that." Brooke pushed.

"But...he's leaving." Eloise went back to washing the bowl.

"Maybe." Brooke shrugged. "Audy says Mike took this

job to fill some sort of hole in his life. Now that you're back, I don't think that applies."

It took her a moment to digest this. She liked Audy's take on things—a little too much. The only way to know how Mike truly felt was to talk to him herself. "I thought you weren't going to do the whole matchmaking thing. Now you sound worse than Mabel. No offense." She smiled Mabel's way.

"None taken." Mabel smiled back. "You really think he's still in love with her, Brooke?"

"It's Mike," Brooke said, as if that explained everything. "Loyal to the end. He was devastated when you stopped visiting, Eloise. And by the fight you two had. He looked for you every holiday for the next two years, at least, hoping you'd show up."

Her heart bounced off her ribcage before twisting one way, then the other. He'd looked for her? Missed her? Then. A long time ago. "That was fifteen years ago," Eloise interjected, refusing to buy into Brooke's romantic notion.

"Fine, don't believe me. He didn't sit in some corner, pining for you. He dated and all, but it wasn't the same." Brooke's sigh was all impatience. "But he is interested now. We've all seen the way he looks at you, Eloise. If you gave him the slightest hint you were interested, Mike would jump at the chance to be with you."

"Stick horses?" Mike repeated. Was Tyson pulling his leg? "How many?" He helped Tyson wiggle the ten-foot bleacher board free from its bracket.

"Oh, at least fifty." Tyson ran a handkerchief over his face. "Probably twice that when it's all said and done."

"They want kids to ride stick horses down Main Street?"

"One of the Ladies Guild members saw something about some world record of the largest group of people riding stick horses and thought it sounded like something we needed to add to the Founder's Day Festival." Tyson squinted as he peered up at the sun overhead. "Why'd it get so warm all of a sudden?"

"It's Texas." Mike shook his head. "Stick horses. That'll be something."

"Yep." He looked his way. "You ready?"

"Yeah." On the count of three, the two of them hefted the ten-foot wooden board onto their shoulders, navigated their way down the stands, and stacked it on top of the pile they'd already removed. "Remind me why I'm helping you with this, again?"

"RJ bailed on me, as usual. It's hard finding people to do physical work. And you're a good friend." Tyson rolled his neck. "And you've been laying low for the last few days and this helps out with that."

Mike glared at his friend.

"Sometimes the truth hurts." Tyson chuckled. "No updates?"

"Plenty," Mike grumbled before giving Tyson the news. His father had been dutifully visiting with Archie for the last week. Every time Mike had planned to visit himself, something had stopped him. From Clifford having tummy trouble to taking his father in for a check-up to having to cover two extra shifts at the hospital, he'd had to make do with his father's updates or whatever he heard around town.

From what he'd heard, Ted Barnes was visiting his kids every day after school, doing good work at the feedstore, and on his best behavior in general. It was good news— as long as Eloise kept her eyes open. She would. He didn't need to be there or to protect her, she was smart and more than capable of handling things. But that didn't stop him from worrying anyway.

"Is that what's eating at you?" Tyson opened his water bottle and gulped down the contents.

Yes, it was eating at him. After Eloise's visit, his heart and his head had been in two very different places. His heart wanted Eloise to be his. His head told him friendship was better than nothing. "You're seeing things." He ran a handkerchief along the back of his neck.

"You want to try that again?" Tyson waved as Audy opened the arena gates. "Before Audy and the high school rodeo team gets here and sees you all riled up like this."

"I'm not riled up," he snapped.

Tyson tried not to laugh, but it didn't work. When he stopped, he said, "I'm sorry, man. I've never seen you this way. Ever. I know it's not funny but…it sort of is."

"I'm going to saddle Chuck." Mike was officially out of patience and energy.

"Hold up." Tyson caught up to him, keeping stride. "Why don't you ask her out? On a date. Her ex can watch the kids, can't he? He must be good for something?"

Mike wasn't sure if Tyson's suggestion was genius or ludicrous. Friends didn't go on dates.

"I'd think, before you leave, you'd want to at least try?" He held up his hands. "I'll stop now, before your face gets any redder."

But Tyson's words caught up with him and Mike stopped walking. "You could hire him."

"Hire who?" Tyson's brow creased in confusion.

"Ted Barnes." He shook his head. "The man said he was looking to find a place of his own. Might help him do that."

"You want me to hire your… Eloise's ex-husband? It's weird enough that he's working for Dad." He scratched the back of his head. "You want him to work here, where you'll see him on a regular basis? Are you feeling all right? Dehydrated, maybe?"

"You need help. He needs a job." Though it was hard imagining Ted out here, sweating and doing physical labor. "And I'm leaving. Soon." Probably. Maybe.

"I guess it might work. I don't need someone full-time." Tyson still looked confused. "But Dad's working him pretty hard. Just remind me why you want to help this man?"

"It's not about him, it's about—"

"Eloise."

"No. His kids." Mike hung his head. "If he's trying to be a better man for his kids, I don't see the harm in helping him. If I'm being honest, I kinda like the idea of him doing physical work—sore muscles, calloused hands, sweating, and being miserable." He grinned.

"When you put it that way." Tyson chuckled. "I can get on board with that. Tell him to stop 'round the store and ask for Dad."

He wasn't going to go looking for Ted Barnes, but he'd find a way to relay the information to him. "I appreciate that."

"Does it make us even?" Tyson nodded at the stack of rotted boards.

"No. Not even close." He put his hands on his hips. "You owe me."

"I figured as much."

"Mike," Rusty called out, his horse trotting across the arena. "Hey, Tyson. You look like you've been up to something."

"Work." Mike stretched. "I'll go get Chuck ready."

"You look worn out." Rusty's horse, Briar, followed the fence line. "You up for this?"

"Not really. He's in a temper, too," Tyson answered for him.

"What's going on?" Rusty asked.

"Are you asking him or me?" Mike glared up at his brother.

"Oh." Rusty frowned. "Tonight'll be fun."

Mike muttered all the way to the corral where Chuck was waiting. He saddled the horse, grumbling the entire time. "Sorry." He ran a hand along the horse's neck. "You're not the problem here." He patted the horse, put his boot in the stirrup, and swung up and into the saddle. "Let's go." With a gentle squeeze, he and Chuck cantered from the corral, between the holding pens, and up and around the arena to the side entrance and paused. The Garrison Ladies Guild was here? From the looks of it, *all* of them.

"What's all this?" Mike asked as he and Chuck pulled alongside Rusty.

"You got me. They wanted to talk to Tyson." Rusty tipped his cowboy hat back on his head. "I'm going to mosey to the other side of the arena."

Mike let Chuck trail after his brother's horse, Nugget, until the expanse of the arena separated the Woodard brothers from the group of women. Staying out of their line of sight wouldn't guarantee they'd escape without notice, but it couldn't hurt.

"How's Dad doing?" Mike drew Chuck to a stop.

"I think hanging out with those kids is good for him. I mean, I'm not happy poor Archie had to have surgery but Dad sure has enjoyed reading to him." Rusty glanced his way. "King Arthur."

Mike chuckled. "His favorite."

"Don't look now, but I think Martha Zeigler is... Yep, she's heading this way." Rusty sighed in exasperation. "Should we make a break for it?"

Mike chuckled again. "She'd only hunt us down later."

Martha Zeigler waved and waved until the two of them

had no choice but to ride halfway across the arena to meet her. "Boys."

"Miss Zeigler," they said in unison.

"You know Hattie is off on her honeymoon for another week and there's been a little problem with Career Day, over at the elementary school."

"What sort of problem?" Mike already felt the hair along his arm pricking up. She was about to ask him for something.

"We had a couple of speakers back out." She pointed at Mike. "You, being an EMT, would make an excellent speaker."

Yep, he'd called it. "I appreciate that, Miss Martha—"

"Good. You can thank Eloise Green for the idea." Miss Martha almost smiled. "She was the one who suggested you—after she agreed to come and participate herself."

Mike's objections faded away.

"I can count on you?" Miss Martha's steely gaze was fixed on his face.

"Yes, ma'am." There was a chance he was going to regret this.

"Good." She gave Mike the date and time and headed off without another word.

"You know she just manipulated the tar out of you, don't you?" Rusty shook his head.

"I do." There was no point denying it. Miss Martha had played the Eloise Green card and he'd gone all in.

"There are probably easier ways to spend time with the woman." Rusty's hands rested on the pommel of his saddle.

"Eloise or Miss Martha?" He glanced at Rusty, then laughed.

Practice went off without any worrisome incidents. Alice Schneider got her pinkie finger caught in the saddle cinch lacing but, after icing it, it turned out to be a sprain and not a fracture.

After practice wrapped up, he loaded Chuck into the horse trailer. Tonight, he wanted his own bed—not the lumpy couch in his father's parlor. He swung by his father's place for Clifford and to give his dad a quick hug before making the drive out of town to his little homestead.

Garrison wasn't a noisy town, but there was quiet in the country that couldn't compare. When he'd found this piece of property, it'd just clicked. Yes, the place was a bit of a drive the two times a day he came by to check on the horses, and the house had a heap of work that needed to be done but, little by little, it was coming together. The barn had been his first priority. His horses, Chuck, Goliath, and Mars, needed shelter from the Texas elements. If it wasn't the brutal heat, it was a flash flood, a tornado— even an occasional ice storm.

The walk from the barn to the house wasn't long, but it was plenty long enough for Clifford to run circles around him until the dog was panting.

They were headed inside when the crunch of gravel signaled someone arriving.

It was the Garrison Gardens van. Once the van was parked and the driver door opened—it was Eloise.

"I come with apology cookies this time." She carried the foil-covered plate up the path to where he stood.

"What did you do?" He smiled. "Did it already happen? Or is it going to happen?"

"Oh, well, I'm not sure." She winced. "I don't supposed Martha Zeigler has reached out?"

"She has." Mike took the plate. "She showed up at the stockyards during the high school rodeo team practice. I was trapped."

She smiled. "I'm sorry."

"It's fine. If Hattie were here, she wouldn't have asked—she'd have told me I was doing it." He shrugged. "Come to think of it, I'm not sure Miss Martha asked, either." He lifted the plate. "You didn't have to drive all the way out here. You could've called."

"Right." Her smile dimmed. "Of course. I should have called." She patted Clifford's head. "I'll get out of your hair—"

"I wasn't trying to chase you off, El." His hand clasped hers. "You're welcome anytime—for as long as you like."

She was staring at their hands. "You're sure?"

He nodded. There was that lump again—making it impossible for him to say a thing. Now was the perfect time to say something.

Her eyes met his. "Are you sure I'm not intruding?"

He nodded.

"Okay. I didn't know you lived out here." She slid her hand from his and turned, inspecting the uneven porch they stood on. "I guess I assumed you lived with your dad. I'm not sure why? Maybe because I live with my grandfather?"

"I needed a place for the horses." He nodded in the direction of the barn. "Dad's yard was too small."

She laughed. "Horses? I'll have to tell Kirby—she'll be so impressed. Samantha Crawley has her becoming quite the horse fanatic."

"You should bring her out and let her go for a ride. Goliath is a gentle giant."

"Goliath, huh? We'll have to see." She tucked a strand of hair behind her ear.

"You want to come in? Have an apology cookie or two? The place isn't much to look at but it's got good bones."

"No, I can't stay. The kids aren't even in bed yet. I left

Grandpa alone with them." She glanced at the van, hesi-
tating. "Mike...the apology cookies aren't the only reason I'm here."

"No?"

"I... I..." She swallowed, her gaze bouncing between
him and the van. "Did I say or do something to make you
upset? You sort of disappeared after I dumped everything
on you—it was too much—"

"El, no. I wanted you to talk to me. I still do." He understood then. "I'm not going to shut down on you. It guts
me that that's what you thought."

"I used to tell you everything and... Well, old habits die
hard." She stared at the ground. "You don't have to be my
friend because of everything I dumped on you... Out of
guilt, you know? I really am okay. I was just having a...
moment." She shook her head. "I was a bit of a mess." Her
attempt at a laugh was forced.

"We all are, El." He stepped closer. "This week got away
from me—work, mostly. But I'll be honest with you and
say I wasn't sure I should come by."

She stared up at him, a V between her brows. "Why?"

Every time he looked into her eyes, he saw something
new. The shades of gray and gold and green were mesmerizing. "Like you said, old habits are hard to break. I've
always been protective of you, El, even though I know
you don't need protecting. This whole thing with Ted is
something you have to do without me trying to get in the
middle of it. I figured giving you space was the best way
to do that."

"Okay." Her eyes swept over his face as she smiled.
"But this is too much space. For me, anyway. I...the kids
like having you around." Her cheeks were a dark red as

she patted Clifford on the head and took a few steps down the path toward the van. "I'll see you later."

He nodded, watching as she drove away. "I can't be sure, Clifford, but I think El-Bell just said she was missing me?" And he, his heart, was oh so happy.

CHAPTER THIRTEEN

"At this rate, you'll be able to go back to school next week." Eloise reached into the back seat and patted Archie's knee. "Isn't that great news?"

"I guess." Archie pushed up his glasses. "I like hanging out with you, though."

She smiled at him. "You know, it's been nice having special time with you."

He beamed up at her.

"How about an early lunch date? Just me and you?" They were passing the Buttermilk Pie Café and it was almost eleven o'clock.

"I am getting hungry." Archie's enthusiasm for food was impressive. He'd inhaled bacon, eggs, a blueberry muffin, and a piece of toast not three hours ago.

She pulled into one of the spaces, parked, and turned off the ignition. "You're sure you're up for it?"

He nodded. "Dr. Rowe said the only thing I can't do is pick anything heavy up. She did say to add more steps."

The doctor had said that, but Eloise wasn't sure walking from the car to a table and back again was what the good doctor had in mind. She came around to help Archie out of the car. He was healing, yes, but he was still tender around the spot where they'd gone in for the laparoscopic procedure.

"Well, if it isn't the one and only Archie Barnes and

his lovely momma," Miss Lucille greeted them. "How are you feeling?"

"Better." He smiled up at the older woman. "That breakfast pizza you made was yummy. I had to hide it from Kirby so she didn't eat it all."

Miss Lucille cackled at this. "I'm glad to know you enjoyed it—your little sis, too. You find a table you like and we'll see what we can whip up for you this morning."

"Yes, ma'am." He pointed. "Look, Momma, there's a booth."

"A booth it is." Eloise loved that he still held her hand. It wouldn't be too long before he'd be too old for such things.

"Hey, Archie. How'd your doctor appointment go?" It was Nolan Woodard.

"Dr. Rowe says I'm on the mend." He smiled. "How are you feeling, Mr. Woodard?"

"Doc Johnston told me the same. I figured I'd have some lunch to celebrate. You're welcome to join me, if you like?" Mr. Woodard indicated the empty chairs. "My boys are supposed to be joining me soon but I'm sure they won't mind."

"No, thank you, sir." Archie looked up at her. "Mom and me are on a date. We don't get to do lots without Kirby, so we're doing this."

"Is that so?" Mr. Woodard's smile was huge. "You go on and enjoy yourselves then."

"Thank you for the invitation." Eloise nodded his way and let Archie lead her to the booth he'd spotted. "That's very sweet of you, Archie."

He nodded. "Yeah."

Which made her laugh.

"What are you going to eat?" Archie started reading over the menu. "I am hungry."

"You said that before." Eloise was still smiling. "Let's

see." It was the softest whisper, but Eloise could make out what was being said.

"Yes, that's the woman." A woman whispering. "And that's the boy. He just had surgery."

"We should go check on him, poor dear." Another woman, also whispering.

Eloise didn't have time to prepare herself for the arrival of two older women. They stood at the end of the booth, wearing looks of equal parts sympathy and curiosity. One, she recognized as Dorris Kaye. The other was tall and thin, with a piled-up white bun on the top of her head. It looked more like a beehive, really.

"Good morning," the tall woman said. "We were on our way out but wanted to see how the young patient is doing. Archie, isn't it?"

"I'm doing real good." Archie smiled.

"I'm happy to hear it. Miss Patsy, a dear friend of ours, was telling us what happened. You've had quite the time of it. Surgery. Hospital stays. Your daddy getting out of jail and coming to see you." Dorris Kaye breezed through her speech as if she was talking about the weather or her favorite kind of ice cream. Not that she'd pulled the pin on a grenade and was standing back to watch.

"You poor thing." The tall woman directed this at Eloise. "It must be hard, your little boy hurting and the talk about your ex-husband being a criminal."

Eloise was so flabbergasted she couldn't come up with a thing to say. But one look at Archie changed that.

"And your grandfather. All this scandal." The first woman kept going. "He's always been such a proud sort."

"Quincy Green is proud as punch of his family," Dorris argued. "Besides, it's not their fault."

Archie's knuckles were white as he held the menu—but

his little face was whiter. "Momma, what are they talking about?"

It was painfully quiet then.

"Hey." Archie slid from the booth and stared up at the women.

Both women looked like they had bitten into something sour—their lips puckered, their brows shot up, and acute looks of discomfort covered their faces.

"You're being rude." Archie was upset. "Making up stuff about people is even worse."

"Archie, come on." Eloise reached for his hand.

"No, Momma. They need to apologize." Archie stood his ground. "You said to use nice words, not mean ones. So, you two should say you're sorry."

"Well, I never." The tall woman clutched her beaded purse to her chest. "And where are your manners, young man?"

"Why should I use them on you? You don't have any." Archie was red-faced. "Are you going to apologize? If you do, I might forgive you."

Dorris Kaye's mouth opened and closed but no words came out.

"Eloise?" It was Mr. Woodard. "Can I help with something?"

"Mr. Woodard." Archie pointed at the women. "They came over and started lying and saying mean things about me and Momma and my dad, too."

"Is that so?" Mr. Woodard straightened, his gaze unyielding and frigid. "Don't you two have something useful to do today? You've done more than enough here."

"And…" Archie shook his head. "Lying is bad."

"I do not lie." The woman sniffed. "But your father does, young man. It looks like your mother does, too."

With that, she brushed past Nolan Woodard and out the front door.

"Oh dear," Dorris Kaye murmured, giving them all a panicked look before hurrying after the other woman.

Eloise steered Archie back to his seat. "Archie?" She dipped the corner of a napkin into the water glass and patted his forehead and cheeks.

"Don't let those old crones get to you, Archie. My father used to say that people who gossip have nothing in their own lives to talk about so we should feel sorry for them." Mr. Nolan's voice was low and gentle.

She glanced up, to thank him, only to find Mike and Rusty standing close by. How long had they been there? Mike's nod was answer enough.

"Momma." Archie's voice was soft. "Was that lady right? Was Daddy in jail?"

"Archie." Mike crouched by the seat. "Let's go home. Clifford's in the truck and he's been missing you. How about you, me, and your mom go home and we'll figure out food later?" Mike ruffled her son's hair. "Sound good?"

Archie nodded.

Eloise wasn't certain how Mike managed to get them out of there without further incident but she was grateful he did. Archie was too dazed to react as she buckled him into his booster seat in the van. He barely responded when Clifford jumped up on the bench seat beside him. Eloise's hands were shaking so much that she handed Mike the keys and climbed into the passenger seat.

Not a word was said all the way home.

There was a vise on her chest—squeezing the air from her lungs and compressing her heart. As much as she hurt, it couldn't compare to what her son was feeling.

There was only one thing she could do. Call Ted. He

needed to be here for his son—to help him understand. If he could.

"We're here." Mike jolted her from her thoughts.

Sure enough, they were sitting in front of her grandfather's house.

"I'll get him?" Mike offered.

"Yes, please." She unbuckled her seatbelt. "I need to make a phone call."

Mike's jaw clenched but he nodded.

It felt like she was moving in slow motion. Every step from the van to the telephone inside weighed a ton. Her brain bounced back and forth through all the "if only" situations that could have prevented this from happening.

She gripped the house phone, one ring. Then two. "Ted?"

"What's wrong?"

"Archie." She sucked in a deep breath. "People…he knows. About jail. He's upset. You need to come and explain this to him. Now. I'm going to call his old therapist—see if she has any helpful tips."

"Okay." The line went dead.

She hung up the phone and headed back into the family room.

Mike sat on the couch with Archie cradled against his chest. He was so small, so young… She'd wanted to do what was best for them. Instead, she'd wounded them.

She was too anxious to sit and too unsteady to pace so she leaned against the doorframe. She shot a quick text to Archie's old therapist and shoved her phone into her pocket.

The thump-thump of Clifford's tail on the floor was the only sound. The big dog was leaning against Mike's knees so Archie could give him long, slow strokes down the neck.

The way Mike was looking at her didn't help. He was disappointed in her, too. She hadn't just lied to her children, she'd been lying to everyone.

She couldn't cry. She couldn't fall apart. She couldn't.

When Ted opened the door, Eloise didn't know how to feel. She was relieved he'd actually come and he was stepping up. And yet, the fear and uncertainty on his face reminded her there was no easy fix to this.

"Hey, bud." Ted sat beside Mike, ignoring the giant man and focusing only on his son. "Archie. Talk to me, okay?"

Archie shook his head.

"Okay." Ted sat back against the couch, pressing his hands to his thighs. "We can sit. Whenever you're ready—"

"Did you lie?" Archie leaned forward, his little face twisted with anger. His voice wobbled then broke. "*Why* did you lie, Dad?"

Clifford whimpered, putting his paw on Archie's leg.

Eloise pressed a hand to her chest, pain rising from inside. She'd give anything to make this better.

"I did. I lied to you and your sister and I'm sorry, Archie." Ted met Archie's gaze. "I was wrong. I was so wrong, son."

"It's bad to lie." Archie sniffed.

"It is. I was ashamed of what I'd done. I didn't want you and Kirby to be ashamed of me, too. I didn't want you two worrying about me, either." He took a deep breath. "But that doesn't make my lie okay. Nothing does. I know that. I've never been so sorry."

Archie stared at him for a long time.

Eloise waited. Archie had every reason to be angry

and reject Ted—reject her. Instead, her sweet, loving boy reached for his father.

As soon as Ted had Archie in his lap, Mike slowly pushed off the couch—Clifford hopped up to take his place. The dog leaned against Archie and scooted down until he'd rested his head in her son's lap.

Mike was watching the exchange, a curve tugging up one corner of his mouth. This big man with broad shoulders and a protective spirit had no reason to stay... Why would he? This was a nightmare—hers, not his. She couldn't leave, but he could. He would. Now. And she had no right to ask him to stay—

Mike crossed to her. His warm eyes swept over her face. "Breathe." He took her hand and gently pulled her down on the loveseat beside him.

"But you…" she whispered. "You don't have to stay. I understand—"

"I'm here for you, El." He slid an arm around her waist. "And for Archie."

She nodded, so grateful for him.

"I know it's hard to understand, Archie." Ted took a deep breath. "Adults mess up and make mistakes, too. I lied to you and I made your mom keep it a secret. She didn't want to, she told me to tell you, but I was too scared."

Archie peered at her.

"I'm so sorry, Archie. More than you'll ever know." She could barely breathe.

"You and Kirby are the most important things in my life." Ted's voice was unsteady now. "I was afraid to lose you."

"You can't lose us. We are your kids." Archie's irritation was oddly comforting.

"I know." Ted nodded. "I know that sounds silly. It is

silly. I made a stupid mistake. A big one. A bad one. And I am so sorry."

Archie took a deep breath. "I wanted that mean old lady to be wrong."

"What mean old lady?" Ted glanced at Eloise for clarification.

"The one that came over and talked to me and Momma at the restaurant." Archie shook his head. "I didn't want her to be right."

"I know. And you can be mad at me for putting you in that position. You should be." He smoothed Archie's hair back. "But I'm not going anywhere. When you want to talk or stop being mad at me, I'll be here."

"You're not leaving?" Archie's expression was far too grave for someone so young. "You won't go traveling or go back to jail?"

"I won't go anywhere." Ted winced. "I promise."

Eloise gripped Mike's hand. As much as she wanted to believe Ted, she had her reservations. Yes, he was saying the right things, but there was no guarantee that would last. And if it didn't and Ted left, Archie would learn how it felt to have a promise broken. It was horrible. *This* was horrible.

She concentrated on the feel of Mike's hand running up and down her back. She could fall apart later—not now.

"Can you go now?" Archie asked. "And come back after school? Later, maybe."

It took a minute for Ted to mask his hurt. "If that's what you want."

Archie nodded and eased himself onto the couch beside Clifford. Clifford waited for Archie to get settled, then lay beside him.

"Okay." Ted sniffed. "I'll come back." Eloise could see how shattered he was when he glanced her way. "Eloise.

Mike." He walked out, gently closing the front door behind him.

"Oh, baby." Eloise couldn't bear it. Mike helped her up and steadied her before she hurried to Archie. "What can I do?"

"Can Clifford stay for a while?" Archie rolled onto his side and draped his arm across the dog. "He makes me feel better."

"Yes, of course." She adjusted the pillows and spread a light fleece throw over him. "Do you need anything else?"

He closed his eyes and shook his head. "Stay close, Momma?"

Eloise sat on the floor beside the couch and smoothed her fingers through Archie's hair. She didn't know what would happen next or if there was anything she could say to make this easier. But this, staying close, wasn't just for him—it was for her, too. There was nothing and no one that needed her more than Archie did, right now.

"Want some tea?" Mike asked. "Coffee?"

"No." She couldn't stop herself from adding, "Stay close? Please."

"That's the plan." He smiled.

This was hard and messy, all of it. Ted, the lie, the talk around town, and being in love with Mike—who was leaving soon. All she could do was take things day by day. Today wasn't the day to worry over her potential heartbreak. Today was the day to be strong for her son and grateful to Mike. So, that's what she'd do.

MIKE PEERED OUT the front window of Quincy Green's house and bit back a curse. A car was pulling up in front of the house. Even from this distance, Patsy Monahan's fire-engine-red hair stuck out like a sore thumb.

Archie and Clifford were piled up on the couch, sound

asleep. Eloise had finally dozed off in Quincy's recliner. This is what they needed. Rest. Peace and quiet.

He slipped out the front door and down the front path to see Patsy wasn't alone. Martha Zeigler was with her. He never thought he'd have to face off against Martha Zeigler but today might just be the day. *This day just keeps getting better and better.*

"Don't you scowl at me, Mike Woodard," Miss Martha huffed as soon as she'd stepped out of the car. "I get that you're standing guard but we come in peace."

Mike didn't budge or relax.

"Like you, I'm furious. Furious, you hear? And I will never call either of those women my friend again." Martha's voice was all indignance. "Not ever. Dorris can't keep her mouth shut but she's harmless. I can't say the same for Pearl Johnston. She's got a mean streak in her. As you saw yourself." She cleared her throat and pulled herself upright. "Patsy and I are here representing the Ladies Guild. Is there anything we can do for Eloise or to help with damage control?"

"Eloise is a good girl—she and her boy didn't deserve all that. How are they holding up?" Patsy Monahan peered around his shoulder.

"They're both sleeping." No matter what the two women were saying, he wasn't going to invite them in. Eloise didn't need more negativity and neither did Archie. "It's been a real humdinger of a morning for them both and they need some peace and quiet."

"Of course they do." Patsy stepped forward. "Is there anything we can do? Anything they need?"

He'd been asking himself that very thing for the last couple of hours. "Clifford's taking the edge off all this for Archie—that boy loves the dog. But Eloise?" He chose his words with care. "She can't seem to catch a break and she needs one."

"Don't you go underestimating that woman." Martha shook her head. "She's weathered fiercer storms than any of us."

"I know she's capable. I'm saying she shouldn't have to go through this." He paused then, looking Martha Zeigler in the eye. "There is something you can do. You can stop the talk. All of it. Nothing about Eloise, her kids, or her ex. At least, nothing *juicy*—or gossipy."

One of Martha's eyebrows rose. "And just how do you propose I go about that?"

"I don't know, Miss Martha. But if there's anyone that *can* do it, it's you." He sighed. "Eloise came here for a fresh start. I don't think that's too much to ask."

"No, it's not." Martha Zeigler glanced at Patsy. "We'll see what we can do, won't we?"

Patsy nodded.

"Before we go, I have one question for *you*." Martha was frowning. "Have you come to your senses yet? About this job? About leaving your home and family?" She nodded pointedly at the Green house.

Mike chuckled. "I've always admired how up-front you are, Miss Martha."

"There is no point in wasting time." She wagged a finger at him. "Are you going to answer me?"

He took a deep breath. "I'm considering my options."

Martha Zeigler smiled. "Fine. Just know the best options are here in Garrison." She patted his arm and nodded at Quincy's house. "Like I said, no point in wasting time. Neither of you are getting any younger." She sniffed. "Now, I promised Dwight I'd make him an apple pie for dessert and it's not going to bake itself." With a wave, she headed back to Patsy Monahan's car. "Come on, Patsy."

Mike managed to slip inside without waking Archie, but the recliner was empty. No Eloise. He tiptoed into the kitchen to find her making coffee. She'd turned the radio on low, the mournful strains of an eighties rock ballad filling the room.

"I can do that, El."

She jumped, dropping the canister of ground coffee and spilling its contents all over the floor. "Oh, no." She stared down at the mess.

"I'm sorry. I didn't mean to scare you."

"You're scary quiet." She glanced at him, slightly accusatory. "I didn't hear a thing."

"I didn't want to wake Archie." He scanned the room. "Broom?"

"In the pantry." She pointed behind him. "I was making us some coffee but…"

He smiled at her. "I appreciate the thought."

Her answering smile was fragile. She gripped the kitchen counter behind her. Tension rolled off her in waves. "I can't relax. I need to *do* something."

He forgot about the broom. "How about a dance?"

"Dance? Here? In the kitchen?"

She didn't argue when he took her hand in his. "Yep." He placed his other hand against her back. "I don't see why not." He started dancing, guiding her effortlessly across the coffee-sprinkled floor. He liked the way she fit in his arms, the way they moved together with such ease.

"There's coffee all over the floor." She glanced down. "And we're in my grandfather's kitchen."

"First, a lot of dance halls put down sawdust so people don't slip. Coffee could do the same? Second, you can dance anywhere if the mood strikes you." He steered her across the room, then circled back around. "We'll clean it up. But this is a good song for dancing." It was a cheesy song—the sort of song that would instantly make him change the station. But, somehow, he knew every word to it.

"It is?" She stared up at him. "I wasn't listening."

He spun her. Her startled laugh was all the encouragement he needed to keep right on dancing. "How's the song go?" He stumbled over the lyrics, but he did try.

"Faithfully." Eloise grinned. "You like this song? *You* listen to Journey?"

"I didn't say I liked it." He shook his head. "I said it was a good dancing song. It's one of those songs everyone knows. An earworm."

"True." She nodded. "My mother loved Journey. She had all their albums. Vinyl records."

Mike chuckled and spun her again.

When she laughed, her whole face lit up.

"You're beautiful, El-Bell." The words slipped out as a whisper but, holding her close this way, there was no chance she hadn't heard. He was okay with it, though. She should know she's beautiful.

She sighed. "You need to get your eyes checked, Mike Woodard."

"I have twenty-twenty vision, Miss Green." He shook his head. "That means my vision is perfect. If I say you're beautiful, you are beautiful."

"Maybe the coffee fumes are getting to you?" But she was smiling and there was a pink hue on her cheeks.

He'd made her blush? And it looked good on her. "Is that a thing?" He cocked his head to one side. "Pretty sure it's not."

"Whatever." She grinned as he spun her twice. "Are you trying to make me dizzy?"

"No. I'm trying to make you smile. It's good for you. When you smile, your brain releases endorphins and serotonin that make you feel good." Where that random tidbit of knowledge had come from, he didn't know. But it was true.

"You're saying this is a medical treatment?" Her brows rose.

"Kirby did say I'm a doctor cowboy." He shrugged. "So, as an official doctor cowboy, I'm prescribing at least one *real* smile a day. All you have to do is find something that makes you happy. Today, it's dancing in the kitchen. Easy."

"You know the song is over, don't you?" But she didn't stop swaying along with him or let him go.

He didn't care about the music. At the moment, Eloise was in his arms and smiling up at him. She was right where she belonged. And, from the way her gaze dipped to his lips and she swayed into him, he thought—maybe—she was feeling the same way.

She stepped closer, her hands sliding up his chest to go around his neck.

He drew in a ragged breath and bent his head. Her lips were so soft, so warm, and clinging to his.

"Momma?" Archie stood in the kitchen door with Clifford sitting at his side. "What are you doing?"

"Archie." She slipped out of his hold. "I—I dropped the coffee and…it spilled."

Clifford's nose was working overtime.

"Stay, Clifford." Mike held out his hand for the dog. "The last thing you need is a bunch of caffeine in your system."

Clifford groaned but lay down on the floor, sniffing the air.

Archie pushed up his glasses and looked back and forth between the two of them. "What were you and Mr. Mike doing?" He wasn't upset so much as curious.

She shook her head but she was smiling. "Mike was trying to cheer me up with a dance."

"Oh." Archie sat in one of the kitchen chairs, staring at Mike with a stern frown. "It didn't look like dancing."

"I'll clean this up," Mike said, pulling the broom from the pantry.

"That's nice. Can we take Clifford for a walk, Mr. Mike? Dr. Rowe said I should walk more and you said Clifford likes to take walks."

"I think that's a great idea," Eloise answered. "I'll find my shoes—"

"Just me and Mr. Mike and Clifford." Archie rested his elbows on the table. "For man-to-man talk time."

Mike stopped sweeping and looked at the boy. It made sense that Archie had some things to discuss; he just hoped he was the right one the boy should talk to. He wasn't a father. He didn't have experience at this sort of thing. But, if Archie wanted him, he'd try. He could only hope he'd figure out the right things to say.

Eloise turned to him. "Do you mind?"

"Nope." Mike finished sweeping the coffee grounds into the dustbin. "I think some man-to-man time is just what the doctor cowboy ordered." He emptied the dustbin into the trash.

Eloise rolled her eyes. "Okay, then. Take it slowly, please. You're still recovering, Archie. When you get back, I'll make us some lunch."

"Okay." Archie climbed out of the chair. "Let's go, Clifford."

Clifford trotted after Archie, his tail wagging.

"Thank you," she whispered. The smile she gave him had his heart tripping over itself.

They were halfway down the block before Archie

said anything. And what he said wasn't what Mike had been expecting.

"Mr. Mike, are you my mom's boyfriend? Levi says you are and that I'm the man of the family and I'm supposed to decide whether you are a good boyfriend or not." Archie frowned up at him.

Mike had nothing. He was speechless.

"Kirby thinks you'd be a good new daddy." The boy shrugged. "And Clifford would be ours, too, and I'd like that." The dog heard his name and trotted back to Archie's side. "I think Clifford would like that. Wouldn't you?"

Clifford wagged his tail.

"I think that means yes." Archie smiled.

Mike was still pondering the whole "new daddy" comment.

"Grandpa Quincy says you're moving. Does that mean we have to move, too? I like it here. Mostly." He glanced up at him. "Dad's here, too. I know he was in jail but he's not a bad guy…" Archie stopped walking and looked up at him. "*Is* he a bad guy, Mr. Mike? Bad guys go to jail, don't they? Not good guys."

Mike was scrambling to keep up. He wasn't going to speak for Ted or address Ted's incarceration, but he respected Archie's questions. Hopefully, Ted would, too. "I bet your father will tell you what you need to know." He paused, then added, "It's important to trust your instincts, too, Archie. You'll know what's best."

"Okay. I know I'm supposed to be mad at Dad, but do I have to be mad at my mom, too? She was just keeping a promise to my dad. She didn't want to lie." Archie started walking, a little slower this time. "I don't want to be mad at either of them."

"Archie." Mike rested a hand on the boy's shoulder. "That's up to you. You don't have to be mad. But if you are, that's okay, too. Today has been a lot. It's okay to feel a lot. It's okay to feel numb, too. Sometimes it takes time for our feelings to catch up."

Archie nodded. "You know a lot about feeling things, Mr. Mike."

"I do?" Mike chuckled. "More like I don't mind talking about feeling things. It's not easy, is it? To share what's going on inside. Sometimes, it's hard to find the right words to say how you're feeling."

Archie nodded again.

"When you find the words or want to talk, you've got me and your mom and dad and Grandpa Quincy to share with."

He smiled up at Mike. "That's a lot of people."

"Yep. A lot of people love you." He loved Archie. He loved Kirby. And he loved Eloise. If he had it his way, they'd be a family. All he had to do was get up the nerve to say as much to El-Bell. Miss Martha was right. Everything he wanted or needed was here. Eloise was at the top of his list.

"Clifford, too?" Archie patted the dog. "He loves me?"

"Clifford, too."

"Can we go back, now?" He rested a hand on his stomach. "My tummy's growling."

Mike chuckled. "Well then, let's go." More importantly, he wanted to talk to Eloise. If she didn't care for him the way he cared for her, he'd take the job. But if she did... If she did, he'd be the happiest man in Garrison, Texas.

"Mr. Mike." He paused before they reached the front steps. When he spoke, there was an edge to his words. Fragile and desperate and even a little scared. "Levi said I'm supposed to decide about you and Momma... And I have. Dad broke Momma's heart and they got divorced. Grandpa said you broke Momma's heart so you can't be her boyfriend. She should be with someone who won't break her heart." He frowned as he shook his head. "I know she's pretty and nice and cuddles good, but you can't have her. My instinct says no and you said to listen to that. I am. No more kissing and stuff." He walked up the porch steps. "That's my man-to-man talk." He shrugged. "But you can be her friend. Ours, too. Okay?"

Mike stood there for a second, his happiness fading. Archie didn't want him with Eloise. After everything that little boy had been through, how could Mike put his wants above Archie's? Maybe, in time, Archie would come to see things differently? Maybe he wouldn't. The only thing he knew was his heart was hurting something fierce when they stepped inside.

CHAPTER FOURTEEN

"STICK HORSE PRACTICE." Eloise read over the flier Kirby had given her. *They needed to have a practice for this?*

"Yep. Samantha said there would be stick horses for all the kids—one for me and Archie, too. And we get to ride them down the street and wear a cowboy hat and say 'yee-haw.' That's what real cowboys say." Kirby took a deep breath. "Samantha said she's going to do a dance, too. Can we go see her dance, Momma? Did you know Miss Gretta is a dance teacher?"

Eloise nodded. "I did." She stuck the flier to the front of the refrigerator and went back to stirring the pasta on the stovetop.

"I want to go to dance school like I used to." Kirby spun in the kitchen. "I like dancing."

"Then you should go to Miss Gretta's," Grandpa Quincy said, helping Archie set the table. "I think that's a fine idea."

"Do I have to ride a stick horse?" Archie was not in the least enthused. "I'm too old."

"You don't have to do anything you don't want to do." Eloise smiled. "Besides, it might not be a good idea to jostle your stomach around."

Archie stepped back, looked at the table, and counted the plates. "Yep. That's five."

"Me and Grandpa and Momma and you and Dad." Kirby nodded. "When is Daddy going to be here?"

"Any time now." Eloise checked the clock. If anyone had told her Ted would be sitting down to dinner with them, she'd have laughed. Now, it was happening.

Considering how rough the morning had gone, there'd been surprisingly little drama since Archie and Mike had returned from their walk. Mike had seemed a little distracted, but Archie had been in a great mood. Mike had been unexpectedly called in to the hospital, but he'd left Clifford to "watch over Archie" for him. Clifford was taking his duty seriously, trailing after Archie or Kirby wherever they went.

"Can Clifford have pasta?" Kirby asked, sitting in the middle of the kitchen floor beside the dog.

"I'm not so sure about that, Freckles. But Mr. Woodard is dropping by some food for him so he won't be hungry." Grandpa Quincy pulled the pitcher of iced tea from the fridge.

"I can't believe we get to have a sleepover with Clifford," Kirby squealed, then lowered her voice. "I can put bows in your hair tonight."

The knock on the door sent Kirby running. "I'll get it."

Grandpa Quincy stood in the kitchen doorway to watch.

"Daddy." Kirby's voice carried down the hallway. "You're here. Guess what. Mom's making chicken fettucine 'cuz it's my favorite. Guess what else? Clifford is having a sleepover 'cuz Mr. Mike had to go to the hospital so we get to babysit."

"All that, huh?" There was a smile in Ted's voice. "He must trust you and Archie a lot to put you in charge of his dog."

"He does." Kirby came skipping back down the hall. "It's Daddy."

"Eloise. Mr. Green." He gave them both a warm smile. "Hey, Archie."

Eloise held her breath as Archie turned to greet Ted.

"Hey, Dad." Archie hugged him. "You look dressed up."

"I came from work." Ted gave him a big hug. "It was a good day."

"A job?" Kirby frowned. "Here or far away somewhere?"

"Here." Ted smiled. "I'm staying right here."

"Oh goody." Kirby went back to Clifford. "Did you hear that, Clifford?"

Clifford wagged his tail.

"Dad wasn't gone because of work, Kirby." Archie sat on the other side of Clifford. "He was in jail."

Kirby frowned at Archie. "Are you sure?"

"Yep." Archie nodded.

"Is he right?" Kirby asked Ted.

"Well…" Ted cleared his throat. "Yes, he is."

"Oh." Kirby kept on frowning but didn't say anything else.

"Are you a bad guy, Dad?" Archie's question flooded the room with tension. "I was talking to Mr. Mike and he said you'd tell me what I needed to know. He said I should trust my…instincts. He also said it was okay if I wasn't mad at you or to be mad and sad. He said I could feel all of it."

Ted smiled. "He's right."

"He knows lots about feelings and emotions and stuff." Archie shrugged. "Are you a bad guy, though?"

For a minute, Eloise thought he'd run. There was a look of total panic on his face. Then, he took a deep breath.

"I did some bad things," he managed.

"Did you wear a mask and have a gun?" Kirby's frown grew. "Did you hurt people?"

An odd strangled sound escaped Ted. "No, Freckles. I've never held a gun in my life. The only masks I've worn have been on Halloween."

Eloise couldn't blame him for avoiding the last question. It was the most complicated of them all. Had he physically hurt anyone? Hopefully, no. But by taking away people's retirement or education funds, he'd taken people's choices and plans away. Eloise knew firsthand how much that hurt.

"Where are you working?" Grandpa Quincy asked. "What's the position?"

"Office manager for Ellis Family Feed & Ranch Supply." He nodded. "Mr. Ellis wants me to update his software and filing system."

"Earl Ellis is a good man. Hardworking but fair." Her grandfather rubbed his jaw.

Her worlds were colliding, and she wasn't sure how to feel about it. Ted. In Garrison. Working for Mike's best friend's father? It was beyond weird that Ted and Mike had run into each other—that they'd had a conversation.

"Eloise?" Ted interrupted her thoughts. "What's this about a stick horse parade?"

Dinner was an overall pleasant event. Archie and Kirby seemed to have put aside the whole jail thing—for now, at least. After Eloise explained how horrible their morning had been, Grandpa Quincy was on his best behavior. Ted even stuck around to take care of the kids' bedtime routine.

"Need a hand?" Ted came into the kitchen.

She was elbow deep in soapy water. "I'm almost done."

"Perfect timing on my part." He grinned. "It could have gone worse. Telling the kids the truth."

"It was pretty bad." She took a deep breath. "But you're right. It could have been worse." She finished washing the pan and placed it on the drying rack. "I'm glad it's out. No more secrets."

"Deal." His blue eyes met hers. "While I'm handing out apologies, I'm sorry for putting all of this on you."

"Thank you." She wiped her hands on the kitchen towel. "I'd offer you some coffee but we're out."

"Yeah, Archie mentioned something about you and Mike Woodard dancing in here—with coffee all over the floor?" He crossed his arms over his chest. "Sounds like a real party to me."

She laughed. "It was…something." Something special. But then, Mike made everything better.

"That's a look." He sighed.

"What look?" She glanced around the kitchen to make sure she hadn't missed anything.

"That one. The one you get when Mike Woodard's name comes up." He pushed off the counter.

"Oh, please." She led him from the kitchen and into the family room. Grandpa Quincy was snoring in the recliner.

"I'll go," he whispered. "Can I borrow you for a couple of minutes first?"

Eloise turned on the porch light and followed him out. "What's up?"

"I'm not sure how to say this." He walked slowly along the path to the gate. "I just… I want you to be happy, Eloise." This far from the porch, it was too dark to see his face and know what he was after.

"I do, too." She wasn't sure she wanted to know where he was going with this.

"What's the deal with you and Mike Woodard?" He cleared his throat. "Are you two—"

"Friends?" She couldn't keep the irritation out of her voice. "Yes. We are friends. That is all. He's leaving Garrison." She took another deep breath, forcing the words out in the hopes that she'd believe them. "Poor guy keeps getting sucked into my drama. It's not fair. Once he leaves, he can get on with his life and I can get on with mine, and the whole town can find some other pair to match up. One that makes sense. Not one that hinges on some tween romance from fifteen years ago." It didn't make sense, not one little bit. But that didn't matter. She loved Mike Woodard and his leaving would destroy her still-fragile heart.

Ted was staring at her, shocked. "I didn't mean to get you upset, Eloise."

She'd overreacted. Ted hadn't meant to send her on some tirade. How could he have known? No one knew how she really felt and that was the way it was going to stay. "I… It's been a long day." She sniffed.

"I know." He opened the gate, then stopped. "The thing is, it's okay if you do care about him."

"Ted." Her eyes were burning—she was going to cry. *No.* She was *not* going to cry over her first love to her ex-husband.

"If he makes you happy, then go for it. The kids love him. He seems like a genuinely good man. And the way he looks at you makes me think he'd treat you the way you deserve to be treated. The way I should have treated you."

She shook her head, her voice higher than she'd intended when she spoke. "Even if I do love him, I'd never ask him to stay. I couldn't do that. If this is something he wants, then I should want it for him. Not ask him to give it up for…this." She gestured at herself. "I couldn't live with myself."

"This—" he gestured to her "—might be what he wants most. You're right about giving the people you love what they want, but how can they know what they want if they don't have all the information?" He shook his head. "You should tell him how you feel, Eloise. If you don't, you'll regret it." He sighed. "Goodnight. I'll stop by tomorrow after school? If that's okay?"

"Sounds good." She closed the gate and lingered there until the chill in the air had her walking back to the house.

When she slowly opened the front door, it was to find Grandpa standing inside the door. "You heard?"

He nodded. "You okay, Sassy?"

She shook her head and sat on the couch. "I will be."

"You want to talk about it?" He sat forward.

She shook her head.

"Are you sure?" He sighed. "I hate to agree with that Ted but, on this, I do. You gotta tell Mike how you feel."

"I'm scared." She wiped at the tears sliding down her cheeks. "I'm scared he'll reject me. Or…or what if he stays and winds up resenting me for losing out on this opportunity? It will hurt to lose him, but it's the least painful option."

"Oh, Sassy. Don't you let fear win. Not now. What if none of that happens and you're just happy? You and Mike and the kids—happy together?"

Archie stepped out of the dark hallway. "Do you love him, Momma? Mr. Mike?"

"Oh, sweetie, I'm so sorry I woke you up." She wiped away her tears, hurrying to calm Archie.

"Momma, do you love Mr. Mike?" Archie grabbed her arm and tugged.

Eloise couldn't read the expression on her son's face.

"I told him he couldn't be your boyfriend because he was mean to you before. I told you you can be friends only." He took a deep breath. "But I didn't know that you wanted him to be your boyfriend or I would have told him it was okay. I like him. I don't know if I want him to be our new daddy like Kirby does, but maybe. And I do like Clifford."

Eloise hugged him close, smiling. "Oh, Archie. I love you."

He nodded. "I want you to be happy. I don't want you to be stressed and needing a spa day all the time."

"I don't want you to worry about all of this." She eased her arms from Archie and smoothed his hair from his forehead. "Everything will be okay, I promise. You don't need to worry about me or Mike or your dad anymore. You need to sleep and get better." She stood and took his hand. "Come on, let's get you back to bed."

She sat by his bed long after he'd fallen asleep. Her sweet, tender boy—too burdened with worry at such a young age. She needed to be more careful around him, so he wouldn't take on problems that weren't his to carry. *Like me and Mike.* She couldn't imagine how the conversation between Mike and Archie had played out, but she'd find out. And, maybe, she'd find a way to tell him how she really felt. If he loved her, she'd never have to protect herself from him. She could love him with her whole heart and he'd keep her, and her heart, safe forever.

He HADN'T SLEPT in days. He couldn't. His dreams were disjointed. From proposing to Eloise to Archie running away to losing El and her kids in a dark fog. Others had him holding Eloise close, and in the next he heard Archie's determined little voice telling him to leave his mother alone.

He'd been avoiding Eloise ever since Archie had put him in his place. He didn't know how to face her without telling her he loved her. He did. So much. He'd been planning to spill his heart to her as soon as they'd come back from their walk… But, after Archie's heartfelt objections, he'd swallowed his declaration and left with a heavy heart. There was no way, no way, he could go against Archie's wishes. He'd never willingly hurt that little boy.

"How's it look? Everything secure?" Rusty was wearing that expression again. He was worried but smart enough to leave well enough alone.

"Yep." He double checked the team harness, making

sure both horses were secure and comfortable. "You're good to go. Have fun." He tipped his cowboy hat at his brother.

"Be safe." Rusty called out, releasing the brake on the wagon and clicking his tongue. The horses responded, keeping a slow and steady pace to the other side of the square and the children and families waiting for the hay-ride.

Mike smothered a yawn as he strode across the street to where he and Terri had parked the ambulance.

Somehow it was Founder's Day. Sure, the last week or so had been a blur, but he couldn't believe it was almost over. Now that his father had been cleared to return to normal activity, Mike was clear to leave. In two days, Garrison would be a speck in his rearview mirror and he wasn't too torn up over it.

"You can go do whatever it is that you…do." Terri waved her plastic spoon at him. "You've got your radio. I can call you if something comes up."

"I'm good." He leaned against the side of the vehicle.

"If you say so." Terri went back to eating her yogurt. "Did you know there are about a million videos of cats doing things on here?" She held out her phone. "Cats knocking stuff off of things. Cats giving hugs. Cats riding dogs. Cats' meows that sound like a person talking." She shook her head.

"I didn't know that." Mike yawned.

"People have too much time on their hands." Terri kept scrolling. "I have an extra yogurt in my lunch bag, if you want it."

"I'm good." He stared across the courthouse lawn.

"Mike." Terri put her phone down. "Don't take this the wrong way, but you've been about to fly off the handle for the last week. I know I didn't do a thing to get you this riled up, so who did? I feel the need to give them a piece of my mind."

Mike shook his head. "I don't know what you're talking about."

"Yes, you do. I'm not going to pussyfoot around, either. And you know it." Terri jumped out of the ambulance and stood beside him. "Last week, you were smiling and happy and thinking about staying put and now you're all grouchy and spitting nails and ready to leave town tomorrow."

Mike sighed.

"Did you tell her?" Terri offered him a piece of gum. "Did you tell Eloise she was the bread to your butter?"

Mike waved the gum away. "I'm going to take a walk."

"Good. That's what I said." She waved him away. "Turn on your radio."

"Yeah," he called back, then adjusted his radio. Terri might be a pain in the rear but she was a good medic. He'd miss working with her.

He sat on one of the wrought-iron benches that skirted the courthouse lawn. He didn't want to get close enough for anyone to think he was looking for company. But he was out of luck.

"Mike." Forrest Briscoe was all smiles as he shook his hand.

"How was the honeymoon?" He held up his hand. "Forget that. I don't want to know. When did you get home?"

Forrest sat beside him. "About a week ago? Give or take a day. Hattie jumped right back into work and, well, you know, things had gotten sloppy around the ranch since I left. For all their complaining about how controlling I am, they can't seem to manage without me reminding them of what needs to get done."

Mike chuckled. "Nice to know you're needed."

"I guess." He slumped back against the bench. "Your

dad looks good. Saw him in his frontier settler getup serving cider to folk in front of the shop."

"According to Doc Johnston, he's as fit as a fiddle." Which meant there was no reason for Mike to stay. His father had a clean bill of health and Rusty was up to speed on helping the high school rodeo team—he'd made sure he'd covered his responsibilities.

"You look a little rough around the edges." Forrest was giving him a hard look.

"Yeah, well, I'm feeling a little rough around the edges, so let's not talk about it." Mike leaned forward.

"Okay." Forrest didn't say a word. The longer he didn't say a word, the more wound up Mike felt.

"Ever feel like things are closing in on you?" He sat back.

"A time or two." Forrest grinned. "Mostly it was me putting off something I didn't want to do. Once I did it, things went back to normal."

"Or maybe I'm just ready to get out of Garrison." He shrugged.

"Maybe." Forrest adjusted his cowboy hat. "I wouldn't know about that. I did hear from Webb, though. He's doing well. Hasn't blown off anyone's fingers or toes yet—or his own, for that matter."

Webb was one of Forrest's younger brothers. When he'd enlisted, the rest of the Briscoes had taken it hard. They were a tight-knit family, after all.

"Glad he's doing well." Mike meant it. "Any plans to visit soon?"

"It'll probably be a year or so." Forrest sighed. "Not soon enough, that's for sure. Missing out on Audy and Brooke's baby being born and, likely, Mabel and Jensen's wedding. The sort of things you don't want to miss out on, you know?"

Mike nodded. He'd miss out on those things, too.

"Forrest." Hattie was waving at him. "There they are. Mike." Hattie kept on waving. "Get over here, you two."

"The wife calls." Forrest chuckled. "You might as well come or she'll march over here after you."

Mike pushed off the bench and followed Forrest. There were too many voices and smiles and people he'd rather avoid than talk to.

"Mike. You're just the man I was looking for. Someone has been trying to find you." Hattie stepped aside. "Said something about having her first hayride with you?"

"Mr. Mike." And just like that, Kirby was hugging him around the knees like her life depended on it. "Where have you been? I looked all over for you. You didn't come."

Her words were like little pinpricks on his heart. He'd missed Kirby's hugs and her sweet smiles—like the one she was giving him now. "I've been working nonstop, Freckles." It was a flimsy excuse, but it was the only one he had.

"You've been working for a long time." She took his hand and started pulling him through the crowd. "Mr. Woodard brings Clifford over to visit, but it's not the same as when you visit. I miss you, Mr. Mike. And Archie misses you, too."

That was the thing about Kirby, she had no guile. She said it like she saw it and he'd missed that. So much. He squeezed her hand, too many words clogging his throat. He knew people were watching them but chose to ignore it.

"Are you being a doctor cowboy tonight?" she asked, inspecting his uniform.

"I am." He chuckled.

"Archie, Archie!" Kirby yelled. "I found him. Look!"

Archie had no right to look so happy to see him.

"Mr. Mike." He came running. "Momma thought maybe

you'd already moved, but I told her you'd say goodbye first. I was right. You're here."

"Should you be running like that, Archie?" He didn't want the boy hurting himself.

"Oh, I'm all better. Back at school, too." His smile faded. "You look kinda sad."

"I'm fine." He was sad. He'd been so determined to keep distance from El, he hadn't thought about how that would make the kids feel. It'd been selfish—and cruel.

"He's been working lots and lots and lots," Kirby explained.

"That's about right." Mike managed a smile. "Maybe even more."

"Grandpa said you need to take better care of yourself." Archie was frowning. "You have an important job and you need to get plenty of sleep and drink lots of water—"

"And eat healthy food. Yep. You do. My teacher says so, too," Kirby finished. "Momma said you took her on her first hayride, so you have to take me on my first hayride." Kirby was still holding his hand. "Samantha says I don't have to be scared of the horses but they're really big. Will you go with me, please, Mr. Mike? Please?"

How was he supposed to say no to that? He couldn't. "I'd like that, Kirby."

"Yay." She tugged him along behind her until they were standing at the end of the line. "I found him so I can go." Kirby hopped up and down. "See?"

Samantha clapped, just as excited. "Hurray."

Mike was beginning to think he might actually enjoy himself. The line waiting for the next ride wasn't that long so the wagon wouldn't be too crowded. Samantha and Mabel were fine. For Archie's sake, he'd put up with Levi Williams and his loud grandfather, Buck. His gaze shifted to the first person in line and his chest caved in. Eloise?

He'd hoped she was working at Garrison Gardens or...
anywhere else.

"Mike." Eloise sounded downright happy to see him.

"Evening," he murmured, refusing to meet her gaze.

"This should be fun." Buck Williams chuckled. "This
is a festival. We're supposed to be festive and celebrate.
You know, laugh and smile and all that."

Mike was having serious second thoughts about this
hayride.

"I'm having fun. Mr. Mike is having fun." Kirby was
swinging his arm with hers. "Are you having fun?"

"I am." Samantha nodded.

The girls started listing off all the treats they'd enjoyed
during the day's festivities so far. Mike would be popping
antacids if he'd eaten half the stuff they had. Archie and
Levi were far more interested in what would happen if
one of the horses pooped while they were on their hayride.
Since Mike had nothing to add to either conversation, he
got to stand by awkwardly and wait.

"Audy said you've been working extra shifts." Mabel
sighed. "You're no use to anyone if you're dead on your
feet."

"What happens if someone calls 911 and there's no one
answering, Mabel?" He shrugged, doing his best not to
look Eloise's way. It was hard not to. She looked extra
pretty in that green sweater. When she turned his way, his
gaze fell. "I'm just doing my job." But he had volunteered
for the extra shifts before anyone else could.

"Time to load up for the hayride." Audy stood beside
the wagon, offering a hand to anyone who needed help
getting up and into the wagon. "Mike. You look like you
could definitely use a hand."

Mike sighed and pulled himself into the wagon.

"I'm so excited." Kirby squealed and climbed into his lap. "Are you excited?"

He nodded. "I am." Kirby's energy was hard to resist.

"Are you ready, Kirby?" Eloise sat in the hay beside him. "Do you need to sit on Mr. Mike's lap?"

Kirby nodded.

He smiled at how quickly she answered. "It's fine." If she wanted to sit on his lap, she could sit on his lap.

"Archie, don't lean over the edge." Eloise's mom voice had Archie scooting away from the back of the open wagon. "Thank you."

"After the hayride, there's going to be a stick horse parade around the courthouse." Kirby relaxed against him.

"Is that so? Are you riding one?"

Kirby nodded. "A pretty red one. It has long sparkly hair. Guess what I named him." She stared up at him, her eyes wide and her whole face excited.

He had a pretty good idea what the name was, but he decided to have some fun. "Red?" Mike scratched his chin. "Tomato? Beet?"

"No." Kirby giggled.

"No? Hmm, Watermelon?" He paused. "How about Ladybug?"

She kept giggling. "No. I named my horse Clifford."

"That's a good name." Mike was laughing right along with her.

Somehow, his eyes got tangled up with Eloise's and he felt like he'd been punched in the throat. She looked happy. Why shouldn't she be? His heart was the one that had been shattered, not hers. And, as hurt as he was, he didn't wish that on her. El deserved to be happy. So did her kids. Even if he wasn't a part of that.

The longer she stared at him, the harder it was to hold on to all the things she'd said.

"Here we go." Kirby clutched at his shirtfront and held on tight. "We're moving."

"Rusty's driving. My brother. He's a good driver. You don't need to worry." He patted her back.

"Oh, I'm not worried." Kirby smiled up at him. "Momma said you always kept her safe so you'll keep me safe, won't you?"

He forced himself to smile. "Count on it, Freckles." A quick glance assured him Eloise was watching the two of them. She'd said that? He glanced at Archie, strengthening his resolve.

Kirby giggled over each bump in the road. When Rusty turned a corner, she and Samantha squealed in unison. About halfway around the courtyard, Levi got upset that neither of the horses had pooped but Archie said it could still happen. Mike had no choice but to relax and find the whole thing amusing. Yes, he was aware of every little thing Eloise said or did, but he could enjoy everything anyway.

When the wagon came to a stop, the sighs and groans of disapproval made him smile. This was what these festivals were all about. New experiences, laughter, and having fun. There was no denying Kirby had had all three. Archie might be disappointed no horse poop appeared, but he'd still had a good time.

He scooped Kirby out of the wagon, then Samantha, too. He offered his hand to Mabel and, gritting his teeth, did the same for Eloise. He wished her touch didn't get to him. He wished he could ignore the jolt that raced up his arm and settled in his chest, but it was impossible. Even after he'd let go, he could feel her hand in his and the pull that tied him to her.

"I've got to get back to work." He crouched by Kirby. "But I had fun, Freckles."

"Will you watch me in the stick horse parade?" She stared up at him.

"Of course." He pointed. "I'll be right over there. Make sure to wave as you ride by and I'll be looking for you and your red horse."

"Okay." She threw her arms around his neck and gave him a tight hug. "Thank you for protecting me from the big horses, Mr. Mike."

"My pleasure." He was smiling as he stood.

"Mike." Eloise tucked a strand of hair behind her ear. "Do you have a minute? I know you're working, but I need to talk to you."

What more could she possibly have to say? He'd had a good time with the kids, and he'd rather leave on a high note. "Now's not a good time." He turned and bumped into Ted Barnes.

"Mike." Ted's ready smile disappeared when he saw his face.

"Ted." He tipped his hat and brushed past the man. He'd played nice long enough. Now, he was done. He quickened his pace as he headed back to the ambulance.

"Have fun?" Terri asked, glancing up from her phone long enough to see his face, sigh, and go back to scrolling. "I'm telling you, Mike, you gotta fight for what you want."

He didn't bother looking at her. "Wake me when the stick horse parade starts, will you?" He tilted the passenger seat back and covered his face with his hat. A nap wouldn't stop his heartache but, maybe, it'd make his world feel a little less bleak.

CHAPTER FIFTEEN

AFTER A NIGHT of tossing and turning, Eloise woke up with a splitting headache. She made pancakes, drank coffee, and tried to keep up with the kids' giddy recount of the festival the night before. They'd had a wonderful time. She, on the other hand, had not.

All night long, she'd tried to make sense of how Mike had treated her. It was obvious he didn't want to talk to her—let alone look at her. Something had to have happened. But what? The last time she'd seen him, he'd seemed happy. Or maybe that's what she wanted to see? Knowing today was Mike's surprise going-away party only compounded the headache—and heartache.

"What's burning?" Kirby asked.

Eloise stared down at the blackening pancake. "Oops, this one got a little overdone." She scooped the scorched pancake aside and poured out a fresh one.

"Want me to take over?" her grandfather offered.

"No." She forced a smile. "Got a little distracted." She waited for the last pancake to brown, added it to the serving platter and carried it to the table.

"Are you distracted because today is Mr. Mike's party?" Kirby set about cutting her pancake into bite-size pieces. "Is he really leaving, Momma? Why?"

"He's got a very exciting new job." She used as much enthusiasm as she could muster.

"A real job?" Kirby's voice lowered. "Not jail?"

"Yes, a real job." Eloise tapped her daughter on the nose. "Mr. Mike has a real, good job that lets him take care of lots more people. And that is what makes him happy so we should be happy for him."

"We get to go to the party, too?" Archie asked, swirling his bite of pancake in syrup.

"Yes." Grandpa Quincy added another dollop of syrup to Archie's plate. "Once the party is underway. You don't want to show up the same time as the guest—it'll ruin the surprise."

"Oh no," Kirby moaned. "I don't want to ruin Mr. Mike's surprise."

"Remind me to pick up a new O-ring for the bathroom sink." Grandpa Quincy served himself another pancake. "The thing was dripping all night. Waste of water."

"Mr. Woodard's bringing over Clifford soon, isn't he? I can go if you tell me exactly what to get." Eloise poked at her food, then sat back. "I'm not really all that hungry so I can go whenever."

"You need to eat, Momma." Kirby pointed at her with her fork. "Or you'll get a tummy ache."

Eloise obediently ate half of her pancake—it felt like lead in her stomach. While she left them to tidy up the kitchen, she walked down Main Street to Old Towne Hardware and Appliances. Grandpa Quincy had called ahead so Mr. Woodard could have the part ready and waiting for her.

But it wasn't Mr. Woodard inside, it was Rusty.

"Eloise." He nodded. "Dad said you were stopping by." He handed her a brown paper bag. "There's a washer in there, too." He opened his mouth, then closed it.

"Thanks."

"Yep." He nodded, barely glancing her way.

"Rusty…" She swallowed. At this point, she had nothing to lose. "Can I ask you something else?"

He nodded.

"About Mike?" She held her breath. "Please."

Rusty ran a hand over his face. "I guess it depends on the question."

"What happened? Did I do something?" She shrugged. "I tried to talk to him last night but he…he practically looked right through me. Now he's leaving and I just… I don't want things to go left unsaid."

He went from wary to sympathetic. "Ah, Eloise, I wish I knew. He's been in a real bad mood ever since the other night. I figured you two had a fight or something. All he said was he didn't want to talk about it. So we didn't talk about it—and he's been in a snit ever since." Rusty adjusted the stapler and pen canister by the register. "I can't say for sure what upset him, but I'm pretty sure it has something to do with you."

"If I don't know what I did, how can I fix it?" She shook her head, more frustrated than ever. Surely, this wasn't over what Archie had said? "He's not leaving until I know what happened. Is he working?"

"Yes, ma'am. Last shift with the hospital."

As tempting as it was to search him out now, barging into the hospital or chasing down his ambulance was wrong. "Then I'll have to wait until this afternoon. At his farewell party."

Rusty chuckled. "I can't wait to see how that goes."

She grabbed the plumbing supplies and walked out of the shop. The whole way home, she tried to make sense of what Rusty had told her. How could he be upset with her when she hadn't done or said a thing to him? He wouldn't invest in gossip. And even if he'd heard something, he'd have come to her to sort it out. If he wouldn't come to her, she'd go to him.

That left Archie. Mike, being the big-hearted wonderful man that he was, was keeping his distance because that's what Archie told him to do. She couldn't decide if she adored him all the more for taking her son's words to heart or irritated that he hadn't come to her to talk himself.

Her mind kept spinning. If she dared give in to the over-the-top romantic idea that was taking shape as she walked, she might be able to sort out what the problem was and tell him what was in her heart all at the same time.

By the time she reached her grandfather's house, she was resolved. She wasn't going to let last night throw her off. Yes, Mike had been a bit cold—and distant. He'd seemed hurt. Maybe even a little angry. And it was up to her to set the record straight and, hopefully, fix it.

She could do this. She should do this. If she did, he'd know how serious she was. Besides, if she started second-guessing things, she'd never get the words out. As soon as she got home, she called Brooke.

"I need your help with Mike." She took a deep breath. "Audy's, too?"

"You've got it. What do you need us to do?" Brooke laughed. "It had better be something sweet and romantic because I'm feeling huge and miserable and need some cheering up."

"I'm hoping it will be both." She swallowed. "There's a chance Mike won't want any part of it but…." She was not going to go there.

"Audy, honey, you owe me five dollars." There was a smile in Brooke's voice. "So, what's the plan?"

Three hours later, Eloise stood under the massive canopy of erste Baum's branches having serious second thoughts. "This is dumb."

"This is sweet," Gretta argued, stooping to adjust a teddy bear.

"I look dumb." Eloise reached up. "I have a clip in my hair."

"You look exactly like you did in the pictures." Mabel held up one of the old photographs. "This is the most romantic thing I think I've ever seen."

Eloise wasn't sure if this was genius or pathetic. "It's too late now."

"Breathe." Brooke sat, fanning herself. "Seriously, Eloise, you're stressing me out."

Eloise took a deep breath. "Sorry. No stress."

"It's okay." Mabel tapped one of the long ribbons that hung all around them. "This is beautiful. All of it."

The idea had been one thing. Yards of ribbon hung from the branches overhead. Each of the ribbons had dozens of photos of her and Mike pinned to them. She'd added lights and flowers, too. Mabel and Gretta had gone above and beyond to find props that fit some of the photos. A teddy bear in a tuxedo. A large, light-up Santa. Some Easter eggs scattered around in the grass. She'd even done her hair to match their *wedding* photo.

"It's too much." She sank into the chair. "You were there last night, Mabel. I've never seen him so…so…upset." Upset with *her*. He could barely look at her.

Mabel sat beside her. "Maybe he was so overcome by your beauty and, knowing he couldn't pull you into his arms and declare his love for you, he was…mad."

"I'm sure that was it." A nervous giggle slipped out. "I'm sorry I commandeered your good-bye party, Mabel."

"Are you kidding me? This is the most romantic thing to happen in Garrison—"

"Since my wedding?" Hattie joined them, holding a large baker's box.

"That's exactly what I was going to say, Hattie." Mabel

winked. "This is the most romantic thing to happen since your wedding."

"I can't take any credit for that either." Hattie's laugh-snort had them all relaxing. "That was all Eloise, too. Just like this." She shook her head. "If the man can't see the love and thought you've put into this, good riddance." She smiled at Eloise. "But it's Mike so he will see it."

Eloise had to hold on to her hope, not her fear. If there was anyone worth risking her heart on, it was Mike Woodard.

"You're right." Brooke nodded. "I, for one, can't wait to see him get all moony-eyed over this."

"I hope so." Eloise's gaze swept over the photos and ribbons again. "Or he's going to think there's something wrong with me."

That had them all laughing again.

Eloise smoothed every tablecloth, checked every extension cord, straightened each bouquet, and tried not to check the time every five minutes. The closer it got to Mike's arrival time, the more people arrived—and the more absurd her decorations appeared. She'd committed and there was no going back. After she'd told Mike her hopes and dreams for the two of them, it was up to him. All she could do was hope that once Mike knew how much she loved him, it wouldn't be a going-away party after all. Just a party.

"WHAT ARE WE doing here?" Mike was having a hard time keeping his eyes open. His last shift hadn't been quiet. From a semitruck accident on the interstate to a kid getting his head stuck between the stair railings, they'd been on the go for a solid ten hours. He'd showered before he left the hospital so he could fall face down into bed as soon as he got home. Unfortunately, his father needed something done before that.

"He said they borrowed that old wheelbarrow for the festival yesterday. We just need to pick it up." Rusty parked the truck on the far side of erste Baum Park.

"You got this." Mike rested his head against the seat and tipped his cowboy hat over his eyes.

"The thing weighs a ton, Mike." He slammed the driver's door closed and, seconds later, opened the passenger door. "I need a hand."

Mike glared at him. "Hurry up then." He stepped out of the truck, rubbed his eyes, and followed Rusty down the path and around erste Baum.

"Surprise!" The cry was so loud and unexpected, Mike jumped back.

"What in the Sam Hill?" He frowned, beyond bewildered. All the faces. The balloons and streamers. A banner that read, Good Luck & We Will Miss You was strung up over some tables. He glared at his brother.

"It wasn't my idea." Rusty held up his hands. "But, you know, maybe try to be nice since all these people are here for you."

Mike tried, he did. He couldn't have been more surprised… Until he was standing face-to-face with Eloise.

"Come with me for a second?" She took his hand and led him to the other side of the tree.

"El—" He pulled his hand from hers but the damage was done. "What is all this?" All around him were pictures of him and Eloise. "What…" He broke off, marveling over the stuffed bear and the Easter eggs and a hundred other tiny things that cut so deep. He drew in a deep breath and faced her. "What is all this?"

"This is us." She cleared her throat. "This is me, trying to tell you how I feel… And, maybe—possibly—going overboard." She fidgeted with the clip in her hair.

He stared at the clip, his jaw muscle working. She

looked a lot like she did when he'd "married" her here all those years ago. "I don't understand."

"I… I love you." She swallowed. "I love you more than anything, Mike."

"You what?" He couldn't have heard that right. "But…"

She stepped forward, taking his hands in hers. "I made a mess of things, I know. I was… I am so scared." She rested a hand against his cheek. "I'm sorry I fought so hard to hold on to my heart. It's yours. I want you to have it—if you want it?"

"Am I dreaming?" That's the only way this made sense. Her sweet smile sent his heart into overdrive.

"No." She cradled his face in her hands. "I love you, Mike."

Her touch was real. "But…" He shook his head. "We can't, El. I can't." And it was tearing his heart to bits.

"Because of Archie?" She slipped her arms around his waist. "He said he wasn't so sure about you being his new daddy but, if I wanted you to be my boyfriend, he was okay with that because he wanted me to be happy."

Mike swallowed. "He said that?"

She nodded.

"And you love me?" When he drew her into his arms, she was soft and warm and alive.

"I don't want you giving anything up, though. We can make it work with your new job… If that's what you want—"

"What I want is right here, El-Bell. In my arms." He shook his head. "It might not have made sense to love you as much as I did when we were younger, but I did. And the truth is, I never stopped loving you."

Her breath hitched and she leaned into him. "You do love me?" she whispered.

"I do." Mike kissed her then. A soft kiss—that turned

into something more. He held on to her with everything he had, breathed her in until he was wide awake. This was no dream. This was real. This was everything he could ever want and more. He broke off to whisper, "I'm glad Archie changed his mind."

"You'd leave?" She shook her head. "Because of Archie?"

"I didn't want to. I avoided you for fear I'd break my word to him." He shook his head. "But, El, we had a man-to-man talk. I don't think I've ever had a more serious man-to-man talk in my entire life. That boy was speaking from the heart. Who am I to break it?"

"Oh, Mike." She smiled up at him. "You are too good to be true. Loving and kind and supportive and…well, you're you. And I love you. I can't lose you."

"El-Bell, you won't." His arms tightened around her. "I'm in this all the way. I breathe easier when you're with me, don't you know that?"

"That you make everything better?" She smiled. "I know that." She stood on tiptoe and pressed a kiss to one cheek. "I know I love you." She kissed his other cheek. "So much."

"That's all that matters." He rested his forehead against hers. "I'm so glad you came back, El-Bell."

"I'm so glad I came home to you, Mike." She ran her fingers along his jaw. "And since Archie is okay with you being my boyfriend and Kirby is okay with you being her new daddy, there's nothing to worry about."

"Not a thing." He kissed her again. "We've got this, El-Bell."

"We do." She tilted her head back. "But, before we go tell everyone you're staying, I'd love another kiss. Or two."

* * * * *

WESTERN

Rugged men looking for love...

Available Next Month

The Maverick Makes The Grade Stella Bagwell
The Heart Of A Rancher Trish Milburn

Nine Months To A Fortune Elizabeth Bevarly
Hill Country Hero Kit Hawthorne

 LOVE INSPIRED

A Companion For His Son Lee Tobin McClain
Hidden Secrets Between Them Mindy Obenhaus

Keep reading for an excerpt of a new title
from the Special Edition series,
THE BACHELOR'S MATCHMAKER
by Marie Ferrarella

Prologue

Sanford Sterling sat in the trailer he had parked at the newest construction site he had set up. He felt incredibly lost and alone. This sensation was nothing new. It came whenever he was alone with his thoughts, looking at the framed photograph he kept on his desk of his late wife. He was contemplating what his life had become in the years since Shirley had died as a result of a car accident, which had left him with their five sons to raise—two of whom were too young at the time when she died to even remember what she had been like.

"Oh, Lord, Shirley, you have no idea how much I wish you were here," he told the woman in the photograph. "Our boys need to settle down, to get married and start their own families. They need your help— *I* need your help. I lucked out when I found you."

He sighed deeply, remembering the day he first saw her. She had walked into his second-period English class on a Tuesday morning in eighth grade. He fell in love with her right then and there—and they had been together ever since. Until the day she had been taken from him. The resulting wound was still fresh even after all these years.

"I want our boys to feel that sort of luck coursing through their veins, but how on earth do I manage to do that for them? I need your help, Shirley. I really, really need you next to me. I don't want to guide our sons into making a mistake, marrying the wrong woman. Otherwise, they'll be sorry for the rest of their lives. I've never been able to even get them to find time for any serious dating." Sanford sighed, shaking his head. "They've always been too focused on getting their degrees and starting their careers. That much I've accomplished." He had a feeling that had been because Shirley was looking down at her sons and guiding their every move.

But this was too much to hope for—and how could he even be able to get all five of his sons to pair up with the right women? The best dating advice he had to offer was "follow your heart."

Sanford combed his fingers through his hair, frustrated and at a complete loss. "Oh, Shirley, I need you now more than ever. The *boys* need you," he whispered into the shadows.

And then suddenly, just like that, it came to him. The answer. From out of the past.

Maizie.

Maizie Sommers had been Shirley's close friend in high school as well as her maid of honor at their wedding. And, just as important, she had been the one who had helped him find a nanny to watch over the boys so he was able to go back to work, to earn a living and provide for his family.

That hadn't been easy, either, but Maizie was right there beside him, despite her busy schedule, weeding out potential candidates for the position of the boys' nanny, promising him he was going to get through this, assuring him that he *had* to get through this for Shirley's sake. And ultimately telling him that if there was absolutely *anything* she could do for him, she would.

For Shirley's sake.

And that was when he suddenly remembered. Aside from being a successful real estate agent, on the side, Maizie also ran a matchmaking service with two of her best friends. She took no money for it, instead gathering a sense of pride and feeling of accomplishment from the matchup.

That was his answer, Sanford realized.

"Matchmaking service," he said out loud, happy for once that his youngest son and business partner was not on-site with him. "Of course. Boy, talk about being thick," he murmured, shaking his head.

The first opportunity he got, he planned on paying Maizie a visit and laying this new dilemma he found himself facing at her feet. He needed help, and he didn't mind admitting it. This needed a woman's touch, he thought.

"Brace yourself, Sam," he said to his firstborn,

the one he was planning on matching up first. "Your fancy-free days are about to come to an end."

He was that confident that Maizie was about to find someone for Sam.

Now that he thought about it, he had heard good things about the enduring matches that Maizie and her friends had made in the last fifteen years. It gave him hope.

"My sweet boys," he said to the image he had in his heart of his sons. "Your lives are about to change— for the better," he said with certainty.

He decided that Sam, as his oldest, was going to be first. It only seemed fair to go that route. He had a feeling that Shirley would definitely approve of this move.

As soon as he was alone—and able—he placed a call to Maizie. It turned out to be the following day. Since she was successful in both her real estate business and this matchmaking, he had a feeling that he would need an appointment to see Maizie in a timely fashion.

Not that the woman would put obstacles in his way, but he wanted to pay her the courtesy of going to her on her timetable rather than his own, even though he was exceedingly busy 24/7.

Maizie picked up her phone on the third ring. "Maizie Sommers, how may I help you?"

He would have recognized that bright, chipper

voice anywhere. "Maizie, this is Sanford Sterling. Would you be available to meet with me tomorrow?"

It had been several years. "Sandy, is that really you?" she cried, clearly stunned. And then she immediately asked, "Is anything wrong?"

The last time they had spoken was at Sean's college graduation. To her credit as a good friend of both parents, Maizie had attended all five of their sons' college graduations, which was why he felt he could count on her to help him to successfully match up his sons.

"No, as a matter of fact, there isn't," Sanford told her. "But once again, I find myself in need of your very unique services."

He imagined Maizie making herself comfortable. "I'm listening. What can I do?"

He took a breath, launching into the reason for his call. "You once told me that you and your two friends had dipped your toes in matchmaking waters. Are you still treading water?"

"Not for a while now," she admitted. "But the girls and I are ready and eager to get back into it. You're not looking, are you?" she asked incredulously.

No one loved their late wife as much as Sandy loved Shirley. "No, not me, but it's time for the boys to find their soulmates. I hear you're really good at that sort of matchup."

He could hear the smile in Maizie's voice. "As a matter of fact, we are. Why don't you come down to the office the first opportunity you get, and we'll discuss the particulars?" she suggested.

"Tomorrow morning too soon?" he asked her.

"Tomorrow's perfect, Sandy. I look forward to seeing you," she told him. "How about ten?"

This was going to be good. "Sounds perfect," he told her.

"I certainly hope so" was Maizie's response.

The shopping center where Maizie's real estate agency was located had changed somewhat since Sanford had seen it last. It had been built up over the years, even though it continued to maintain its warm, friendly, welcoming appearance.

As he pulled into the lot, he felt as if he had butterflies in his stomach, a strange feeling for a grown man to have, he thought. But this was important. Very important, he told himself. If this visit went well, the ones that would follow would, too.

Parking his vehicle, he made his way over to the recently renovated real estate building. It looked inviting, he thought. That was a good sign. Taking a deep breath at the front door, he knocked once, opened it, then went inside.

There was one person inside. It wasn't a client. He flashed a quick smile in greeting, then nodded.

The woman came straight for him, her arms outstretched. "Sanford?" she asked.

"Maizie, you haven't aged a day since I last saw you at Sean's graduation," he told her.

"And you are still spreading it as thick as you ever did," Maizie said with a laugh, planting a kiss on Sanford's cheek. "How have you been, Sandy?"

"Busy." And then he admitted, "Lonely."

"Do you still have Sunday dinners at the house the way you all used to?" she asked him.

He nodded. "It's a tribute to Shirley."

Maizie smiled broadly. "She would have been very proud. Come, sit," she urged. "So are the boys ready for something serious?"

"Absolutely," he answered. "And I realize that I'm just not any good at matchups. But word on the street is that you and your two friends are extremely good at it."

"Well, I don't mean to get your hopes up," Maizie confessed, "but so far, my friends and I have been batting a thousand."

"I'd say that's pretty damn good," Sanford told her. "Do you think you could do it a few more times?"

Her smile all but lit up the room. "Absolutely," she told him. "I just need to ask you a few preliminary questions. But first, how is everyone?"

"Busy," he said again. "That's the problem. The boys are too busy at the moment to do the ordinary things that men their age normally do. That's why I need you, Maizie. They just don't seem to be able to find the time to sow their oats, wild or otherwise.

They seem obsessed with laying the foundations of their various careers. Sam is a veterinarian, Simon is a divorce lawyer, Sebastian—"

Maizie held up her hand, stopping Sanford mid-sentence. "You don't have to go through all their vocations. I was there at each of their graduations, remember?" she reminded her late friend's husband. "I can take it from here," she assured him. "Are they happy in their chosen fields?"

"They never gave me any reason to doubt that they were very happy," he told her.

Maizie frowned. "Not exactly a ringing endorsement."

"They're not exactly a talkative bunch, at least not around me," Sanford told her.

"Boys have trouble making their feelings known around their father, especially when he sacrificed so much for them," Maizie pointed out. She made a notation on her folder, then looked up. "Are they still as handsome as ever?"

He felt the usual fondness whenever he thought of his boys. "I'm sure that their mother would say that they are."

Maizie flashed a warm smile at him. "Just like their father," she pointed out.

Sanford gave her a look. "I'm not fishing for a compliment."

"I know that," the potential matchmaker told him. "You were never that vain. That was one of the things that Shirley liked about you. She would have approved of you trying to match up your sons to their potential soulmates. So, is Sam dedicated to his vocation?"

"If he could, he would care for animals for free," he told Maizie.

"Selfless and dedicated. There's a lot of his mother and his father in him," she told Sanford.

"But I know my limitations, which is why I've come to you for help," he told her.

Maizie nodded. "Tell me, do I have a time limit on this?"

"Just sometime before I die would be nice, although I need to tell you that I would like to be able to enjoy my grandkids," he told her.

Maizie smiled, probably thinking of her own grandchildren. "Oh, they are just the very best," she assured him. "You get to play with little people and enjoy them without worrying that you're doing things wrong. Because you know you're not." She patted her friend on his broad shoulder. "Smile, Sandy. It's going to be all right, I promise," she said, leaning over the desk and squeezing his hand. "Are there any physical preferences? You know, blonde, brunette, tall, short, that sort of thing."

"Only that she's breathing," Sanford specified.

Maizie nodded, lips pursed as if to keep from laughing. "Definitely breathing," she agreed. She leaned back in her chair, reviewing the notes that she had taken. "Well, I think I have everything I need. I take it you want to match up all of your sons?"

"Most definitely yes," he answered.

"In order?" She knew him well.

"Well, I think that would only be fair," he pointed out.

Maizie nodded. "Wouldn't want any of the boys to think that you're playing favorites," she said, "putting one above the other."

"Just like doing things in their proper order, that's all," Sanford said. "I always have. Will that be a problem?"

"Not for me," she answered. "If we find someone more suited to one of the other brothers, I'll just make a note to get back to the woman at a later date—unless, of course, there's a danger of losing the woman, and if we come up against that, then we'll take the proper precautions."

Sanford smiled. "That's why I came to you, Maizie. You know how to juggle things and keep all the balls up in the air at the same time. If you need anything to make this happen, just let me know," Sanford said. "Also, that goes for any payments."

"Payments?" she questioned, looking at him oddly.

"For possibly the initial outlay," Sanford specified.

She was still confused by his meaning. "Such as?"

"I'll leave that to your imagination," Sanford told her.

She flashed a smile at him. "Not to worry," she answered. "I have plenty to work on in my notes. Let me talk to my friends Theresa Manetti and Cecilia Parnell. We'll put our heads together and see if we can come up with a good candidate for Sam. There'll be a good backstory—all true," she specified. "And once we find the proper candidate for Sam, we'll go from there."

"She needs to be an animal lover," Sanford told her.

"Most assuredly. I wasn't born yesterday, Sandy. This is for my friend's son—as well as my godson," she said. She saw the look on Sanford's face. "You forgot that part, didn't you? Well, I didn't. I remember how he wiggled and wriggled as I held him while he was being baptized. Out of all the matchups I plan to make, Sam will be my very best," she promised. "You have my word on it."

Sanford took heart from the look on Maizie's face. "You've made me very happy, Maizie," he told her as he rose to his feet.

"Good. Then I'll get in contact with you once all the pieces come together," she told him. "My advice to you is to prepare for a wedding."

"You can be that sure of the outcome?" Sanford questioned.

Maizie flashed a bright smile at her friend. "Oh, I can be that sure," she told him with unshakable certainty.

Sanford smiled at Maizie. "Then I'll go home and wait for your call."

Her eyes sparkled. "You do that," she encouraged her friend.

She couldn't wait to call her friends with the news. They were going to be thrilled.

BRAND NEW RELEASE

Don't miss the next instalment of the Powder River series by bestselling author B.J. Daniels! For lovers of sexy Western heroes, small-town settings and suspense with your romance.

RIVER JUSTICE

—R—

A POWDER RIVER NOVEL

PERFECT FOR FANS OF YELLOWSTONE!

Previous titles in the
Powder River series

September 2023   January 2024   In-store and online August 2024

Don't miss out!

Limited edition commemorative
Anniversary Collections

In honour of our golden jubilee, don't miss these four special Anniversary Collections, each honouring a beloved series line — Modern, Medical, Suspense and Western. A tribute to our legacy, these collections are a must-have for every fan.

In-store and online July and August 2024.

MILLS & BOON

millsandboon.com.au